I0522516

I knew I had no business here, but was it going to cost me more than I'd thought?

Closer in, I could see the yellow tape was broken or missing in places, but still cordoned off a circular area of dirt and mud, about twelve feet in diameter. The tape had been stapled to stakes pounded into the ground, but many of them had fallen over. This crime scene had already been worked. Two dirty latex gloves and a staple gun had been left outside the perimeter, and multiple footprints marred the mud. The absence of a patrol officer protecting the scene implied the clean-up crew was on their way.

Inside the partially taped-off area, someone had outlined where Jimmie Lee's body had been. Instead of the typical chalk line, plastic pegs were pressed into the mud about six inches apart, marking where the body had fallen.

I stepped high over the tape and into the mud, grateful I'd worn jeans and flat shoes for that dress-down Friday. Trees towered behind me, the interminable water before me. I caught a whiff of mildew.

I was no sooner inside than a rustling sound came from the tangle of maples and I twisted around. The noise disappeared and I turned back, catching a glitter in the mud. It came from the waterline where the soft waves of the Mississippi Sound licked against the cryptic outline of the corpse. That noise again.

I spun around to the whooshing sounds in the maples, my heart palpitating, but I still didn't see anything. When I turned back, the glitter had disappeared. I stooped. I was in a race with the sun, not to mention wanting to be long gone before the clean-up crew appeared. With one hand, I frantically ran my fingers through the muck. Then a final spray of sunlight illuminated the spot and the sparkle reappeared. This time, I kept my eyes fixed on it, bending, reaching, touching. Gently, I lifted a metal object, close to an inch long and about half that in width. Heavy for its size. Twilight had deepened into dusk. I stood up and whirled round to the same rustling noise, but this time a crackling blast followed. A gun?

At long last, she lands a job with a good employer, but the trouble is just beginning…

Human resources manager Judy Kenagy hopes her days of running from bad bosses and guilt-ridden memories are over. But alas, she's barely settled in when a young female employee is found shot to death, spinning her new workplace into turmoil. Small-town police chief, Carl Bombardier solicits Judy's help in her role as the company's HR Manager. While working with Judy, he shares his fanatical interest in a twenty-five-year-old double homicide he believes is linked to her last and worst bad boss. To make matters worse, the trusted assistant of her monster ex-boss starts showing up, keeping the unwanted connection going. When the pesky trusted assistant turns up murdered, Judy learns there's a connection with the shooting death of the employee. She starts sleuthing at the crime scene and stumbles upon an important piece of evidence. Can she solve all of the murders with this single find? If she does, will she finally be freed from the demons of her past? Or are things not as they seem?

ACKNOWLEDGEMENTS

I can't name all of the people who have helped me through my long journey with this book, but I do remember each and every one. So if you've ever pointed out an awkward sentence, a boring segment, or suggested I start my chapter in the middle rather than where I started, I am thinking of you and thanking you with all my heart.

Thanks are due to the Nashville Writers Meetup. Especially appreciative for the help I received at Alan Lewis's Novelist Meetup, and then later at the Mystery, Suspense and Thriller Meetup with organizers, Kathleen Cosgrove and Lily Wilson. Also wish to express my gratitude to everyone at the Middle Tennessee Sisters in Crime organization.

Writer, speaker, and teacher, Jaden (Beth) Terrell took the time to show interest in my book a few years ago and gave me advice and assistance. I thank her for her time and invaluable input.

Then there are all those folks I met in the early years of this book when I lived in the Central Valley of California: The San Joaquin Valley Sisters in Crime in Fresno, the Kings County Writers Support Group in Hanford, and the Visalia Writers Group.

Last, but not least, is Sunny Frazier who I give the most credit and thanks to. Sunny was there at the beginning with her guidance and kick-butt attitude. She was there at the end too, telling me I needed to stop revising and get published. She recommended Black Opal Books, a publisher I am proud to be associated with.

JUST ANOTHER TERMINATION

Linda Thorne

A Black Opal Books Publication

GENRE: COZY MYSTERY/WOMEN SLEUTHS/WOMEN'S FICTION

This is a work of fiction. Names, places, characters and incidents are either the product of the author's imagination or are used fictitiously, and any resemblance to any actual persons, living or dead, businesses, organizations, events or locales is entirely coincidental. All trademarks, service marks, registered trademarks, and registered service marks are the property of their respective owners and are used herein for identification purposes only. The publisher does not have any control over or assume any responsibility for author or third-party websites or their contents.

*For my husband, Dave,
who believed in me every step of the way.*

Author's Note

Just Another Termination is set on the Mississippi Gulf Coast prior to Hurricane Katrina. The characters are fictional, but many of the landmarks and structures in the story existed before Katrina barreled through the region in August of 2005, devastating the coastline. Although some of the structures survived, many did not but are preserved the way they were within these pages.

CHAPTER 1

October 2004:

When the plant manager told me Alma Guerra hadn't shown up for work, I should've walked away from my quarter-century long career in human resources right then. But the thought didn't enter my mind. Why would it? I couldn't recall a single incident of a no-call-no-show amounting to much more than some trifling issue. Sure, you get those who quit without notice, but they're always the ones you're glad to see go.

Not more than an hour after his announcement, Andy Holman waltzed back into my office with a new issue. "Judy, we've got to term Lester Robichaux."

"What now?" I asked. In Lester's mere six-weeks of employment, he'd already damaged two machines, putting them out of operation for weeks.

"He dropped a motor on the plant floor. It's done for, and so is he."

I rolled my eyes and sighed. "I'll prepare the discharge papers and meet you in your office."

I'd gotten as far as opening the blank termination form and typing in Lester's name when Millie Landry rapped on my doorframe. "I'm worried about Alma. I've been calling her all morning."

Having a bout of hot flashes, I didn't want to deal with it

so I waved her off. "Maybe she overslept, or had car trouble."

But I knew Millie couldn't be pacified. She was Alma's supervisor, and a motherly one at that. No doubt she had visions of Alma getting in a car accident, or a random fire at her house.

Millie cited a list of possible calamities before dropping dramatically into one of my straight-back chairs. "Alma was due in at seven. Judy, I'm telling you something's wrong." Her Southern Mississippi drawl cut across my desk without losing a note. "For land sakes, the girl's worked here ten years with no attendance issues."

I gulped. "Ten years?"

"Yes. If you knew her, you'd be in a panic, too."

I'd only worked for this packaging manufacturer for less than two months and hadn't met most of the two hundred plus employees yet.

Millie scooted closer, her dark hair, chocked-full of gray, hardly moving. "I'm going to drive over."

I held up a hand to keep her in her seat. "Let's pass it by Andy first." I leaned toward the phone, hit the speaker button, and tapped in Andy's extension. When he answered, I said, "Millie's here, upset about Alma, and—"

"You mean she still hasn't shown? Alma's never late."

"I want to check in on her," Millie piped in.

"Hold off," he said. "Judy, look through Alma's file. Try her emergency contacts first. Millie, we'll get back to you, but we've got another issue at the moment."

✧✧✧

Alma had listed her parents on the company's personal information form. At the time, they'd lived here on the Mississippi Gulf Coast, but she'd noted a change later, showing their address now in Texas, along with a new out-of-state phone number. I flipped through the rest of her file, looking for local contacts, then went back to completing Lester's termination form.

With the papers in hand, I pushed open the door leading

out to the plant. Rows of machines stretched out before me. Their warning lights flashed, reflecting off the rusting, thirty-foot ceiling, while an array of noises roared in my ears.

Millie stood near a cluster of box-folding machines, holding a clipboard, a stocky, uniformed woman beside her. "Millie!" I called over all the grinding and clacking. She glanced up then transferred the clipboard to the woman and serpentined around the machines.

I led her to a slightly quieter spot. "Her parents are her only contacts, but they're out of state. I'll get back to you after Andy and I handle this other matter."

Millie bit down on her lower lip. "I don't like this. I don't know of anyone who could look in on her 'cept me or one of her co-workers."

I had to admit I didn't like it either. The memory of another young woman surfaced for the first time since I took this job, intensifying my feeling of unease. I'd hoped to shake the tragic memory by changing jobs, yet here she was with me once more. I shuddered and rubbed my brow.

"Are you okay?" Millie asked, laying a hand on my shoulder.

"It's kind of hot in here," I said. Memories of Jolene Cromwell threatened to permanently carve themselves into my psyche, my being. I shook my head to clear it. I couldn't let myself get trapped in the past. I had a termination to deal with. Holding up the papers in my hand, I said, "Anyway, I'll get back to you once I've taken care of this."

I walked away and headed for the long corridor to the back offices. Stopping before the door with a plaque that read *Plant Manager*, I gave a quick knock then pushed the door open. Inside, Andy sat at a small table.

I pulled up a chair. "Did you send him for a drug screen?"

"Yeah, but I'm not waiting for the results," Andy said. "This is a terminable offense."

"Shouldn't we include Bert? He is Lester's supervisor."

"Bert's at a doctor's appointment. He'll be here soon, but we don't need him."

I was handing Andy the termination form, when Millie

passed by the open door. Andy leapt out of his chair and stuck his head into the hall. "Hey, Millie. Could ya run by the machine shop and send Lester in?"

While we waited, I told Andy about the no-show employee's contacts not being local.

He heaved a sigh. "I know Alma. She's in trouble or she'd be here. Something must have happened."

Unlike the last couple of places I'd worked, this management team showed respect and concern for their employees, traits I admired. And I'd already begun to feel camaraderie with my co-workers, as well as my boss.

Lester peered in through the open door. The scowl line across his forehead looked deeper than when I'd hired him. He lumbered forward, a shrunken man who wore his pants hiked halfway to his chest. He plopped into a chair, gravity tugging at the corners of his mouth. His dishwater-blond hair looked tousled, unkempt like the gray stubble on his face. His gaze caught mine and he swiveled his head twice in reaction, realization dawning on his face. "You're the HR lady."

"You've had one too many accidents, Lester," Andy said. "And you're still in your ninety-day trial period. So, I'm sorry, but your employment ends today."

"No. Please, Mr. Holman. Don't fire me."

I looked across the table at Andy. Since I'd started, no one had ever addressed him as *Mr. Holman*. I figured it was due to the fact that he didn't look old enough to be a plant manager.

Andy sighed and handed Lester the discharge papers. "Unfortunately, it all comes down to numbers, I'm afraid. It's costing us more to fix the damage you've caused than what your salary is worth. Sorry, but this is irreversible. If you have comments, please write them here and sign."

With an uneasy feeling, I led Lester down the hall to the supply room. I'd endured more than my share of bad terminations and had a feeling this one wasn't over yet. I just hoped my gut feeling was wrong.

I pulled out a checklist while he transferred any company property from his locker to the supply table—spare uniforms, keys, and gloves. When he turned over his name badge, he started mumbling incoherently.

I gritted my teeth, trying to not let my anxiety takeover. "Let's stay focused, Lester. You're almost done."

"I am done," he muttered. "I'll have to eat a bullet now."

My efforts at remaining nonchalant flew across the room, along with the pen I'd been holding. Feigning calm, I said, "I'll be right back."

Dropping the checklist, I sailed down the hall to Andy's office, slammed my hands against his doorframe and swung my head in. "He's threatening suicide," I said, shouting over Andy's telephone conversation with someone on speaker-phone.

Without waiting for a response, I shoved off and sprinted back to Lester. The poor man was folded over the supply table, sobbing.

A moment later, Andy burst in. Resting his hand gently on Lester's shoulder, he sat down beside him at the supply table. "This isn't personal," he said. "But you had another accident, and it's our policy—"

Lester looked up, his face dripping with tears and his shoulders heaving. "This always happens to me."

Andy put one hand out, palm up. "Lester, try to calm down. We'll get you some help. We have an employee assistance program—"

"But you fired me."

"You're covered through the end of the month." Over Lester's head, Andy signaled to me and I quick-stepped to his side. "Get the EAP on the phone," he whispered in my ear. "Speed-dial number three."

Once more, I hurried down to Andy's office. A woman who introduced herself as Dottie Salazar answered after the second ring.

"I'm Judy Kenagy, the new HR manager for Rockhold Packaging in Ocean Springs, Mississippi," I said in a rush, gripping the receiver with both hands. "We just terminated an employee, and now he's threatening suicide."

"Can you get him on the phone?" she asked in a choppy tone.

"I–I'll try," I said, my voice trembling. *This can't be happening. Not again*, I thought.

Shoving images of Jolene's tortured face from my mind, I put Dottie on hold and stepped into the hallway. Just then Lester came out of the supply room, Andy steering him toward me from behind.

As they approached, I fell into step beside them. "We have someone on the phone you can talk to," I said.

Together, we nudged Lester into Andy's office, sitting him down in Andy's desk chair. I took the phone off hold and handed him the receiver then we returned to the hallway, leaving the door open.

"I don't think he's leaving without a police escort," Andy whispered.

Hearing a clicking sound, we looked back at the door to find it closed. We swapped glances, but before either of us could move toward the door, an earsplitting *crash-bang-clank* came from inside the room. We jumped back just as Lester bounded out, bumping my shoulder and knocking me backward into Andy. He paused long enough to shake a fist at us, his tear-streaked face tensed and pink, then he turned and sped toward the back of the plant.

"Don't leave," Andy hollered after him.

Lester steamrolled past his supervisor, Bert, who had just arrived through the back entrance. Bert tumbled to the floor as Lester bolted out the door and into the parking lot.

"Wait," Andy yelled as he sprinted past Bert sprawled on the floor.

"Shove it up your ass," Lester shouted. "I ain't talkin' to you people no more."

I joined the chase, scolding myself for wearing heels to work that day. When I got to Bert, I stopped and offered a hand, helping him into a sitting position. He dangled a pair of crushed eyeglasses in my face and groaned. I patted his shoulder then stumbled back into a run.

By the time I reached the parking lot, Lester had climbed

into a rust-colored Ford pickup at the far end of the lot. Andy stood near the truck, jotting the plate number onto a tiny notepad.

I darted down the ramp then knitted in and around parked cars, jogging over a long stretch of empty parking spaces to the outer edge of the blacktop. The little truck coughed and choked, vibrating in tune to the clatter of its engine.

The driver's side window rolled down and Lester stuck his head out, his face burning red, his scowl line compressed into a dark, double-fold. "Andy Holman, you bastard! I'm going to git' my gun and come back here and kill you! No faggoty-ass sonovabitch is gonna fire me."

The pickup reeled forward, its tires squealing as he raced out of the parking lot.

Andy cocked his head to one side and gave me a lopsided grin. "Hmmm. So much for thinking Alma Guerra was the problem of the day."

I'd forgotten all about Alma but now my earlier dread returned. Praying whatever had kept her from work that day was trivial, I glanced back at the building a football field away. I felt small standing beside Andy on the vast expanse of asphalt, watching the pickup careen out the front gate and out of sight.

As we walked back, Andy had his cell against his ear, talking to the police. After reading off the license plate number, he hung up and sighed. "They've got an ABP out for Lester so hopefully they'll pick him up before he can hurt anyone. And they're sending a patrolman over to get our story."

Once back inside, Andy heaved the back door closed, sliding the thick steel bolt into place.

"What a reversal," I said. "The man was crying suicide one minute and threatening to kill you the next."

"And he called me a faggoty-ass."

"But you handled him as any practiced manager would."

Andy threw his hands out, palms up. "Call me the consummate professional."

I laughed. I'd gotten used to his flippant remarks. They

could take me out of a serious situation in a flash, but only for the moment. We still had another issue to deal with. "Call Millie and see if she's found out what's up with Alma Guerra yet."

"Let us worry about her. I need you to brief George before the cop gets here. Oh, and update the EAP rep about Lester." Andy whipped around and headed for his office.

Going through the plant on the way to George's office, I tripped on a wooden pallet. Stumbling to get around it, I stepped inside the yellow caution lines on the cement floor and had a near miss with a forklift.

God, what else can go wrong today?

"Are you h–hurt?" Bert asked, standing next to a cutting machine. Cardboard dust covered the floor at his feet.

"No, but I could've been." Pointing, I said, "That pallet needs to be moved."

"Sorry. Without my glasses, I c–can't see much m–more than the brightness of the lights. Heard the forklift's horn and barely made out your image." Turning his head toward another employee, he raised his voice to be heard over the cutting machine. "D–Dixie, c–could you help me over here with this p–pallet?"

A huge shadow fell over me and I looked over to see a muscular hulk. He skulked over and plucked up the stray pallet with one hand. Dangling the pallet against his side, Dixie took it to a nearby stack and dropped it on top. Then he returned to his machine in silence, not looking at either of us.

"Is that R–Robichaux fellow g–gone?" Bert asked.

"Yeah. Andy had to report him to the police."

He shook his head. "Sure c–caused a r–ruckus. And my glasses…" He sighed. "Pulverized."

With all Bert's stuttering, I found it interesting that he could throw out a big word every once in a while and have it come out as smooth as silk. "Well, you can't work if you can't see. How are you getting home?"

"My w–wife's on her way."

"All right. I'll help you out to the front." Taking him by the arm, I led him to the front entrance where I left him waiting on a bench then headed to George's office. As general manager, George Nichols was my direct boss, overseeing our plant in Ocean Springs.

I updated George on the sequence of events leading to Lester's discharge and what followed, expecting some kind of concern for what we'd been through. I also told him about Alma Guerra's absence.

The mention of Alma's name instantly brought George to his feet. "Why wasn't I informed?" he said. "If Alma hasn't shown up or called, something bad's happened."

Considering I'd been hit with surprises all morning, I shouldn't have been shocked that my boss seemed more concerned about Alma than the impending interview with a police officer over a potentially violent ex-employee. "She may be in now," I said. "Andy's getting an update from Millie." Leaning forward, I spun George's desk phone around, punched in Andy's extension, then pressed the speaker button. Andy's lack of any news didn't help matters.

I set the phone back in place. "I'm sorry, George. At first, this seemed like a regular no-call-no-show. And then we had the whole Lester Robichaux fiasco."

George just stared at me in silence.

Backing out of his office, I tried for a reassuring smile. "I'll try calling her house again. If she doesn't answer, I'll go over there myself."

લજલ

Alma's house was in an older section of Ocean Springs, where the homes were modest but maintained with pride. Most had only slender driveways and no garages, as they were built at a time when owning more than one car was common only for those in upper middle class or rich neighborhoods. As expected in the midst of a work day, the majority of the driveways were empty, so the sight of the Honda Civic in Alma's set off an alarm inside my head.

I parked at the curb. A sign stuck into the small front lawn read *John Kerry for President*. I glanced around. Across the street, a man unlocked his front door and let himself in. A young couple, with two dogs, strolled by. Down the block, a mail truck stopped in front of a house, the driver hurrying up the front walk to deliver a package.

Nothing out of the ordinary, I thought. Nothing to warrant the sense of impending danger I kept feeling. Was I still that traumatized by my memories of Jolene?

Only the presence of the Honda suggested Alma was home. The heavy curtains covering the large picture window were still drawn, not leaving so much as a half-inch gap.

I climbed out of my car and crossed the lawn to the wooden porch. Taking the three steps up, I made my way to the door, the planks squeaking beneath my feet. I nervously looked around once more then knocked.

The door drifted open on the first rap with a sharp squeal from the old hinges. I shrank back, my breath catching. *It's okay*, I told myself. *This isn't like that time.* Steeling myself, I peered through the opening and called inside. "Alma Guerra? This is Judy Kenagy, the HR manager from Rockhold Packaging. We were worried about you."

I touched the door lightly and it creaked open farther. I stepped in and froze, staring in horror and disbelief.

A woman's body lay sprawled out on her back right there on the living room floor. As much as I wanted it to be otherwise, she had to be Alma Guerra. She wore the company's standard issue brown uniform and black safety shoes, Rockhold's logo embroidered across the chest pocket. Her head was cocked at an odd angle, her face covered with a mass of coagulated blood. Long, black hair, splotched with dark red goo, fanned out around her head.

I covered my mouth, stumbling backward until I bumped into the doorframe. Then turning, I bounded down the porch steps and bolted across the lawn.

Chapter 2

Ignorant of oncoming cars, I raced across the street and pounded on the neighbor's door. My heart beat a fast staccato, my breath coming in pants like a hound after a two-mile run in the Arizona desert.

Come on! I thought, knocking again. *I know you're home. I just saw you go inside!*

Finally, a slightly older man opened it, leaving the screen door latched. My panic and vulnerability must've shown on my face because the moment I told him I'd found a body, he flipped the latch, pulled me inside, and locked the door with its deadbolt. He brought me a bottle of water while my shaking hands reached for his phone and called the police.

I was barely able to give the operator the needed information. The man finally relieved me of the responsibility and handled the rest of the call. After he'd hung up, he insisted I sit at a small wooden table by the window. I stared through the glass at Alma's small bungalow, memories of Jolene overlapping with the fresh ones of Alma.

What felt like an eternity later, two patrolmen finally arrived. "Where's the body?" the younger one asked as they flashed their badges and entered. I pointed toward Alma's home. "Is there anyone else inside?" he asked.

I shook my head. "I–I don't think so. That's my Camry parked out front."

Without another word, they left. I watched through the

window as they drew their guns on Alma's porch, paused, then disappeared inside.

A moment later, a black Crown Victoria pulled up, parking behind my car, and three men in suits climbed out. As the three made their way onto the porch, the two cops exited. The younger one began wrapping yellow and black crime scene tape around trees and fence posts, cordoning off Alma's property, as the other joined the three men in suits. The cop paired up with one and headed back across the street while the other two suits snapped on latex gloves and ducked under the tape.

"Are you all right, ma'am?"

I looked up to see the patrol cop and the suit standing over me. Realizing my hands were pressed against my cheeks, I let them fall. "I was, then I wasn't…and then I was again, but…"

The two gave me looks as though they thought I was nuts. *Perhaps I am*, I thought.

"Ignore that," I said. "Alma should've been a regular no-call-no-show. All the statistics will tell you that, but…she was killed. Why?"

While the officer jotted down notes, the other man asked, "*Why* as in why did this happen to you?"

"No." I put my hand up, palm out. "This shouldn't be on the report." But now, both men were scribbling notes.

I sighed. I had meant *why me*, but he didn't need to know that. Not only did it sound childish, it was irrelevant and would only make them ask questions I'd rather not answer.

I'd worked hard to escape bad bosses, dreadful work environments, and the tragic past that still haunted me, but my luck just kept running out, no matter where I went.

Taking a deep breath, I tried again. "You see, this morning I found out that Alma Guerra, uh, the woman over there—" I tipped my head toward the window, "—hadn't shown up for work. I'm the HR manager for the company she works at—I mean, worked…" I swallowed hard. "I didn't think much of it—no-shows are pretty common occurrences—but everyone else kept insisting her absence was like the sun not rising. Then what should've been a routine discharge spiraled into chaos."

I told them about the events surrounding Lester's termination, followed by how I'd ended up here. They scribbled faster, flicking notebook pages at a regular beat.

After asking every question imaginable, they sent me on my way, calling the neighbor over to question him.

As I slowly walked back outside into the hot afternoon sun, a WLOX TV news van pulled up. I quickened my pace, getting into my car just as a newswoman with a cameraman at her side approached.

"Ma'am? A few questions, please," the reporter asked.

Not on your life. "Sorry," I said. "The police asked me not to discuss anything with anyone."

As I drove away, wailing sirens announced the arrival of another black and white. As I turned onto a side street, an Alabama TV news truck fishtailed past me.

Knowing a phone call would be easier to handle, I pulled over and called George, bracing myself for the news I had to deliver. When he answered, my vocal cords shut down.

"Judy?"

"Yeah, I'm here. I, uh, found Alma, but–she–the body—" I lost it. Tears spilled down my face as I blubbered into the cell phone. "It was so horrible. She didn't have a face. Oh, God! Someone brutally murdered that poor girl."

"*What*? But–I just talked to her yesterday. This can't be."

"She's dead, George. The police already confirmed it." An image of the woman's mutilated face surfaced. *No. The police didn't need to confirm it. There was no way someone could have survived that.* I took a deep breath, trying to calm my emotions. "I'll tell you everything when I get back."

"No. Judy, I don't want you to come back to work right now," George said. "Go home and get yourself together. We'll talk tomorrow."

"But Andy–Millie."

"You're in no condition to do anything right now. Just do as I say. I'll tell them."

I knew he was right. If I couldn't do a decent job of

telling George, what business did I have dumping all these emotions on Andy and poor Millie? "I'm sorry, George," I sniveled. "I'm not thinking straight. I'll see you tomorrow."

When I got home, I called my husband, Dan, at work. Still crying, I went through the whole horrid sequence of events.

Exhausted, I collapsed onto the couch. Close to four, I awoke to the phone ringing.

"The police called, looking for you, and ended up with me," George said on speakerphone, Andy, Millie, and Bert in his office for the conversation. "They haven't made a positive ID yet, but wanted Alma's parents' names and phone number in the event Alma is the victim." He sighed over the line. "Had to unlock your office to get her file. Hope that was okay. They asked about her friends and relatives, job performance, that sort of thing."

"I'm sure that helped," I said. "I didn't give them much."

"How are you holding up?" he asked.

"Okay, I guess. It was just so awful." My hand flew to my mouth. "Sorry. You guys must feel dreadful. You all knew her. I didn't. And sorry again for losing it earlier, George."

The line was silent for a moment then all four of them came on at once, bombarding me with questions.

"Do you know what weapon was used?"

"Did you see anything near the body?"

"Do you know for sure it was her?"

"Wait. Wait," I called over them. "Remember, all I really knew about Alma Guerra was that she worked for us. Seeing her…well, I assumed it was her. She was wearing our uniform, and according to the address listed in her file, it was her house."

"Did she have long b–b–black hair?" Bert asked.

"Yes. But I, uh, couldn't tell much from her face."

Millie moaned into the phone.

"You sure you guys want to hear this?" I asked, praying they'd say *no*. I really didn't want to go through it again.

"Absolutely," George responded. "Tell us everything."

Taking a deep breath, I said, "Okay. Well, it was probably

gun shots, but I'm only guessing. The wounds messed up her face pretty good, which is why the police haven't ID'd her yet." Reluctantly, I pulled up the scene in my mind. "I didn't notice anything near her, but I didn't stick around there staring. Do any of you have guesses on who could've done this?"

"No, but we've been tossing possibilities around," George said.

Andy jumped in. "We learned she knew Robichaux. One of the employees told me they sometimes sat together in the break room. The two of them together freaks me out."

"Yes," Millie said. "From what I've heard of Lester, he was hardly someone Alma would take up with."

Their comments triggered a shadowy thought—pieces of a conversation in the break room. Lester was there, smiling. The voices floated in my subconscious, so close I had a sense of them, but they fizzled into nothingness.

"Judy? Ya' still there?" Millie asked.

"Uh? Oh, yes. Sorry. The police were working the scene when I left. They said to expect them at Rockhold soon, so we should know then if they found anything. They were glad I didn't go farther into the house and contaminate the crime scene." A chill snaked up my skin. "Believe me, the view from inside the door was more than enough."

"I bet," Andy said.

"Well, we'll meet tomorrow," George said. "In the meantime, try to get some rest."

෴

Unable to sleep, I sat in bed until almost midnight, sipping bourbon and talking to Dan. Finally, exhaustion overcame the horrors I'd seen that day and I fell into a deep sleep...

Dark things—faces and sounds—tumbled through my head. Then, with a strange clarity, someone called my name and I was gone, down a vortex, suddenly sitting on the edge of my bed, adjusting my eyes to the dark.

I was eerily alert, but still lost inside the dream. I got up and moved down the long hallway. In the family room, I stopped and looked around. All was as it should be. The stone fireplace in the corner, the overstuffed chairs nestled beside the sofa.

The air loomed with a harsh silence that slowly began to take on a life of its own, stabbing, tugging, and swirling around me. I stumbled past the sofa to the window and gripped the sill. In the darkness, the lawn, three stories below me, looked like a gaping black hole.

I pushed off and turned the corner into another hallway, my nightgown sweeping against my legs. A *click* shattered the silence and I swiveled toward it. Then, to my relief, the air conditioner began to whine and a blast of artificially cold air cut through my thin gown.

At the end of the hall, a door creaked open. I tiptoed over and peeked out onto an unfinished balcony, its balustrade missing. A plump young woman in a pink sleeveless blouse and tight-fitting jeans that framed her large buttocks, stood on the ledge. She turned her head to one side and, in the dim glow of an outside light, I recognized Jolene.

"Don't move," I whispered.

She glanced back, giving me a quick, sweet smile. The fullness of her face didn't affect her beauty, but the lingering sadness robbed it of all warmth and life.

I dropped down on all fours, cat-like. "Don't move, Jolene," I repeated, shuffling forward. Yanking at my nightgown caught under my knees, I moved farther and farther out toward her. "Be still."

A whooshing sound came from below. Leaves swirled in the dirt, quickly becoming a whirlwind that strengthened and grew until it towered above the trees in the garden.

Then, just as suddenly as it began, the cyclone vanished and Mrs. Briscoe appeared on the lawn, twenty feet below. She beckoned Jolene with open arms, her fingers wiggling like talons. Even in the dark and at that distance, malice was evident in the smirk on her face.

I crawled as fast as I could, stopping within inches of Jolene's legs. "Step backward, carefully."

She didn't budge.

I reached up to grab her hand, but only grazed the tips of her fingers. I tried again just as she took a step forward into empty space. I gasped and lunged, stretching my arms over the edge after her. But she was gone. "No!" I screamed. "Jolene!" I covered my eyes as my stomach sank with a sickening sense of powerlessness.

"Judy? Judy?" A voice came from the shadows, far away at first then closer.

I began to drift into a haze.

The voice calling my name echoed again. I blinked my eyes open to find myself in bed beside Dan.

"Judy? You okay, honey?" he asked.

I brought myself up onto one elbow and faced him. "What a dreadful dream. It seemed so real. I was here—" I pinched the cotton fabric of my nightgown and pulled it toward him, "—wearing this." I let the material drop back against me. "I thought for sure I'd just woken up. Everything here looked the same, the family room, too. But the rest of the house was different, and three floors instead of one." I took a breath. "Jolene Cromwell was on a balcony and Mrs. Briscoe was in a garden."

He lifted the blanket and pulled it over my shoulder. "With the day you've had, who wouldn't have nightmares."

"But Jolene had nothing to do with my day."

He frowned. "By now, Jolene should have nothing to do with anything, and that ridiculous Mrs. Briscoe—" He shook his head.

I knew he was right, but still I couldn't go back to sleep. Troubled thoughts kept spinning in my mind. Memories of being back in California working with Jolene Cromwell. Her termination almost two years ago and subsequent suicide. Then working for Mrs. Briscoe right after moving here to Ocean Springs.

Like the dream, everything morphed together as my thoughts continued to spin out of control, memories of what I'd seen at Alma Guerra's tiny house blurring with Jolene's leap and Mrs. Briscoe's toxic personality.

I slipped out of bed, careful not to wake Dan, and escaped to the guest bathroom at the other end of the house. Closing the door, I sobbed into my hands.

CHAPTER 3

The victim was shot at close range with one bullet to the face. The gun is missing." ~ Police Chief Carl Bombardier, the *Sun Herald.* Wednesday, October 20, 2004.

The next morning, Andy and George were waiting outside my office. I unlocked the door and they followed me into the room, closing the door behind them.

Except for a similar shade of dark, almost black hair, the two men were poles apart in appearance. Andy fell on the small side for a man, lean and wiry. Pushing thirty, he looked barely twenty, his skin color so fair I wondered if he lived in a cave. Andy's exact opposite, George was a hefty older black man, tall enough to look down at just about everyone at Rockhold Packaging. For a big man, George spoke with a compassionate tone, his manners impeccable and his eye for detail always open.

They settled in the chairs facing my desk.

George leaned forward. "I got another call from the police yesterday. The victim is Alma. A general comment hit the morning news, but they've yet to make her name public."

"I'm so sorry," I said.

George nodded. "We all are. I hate to say it but I'm glad

the police have the hard job of notifying her parents. But we've still got to tell the employees. Many of them work with Alma or did at some point over her years here and they're already asking about her. Would you see about getting a grief counselor? And call Corporate. God knows they'll be miffed if this hits the news, and we left them out of it." He rolled his eyes.

I stared at the two long faces. "Well, that shouldn't be an issue. They're an hour behind us in Phoenix so, they won't be in yet. Our EAP rep works there, too."

Tears welled up in Andy's eyes. He sniffed, no doubt trying to keep them at bay, but one got loose and he wiped it away.

"Did they find Lester?" I asked, desperate to change the subject.

"Actually, Lester found them," Andy said, sniffing again. "He rammed into a patrol car as the cop was on his way here. No one hurt. Jena witnessed the whole thing."

"Who's Jena?"

"She works in the folding department. She's best friends with Alma—or she was." Another tear slipped down his cheek.

"Is Millie here?"

"Yes," George said. "She should be at home though, with the way she looks. Get back to us with a schedule for the group sessions."

I hadn't slept more than a couple of hours and had come to work feeling slightly sick. On top of that, I couldn't shake the poignant residue from the dream. When I started my job at Rockhold, I'd gotten a short reprieve from the guilt that had torn at me for two years, guilt for my role in Jolene Cromwell's termination. For whatever reason, the murder of Alma had prompted its return.

After Jolene's suicide I'd stayed in a hospital, knocked out on sleeping pills. The dreamless sleep and waking up rested, with my last memory being my head hitting the pillow, sounded good right about now.

At close to nine, I called the vice-president of human resources at the corporate office. He didn't ask what we planned to do, just instructed me to send a memo. *A memo*? I thought, trying to visualize it in my head.

MEMORANDUM
TO: All Employees
FROM: Rockhold Packaging Management
SUBJ: Murder of Co-Worker

I shook my head. No matter what information I shared with the folks at corporate, they inevitably made some idiotic recommendation. I'd seen the horror of what was left of this young woman's face, seen the hurt in George's eyes and the tears in Andy's. I wasn't about to witness her co-workers' reactions to such an insensitive solution and felt like telling this guy to shove it. Instead, I hemmed and hawed about his directive then got off the phone, planning to ignore it.

I phoned Dottie. She needed more notice than this to be able to set up large group counseling sessions, but we'd just have to make it work somehow.

"Please try," I said. "I should've been here yesterday making arrangements, but the whole thing knocked me for a loop."

"I can imagine." She sighed heavily into the phone. "Well, I'll see what I can do. A lot of our counselors have day jobs and have to request time off from their employers in order to work for us. And their wages aren't so good, so they're not that keen to ditch their regular job for us. We have the psychologists, but they cost more and we don't use them for grief counseling." I could hear a soft tapping sound through the line. "You know, Judy, after what you've been through, you may want to consider—"

"No. I'm fine." I cleared my throat and redirected the conversation. "The first shift is the biggest. We'd need three, maybe four meetings to get to all of the employees. Try to get a counselor here by one o'clock, one-thirty at the latest. We could catch all of the second shift at four, and then reach out to third shift employees in the morning before they go home."

"We'll see," she said, "but I recommend you have a back-up plan."

Like what?

I dialed George's extension. "Getting a counselor's not looking good."

"Keep at it," he said. "Andy will lead the meetings, communicate the bad news."

An hour later the human resources vice-president phoned to ask what we'd done.

I felt like screaming, but managed to bite my tongue—barely. "Nothing yet," I said after taking a calming breath. "We're trying to pull the employees together in groups."

"What about the memorandum?" he asked.

"What was that? Sorry, I can't hear you. I think something's wrong with our connection," I lied and hung up.

ℰↈℰↈ

At the first meeting, Andy told everyone what little we knew about Alma's death then shared his feelings about Alma as a friend and co-worker. The room was somber, the employees listening quietly. When he finished he took a seat beside me, allowing the grief counselor to take over.

With head bowed and hands clasped, she took slow, short strides to the front. She'd appeared in our lobby not ten minutes ago, with the message she'd been sent by Dottie Salazar. "We are here today to say goodbye to a loved co-worker."

Her words and tone crystallized the permanence of the violent act that took our employee's life, and I could hear several people sniffling.

"Tell me things you remember about her," the counselor said.

A middle-aged woman with frizzy red hair stood up and glanced at those seated around her. "Alma had the sweetest smile," she said. "She was always so light and happy." She sat down in a slump, her face twisted in despair.

A young black man described Alma as determined to the point of being stubborn. He was quiet a moment, then said,

"Alma had faults like the rest of us, but her greatest attribute was her kind heart. She had a way of raising your spirits when you were down. Just being in the same room with her was a gift."

That did it. The dam cracked.

Most of those not already crying broke down. Andy wiped tears from his face as Millie bawled into a handkerchief. I muffled a moan. My face tensed as I tried to control my own emotions. I hadn't known Alma, but the overwhelming sadness and loss had gotten to me. I looked at George with his head hung like a beaten dog and hoped I'd never see him like this again. Dixie, that hulk of a man I'd met the day before, sat in the row behind George, looking around. He kept glancing at his watch, obviously agitated.

Remembering Jolene, alive and well, I almost cried. It didn't seem right to bypass the murder victim and feel for someone else, but I couldn't help myself.

When the session ended, the counselor distributed employee assistant program cards, letting them know they could contact a grief counselor if they ever needed to do so.

The next meeting went about the same, different faces yet similar stories about Alma. After the last of the first shift meetings, I noticed a young man exiting the break room and making tracks for Andy. He caught up to him near the plant entrance and they chatted for a while.

I passed them and pushed through the door, weaving around a maze of cardboard stacks. At the main walkway, I strode passed a half-dozen cutting machines before I felt the chilling sensation of being watched. A half-glance over my shoulder confirmed it. Dixie was bent over his worktable, his sullen blue eyes turned up at me. He lowered his lids and with slow, mechanical movements, guided his cutting machine across the worktable, his huge suntanned biceps pulsating.

I turned back and picked up my pace. I found Millie in the folding department, her right hand resting on the only folding machine not running. Alma's machine. Her gaze stared off out into the plant, vacant and lost.

I hurried over and stood beside her. "Are you okay?"

She hung her head and gulped back a sob. "No, but I'm trying to hide it for the sake of the employees."

I gave her a comforting hug and she hugged me back, hard, as if she'd known me for years.

"Soon as the second shift meeting ends, I'm outta' here," she said, pulling a tissue from her pocket. She blew loudly, like an old man, then stuffed it back into her pocket. "Let's not talk about her for a while."

I nodded and we started walking.

"What was the hubbub with Lester?" she asked.

"Nothing much." Even if I'd wanted to talk about that fiasco, company policy forbade it. So I changed the subject. "Who's that guy in the cutting department with the brassy blond dye-job?"

"Who? Dixie?

"Is that his real name?"

"No," Millie said. "We call him Dixie but his real name is Michael Ledet." We stopped in the corridor. Millie's pixie face and pug nose brought youth to her appearance. But up close, her eyelids sagged and wrinkles creased her flesh. "He's worked here twenty-four years, same machine. Pretty much keeps to himself."

I leaned against the wall and stared at the tips of my shoes. "He gave me the crawly creeps the way he was looking at me a minute ago. And at one of the meetings, he seemed anxious, like he wanted to leave in a hurry."

"He's okay. Just a bit odd, that's all. Pay him no never-mind."

A clap of thunder boomed in my ears and the wall vibrated. I jumped back. "Sheesh. That sounded close."

"I'm gonna check out back. We might've been struck," Millie said, hurrying away. "This storm's a real gulley-washer."

By the time we caught the second shift at four, the rain had picked up, beating on the fabricated metal roof like shots from a machine gun. The grief counselor raised her voice to compensate. The meeting ending with the earsplitting noise of the storm still going strong.

Employees were leaving, the buzz of their voices rising like a locust-storm. The last few second shifters were leaving the break room. At the door, Andy tugged at my elbow and pulled me back in. "I got a snippet from Eddie Sutter," he said.

"That kid with you by the plant entrance?"

"Yeah. He said Robichaux was hot after Alma."

"I may have something, too." I swept my gaze around the empty room. "When you mentioned you'd heard Alma and Lester sat together in the break room, I remembered bits of a conversation I'd overheard. I didn't say anything then because I wasn't sure who Lester had been talking to and the memory was so faint I wasn't even sure it was real. But while I was getting dressed this morning, the break room discussion niggled at me once more. Was Alma pretty?"

"Beautiful," Andy said without hesitation. "Dark features, long hair."

"Well, I'm pretty sure I heard a young woman invite Lester to her home. I think that may've been Alma. I heard her and then saw a woman of her description write down her address on a napkin."

"I can't imagine," he said. "All Eddie mentioned was Lester's interest in her. Not a word about Alma liking him back. Did you hear the reason for the invite?"

I thought for a moment then shook my head. "I'm certain there was one, but for the life of me I can't remember."

"Well, it's a good thing he's in the slammer now. He's volatile, even threatened to kill me."

I waved him off. "Volatile, yes, but a broken man, that's all. We'll file a restraining order to keep him away from you and all the other employees." Seeing he was about to protest, I held up a hand. "That's protocol after the scene he made."

⌘

I finally got back to my office at a little after five, exhausted and grateful the last meeting was tomorrow morning.

A pink message slip had been dropped on the seat of my chair. I picked it up and sat down.

"Hell of a day," Andy said, drifting in and sinking into a chair. I handed him the slip of paper. He read it and smiled. "Wilma's up to her tricks. She knows to transfer your calls to voicemail."

"Since it's from the police chief, I'm sure she pumped him for information."

"Didn't take you long to get her number."

"Someday I'll tell you about it," I said.

He clasped his hands behind his head and leaned back. "Chief Carl, huh?"

"You know him?"

"Used to work with him. I was a part-time clerk at the Biloxi Police Department during my last year in high school and all the way through college. He was a commander then."

"What's that?"

"A high level detective. He was a workaholic and a real micromanager, but the best detective the City of Biloxi ever had."

"I think I've seen him on TV," I said. "Commander to chief, quite a jump."

"Nah, not in Ocean Springs. His title may've changed, but Ocean Springs is so small, I doubt his responsibilities did." Andy yawned. "Can you believe Bert? Made only two meetings."

I chuckled. "Did you see his new eyeglasses?"

"Yeah. Why would he pay for glasses as ugly as that? Common sense should've told him to jump at a chance for decent frames."

"An–dy," I scolded in a motherly tone. "Poor guy got knocked flat on his only pair. He was probably in a hurry."

"But Judy, I didn't think they make coke bottle glasses anymore. And those thick, dark frames, he'd have to go to some black market to find them."

My face tightened from the strain of my grin. "Heaven forbid we say anything good about them."

We laughed, hard, unrestrained in that giddy way folks do when they've been through trauma. It wasn't even that funny, but releasing the tension, even just a little bit, felt so liberating.

The laughter wound down and I wiped my eyes. "You know, there was one time, I'm trying to think when—" I pressed my fist to my chin. "Bert looked kind of handsome."

"Girrrl," Andy drawled, "you've gotta be kidding."

Ignoring him, I continued to search my memory. "Yes. I remember you were there." I looked over his head at the wall as if the answer might be posted there. "Bert had taken off his glasses. Must've been a dress-down Friday because I remember him wearing a vibrant shirt. Color's what he needs with his pale skin and that thin light hair. Darn, when was it?"

Andy looked up at the wall clock. "I don't know, but I've gotta' go." He rose. "Jena Doggett went home early."

"Well, I can understand why."

He ambled backward toward the door. "She'll milk this." At the threshold, he whirled around. "Mark my words," he said with a wave over the back of his head.

Glancing at the pink paper in my hand, I debated returning the call in the morning. Figuring I'd just get the voicemail since it was after five, I dialed the number.

The police chief answered after the first ring. "Wanted to forewarn you we'll be stopping by in the morning," he said and I caught the sound of Cajun. "About this Guerra death."

"We've been expecting you." I didn't like the idea of having cops roaming the plant just when the employees were trying to grieve but I knew there was no way around it.

"Ya have any suspicions yet, company gossip?" he asked.

"We learned our problem discharge from yesterday, Lester Robichaux, knew the victim. Apparently he was attracted to her. Do you have a picture of Alma you can bring tomorrow? I didn't know her, but I remember hearing a female employee invite Lester to her home. After hearing our plant manager describe her, we think it might've been her."

"I do. We'll want to talk to your general manager and then the other management staff. Maybe others. We'll be there around nine." He hung up without another word, leaving me with the dial tone and wondering why he'd called it *death* instead of *murder*.

At Rockhold we all depended on speed-dial for regular

phone contacts. I jabbed the third speed-dial button, reaching Dottie and briefing her on the meetings. I glanced at the button for Corporate, ignored it, and pulled out Alma's personnel file. Even dead people have to be terminated.

On the personnel status change form, I entered the name, social security number, and a term date of October 19, 2004. It wasn't until I was separating the copies that the error jumped out at me. I'd printed *Jolene Cromwell* on the name line. I ripped the form up and threw it away, then looked at the wall for a long, empty minute. I dug the pieces out of the waste can, shredded them more, then tossed them back in.

I reached for another form, but a flood of emotions ran through me, hard and riveting as the rain that pounded on the roof. My hand trembled and I dropped the pen. Tears filled my eyes. I grabbed my purse and ran out into the rain, trying to remind myself this was just another termination.

❧❧❧

Dan had already eaten by the time I got home. I wasn't hungry. I hung my wet coat in the closet by the door then patted Buffy, our golden retriever's head. Dan got a two-sentence summary of my day before I went into the bedroom. I changed into lounging pajamas and settled into a chair with a book. Two pages into it, I fell asleep.

The phone rang then stopped. Dan came in, Buffy at his side, her sweet face turned up. "It's for you. Some guy," he said then went back out to the living room with Buffy.

I picked up the phone beside the bed. "Hello?" No answer. I could hear a click as Dan hung up the line in the other room.

Thirty seconds passed. I repeated myself only to hear light wheezing coming through the line. Then, with a muffled voice, the caller said, "It's not an employee. The murderer is her secret friend."

Chapter 4

Taken aback, I set the phone on its cradle and left the bedroom to find Dan. He was playing a war game on the computer in our little office off the family room. I recounted the caller's ominous words. "I don't like this," I said. "I'm being pulled into this murder case. Hon, I have a feeling this is only the beginning."

But was it? Somehow, it felt tied to the other events in my life over the past few years.

Later, while Dan slept, I stared at the ceiling, thinking about Valerie Kelm-Briscoe, owner of Kelm Machinery here in Ocean Springs. Dan had taken a job in Biloxi and was living in temporary quarters until I could either sell our LA home or find a job on the Gulf Coast. I managed to get a phone interview with Mrs. Briscoe for an HR opening at her company, and I accepted a job offer, sight unseen. Yes, I thought it strange to be offered a job after a phone interview, but I was blinded by my desire to join my husband, along with my desperation to leave that nightmare job in LA—the place where I'd worked with Jolene.

Within the swirling ceiling fan, Mrs. Briscoe appeared. I saw myself, too, sitting before her in one of the leather high back chairs. I watched her naturally pretty face redden then morph into a vein-bulging mass of lined flesh.

Her soft blue eyes turned mean and squinty, darting about wildly. "What are you doing here?" she screamed down the hall at one of her employees. "Get back to the plant." As quickly as she had tensed, the lines disappeared and she fell back in her chair, her face returning to normal.

"Mrs. Kenagy, do you see what I have to put up with? I'm surrounded by dimwits."

Her behavior didn't surprise me. Any expectation I'd had that this might be a normal place to work was gone, obliterated in my first week on the job.

∽∾∽

December 2003:

Mrs. Briscoe's assistant, a willowy young woman with her face always caked in makeup, had greeted me in the Kelm Machinery lobby that first day. In a child-like voice, she'd introduced herself as Nora Flint.

"Well, Miss Kenagy," she'd said, "Mrs. Briscoe will certainly be happy you've started."

Nora led me past the reception counter and down a short hallway. Turning into an office on our right, she said, "Here's your office." Then she hurried out, returning with a policy manual and office supply booklet. "This will keep you busy," she said with a sweet smile.

I thanked her and she moved gracefully across the room, closing the door behind her.

Thirty minutes later, she returned with an urbanite man, tall and stately.

"Hello, Ms. Kenagy," he said. "I'm Keith Briscoe."

"Oh, you must be—"

"Yes, I'm the husband. I don't work here. My wife asked me to stop by to meet you." He spoke with an upper New England clip and his graying black hair complemented an angular face, balanced with dark features. He was handsome, but his smile felt plastic, not quite reaching his eyes.

Keith and Nora left and I roamed the halls, found the break room, restroom, and the door leading out to the plant. I introduced myself to a few office employees, all of them somber and standoffish. No matter how many times I went out to look around, I found myself back at my desk, feeling oddly safe there. Nora stepped in every once in a while to see if I needed anything.

On one of her visits, I said, "Thanks for asking, but I'll wait to talk to Valerie."

Nora's heavily mascaraed eyes widened. She looked bowled-over and I instantly felt I owed her more of an explanation. Not that I had any idea what that explanation should be.

"I mean, I'll know what I need after I learn what's high on the boss's agenda."

"Ummm," she said, kneading her hands, her face ashen. "Maybe I should explain—tell you how it is here."

"Is something wrong?"

Nora gave a squeaky little yelp. I sprang out of my chair and went to her.

She took a step back and studied the top of her hands. "Well, it's just—I mean—no one calls Mrs. Briscoe *Valerie*. It's a matter of respect for such a fine lady, if you know what I mean."

"Seriously?"

"Yes. Sorry. We're always serious around here." She turned and sped out the door.

ひつびひ

Mrs. Briscoe arrived mid-morning the next day and walked passed my open door without so much as a glance. I recognized her from photographs plastered all over the break room walls.

A few minutes later, an authoritative Southern voice came over the paging system. "Mrs. Schneider. Mr. Thornton. Mrs. Kenagy to my office."

Before the summons ended, Nora leaned in, her shoulder-length golden locks falling forward. She waved me toward her. I got up and went over, inhaling her rich perfume. "It's Mrs. Briscoe," Nora said in an urgent whisper.

She pointed to another office behind the lobby, across the hall from mine, and nudged me forward. After a quick knock, I entered the room, immense for an office. No windows and a ceiling at least fourteen-feet high. Tight-looped Berber carpet covered the floor in a feminine pastel blue. Valerie Kelm-Briscoe seemed small, seated behind the ample oak desk. A man and a woman sat, facing her, in two of five throne-like chairs.

"Well, don't just stand there," she said with a wave of her hand. She wore a long-sleeved burgundy dress with a low neckline. "Come on in."

The white walls were suitably bedecked with large pictures in ornate frames. Even with colossal wall hangings and big furniture, the gaps of open space gave the room an empty feel.

Mrs. Briscoe had fair, creamy skin, high cheekbones, and eyes a true definition of blue. She watched me look around, then stood, and pointed to an enormous painting on the wall behind her.

"That's the Kelm plantation in Vicksburg. It's been in the family since before the Civil War. My daddy told me stories of how the Yankees tried to burn down the old mansion. The family's devoted servants chased them off."

She fell back into her seat, her dyed blonde hair curling around her face like a pair of parentheses. Serrated bangs sprang from her evenly cut hair and curved over her smooth forehead.

She pressed her lips shut, forming a thin line, her finely arched eyebrows pulled together. "Those servants were the last of their kind. We certainly don't get that sort of loyalty from the employees around here."

I hunched my shoulders, an instinctive reaction I'd picked up in LA when my bosses criticized their staff. I strode over to the big chair next to the woman and eased into the seat, still gazing about the office.

Mrs. Briscoe introduced the lady beside me as Mrs. Schneider, one of the managers. A birdlike woman with sallow skin and stringy hair, Mrs. Schneider made an attempt at a smile. Her dark pinstriped suit hung loose, suggesting she'd once weighed more. A chubby-cheeked caricature of a young man stepped up to the corner of Mrs. Briscoe's desk, drawing my attention away from Mrs. Schneider. He wore a long-sleeved T-Shirt and dingy overalls with a patch on one leg. He was short enough to rest one elbow on the desk while still standing.

The man in a gray suit, sitting two chairs over, leaned forward. "I'm Jack Thornton," he said, a hundred and fifty watt beam of a smile crossing his face. "Plant manager. Glad to have you aboard."

"Likewise," I said, returning the smile.

Nora fluttered in and out, her colorful, thin dress floating around long, slender legs. She brought Mrs. Briscoe ice water, making a separate trip for a side glass of ice then a couple of napkins, not the ones with the flower print, but the thicker ones from the break room.

Mrs. Briscoe ignored Nora, her attention still on the odd young man in the overalls. His ginger hair was full and cut long enough to cover most of his ears and part of his brow.

"And this is Jimmie Lee Albright," she said, cocking her head and grinning.

He removed his elbow from the desktop and straightened, allowing his short arms to dangle at his sides. He grinned like one of those yellow smiley faces with the words *Have a Nice Day* printed below.

"Jimmie Lee does a little bit of everything 'round here," she said. "Don't you, Jimmie?"

I figured he couldn't be older than his early twenties, but he sported one of those worn, rode-hard looks, suggesting he'd begun a career in heavy labor at a rather tender age. I pictured him as an eleven-year-old, tramping into a sawmill swinging a rusted lunch pail.

He stared at her in adulation. "I can do everythang," he said. "Mizz Briscoe uses me in 'bout any job if they're short o' help."

She gave Jimmie another quick grin then emptiness fell over her face, as shallow as the words that followed. "Our last human resources manager, Miss Crandall, was a bit of a twit." Sizeable earrings tugged at her ear lobes and knocked about with the shake of her head, while her hair bounced in sync with her speech.

Jimmie Lee put his thumbs under his overall straps and took over, launching into his own version of the story. "Miss Crandall drove down a street behind the company, not an open thoroughfare, but one that dead-ended at Kelm Machinery. I recognized her car right off and jumped into my pickup and roared after her. When I got close, I swerved side to side, comin' close to her rear then backin' off, gittin' closer. Over and over." His hand swerved in graphic movements, like a kid describing planes in aerial combat.

Mrs. Briscoe's attention stayed on Jimmie Lee, her eyes gleaming as she nodded in approval. Mrs. Schneider watched with a smile so tense you'd think her boney face would crack in two. Jack Thornton's smile shriveled into a counterfeit one, the corners of his mouth quivering under the strain.

"Why, I saw the tracks Jimmie Lee left in the road," Mrs. Briscoe said, leafing through the mail. "That'll teach her to prowl around my company. Mrs. Kenagy, I've told Callie— she's our switchboard operator—to listen for Miss Crandall's voice on incoming calls and not transfer her to anyone. Although, I'm not sure I can trust Callie—I heard that when Miss Crandall quit, Callie cried."

Miss Crandall quit? From all this to-do, I assumed they'd fired her.

Jimmie Lee glowed gallantly. "And I really got her good when I rode over to her new job and told 'em I needed to collect the thirty dollars she owed Mizz Briscoe. She didn't have it then but said she'd send it postal. Well, I told her I'd be comin' back every day till we got it, and guess what? A check was under our door next mornin'."

"Jimmie Lee's the best," Mrs. Briscoe said.

Confused, I gaped at them. *So, she quit but they continued to harass her?*

"Why, if my other employees were half as loyal as Jimmie Lee, I'd be in my glory. I can't begin to tell ya'll how ungrateful they are. I give them bonuses at Christmas and Jimmie Lee tells me they call them puny." Her hands and arms moved about wildly. "Why, my daddy, God rest his soul, would turn over in his grave if he knew."

She continued to complain about her employees, sounding strikingly like my bosses back in LA. At the thought of them, poor Jolene Cromwell popped into my mind.

"Now we've hired you, Mrs. Kenagy, and I'm sure you'll straighten them out. Why, you're not anything like that other HR person."

Heat flushed my cheeks. *Excuse me?* I thought. *How does she know what I'm like or not?*

"Val-*er*-ie," I said, articulating each syllable of her name.

The blue of Mrs. Briscoe's eyes fired at Nora walking toward her with a tall glass of lemonade. Nora came to an abrupt stop, teetered, then dropped the glass.

I continued, "Can you please tell me what Miss Crandall did that was so bad?"

Nora raced out, quickly returning with an armload of white towels. "I'm sorry. So sorry," she said in her little girl voice. Dropping to her knees, she scrubbed the carpet with vigor.

Flicking her gaze to me, Mrs. Briscoe said, "My problems with Miss Crandall were many. One that comes immediately to mind is that I couldn't figure out what she did all day." She swung her head to the side and glanced at the wall mirror. "Miss Crandall argued that the staff wanted to do a good job. All we had to do was provide them with the tools. Can you believe that? She obviously didn't know a thing about *my* employees."

While she spoke, Jimmie Lee's mahogany eyes stayed focused on her. With her first pause, he turned to me and said, "Mizz Crandall wuz reeel stupid."

Opened and stacked mail sat in orderly rows in front of Mrs. Briscoe. She began to divvy out each piece one by one, what seemed to me an odd and inefficient procedure. Noticing my scrutiny, she said, "Daddy taught me this." She flattened an envelope above her heart, launching into a soliloquy. "My daddy was a wonderful man. Always told me, 'never let anyone get the mail, little girl, until you've seen it first. The mail will tell you everything going on in your company.'"

The sorting ritual done, she divvied out the piles. My batch included an unemployment hearing notice. A Mr. Mooney was appealing a claim he lost because he'd resigned voluntarily. He argued he was brutalized into quitting, a constructive discharge by the owner.

As I glanced over the notice, Mrs. Briscoe shrieked about all the ill-will Mr. Mooney had caused her and why she should sue him. And the nerve. Oh my god, how she went on about his nerve. Her voice, already at a sharp pitch, rose as her head jutted forward. "And, Mrs. Kenagy, they must be told how he barged into my office that day. Then there's the time he questioned my authority—*my* authority. This has to be on the record."

She waved her hands in front of her face before balling them into fists. With the movement, a trinket clattered across the desktop and fell at Jimmie Lee's feet. He bent over and picked the thing up then, stretching his arm and half of his body across the desk, dropped it into Mrs. Briscoe's open palm.

"Thank you, Jimmie Lee," she said, pressing her fist, tightly wrapped around the object, against her heart. "My, I must watch myself or I'll surely lose one for good." She clasped it onto her bracelet. Holding her wrist up, she said, "Mrs. Kenagy, these are from my daddy. With each new invention, he took the first machine parts produced and made pieces of jewelry for his family. I got charms." She held the little nugget up. "See? There's a tiny screw inside."

"Yes," I said. "Smaller than any screw I've ever seen."

"We make and market unique products at Kelm. The micro parts my father invented are renowned worldwide. Although small, they're stronger and more efficient than those of our competitors. And they're cheaper to ship, handle, and store. My daddy took some of these industrial fasteners and plated them with silver, making jewelry pieces out of them. They're keepsakes to remind us of the basic Kelm family principles—hard work, honesty, and dedication to tasks results in success."

Jimmie Lee beamed and the roll of fat around his middle wobbled. "And Mizter Kelm marked the ones for his kin in the order they came offa' the production line."

Mrs. Briscoe fingered her bracelet, gazing at it proudly. She looked up with a pleased, childish grin. "Mine were always the second ones from each new run."

❡❡❡

Each day I went to work for Valerie Kelm-Briscoe felt like the same day. She'd arrive late, pass by my office, then page me into her office with the others. Every night I'd go home, pound down a martini or two, and tell my husband that Mrs. Briscoe's office was the Queen's court and Jimmie Lee was her court jester.

He thought I was exaggerating. He'd laugh when I told him I wished the Yankees *had* burned the Kelm plantation to the ground.

Every day she'd snap her fingers at Nora who flitted nervously in and out of her office. "Get me some tea. This time, use the crystal from the kitchen. And make sure you bring the patterned napkins."

Mrs. Schneider and Jack Thornton would always be in the room, along with the ever-present court jester. She was never without her audience and her servant.

How could she say she didn't know what Miss Crandall did all day? This was what Miss Crandall would've done all day, every day.

Chapter 5

I try to do the best job I can. If I'm doing something wrong, please tell me so I may correct the problem. I was to be discharged yesterday for a mistake on the loading dock until I proved I was out on my scheduled day off. Please put this in my personnel file." ~ Jolene Cromwell, one month before she was fired.

∽∾∽

October 2004:

I drove down narrow, twisting roads, flanked with foliage, and zipped across a squat cement bridge before turning onto Washington Avenue, the main thoroughfare of downtown Ocean Springs. Unlike the dying downtown areas in large cities, this hub was thriving. Old, wood-framed buildings, painted in loud colors and with numerous trees, lined the street.

Normally I took my time, savoring the beauty that glided past my windshield, but not this morning. I had to get in early for the last of the grief meetings.

I ground to a halt at the stoplight where Washington intersected with Highway 90. An eddy of wind scattered leaves across the road while I impatiently kept my foot on the brake. The light changed and my Camry lurched forward, taking a right onto Highway 90 East, away from the little city center.

Ten minutes later, I sprang from my car and hurried across the pavement to the main entrance of Rockhold Packaging. The twenty-some third shift employees were already seated in the conference room. The grief counselor, prepped for her part, waited in the first row. I sat down in a folding chair next to Millie and George. Andy walked to the front to begin once again.

At close to nine, I clutched my report of last night's anonymous caller and took off for the front of the building, my heels clacking on the cement floor. Police officers stood in the undersized lobby while the receptionist, Wilma, stared at us. Clearly, I would need to move them to someplace more confidential.

The police chief flashed his credentials then extended his hand, not for an overzealous arm-pumping shake like some Southern folks, but in what I'd call more of a California handshake—pure business. "I'm Carl Bombardier."

He wasn't as tall as I'd expected, and heavier, but then people you see on TV always look different in the flesh. If this were LA, he'd pass for Portuguese with his black hair and smooth olive complexion. But here, on the Gulf Coast, I'd say he was of French descent. I put him at around forty-five years old, his hair showing the salt and pepper signs of age. He was handsome for a moment then not the next. His eyes were the root of the variation, liquid black. They alternated between radiant and murky.

With him were two lieutenants. I'd heard they were the only ones of their rank in the city, both next in line to the chief. The city of Biloxi had the higher rank of commander, but Ocean Springs' budget was too small to justify the position. Ocean Springs had a handful of sergeants and the usual contingent of street cops. Whether any of this was accurate, I could only guess as I'd gotten my information that morning from Millie who, apparently, had a friend inside the police department.

The police chief turned toward the younger of the two men and introduced him as Lieutenant Kevin Young. Tall, with the build of a former jock, he had clipped ash brown hair and a high forehead. Like the others, he was dressed in a suit and tie.

"And this is Lt. Johnnie Leblanc," the chief continued. "You've already met him, of course." The chief gestured to the detective who had interviewed me the day I found Alma's body, a somber Joe Friday type with light red hair, trimmed in a marine crew-cut.

I shook his hand then ushered the trio down the hall to the administrative offices and into the conference room. George sat with his back to us, his attention on something written on the whiteboard. From that angle he could've been mistaken for James Earl Jones. The comparison extended to George's voice, mannerisms, and personality, exhibiting the same strong moral fiber portrayed by Jones in the characters he played.

George stood up, facing us. Except for his dark skin and hefty build, the resemblance disappeared. His wide mouth curled up naturally at the corners.

Introductions made, handshakes and small talk behind us, we all claimed seats around the long oval table. Bombardier started by requesting approval to review employee files and question whomever he chose. George gave him carte blanche.

When Bombardier asked if anyone had anything new to share, I sat forward. "I got an anonymous call last night," I said, handing my report to the police chief.

George leaned forward, his chair groaning in protest from the shift of his weight.

"My husband tried *star sixty-nine* and got nothing," I continued before anyone could ask the obvious question.

Bombardier studied the report. "Hmmm." Then he read the caller's statement out loud. "'It's not an employee. The murderer is her secret friend.' I wonder why he called you?" he asked, more to himself than to me. "Based on this, we can't rule out employees."

"Did you recognize the voice?" George asked.

"Well, as it says in the report, Dan took the call and swears the person was male. When I got on, I couldn't even determine the caller's sex. Their voice was so muffled."

"Well, I don't see any reason to keep ya," Bombardier said to George. "We'll start with Judy, look through some files."

George started to speak, but I cut him off. "Do you have any clues yet in the murder?" I asked Bombardier.

His dark eyelashes fluttered. "We don't know that it's murder."

"But she was shot in the face."

George stared at me, furling his brow.

"Her death could've been an accident or even suicide. Can't rule anything out," Bombardier said, Cajun leaping in and out of his voice.

"But you can't find the gun, right?"

George harrumphed and I sagged back into my seat.

Bombardier worked his gaze around the table. "Correct. The gun's missing and this is likely murder, but I've seen it all. Someone's accidentally shot and killed and the shooter panics, takes the gun, and runs. Or family members of a suicide victim remove the note and weapon to ensure payment of life insurance or, to bury the stigma of the act. I could go on."

Sighing, I stood up. "I'll take you to my office."

The chief started to rise then sat back down and looked at us. "Oh, we just learned Guerra wasn't sexually assaulted. That'll hit the paper tomorrow."

No one commented, but George heaved a heavy sigh as if this tragedy had become easier to swallow. He left quietly.

Bombardier used his arms to push himself up to standing. Lieutenant Leblanc followed, but Lieutenant Young remained seated, toying with a gold band on his left hand. Bombardier stared at Young until the lieutenant caught on and rose.

I led the threesome to my office where we settled at a little round table. I reached behind me and grabbed Lester Robichaux's file from atop my desk. "I figured you'd want this."

"Yes," Bombardier said, taking the file from me and leafing through the paperwork inside. "Why did you hire this guy? He has a terrible work history."

"Experienced machine adjusters are in short supply. We hire just about anyone who has any."

A mocking grin appeared on his circular face and he bounced a glance from Young to Leblanc. "I guess you do." He handed the file to Lieutenant Young. "I noticed you submitted a background check. Where's the results?"

I shifted in my chair. "He lives in Hancock County—Bay St. Louis. They take their time, so we hired him contingent upon the report being okay when it comes in."

He looked at the detectives. "Dig up information on Robichaux's background and find out his whereabouts when Guerra was shot. Now, let's start the interviews."

"I'll call Alma's supervisor. She's worked here forever."

They stood in unison, the chief appearing rotund in comparison to his sidekicks. Before returning to the conference room, Bombardier asked me for time records for October eighteenth and nineteenth.

Millie must've been waiting for my call since she answered on the first ring. "Do they want me in the conference room?"

"Yes. They're expecting you."

I hung up the phone and walked out, crossing a stretch of floor dotted with cubicles, then went around a corner to the payroll department. JoAnne Necaise was digging through one of the file cabinets behind her desk and didn't see me come in.

When I called her name, she pulled a stocky arm out of a drawer and glanced back at me. "Oh, Judy. You poor thing. I heard all about it." JoAnne had returned that morning after a few days off, out of state for a niece's wedding.

"Yeah, well. The police are here and want time records for Monday and Tuesday."

Her auburn hair, brushed back hard and sprayed into position, emphasized big cheeks on a podgy face. "This is such a tragedy. I'll pray for Alma's family—as soon as I get home that is."

George and I had spoken to JoAnne about praying publicly during work hours.

She turned to the wall unit behind her and lifted a thick binder off the top shelf. With round, ringed fingers and manicured nails, she opened the binder and placed a yellow sticky on one page then another. "Here. I've marked the dates," she said and heaved the bundle into my arms.

"Thanks—appreciate it." I turned to go.

"Now, Miss Judy," JoAnne said to my back. "If there's anything I can do to help you, dear, don't hesitate to ask. I don't want to see you fold under the pressure."

"No, I'm fine," I said, making a reassuring face and hurrying out.

Millie sat at the conference table across from the chief and his detectives. I placed the binder in front of Bombardier then left to look for Andy, finding him in conversation with Bert by the time clock. He looked relieved to see me and escorted me to his office.

"What's wrong with Bert?" I asked. "He looks miserable."

Andy sat down and began shuffling through the papers on his desk. "He *is* miserable. Today it's about being trapped into a weekend visit with his in-laws. It's not my fault he married one of those *momma's girls*. Talks about how great things were when he lived in St. Louis. Problem was she nagged him about moving close to her parents the first few years of their marriage. Finally wore him down. He's stuck now. Has five kids. Five friggin' kids. The oldest—she's fifteen and causing trouble."

"That's tough," I said sympathetically.

"Yeah, but he pulls the rest of us down, too. I wish he'd pack up and go back to St. Louis for Pete's sake."

I had little doubt that deep down he felt bad for Bert, but Bert's weaknesses seemed to rub Andy the wrong way.

"Well, Chief Bombardier is speaking with Millie right now. You're next." I glanced at my watch. "You told me he was a good detective when you worked with him, but he's kind of rude. He made a big deal about our hiring Lester Robichaux, which we already know was a mistake, but what business is it of his? Honestly."

"That's him. Never yelled at anyone that I can remember. That wasn't his style. But he had a surly side he thought nothing of showing. Oh, by the way, Jena Doggett called in sick.

I'm telling you now, she's going to be a problem."

Back in my office, I dug into my paperwork, mostly filing and sorting. The Christmas party was less than two months away. I needed to clear my desk of the trivial, but necessary tasks then spend some serious time on planning the party. I nibbled on a tasteless day-old bologna sandwich while I worked. I'd just choked down the last bite when the phone rang.

"Chief Carl and his men went to lunch," Andy said. "So, they'll be out of our hair for a while."

"Great. Thanks." I returned the receiver to its cradle and examined my desk, choosing which file to dive into next. Between the murder and grief meetings, I'd gotten behind. I zipped through segments of time, completing forms, sending e-mails, doing two, sometimes three things at once. My arms propelled around in a blur. I'd spent the better part of an hour in this frenzied state when I sensed a presence. Bombardier stood just inside the doorway, cradling his notebook against his abdomen.

"Have you been there long?"

He smiled, the amusement in his eyes giving me his answer. "You're one busy lady."

My cheeks warmed as I pictured myself—body parts flailing, elbows up and out, beating on the computer mouse. I'd slammed completed forms onto my desk instead of stacking them neatly. The sight might've been cute for someone in her twenties, but I was forty-nine.

I gestured to the chairs in front of my desk. "Come in."

He pulled out a chair, made himself comfortable. "I didn't want to interrupt. You seem to be...well, let's say, focused." He gave me a playful grin, this time without the mockery. Dropping his notebook on the desk, he pulled out a folded piece of paper from his shirt pocket. "Brought this picture of Guerra. Her parents e-mailed it." He unfolded the photo and laid it before me.

It was the woman from the break room.

Alma Guerra had been as beautiful as Elizabeth Taylor in her late twenties. In the picture, Alma wore a turquoise top made from a soft-woven fabric hanging loose over her arms and body. The delicate material complemented everything feminine about her. Long, black hair cascaded down her back. A few strands hung in wisps that framed her heart-shaped face. Naturally black lashes and eyebrows enhanced her deep, brown eyes while her red-painted lips added sensuality.

"You recognize her?"

"Yes. She's the one I overheard inviting Lester to her home. I think the interaction caught my attention because she was pretty and Lester…well, you'll see."

"Do you remember anything else?"

I stared at the picture again with a sense that something was amiss. I couldn't summon more than the same feeling of incompletion I'd had when I told Andy what I'd seen and heard in the break room. There was another piece to it, but I didn't know what.

I glanced up to find Bombardier glaring at me impatiently.

"Yeah, that's all," I said.

"Tell me about Millie Landry. What's her function here?"

"She's in charge of the folding and printing departments. She's worked here the longest—twenty-some years."

"What does Bert Axelrod do?"

"He's Millie's counterpart, supervising the machine shop, warehouse, and cutting departments. They both work days. Lead-persons oversee the second and third shifts, and once a month Millie and Bert work part of shift two and three. Jo-Anne Necaise manages the local accounting and payroll functions."

"How long have you worked here?"

"A little over two months."

"Where'd you work before?"

What does that have to do with this case? I wondered. "Kelm Machinery. Short-term—eight to nine months."

"Hmmm. Valerie Kelm-Briscoe's turf."

My heart beat quickened as Valerie's face appeared in my mind, along with the urge to slap it. "You know Mrs. Briscoe?"

"Not really. I know about the Kelm family, but then most folks do here in Ocean Springs," he said. "Go on."

"We moved here from Los Angeles. My husband first, then me when I got the job at Kelm. After my first week there, I was already looking for another job. Rockhold's a place I'll stay. Kelm Machinery…well, let's just say it wasn't."

"Why?"

I wasn't about to dive into that story, a far-fetched sounding one to begin with since most people around here seemed to have a very different impression of Valerie Kelm-Briscoe than I did.

"Hard to explain," I said with a smile then turned the conversation back to him. "Are you a Gulf Coast native?"

"Yup," he said. "Long line of family history—Biloxi, Gulfport, Ocean Springs." Without missing a beat, he turned the conversation right back. "Can I ask why you'd leave a big city for this podunk town?"

I sighed. "Desperation. My husband had been out of work for a year and a half and, honestly, I would've practiced HR in Tiananmen Square to get away from my employer. Right when we were at a breaking point, Dan found a classified ad in the *Los Angeles Times* for an operations director at Biloxi's Gulf View Hotel and got the job." I scrunched my mouth sideways. "I must sound like an awful employee, running down the last place I worked along with the place before that. Sorry." I waited for him to comment, but he didn't. "I swear I liked my other employers and I've worked in HR for twenty-five years. I had a great job in LA, but the company went through a wicked restructuring and eventually went out of business while my husband was unemployed. I grabbed the first job offer I got but it was a horrid place to work." I chuckled at the irony. "Then I came here, ditching one evil for Valerie Kelm-Briscoe."

Bombardier grinned. "I heard most of the employees liked the old man. He had a gentle way with them." He stared for a moment at the picture on the wall behind me. "But rumor has it he came up short in matters of moral principle. Some pretty nasty stuff."

"Really? Mrs. Briscoe always gushed about *Daddy* being

some fine role model, decent and kind. What was this nasty business?"

"Stealing intellectual property from a competitor and…other alleged illegal deeds."

I leaned forward. "Sounds serious."

"Perhaps I shouldn't say since they're all allegations. Of course, the case can always be reopened, even though the old man is dead. Takes some of the fun out of catching him, though. His wife, Eleanor Kelm, is still around."

"Yes, I met Mrs. Briscoe's mother last December at Kelm Machinery's Christmas party."

"Before Eleanor married Paul Kelm, she was a Tillery."

"Tillery?"

"Ah, I forgot. You're not from these parts. The Kelm family was prominent along this coast, but the Tillerys were thought to be part of the Dixie Mafia."

"Never heard of it."

"Read the book *Mississippi Mud*. The organization's no longer around, but when they were, some politicians and police officials looked the other way when dealing with them." Bombardier glanced at his watch. "I'd like to look at Guerra's file."

"Sure," I said, getting up.

"Oh, also pull files for…" He scanned his notepad. "Keisha Davis, Jena Doggett, Eddie Sutter, and Rusty Shaw."

I crossed to the filing cabinets as he moved to the table, dropping his pen and notepad on top before taking a seat. I stacked the files in front of him and returned to my desk.

We both worked quietly until, a half-hour later, knuckles rapped harshly on the doorframe, shattering the silence. Lieutenant Young gripped the doorjambs and leaned in. "Chief, we've got something."

Bombardier twisted a hundred-eighty-degrees in his seat to look up at Young. "What is it?"

The lanky detective released one hand, moving it about as he spoke. "We need to talk to Jena Doggett. I understand she's home sick today."

"Can we get Doggett's contact information?" Bombardier asked, climbing to his feet.

I gave him her phone number and address, eying them with curiosity as they hurried away.

CHAPTER 6

The garage door opened and I slammed my fist against the steering wheel. "Damn." My husband's Buick LeSabre had taken over more than its share of space. Again. I wedged in on the right and struggled to get out of my car.

Buffy welcomed me at the washroom, her golden tail wagging, and I paused to ruffle her ears. Dan was in the kitchen, pouring Tanqueray gin into a tumbler. His purple, green, and gold sweatshirt complemented his full head of paper-white hair. While white hair looked handsome on him, I wouldn't be caught dead with any white in mine. Thanks to a monthly dose of L'Oreal Preference, I'd always been some variation of brunette.

"How was work?" he asked, adding ice, a smidge of vermouth, and a dab of olive-juice.

I sighed. "The police were there most of the day. They left suddenly to visit an employee who'd called in sick so I called it a day." I set my bag down on the dining table with a thud. "Dan, what is it with your car—"

"Can I entice you into a cocktail before dinner?" he asked, cutting me off. His wide golden brown eyes smiled as he covered the tumbler, shook it, then strained the mix into two glasses.

I smiled, lifted myself up on the balls of my feet, and gave him a light kiss on the cheek, forgetting his garage-hogging car. "How long have you been home?"

"Since three," he said, dropping a toothpick with two olives into each glass. "I snuck out early."

After a quick change into sports pants and a T-shirt, I plopped into the soft, oversized chair in the family room. Dan brought the drinks in, handed me one and sank into the sofa, taking a chug from his before bending forward and placing the drink on the coffee table.

"I've had a very good day," he said.

I sipped the drink. The gin warmed my insides as it went down, instantly easing the tension from my shoulders, so I took another. "Tell me about your good day." I set my glass on a side table and propped my stockinged feet on the ottoman.

"I told you about having the pictures in our office re-matted in burgundy."

"At Georgina's Hobby Shop," I said.

"Yeah. I went to pick up the last one. Georgina was working the counter."

"She's the one your boss ranted about at your company Christmas party, right?"

"Uh-huh. Fred's still pissed. Claims he'll never go back to her store. You've seen her. The reddish-gold-haired woman, late thirties."

I nodded and reached for my drink.

"She brought the picture out and stood it on the counter. The matting was blue instead of burgundy." He shook his head. "I showed her my pick-up receipt with the color noted and she got mad."

"What?"

"Yep. Rolled her eyes, gave me an annoyed sigh, the whole bit. And she wasn't planning on fixing it either."

"Ever?"

"'You'll have to take this one,'" Dan said, mimicking Georgina. "'I won't charge you.' I told her the picture was useless to me."

"The last time we bought something there she shoved it into a bag and grumbled that it was closing time." I swigged my drink. "When I checked, she was five minutes off."

"That was nothing. Today, she might as well have been a raging bull in charging mode—nostrils flaring, bushy head see-sawing."

"Mrs. Briscoe personified."

Dan nodded. "I had to grab the re-matted print for fear she planned to hurl it."

I chuckled.

"She didn't, but she shook her head so hard her hair floated up and out on all sides. 'I have things to do—things of considerable importance. Good day, sir.'" He rolled his eyes. "She released the picture so suddenly, I almost dropped it. Then she snagged her bag out from under the counter and left through the backdoor. Then—" His grin turned devilish. "—a dark, hefty young woman appeared from the back room—feisty smile, cookie face. She said, 'Miss Georgina knew I was back there. I could've changed up your picture in no time. Miss Georgina likes being a martyr.' Man, she was sassy."

"That's soooo Valerie Kelm-Briscoe of Georgina," I said.

He laughed. "I knew you'd connect the two."

"Yeah, thank God she's in my past."

Dan tempered his expression. "That's a point of contention." Diving back into his chronicle of events, he said, "So, Georgina's employee took my picture to the back and changed the matting to burgundy, returning in a matter of minutes, her smile unchanged. But when I put my charge card on the counter the smile disappeared."

Before I could ask why, he began mimicking her voice again. "'Lawd, mister, I can't take money for this. Why, Miss Georgina would toss me into yesterday if she thought I'd made ya' a satisfied customer. She's as bad at being a boss as she is at customer relations.'"

I felt the strain of my smile as I pictured Georgina's employee shifting her weight in a rapid wiggle, swapping hips, and switching hand.

Dan stopped to catch his breath before going on. "I slapped ten bucks on the counter and asked her if she took tips. She boosted the bill, rolled it, and in one slow, defiant motion, stuffed it into a blouse pocket. I handed her my business card and told her I could get her a better job at the hotel. She beamed and we both laughed."

I chuckled. "A don't-get-mad-get-even moment. And to think Ocean Springs' Chamber of Commerce voted Georgina the small business woman of the year." I took another swig of my drink and a wave of wooziness followed.

"It won't last, Judy. Bad bosses lose in the end."

An image of my awful bosses in LA cropped up in my mind then poor Jolene Cromwell appeared. I thought of Mrs. Briscoe on her queen's throne at Kelm Machinery.

"Why do you look so sad, honey? I thought my Georgina story would make you laugh—the comparison to Mrs. Briscoe and all."

"Because you're wrong. Bad bosses don't lose—not the ones you and I have worked for."

"You're not going to blame me for losing my job and you being stuck at that company in LA, are you?"

"How can I blame you? Unlike me, you raised holy hell to help someone. I did nothing and got to keep my awful job."

"What I did turned out to be worse than nothing," he said. "I couldn't get the employee's discharge overturned and lost my job trying. I only made matters worse for me and you."

"At least you tried. You didn't know it wouldn't work. But I did nothing." I took what little remained of my drink to the kitchen and poured it out.

"What are you going to do?" he called after me. When I didn't answer, he tried again. "Judy?"

I went into the bedroom and slammed the door. Falling into the chair, I dropped my head into my hands. Where had the anger come from? Dan hadn't deserved my ire. I didn't feel well and didn't want to think about anything. To distract myself, I picked up my book from the side stand and began to read.

CHAPTER 7

I went to work the next morning, determined to put some serious hours into the Christmas party project. I'd no sooner settled in than Andy called, his voice bellowing through the speakerphone. "Surprise, surprise. Jena Doggett called in sick—again."

"She may have reasons, Andy."

"Not reasons, excuses. She can produce a whole string of them in the bat of an eye."

I took it off speaker and lifted the receiver. "Let's go easy on her. Her best friend's been murdered. And yesterday, the police tore out of here heading to her place."

He was silent a moment. When he spoke, the sharpness was gone from his voice. "Hmmmm. Re—eally? I mean, what could Jena know that would excite the police?"

"Who knows? But I don't recommend writing her up."

"Girl, check her record. We need to meet with her. How 'bout four? Wait, it's Friday. Make that three. Call Vicky Coupe in, too, before her shift starts. She left her workstation last night with her machine running. Not the first time."

Sighing, I disconnected but almost immediately the phone rang again.

"Wanna have dinner at the Biloxi Yacht Club tonight?" Dan asked.

"Where did that come from?"

"Out of nowhere. Fred Ratzel's a member and invited us."

"Common sense is to accept any invitation from your boss," I said. "Sounds fun. I heard the mayor's a member, too."

"According to Ratzel, all the big names are. Plan on six-thirty."

"Okay," I said and clicked off.

I swiveled round to the file cabinet behind me and pulled out files for the Christmas party. I needed to catalog what parts of the project were complete and what still needed to be done. I'd spent two hours transferring the information onto index cards when Millie glided in and pulled up a chair.

"How's it going?"

I stared at her Rockhold uniform, wondering why she'd worn it even on dress-down Fridays. "So, so," I said, jiggling my hand back and forth like a swaying airplane. I closed the party project file and pushed it to the side. "Dan called. Said we're invited to the Biloxi Yacht Club."

"I heard they serve a supper to die for," Millie said. "I'm fixin' to go on break. Wanna come?"

I wrinkled my nose. "Let's get coffee and bring it back here. I'm under siege when I go into the break room."

"Me, too, but Andy expects Bert and me to spend our break time there. Calls it 'being available to the employees.'"

I flashed Millie a playful grin and got out of my chair. "I'm using the excuse I'm new and still settling in."

"Won't last forever."

The coffee pots and accompaniments sat out on a cluttered table between the snack and soda machines. I poured myself a cup, avoiding looking at the colorless, stain-splattered wall. Scratched-up bi-fold tables, surrounded by metal folding chairs, were scattered about the room.

Millie dumped a packet of sugar into her Styrofoam cup. "It's always a mess in here."

I did a double-take when an ample young woman pressed toward us. She looked much like Jolene had, only a little older and wearing the company uniform.

"Miss Millie," the young woman said, wringing her hands. "I really need next Thursday off. See, I have this thing with my family and it's just that…well, I realize I've been off a lot lately, but something's come up, and—"

"I'll meet you at your workstation in half an hour," Millie said. "We'll talk then."

"But this time the reason's different," the brunette continued. Her short hair rose and fell with the bobbing of her head. "And, Miss Millie, I was hoping—"

Millie patted the girl's hand. "I won't forget about you."

We headed out of the break room, steaming cups in hand.

"See? It happens to us all," Millie said, speaking in a whisper.

"I know, Millie. I know."

Settled into a chair in my office, Millie leaned over and said, "Lidia Trash called." The words were barely out when her hand flew to her mouth, her eyes wide. "Oh, I probably shouldn't say anything."

I waited, knowing Mille would eventually spill, even if she *shouldn't.*

Millie scooted closer. "Can I trust you with some really sensitive information?"

"Of course."

Glancing over her shoulder at the still-open door, she leaned over the edge of my desk, her dense, gray-streaked hair coming within a half-inch of dipping into her coffee. "I got a driblet from Lidia."

"A what?"

"Now, remember, Lidia'll be in a heap of trouble if the chief finds out she's talked about the case." Millie brushed her hair back. "Lester Robichaux isn't a suspect. He has an iron-plated alibi." She paused, her dark eyes drifting back to the door. "What was all the foofaraw with him anyway? You know, the day you found Alma?"

"He simply went off the wall. I'll tell you later. What's his alibi?"

"Some folks in Bay St. Louis reported him as lewd and lascivious. He was picked up shortly after leaving work the day before we discharged him."

"Huh?" How come I'd never heard about that?

"Yes. The police arrested him and he spent Monday night in the Hancock County Jail. They let him go the next morning, early enough to get to work. He has to appear in court next month but since he was in jail all night and at work all day, his alibi is as solid as a…kidney stone." Millie's soft, southern accent never disturbed her articulate delivery of words.

"I never considered that lost soul capable of murder, but I hadn't considered lewdness either."

"Oops. That's another thing," she said. "The chief reviewed Lester's criminal record. Lidia said he snickered and told them we'd be embarrassed when our overdue copy arrived."

"Millie, Bombardier means I'll be embarrassed. What were the lewd and lascivious acts he was charged with?"

"Lidia didn't know."

Just then, JoAnne peeked in. "Can I give one of my employees an extra day of paid vacation?"

"Sorry, JoAnne," I replied. "It doesn't work that way. They have to accrue it just like everyone else."

She glowered at me and left.

"Gaaahh," Millie said. "Is she for real?"

"I'm afraid so." I shared a smile with her then glanced at the wall clock. "Whoops. I need to meet with Andy. We're giving Vicky Coupe a written warning."

"Did he plan to tell me?" Millie said.

"Oh, yes. Of course. If you ask me, you should be glad he handles some of your disciplinary actions. He said he wants your second shift employees to see the positive side of you. They don't work with you as often as the first shifters."

Millie sighed and shook her head. "I bet she left her equipment running again."

I nodded.

Millie stood up to leave. "Well, I'll see you back there when Jena arrives. Remember, mum's the word on what Lidia told me."

Apparently, Vicky Coupe had rushed to the break room to buy a soda, leaving her folding machine running. She'd pulled it off this time, and the last time, too. No damage, no mess.

Vicky, a thin, dark-haired, giggly girl—all of twenty-one, a generation Y employee—signed the form and apologized.

Vicky opened Andy's office door to reveal Millie standing at the threshold. Vicky gave her a squeaky, "Hi, there," then brushed past her.

Millie watched her leave then stepped in and closed the door behind her. "How'd it go?"

"Easy," I said.

"Yeah, but I doubt Vicky will learn from this," Andy said.

Millie joined us at the small circular table in front of Andy's desk, her uniform dowdy-looking next to Andy's crisp wine-colored polo shirt and gray khaki pants. I glanced down at my navy polyester pantsuit and made a mental note to hit Edgewater Mall before our next dress-down Friday.

A knock sounded then a young woman in tight, white stretch jeans walked in. A light-weight jacket hung open and loose over her orange tank top, her midriff bare. As she turned to close the door, her messy ponytail swung wide. When she looked back, her gaze settled on me. "What's HR doing here?" she asked, her eyes snapping to Andy.

"Just have a seat, Jena," Andy said with a sigh.

She jerked a chair out and plopped down into a slouch. "Am I being fired?"

I moved my legs to make room for her sprawling ones, pondering the irony of her being Alma's best friend. From everything I'd heard, Alma had been positive, productive, and dependable while Jena seemed her exact opposite.

Andy read the disciplinary statement then said, "You've accumulated enough absences to warrant discharge."

Jena rolled her eyes. "But Alma's dead. Aren't I allowed a grieving period?"

Andy hung his head and took a deep breath. "I understand. It's been a tragic week for us all, but you used up all your chips on frivolous absences well before this week began. You know the policy, Jena."

"So, fire me."

Andy tapped his finger on the form. "I want your comments."

She glared at him then seized the paper. Scribbling quickly, she thrust the form back to him.

"Thank you. Now please wait in the break room while we discuss this," he said, gesturing to Millie and me.

Making a great deal of noise, she left, her thin, baggy jacket flapping behind her.

Andy shook his head then read from the disciplinary form. "'This week has been hard on me. If you will give me one more chance, I promise to improve. Jena Doggett.'"

"Wow," I said. "Unexpected."

Millie and Andy swapped grins.

"Judy, this is the norm," Andy said. "Jena always comes in copping an attitude, but when she puts her comments in writing, she sounds like Mary Poppins."

After some discussion, and minor resistance from Andy, Millie and I prevailed. We'd give Jena one last chance. Her best friend had been killed and discharging her now wouldn't bode well for employee morale.

Millie got to her feet. "I'll get her."

"Wait," I said. "Do either of you know what the police wanted with her yesterday?"

"I didn't even know they spoke to her," Millie replied.

"Lieutenant Young had been interviewing employees when he suddenly came to my office in search of Bombardier. Someone must have told him something. But all I know is that the lieutenant told him they had to get to Jena's house. The moment I gave them her address, they split."

Andy looked at Millie and his eyes glowed green-hazel. "Jena normally confides in you. Has she told you anything the police might be interested in?"

"No, nothing. But it's possible she told a co-worker something."

Telling Millie to stay put, I went and found Jena, leading her back to Andy's office.

"This is another written warning," Andy said as Jena sat down.

She looked at him blankly for a moment, seemingly unfazed by the punishment.

"I heard the police went to your home yesterday," Millie said, drawing Jena's attention.

"Yeah. They just had questions."

"They seemed to think you knew something," I said, "something that might provide clues to Alma's murder."

She shrugged. "They won't let me talk about it. It's as important to them as my attendance is to ya'll. When I get home, I push a chair under the doorknob and don't move it 'cept to leave." Her voice began to quiver. "I'm always looking behind me when I'm going to my car, when I'm going anywhere."

"If you're afraid of one of the other employees," I said, "we need to know."

"I can't. He'll—the person will know I told."

I leaned closer, making sure I had eye contact. "But if whoever you're scared of is a co-worker, this falls under our workplace violence policy. And I'm sure the police could put you in protective custody."

She fluttered her hands in front of her then shook her head. "I'm not talking. Alma had me cross my heart and hope to die that I never mention the person's name. I'm not saying no more, 'cause ya'll could find out through the process of elimination."

"But you told a co-worker about it, right?" Millie said.

Jena's head whipped left then right and back again. "Un-uh. I told nobody 'cept the police yesterday. But I told someone 'bout something else Alma'd done, which is why they came to my apartment."

Millie touched the top of Jena's hand. "If you're this scared, you're welcome to stay with Red and me. We have an extra bedroom for when the grandkids stay over."

Jena shook her head. "Thanks, Miss Millie, but I don't want anyone else involved."

I glanced at Andy then leaned back in my chair. "Thank you for coming, Jena."

"Yes," Andy said, "but remember, the 'zero tolerance' status for any absence or tardy is in effect for the next thirty days."

Jena nodded then pushed back from the table. She left the room, looking considerably younger than when she'd first arrived.

Millie placed her hand below her throat. "Lordy be, that girl looked like she'd been put through a wringer."

Andy leaned forward. "I'd say the police are probably hushing this up to protect Jena. I doubt they have enough yet to arrest whoever this jerk is."

"You're probably right," I said.

Andy rose and began pacing the perimeter of the room. "Hmmm. That's it. They won't endanger Jena, so we're all just waiting. We've got ourselves a paper bag full of water moccasins right here at Rockhold and that bag just got wet. The killer works here, I'm sure of it."

"The anonymous caller said the murderer was some secret friend," I said, "and not an employee, remember?"

Andy stopped and glared at me. "Yeah, and I bet the son-of-a-bitch only said that to throw us off." He trekked forward then turned around and retraced his steps, stopping a moment, only to repeat the pattern.

I turned so I could keep him in view. "Remember she kept saying *person*," I said. "Except one time, she said *he,* or was it *him*?"

Millie's eyes followed Andy as well. "It has to be a man. How many times is a woman afraid of another woman?"

Too often, I thought.

"Andy, please sit down. You're making me dizzy," I said.

He fell into his desk chair, a semi-pout on his face.

"I saw this movie years ago," I said. "A murder mystery. In it, the police said that women don't shoot women in the face—some vanity thing connected to the feminine psyche."

"The dickhead's an employee, all right," Andy said, ignoring my comment. "Why else would Jena worry we might identify him through the process of elimination? You can't eliminate anyone unless you already know them."

"I'm tired," Millie said, rubbing her temple. "Let's get out of here and try to forget this creepy stuff. It's bad enough we have the funeral tomorrow."

Millie and I rose from our chairs at the same time while Andy remained slumped in his.

"Sure, see you tomorrow," he muttered, his empty gaze drifting off into the distance.

Millie stopped at the back exit, her hand on the knob. "Have fun at the Biloxi Yacht Club tonight."

"Thanks, Millie." I turned and strode down the corridor then out into the noisy factory. Walking through the plant, I stared into the face of each employee I passed. *Could one of these people really be a murderer?*

Chills rippled down my spine. Then I remembered how safe and free I felt when I'd left Kelm Machinery to work here. I'd been so sure nothing else would ever hurt me.

Please tell me this isn't happening to me again. Not here at Rockhold Packaging.

CHAPTER 8

M s. Kenagy, could you help me with a transfer? I'd like to work under one of my prior supervisors, who isn't a family member or owner. I was written up again today for an error that occurred on the dock when I was nowhere near there. Thank goodness I was able to prove I was collecting an order from the canning department when the error occurred. All of the other supervisors liked working with me. I try hard to be a good employee. Please put this in my personnel file." ~ Jolene Cromwell, two weeks before she was fired.

⌘

2003:

I worked for Kelm Machinery for eight months, five days, and four-and-a-half hours. A long, agonizing stint in which every day felt like a replay of the day before. Finding the job at Rockhold Packaging was a definite stroke of luck, or so I'd thought.

By the end of my first week at Kelm, I had a pretty good idea of what prolonged employment there would do to me. I began looking for another job, mailing my first batch of resumes the following Monday.

At close to ten that morning, I removed a handful of

stamped and addressed envelopes from my purse and marched across the marble floor of our company's lobby.

"I'm going down to the mail drop," I said, glancing back at our switchboard operator, Callie. "I'll be right back."

But Callie wasn't the one who answered.

"Whatcha' mailing?"

I whipped around to find Jimmie Lee leaning on the reception counter like a West Texas cowboy propped against an old saloon bar.

"Just bills," I said, swinging the cream-colored envelopes behind my back.

"Why don't ya leave 'em here with Callie and the other mail?"

From behind the counter, Callie bobbed her head. "The mailman is due anytime."

My face flushed. "I–I need the air," I stammered. "And I like using the mail drop."

Jimmie Lee strode over and peered behind me. "Hmmph. Don't look like no bills I seen."

I spun around and pushed through the glass double doors, taking a sharp left then walking briskly down the sidewalk. I passed a printing company and Jay & Jay's tax preparation office then stepped up to the blue US Post Office box. I deposited my resumes, opening the collection box door a second time to assure they'd all gone down.

When I turned back, Jimmie Lee stood on the sidewalk outside Kelm Machinery, staring at me. He turned and went back into the building.

Why do I let the little urchin bother me so? I took a deep breath before heading back.

Ten minutes later, I sat in Mrs. Briscoe's office with Jack and Mrs. Schneider, the three of us in our assigned seats. Jimmie Lee stood where he always did, at the edge of Mrs. Briscoe's desk while Nora whizzed intermittently in and out.

From behind the flat oak surface of her desk, Mrs. Briscoe lifted her perfectly-shaped nose and looked down at us with condescension. "I'll be on vacation the rest of the week," she said. "I want ya'll to keep busy, so I made to-do lists.

Nora!" she yelled out the door. "This tea's too watery." She shooed the glass away with a wave of her hand then gave us each a list. Waggling a finger at me, she said, "Mrs. Kenagy, add our switchboard operator to yours. Her earrings need to come off."

"I like her earrings," I said.

"They don't look good on her. Too garish." Then she turned to Jack. "Mr. Thornton, Jimmie Lee overheard Candy Cumin complain of being overworked. I want you to write her up." She ordered Mrs. Schneider to deal with two of her employees, also for trivial reasons. Mrs. Schneider made one meek attempt in their defense before giving up. Then Mrs. Briscoe ordered us to counsel or discipline employees who weren't problems.

I raised my hand at half-mast like a schoolgirl.

"Yes, Mrs. Kenagy?"

"While you're out, how will we get our mail?"

In an eruption of movement, Mrs. Schneider uncrossed her arms and legs and dropped her gaze to the floor. Nora came to a standstill like a statue while Jimmie Lee rolled his eyes.

I worked my gaze around the room, yet no one said a thing. Jack offered a small, cautious shrug.

Mrs. Briscoe tapped her nails on the desk. "Mrs. Kenagy, what is it you don't understand about our policies? You've been here a full week already."

"I understand the policies. You disperse the mail. But how do we get it when you're gone."

"You won't see the mail until I see it first. So, what is it that you don't understand about our policies?"

I glanced around the room again, hoping for a sign of support. Medusa may as well have frozen them. "I assumed you'd have a back-up plan for when you were out of the office."

"I would never disregard my daddy's rules," she spat out. "The mail can wait until I return. So again, Mrs. Kenagy, do you understand our policies?"

This is ridiculous, I thought. I'd asked a legitimate question and her answer was daft. So I smirked. "Gee, I hope nothing important comes in." It was all I could do to keep from laughing.

Mrs. Schneider asked about production requirements. Mrs. Briscoe answered while her eyes shot death wishes my way.

Jack Thornton started to speak, but stopped. He rubbed the loose skin under his chin, contemplating something for a moment then said, "Mrs. Briscoe, one of my employees, Tommy Wilson, is interested in the tuition assistance program, but our policy is vague on how we reimburse employees—"

"I'd eventually like to rewrite it," I said, cutting in. "Right now, we can interpret it almost any way we want."

"He's broke," Jack said. "He'd like us to pay up front and is willing to sign an agreement to continue employment for a minimum period after the completion of each class."

"Why, I think that's wonderful," Mrs. Briscoe said.

Jack and I swapped glances.

"Have him discuss it with me," she said.

"Wait," I said. "I don't recommend he sign anything promising continued employment. That is, not until I can include some legal wording that will retain the company's 'At Will' employment rights."

"I don't understand," Jack said.

"If we accept an employee's promise to remain employed for a period, we're guaranteeing his job for that same time frame. If we do that, we lose the 'At Will' right to terminate him. He could basically do anything he wanted and we couldn't fire him until that period of time was up."

"I get it," Jack said.

Mrs. Briscoe's stare bounced from me to Mrs. Schneider to Jack then back to me. "Why, Mrs. Kenagy, I've never heard of such a thing. Have you lost your mind?"

I started to speak, but reconsidered.

"I'll tell Tommy to make an appointment with you, Mrs. Briscoe," Jack said, saving me from replying.

"Why, no appointment is necessary. Tell him to drop by on one of his breaks."

Jack tossed me a smile then turned to share the smile with Mrs. Schneider, but she looked at him blankly, her face one big question mark.

Jack and I found Tommy at his workstation and pulled him aside. He was young, clean-cut, dark-skinned.

"Do ya'll think this'll happen?" Tommy asked in the way people do who are used to disappointment.

"Yes," I said. "On your break, go into Mrs. Briscoe's office."

"Will one of you go with me?" he asked.

"I don't think she'd want that," Jack said.

Later that day, Mrs. Briscoe summoned me back to her office. I went in as she was giving Nora money with instructions to pick up her dry cleaning and buy tampons from the drug store.

As Nora left, Mrs. Briscoe rounded the desk, dropping into her chair. She stared at me, lapsing into an uncharacteristic silence. When one corner of her mouth began to quiver, I took refuge behind one of the high back chairs lined in front of her desk.

"Mrs. Kenagy, I just came from the reception area and Callie is still wearing those gawd-awful earrings."

I gripped the top of the chair. "I'm sorry. I thought you meant for me to handle her earrings after other more important matters were dealt with."

Her blue eyes blazed. "Mrs. Kenagy, I can't stand to look at her. Why, that snooty air about her is worsened by those…those ghastly thingamajigs." She scrunched up her face as though she'd just smelled something horrid and wriggled her claw-like fingers in front of her.

God, her earrings are smaller and more demure than yours, Val-er-ie.

"I want them gone. Why, what on earth will people who visit us think of the good Kelm name?"

I thought about pointing out that virtually no one ever visited the plant. We worked in a manufacturing company, not a bank, but held my tongue. "I'll take care of it," I said.

Mrs. Briscoe's gaze moved behind me and I turned

around. Tommy Wilson stood in the doorway, quiet and rigid. I started for the door.

"Wait, Mrs. Kenagy. I'm not through with you."

I turned and grabbed hold of the top of the chair once more.

Her eyes shifted back to Tommy, her annoyance rising visibly. "What do you want?"

He shuffled his feet. "Miss Judy told me to see you 'bout the education assistance program."

"Miss Judy? You call your HR Manager by her first name?"

"Yes, ma'am. That's what she told us to call her. Actually, she said to call her Judy, but it's hard not to say *Miss*."

For the umpteenth time that day, she hurled a fuming glare at me. "Is your name Tommy Wilson?" she asked.

"Yes, ma'am."

"Well, come in. Don't just stand there gawking."

O-o-oh. My fingernails dug into the chair's fabric.

With a crooked index finger, she pointed to the chair next to me and he walked over, but didn't sit.

I watched and waited, hoping she'd go easy on him, show him a touch of compassion, anything to dispel the look of humiliation developing on his face.

"Sit down, Tommy," she said with an aggravated sigh. He complied while my stomach churned. "So, I hear you don't have the money to pay for technical school."

"No, ma'am."

"And what makes you think Kelm should pay for it?"

"Well, there's the education assistance program—I just thought the company would benefit from me getting more training."

"Are you saying we don't train our employees?"

"No, ma'am. I'd like to have more education—be in supervision one day and make more money for my family."

"How many people are in your family?"

"I have my wife and three kids. She's pregnant again. We're expecting twins." His youthful face lit up in a smile that was half pride, half trepidation.

"Are you Catholic?"

I winced.

"No, ma'am. Baptist."

"Baptists believe in birth control, correct? So, why would you have more kids than you can afford?" She gave him a hard stare. "What stage is she in her pregnancy?"

"First trimester."

"Do you believe in abortion?"

My nails dug deeper.

Tommy shifted nervously. "We wanted kids," he said. "We really didn't expect twins but now that they're—"

"Well, it's not my problem if you have a family you can't afford. I don't see any reason we need to pay for your college. If you're having financial difficulties, I strongly recommend you look into birth control."

Tommy stared at her a moment then tipped his head. "Okay, ma'am. I just thought I'd try." He stumbled awkwardly out of the room, head bowed.

I wanted to release my grip on the chair, stomp around to her side of the desk, and put my fist through her face. Instead, I listened while she berated me for allowing employees to call me by my first name and why I must demand their respect.

"Never admit to an employee you've made a mistake either," she snapped. "That's one thing Daddy taught me. If they think you're vulnerable, they'll walk all over you. Now, go on and tell Tommy we'll pay for his class." She shook her head. "I certainly hope he's grateful since he's the one who chose to have all those babies."

She was going to approve it? Then why the mind games? But I already knew the answer. This wasn't about Tommy. When she'd been speaking to Tommy, her eyes moved from mine to his, watching for my reaction.

"What are you still standing there for? Go on and tell Tommy."

I kept my hold on the chair. Something came and went in her face—a realization of sorts.

I opened my mouth to speak then closed it. Anyone with a shred of decency would've told her what they thought of her treatment of Tommy. But her mind game was meant for me and in it she'd planted a paradox. If I said one negative word, she'd renege on approving the funds for his classes. So by defending Tommy, I would end up hurting him. Any satisfaction I'd feel in releasing my anger would be smothered by a painful sense of guilt that I'd caused this employee financial loss. She was sly, all right, creating the ultimate *screw you.*

I let go of the chair and left quietly. A few minutes later, bent over some forms on my desk, I heard a sound and looked at the open door. A shadow appeared on the floor. From the left side of the doorframe, I caught sight of a strand of blond hair, followed by the gleam of an earring. I turned and pounded gibberish into my computer.

From the edge of my peripheral vision, I saw her peer in then retreat, all in a nanosecond. After she left the building, I looked for Jack, finding him standing next to a trimming machine. I steered him to his office where I told him what had happened.

We called Tommy Wilson in and attempted to salvage his self-esteem.

"I'm so sorry, Tommy," I said. "We had no idea she'd act that way. At least she changed her mind about the tuition."

Jack placed his hand on Tommy's shoulder. "You're a good employee and far removed from the boss lady."

"Except, sir, if I ever get into supervision, I'd have to deal with her directly and…I dunno."

"Well," Jack said, "you'd have the education and the credentials to apply for higher level jobs at other companies."

We convinced Tommy to take the money and, for an added bonus, I advised him not to sign any agreement. "You see, Tommy," I said, "if you take these classes and then find another job, you can leave anytime you want, without owing this company a thing."

Tommy left and Jack sat down at his desk while I crashed into a chair before him. I felt so wrung-out.

"How have you tolerated it here?" I asked.

"I haven't. I started a month before you. Longest damn month of my life."

"I thought you'd been here longer." I looked into sane, understanding eyes and welcomed the camaraderie.

"I came here kind of like you. I lived in another state, Minnesota. Had a reasonable life, quiet, making average money, and I see this ad on the Internet. I discussed moving with my wife, leaving the cold and snow behind. If we were going to make a move, the time was now while the kids were young enough to move with us."

I nodded in sympathy. "We didn't have to factor children in," I said. "I was pushing forty when Dan and I got married. Timing for children didn't work out. Jack, what are you going to do?"

"I'm sending out resumes all over the coast. Have you ever worked for anyone this bad?"

I hesitated then wondered why. "Yeah. The place I worked for in Los Angeles was…brutal."

"This bad?"

"Yes, but in a different way. My previous employer had gone belly-up right after my husband lost his job. He was having trouble finding work, so I had to take the first job I could get to make ends meet. The owners were vicious, disciplining employees out of spite or on a whim, depending on which way the wind blew. Nothing was ever about business. It was always personal. And there was this young woman—" My stomach sank and my mind drifted to a different time and place.

"What about her?"

I looked past him at the wall clock, watching a fly skywalk around the circular rim.

"Judy?"

The fly flew away and I blinked. Then with some effort, I lifted myself from the deep waters of my thoughts back to the refuge of the shallows. "Sorry. Jolene was an employee there. Everyone loved her, except the owners. They made fun of her because of her weight and pinned any mistake they could on her."

"Sounds pretty similar to this place."

I slumped forward, propping my elbows on my knees, and dropped my face into my hands. "The place was the pits. They were barbaric, but made no attempt to hide it. Here, it's an obscured subtle brutality, stemming from Mrs. Briscoe's deep-seated need to be revered."

"Go on."

"Well, once I tried to help Jolene by polling her prior supervisors. All were eager to have her back. She was a hard worker, dependable, and customers loved her. Yet, when I took the information to the owners, it backfired. They discharged her two days later."

I couldn't tell Jack the rest. Whether the subject was too painful for me to verbalize or my shame got in the way, I wasn't sure. All I did know was that I might've prevented what happened. Yet, I did nothing.

A week after Jolene's discharge, her parents found her dead in their garage, her car running.

I couldn't say I practiced my profession differently after that incident, but a hole was left somewhere inside me, a hole still unfilled. I'd left that place with pent-up anger and guilt over things I'd been bullied into doing, things that weren't right. Like I told Jack, I was stuck.

"You can't blame yourself for every discharge, Judy. It'll just make you go mad."

I sighed and met Jack's inquiring gaze. "No, you're right." But even as I spoke the words, I knew I didn't mean them. Jolene Cromwell was dead for one reason only. I didn't stop her termination.

"This is the second mistake for me, Jack. I can't take a third."

Almost eight months later, I had the job at Rockhold Packaging, leaving Jack behind.

CHAPTER 9

2004:

We pulled in at the Biloxi Yacht Club, our headlights spilling over a tabby cat resting under a willow tree. The cat looked into the light, its eyes glowing discs for a moment before it ran away.

Dan switched off the headlights, climbed out then leaned against the car. I walked around to join him.

He pointed down the beach to the other side of Highway 90. "See the boat dock over there?"

I stood beside him and stretched my neck. "Yeah."

A wooden walkway followed the beach up to a small vacant outdoor bar. A pier extended out to the gulf with security lights lining the handrails. The misty water reflected a luminous trail from the summer moon and transformed dock lights into floating stars. Tethered to the pier, cabin cruisers, yachts, and sailboats swayed gently on the water.

"That's where the Yacht Club used to be," he said. "Until 1969 when Hurricane Camille barreled ashore. The winds were in excess of one hundred and fifty-five miles per hour. To ward off a recurrence, they rebuilt the club here on the north side of Highway 90."

I tossed him a crooked grin. "Interesting. But if any storm that strong hits the Gulf Coast again, I doubt the hundred-yard move will help."

"I know. People lost their homes. Some were permanently displaced."

A distant birdcall broke the night silence and a southern breeze brought a chill to the air. I put my arm through Dan's, squeezing close as we strolled toward the club entrance. My arm fell away when he opened the door to the cacophony inside.

Dan's boss towered over the others in the crowded bar, his eyeglasses reflecting the movement in the room. I had met Fred at last year's Gulf View Resort and Hotel Christmas party.

Fred saw Dan and instantly sped over, shaking our hands in that vigorous Southern way. "What can I get you?"

"A couple of Jim Beam's on the rocks with a splash of water," Dan said.

The bartender nodded then picked up a fifth and went to work on our drinks.

Fred tipped back his head, letting his voice carry around the bar, alcohol already slurring his words. "That's what I like to see, real drinkers."

When the drinks came, Dan handed one to me and took a sip from the other.

"Let's sit down," I said, tugging on Dan's sleeve.

He placed an elbow on the top of the bar and leaned one knee in against its base. "Go ahead and find a place. I'll join you in a minute."

I seated myself at a table by a window, finding comfort in the tranquil, dark view outside. Across the highway, soft black waves stroked the edge of the pier, flickering as if they carried fireflies.

Hearing someone call my name, I turned around and saw Andy walking toward me with a bottle of Bud in his hand. He put a hand on the back of my chair and leaned into my ear. "Are you here alone, pretty lady?" He straightened and wriggled his eyebrows in a Groucho Marx fashion, a routine so old I'd never have figured Andy to be one to know it.

I laughed. "What are you doing here?"

"Sweetheart, I'm a member."

"Really? I left you sitting in your office not two hours ago. You certainly look more relaxed now than you did then."

"That's because I don't take work home," he said. "And I'm not ruining my weekend worrying about a murderer amongst my employees. And he *is* an employee, or ex-employee."

"If you're thinking of Lester, Millie gave me inside information that he has a solid alibi."

"Damn. That means we're looking at a current employee." Andy made a face. "Is your other half here?"

"Yes. Dan's boss invited us." I took a quick look around the club, spotting Dan still over by the bar, then tapped my hand on the seat cater-corner to me. "Sit down," I said with a smile. "He may be awhile. He was settling into his drinking posture when I left him."

As Andy sat, I spotted Keith Briscoe lurking in the crowd. Andy twisted in his seat to follow my gaze.

Briscoe dusted something invisible off the sleeve of his Ralph Lauren polo shirt and began to move across the room, chin up.

"Who's that?" Andy asked.

"Oh, just the husband of my old boss. Gawd, I hope she's not here, too."

"If you come here often enough," he said, "you'll run into every wealthy, prominent, or notorious person on the Mississippi Gulf Coast. What's the story with your old boss?"

I gave him a never-mind wave and took a sip of my drink.

"Ah, c'mon. Tell me," he said pleadingly.

I sighed. "Okay, but it's nothing exciting. She just loves to play mind games."

A loud burst of laughter came from behind us. Andy leaned closer in, crossing one leg at the knee.

"She has this little gopher," I continued quietly, "Jimmie Lee Albright. She sends him on errands to spy on and annoy employees, as well as ex-employees."

"This is someone's boss?"

"She's the owner of the company, Andy."

"Re—eally."

"Yes. Right after I started with Rockhold, she sent Jimmie Lee over. Wilma called to let me know he was in the lobby asking how to get to my office. I went up there and found Jimmie Lee and Wilma face-to-face, whispering. The moment they saw me, they stopped, so I know they were talking about me. Then Jimmie Lee planted his hands on his hips—" I held up a hand. "The rest is going to sound like I'm making it up, but I'm not."

"Let's hear it."

"Jimmie Lee said, 'Mizz Briscoe wuz looking for her burgundy three-hole punch. Ya' know, the one matches her other office stuff. An' she wants to know if you accident–al–ly took it with ya' when you left.'"

"Someone talks like that?"

The racket in the club stalled and I heard a snippet of an old Paul Simon song. "Oh—yes. I told him that hole-puncher must weigh fifteen pounds, so why did he think I accidentally took it? With his hands still on his hips, he said, 'Don't git testy with me. It's Mizz Briscoe who—' I ordered him out and returned to my office, hoping the operator might be discreet. She wasn't."

"Wilma? Of course not. But your old boss. What's her problem?"

"You're lucky, Andy. You've obviously never had a monster boss."

"I've worked for a couple of trolls, but not too bad." He clasped his hands behind his head and leaned backward. "What else did she do?"

"Where should I start? She would encourage the factory workers to come to her for advice on very personal matters— totally inappropriate by the way, considering she's probably never even looked at a psychology book, let alone had a degree in the field. I sat through some of the *sessions*." Catching sight of a young woman across the room, I froze. *It's not Jolene*, I told myself. It couldn't have been.

My eyes still fixed on the other side of the room, I watched as Keith Briscoe stepped up to a pretty young thing poured into a red strapless dress. She stood with her back to the woman I'd mistaken for Jolene. Keith said something and the leggy woman in red laughed.

Andy leaned into my sightline, drawing me back. "And?"

"Well, Mrs. Briscoe would—" There was a tap on my shoulder and I turned.

"Here you are," Dan said.

Andy stood and introduced himself, shaking Dan's hand.

My husband grinned. "Glad to meet the infamous Andy Holman."

I expected Andy to do something outlandish like curtsey, but he only smiled.

"Here comes the man I met at the bar," Dan said. "Vernon Stiff."

I muffled a giggle and whispered, "Stiff?"

A red-faced man with a mouthful of teeth came toward me, thrusting a hand forward. I got out of my chair and sidled close to Dan and Andy.

"I hear you and Dan are from out of state," he said, his words coming out on fast-forward, his Southern twang a match for Jimmie Lee's. "I wanted to welcome you Yankees to Mississippi." He grabbed my hand and pumped my arm.

"But we're from California." I turned with a gesture toward Andy. "And Andy here's a native."

Vernon chortled. "Good for you, young man. Damn Yankees have been taking over ever since the casinos moved in." He slapped Andy on the back so hard Andy choked on a cough before he rolled his eyes. Vernon turned to me. "Dan here tells me you used to work for Kelm Machinery?"

Oh, for God's sake. I shot Dan a warning glance. "Why, yes. I did."

"I know Valerie Briscoe from the gun club. I don't see her too often, but she's one of our few lady members. We don't let many girls or democrats into the gun club." He unleashed more guffaws and I recoiled farther behind Dan.

I looked from Dan to Andy then back to Vernon. "The gun club?"

"A real straight shooter, that woman. For a long time her daddy took the whole family. Her two older brothers—well, one kind of dropped out of sight—they were regulars."

"I thought she had only one brother," I said.

"No. The other one must've left or something. I'm showing my age. It's been a long time—some twenty years plus." He rubbed his chin. "Paul Junior—that was his name. The eldest. Nice fella. Haven't seen him since he was a college lad. Attended the University of Southern Mississippi in Hattiesburg. Saw the other brother from time to time, up till 'bout five years ago when he got a job outta state. Up north—Ohio, I think." He hesitated. "Anyway, Valerie's 'bout the only one who practices now, 'cept sometimes she brings her momma. You know, the old man is dead."

"Yes, I'd heard." *Like a thousand times already.*

"Weeel, ya'll need to think about joining one of these clubs down here if you want to become part of the community. If ya' like guns, I'll recommend you for membership. I'm in the phone book." He winked at me then strutted off, taking his raucous laughter with him, his beer belly guiding the way.

Dan glanced at me then Andy. "Mrs. Briscoe in a gun club?"

Andy took a swallow of beer. "Oh, that doesn't mean much. It's a prestige thing down here. My next-door neighbor's a member and brags about it all the time. It's probably considered redneck where you're from but here, it's a status symbol."

"She never said a word about a gun club or even owning guns while I worked for her. I wonder why?" I asked, more to myself than to them.

Andy sat back down in his chair and I followed suit.

"I know Stiff sounds like a hick, but he's an attorney," Dan said, taking the seat beside me.

"A lot of people 'round here talk that way on purpose," Andy said. "Sometimes it's no more than an act before it becomes a habit."

A waitress passed by and Dan held up his empty glass, wagging his finger around to Andy and me. She nodded and kept going.

I gazed out across the highway at the moonlit water and

thought about Alma's funeral tomorrow. How glad I'd be to have it behind us. I tried to picture Mrs. Briscoe shooting a gun, but simply couldn't get that into my head. I thought about the murderer being a Rockhold employee, but despite Andy's belief, I couldn't get that into my head either.

I began to daydream about being the heroine who caught the killer. Calling 911 and chasing him through the plant, crouching behind folding machines when he shot at me. News cameras were on me while I explained how I'd used deductive reasoning, or Jena's process of elimination to find him. How I'd confronted him in the plant during a shift change.

Then, as if by instinct, I muttered the words of the anonymous caller, "It's not an employee. The murderer is her secret friend."

CHAPTER 10

December 2003:

Our Buick LaSabre bounced over the Ocean Springs Bridge and I looked out through the passenger side window. The bridge's lights reflected off the dark Mississippi Sound, flickering in time to the water's languid waves.

"Three weeks," I said. "I've worked at Kelm Machinery for three long weeks and now I'm going in on a Friday night."

Dan flashed me a cheery grin. "But this is a Christmas party." He looked back at the road. "We'll have fun."

"Nice try."

The bridge ended in Biloxi and we drove a couple more miles, turning right, and passing the Ohr-O'Keefe Museum of Art. Another right onto Jackson Street and the brightly lit century-old Greek revival house burst into view.

"Wow," I said. "So, this is the Redding House."

We stepped out of the car, heads up, taking it all in. Outdoor floodlights and low-hung porch lamps illuminated the tall two-story structure. The balcony and porch balustrades were decked with yellow Christmas garlands.

A crisp chill hung in the air and I cinched the wrap draped over my shoulders tighter, tucking my arm through Dan's to nuzzle closer. The still night amplified faraway noises. A car door slammed from over the hill, voices echoed from down the block, and the footfalls of unseen people clicked and pattered.

"Miss Crandall organized the party," I said as we walked. "One less thing."

Dan smiled. "Ah, the advantages of being a new employee."

He reached for the door and my arm fell away as he pulled it open to a frosty, crystal-chandeliered interior warmed by heart-pined floors. Cypress millwork and custom mahogany ran the perimeter of the main floor, packed with evenly spaced white-clothed tables.

I lowered my head and whispered, "I don't know most of these people."

Dan nodded, nudging me forward.

We'd almost passed Nora when I stopped him. "Nora. Hi."

She glanced at me then Dan and gave us a pretty smile. She wore a blue-black velveteen dress and clung to the arm of a fair-haired young man who kept his gaze on her. Nora had pulled her hair up into a tidy bun, but her makeup was heavier than usual, giving her a comic-book character appearance. We exchanged pleasantries then moved on.

"Is that woman over there ill?" Dan murmured, his hand half covering his mouth.

I turned to see Mrs. Schneider, her skeletal frame drooping against a cherry-wood banister. I sent her a greeting nod before shepherding Dan her way. She squared her shoulders and produced an obligatory smile.

"This is Dan, my husband," I told her. "Dan, this is Mrs. Schneider. She's on the management team."

"Nice to meet you," Dan said.

Mrs. Schneider nodded.

"Isn't this a beautiful place for a party?" I said.

Mrs. Schneider nodded again.

I looked all around. "Is that wood I smell?"

"I don't think so," Dan said. "Might be wood polish."

"Oh." I glanced at him then Mrs. Schneider. "Well, hope you enjoy the party. Talk to you later."

We moved behind her and up the winding staircase.

"E-gads, that was painful," Dan said.

"Always is with her."

On the second floor, rows of folding chairs faced a stage with a microphone propped atop a podium, a flip chart off to one side. I winced. "I don't even want to know." We turned and headed back.

Downstairs, we crossed the base of the stairwell over to the bar, getting drinks and taking them to a table. Dan set his down and straightened his suit jacket. "I'm going to hit the head."

He turned and strode toward the back of the manor. At the same time, Jimmie Lee appeared from the opposite direction, waddling toward me. His hair, cut in an old Beatles-style, bounced in time with his steps.

"Jimmie Lee, you're dressed to the hilt."

"Mizz Briscoe got me this sports jacket and pants. Her taste is lots better than mine."

"She's good to you, huh, Jimmie?"

"Yah. 'Cause I'm an orphan an' that seems to be a big thing with her, but it ain't been hard on me or nothin'."

"Maybe she sees you as a good pers—oouch!" I sprung out of my seat as pain shot through my calf. I grabbed my lower leg, rubbing it with fervor.

"What's wrong, Mizz Kenagy?"

"Ow, that hurt," I said, still massaging my calf muscle. "A charley horse. I went jogging this morning. Probably overdid it. Seems fine now."

The sharpness of the pain moved on, but the ache lingered. I remained standing, hoping to counter any recurrence.

"Where did ya' go joggin'?"

"I found this out-of-the-way place called East Beach. Only about a mile long and often empty. Dogs are welcome, so I take mine and let her run free while I jog on the pavement above the beach."

"I know where 'dat is. It's by the Gulf Coast Research Lab, huh?"

"Yes."

"I'll tell ya' a secret. I got a rowboat hidden between East Beach and the lab."

"Really? I've never seen a boat there."

"And ya' won't. It's hid real good. Don't take it out much. Keep it mostly for emergencies. Went a couple times to scout out the island jus' south of East Beach."

What kind of emergency would he need a rowboat for? I wondered. "That teensy uninhabited island?"

"Yep. That's why I picked it out."

"Picked it out for what?"

He shrugged. "Who's to tell? Never know when I might need ta run from somethin' or someone. Maybe there'd be terrorists and I need be saving Mizz Briscoe. She laughs when I tell her that, says she'd rather deal with terrorists than walk in quicksand."

"You mean you row all the way to that little isle alone? It looks like a dangerous place. It's got to be a half-mile away, and there's so much brush."

"I hafta watch out for them gators, but it jus' takes me forty minutes. It's mostly mud, 'cept there's one bare spot where the ground's harder and got some rock. I've stashed rations jus' case I ever need to stay hid awhile."

While I stared at him blankly, unsure of what to say, Dan returned. I introduced him to Jimmie Lee who trundled off to new territory, the tube of fat that circled his middle jiggling.

"The notorious court jester?" he asked as we sat down.

"Yep," I said, taking a sip of my drink.

"Your descriptions are thorough. I'll give you that."

"Dan, look. Jack's here. That must be his wife."

Jack had just stepped through the entrance, a woman at his side. I popped out of my chair and waved. Jack's face split into a grin and he waved back. They stopped at Mrs. Briscoe's table, smiling, shaking hands, and talking. They nodded and gestured to the folks at the table, then backed away, shaking hands with others while in route to us.

Dan and I stood for the introductions then Jack left to get drinks.

A slender waitress in a black and green uniform placed a plate of hors d'oeuvres in the center of the table. A moment later, Jack returned, two gin-and-tonics in hand.

"I'm glad you're here," I said, filling my plate with cheese and crackers. "I hardly know anyone."

He dipped a shrimp into cocktail sauce. "You're not alone."

His wife, Carolyn, bit into a cracker with jalapeño cheese spread. "At least the company throws a good party," she said in an accent unique to Minnesota natives. Her heavy brown hair was similar to mine, but two inches longer and clipped up away from her face.

Dan grinned. "At least?"

"Sorry, that just popped out—result of Jack's war stories. My guess is you hear them, too."

"Oh, yes," Dan said, shooting a smile at me.

She gave Jack an affectionate pat before turning back to Dan. "And your wife's been at Kelm for less time. It gets worse."

"Who're those people sitting with Mrs. Briscoe?" I asked. "I've met her husband, but who's the elderly woman and the other man?"

"The man," Jack said, "is Mrs. Briscoe's brother. He flew in from out of state for the holidays. The woman is their mother, Eleanor Kelm."

"Does she have other family?" I asked.

"Not that I know of," Jack said. "Only a mom and a brother."

Dan scanned the mansion from floor to ceiling, his eyes sparkling. "Isn't this spectacular?"

Carolyn's gaze followed his. "Yes."

"Judy and I took a tour. I suggest it. There are nine fire-places and the woodwork—"

"You may want to do it soon," I cut in, lowering my voice to a whisper. "Upstairs, there are rows of chairs set up in front of a stage."

Jack half-choked on his drink. "Surely she won't put us through one of her performances at a party."

A wild-haired woman in a purple sweater appeared in the midst of the room and announced, "The buffet is ready."

Mrs. Briscoe turned to look at her and, in doing so, saw me. She nudged her mother, whispered something then the two of them stared. Mrs. Briscoe seemed to have a natural hatred for HR managers. She and her mother rose as one and started for the buffet table, the difference in their height noticeable. Mrs. Briscoe was about as tall as me, a little over five-foot-four, but her mother had her beat by a good three to four inches.

I turned back to an empty table. Hooking my purse straps around the back of my chair, I left for the buffet line as well.

Forty minutes later, the woman in purple returned. "Please proceed to the upper level," she ordered. Jack and Carolyn had left to explore the property, so Dan and I joined the other guests, ascending the stairs like sheep to the slaughter. We all settled into seats or found places to stand along a wall.

The hubbub softened as Valerie Kelm-Briscoe bounded onto the stage, seizing the microphone as though she were rock star, Mick Jagger. Then she pounded a gavel on the podium. "I'm calling this party to order," she said, sniggering.

Forced laughter floated awkwardly around the room.

"I want to show ya'll the grand year we've had." She flipped a page over the easel and with a long slender pointer, poked at numbers. She read profit margins, generated revenue, and year-to-date gains aloud. Then she turned another page, jabbing at charts showing the volume of sales and deliveries. "Ya'll are lucky recipients of generous wages and benefits resulting from our profitability year after year."

So generous, I thought, trying to keep from rolling my eyes.

Following her review of the company's finances and our reminder to be grateful, she invited Jimmie Lee onto the stage. "He's my second set of eyes," she said, cackling. "If I don't find out what ya'll are up to behind my back, he'll do it for me."

Jimmie Lee posed beside her, displaying his full four-foot-eight inches of height. He puffed out his chest like a rooster ready to crow and gave the audience a gloating smile.

Dan leaned into my ear and whispered, "You've got to be kidding."

"I told you."

As if we were back in one of her meetings, she talked about "Daddy" then pointed to Keith Briscoe who rose and nodded. "My husband, Keith, is working on an MBA at the University of South Alabama. The college is costing me a fortune." Another wave of her hand dismissed him.

"Mr. Valerie Kelm-Briscoe?" Dan whispered again.

"Uh-huh."

She went on to thank her sister-in-law for good advice, her brother for getting her out of jams, and her mother for years of moral support. Her nonsensical rhetoric droned on and I tuned her out, seeing only the movement of her mouth.

Then Jolene Cromwell's smiling image appeared behind Mrs. Briscoe. She almost looked real. She began to move closer, her smile fading. I sat up straight and covered my mouth. I wondered what she planned to do, but the apparition of Jolene saw me watching. Hurt appeared in her eyes a moment before she disappeared and I smothered a gasp.

"What is it?" Dan asked, gaping at me.

I dropped my hand. "Nothing." It took several tries before I could catch my breath.

He glanced at me repeatedly while I worked at gathering myself.

Mrs. Briscoe's brother, in a dark Armani suit and black Cole-Haan shoes, stepped up onto the platform. He took the microphone away from Mrs. Briscoe and she treaded softly down the steps.

He raved about his father and founder, Paul Kelm, about his good character and philanthropic deeds. You would never have guessed he was her sibling if not for her announcement, what with his bulging eyes and that hawk of a nose.

He introduced Eleanor Kelm as his mother and Paul Kelm's dear wife. Then, in the same vein as Valerie's depictions of her father, he described his mother as a loving woman—wonderful, endearing, and refined. A spotlight found Eleanor Kelm seated in the front row, a plum-colored Gucci bag perched on her lap. Her son asked her to stand.

Placing her bag on the floor, she rose slowly, like anyone whose age fell on the downhill side of seventy. She stood tall in a blue knit dress, its length hitting below her knees and a neckline that stopped just under her chin. With its long, tight sleeves, it looked severe and restricting. She waited, looking over her audience as though making eye contact with each and every person there. Then, in an old voice, she said, "I want to thank you. If it hadn't been for ya'll, we could not have been as successful."

"Well, finally," I whispered to Dan. "Someone's giving credit to the employees."

Combining the kind words with her frail frame and the quiver of age in her voice, Eleanor Kelm seemed to be a considerate woman. Her blue-gray eyes set under drooping lids, complemented dyed-silver hair. Her nose was crooked in the same manner as her son's, but the distinguishable bend not as imposing on her.

She brought the likes of Valerie into this world? It hardly seemed possible until I made a subtle observation.

Eleanor Kelm seated herself, delicate and deliberate, purposely taking her time. In an even slower movement, while everyone's eyes remained upon her, she placed her arm across her lap so that her left hand touched her right thigh. Gently positioning her right hand over the other, she arched her back and held her head high, turning from one side to the other to peer snootily into the crowd, her lips pursed, her eyes nefarious.

In that instant, I knew. Like her daughter, Eleanor Kelm considered herself a very proper Southern woman, one oh-so-much finer than all the peons in the room.

CHAPTER 11

I threw my legs over the side of the bed and padded to the window. Alma Guerra's funeral was set for eleven, with rain in the forecast. I clutched the curtain panels and hesitated, glancing down at my cold, bare feet. Behind me, the sound of Dan's steady breathing tempted a return to the warmth of our bed. Instead, I steeled myself and flung open the curtains.

"Whew," I said under my breath at the sunlight pouring in, warm and inviting. There was a good chance the funeral would be rain-free, and the weather was perfect for jogging.

I tossed on running clothes, hiding my tangled hair inside a yellow-knit ski cap, then signaled to the dog that we were on our way. She scampered ahead and, when I opened the car door, she landed in the passenger seat with an easy bound.

General Pershing Avenue turned into Shearwater Drive and ducked into a long, shaded tree tunnel. The road curved east and the name changed again, along with the scenery. East Beach Drive offered the Mississippi Sound on my right and good-sized Southern homes on my left. I pulled off before it dead-ended at North Halstead Road.

I eased the car over to a bare spot of ground where I normally parked, close to the beach. A stand of maples shaded my windshield, but didn't block the view of the Gulf Coast Research Laboratory, a collection of single-story brick buildings. The buildings were separated by cement walkways that fed off one another. The GC Research Lab faced south, its backdrop a dense patch of dark green woods.

Buffy bounced onto my lap, eager to exit, and when I opened the door, we both tumbled out. I reached back inside for her leash, snatching it too hard and stumbling backward, falling against the little wooden fence that ran along the beach.

A jogger whizzed past and grew smaller as he turned north on Halstead Road. Buffy barked at him, taking a few steps in reverse. At the end of the fence, she lost her footing and slid down a short embankment, landing sideways on the beach. In a flurry of legs, she pulled herself up, shaking off sand.

I walked down after her, craning my neck toward Biloxi at the curve of the bay. Casino Row began at Point Cadet, an area of Biloxi at the west end of the Ocean Springs Bridge. From where I stood, the riverboat casinos looked like cereal box trinkets.

I returned to the fence, flinging the leash over it, and began my warm-up routine, using the fence as my prop. Buffy began to sniff the sand, gradually moving away. When I sprinted up to the road and began to jog, she fell into step beside me. I stayed on the pavement while she ran along the beach side of the fence.

Twenty minutes later, I garnered the leash and was hoofing my way up the slope to the car when a rustling stopped me. Buffy stopped, too, lifting her ears and raising a paw like a hunting dog in prime position. I went for her, swinging the leash, but she was already on the move. "Buffy! Buffy!" I yelled, catching up as she started forcing her way into the brush under the maples.

I grabbed her backend and drew her close enough to grasp her collar, but she broke free and ran behind me, barking frantically in the direction of the shrubs.

Some kind of rodent sat on its hind legs, sizing us up. I screamed then covered my mouth with both hands. Its feet were webbed like a duck's yet its face resembled a monkey and its tail that of a rat. It had to be twenty-five pounds at least, with a grimy gray-black body and white fuzz about its face. Two upper and two lower incisors looked like they'd been hand sharpened to icepick points.

The creature dropped onto all fours and stalked toward us. Buffy went ballistic. I recoiled, lost my balance, and fell on my back. I thrashed about on the ground, looking for something to throw, but while Mississippi had an abundance of mud, it was severely lacking in rocks.

Buffy and the beast locked eyes and circled. I propped myself up, feeling like a bystander watching the events unfold. The thing jumped up six inches and hit ground with a belly flop.

"G–get out of here," I stammered, contorting myself back to a standing position. I lunged again for Buffy's collar, not making the connection. Buffy chased the rat and burrowed into the thicket.

My heart sank at the sound of a hollow thud, followed by my dog's shrill scream. The monster emerged, took a few swift looks around, then slithered toward the boat launch. It ducked into the gulf and splashed away, its long, cord-like tail battering the water.

I covered my face with one arm and broke into the underbrush. Wet earth and tangy weeds filled my nostrils. A couple yards inside, pricked and poked by foliage, I found Buffy in a clearing. She rubbed her bleeding brow with a front paw. I went to her, my hands trembling. I moved her paw aside, exposing a shallow gash above her eye then with a heavy sigh, crumbled down beside her.

But my moment of relief was short lived. My guard went up and I took a quick look round. No more creatures crawled out of the surrounding brush, but we weren't alone in a hollow space in the thicket either. Someone had hidden an old dusty rowboat here. What on earth?

Inside its aluminum shell, liver-colored oars crossed one over the other. Fresh blood dripped from the boat's bow and I realized Buffy hadn't been bitten. She'd run into the boat.

Then I remembered my conversation with Jimmie Lee at

the Christmas party nearly nine months earlier. This had to be his getaway boat.

I put my arms around my dog, hugging her while I stared at the odd little dinghy. A spider web descended from one side into the middle of the teeny seat, a handful of dead bugs dangling in the web. The skiff obviously hadn't been used for some time and, as Jimmie Lee had said, was well hidden.

I returned to the house worn out, scratched up, and filled with questions. Who was Jimmie Lee really? And why did he feel the need to keep a boat in hiding as a means to run, a means to save Mrs. Briscoe if need be? I shivered at the oddity of it all. He was in his early twenties, but his motivation and reasoning seemed that of a child's. I pictured him boasting about the hidden vessel. The boat was something of great importance to Jimmie Lee.

Dan had left me a note saying he'd gone into work. I tossed it and took Buffy into the bathroom, gathering first aid supplies and setting them on the counter. I sat on the toilet seat lid and dabbed Buffy's wound with peroxide before wrapping gauze around her head.

The shower's stinging hot spray calmed my nerves, but my mind continued to spin over the morning events. I put on makeup, blow-dried my hair, and changed into my darkest colored suit, a Liz Claiborne navy blue knit with matching two-inch pumps. I grabbed my keys and purse and had the presence of mind to say "Goodbye," to Buffy.

CHAPTER 12

The words *The Bradford O'Keefe Funeral Home* were carved into an ornate wooden sign posted beside the entrance gate on the brick fence. If *Funeral* hadn't been part of the name, the structure would have easily passed for a classic southern mansion, the kind normally given to the state and converted into a museum in honor of a civil war hero or some other historical figure. I let up on the gas and rolled my Camry onto the red-brick drive, stealing glances at the white, two-story building. Imposing columns and gracious balconies accentuated the grand architecture. I eased past a daunting oak tree toward the parking lot, admiring wisteria vines clinging to the inside of the fence.

I had just put my Camry in park when Andy pulled his red Mazda RX-8 into a space across from me. He stepped out, straightened the jacket of his dark silk suit, then shook one leg as if ridding his slacks of wrinkles.

I clicked the lock button on my key fob and called his name, taking long strides toward him.

"You're out of breath," he said.

"I know," I replied with a sigh. "Something crazy happened this morning."

"Something to do with the funeral?"

I shook my head. "No."

He boosted a pack of cigarettes from his shirt pocket, shook one out, and slipped it between his lips. Then, shifting the pack, allowed another cigarette to slide halfway out. I hadn't smoked in years, but a cigarette sounded good so I took the one he presented. He lit his then mine. "Dish."

I gave him the rundown about my encounter with the creature. As bizarre as it was, still simpler to explain than discovering Jimmie Lee's boat.

He tapped off ashes. "You just ran into your first nutria rat."

"A what? I've never heard or seen such a thing, not on TV, *National Geographic*—nowhere."

"Down here, they're all over." He took a long puff, sending a slender stream of smoke skyward. "There's more in Louisiana. The Cajuns eat 'em."

"Gross."

He nodded. "Some restaurants in New Orleans use the meat in their sausages and gumbo, stuff like that. I had a nutria rat burger once. Pretty good."

A streak whooshed past us then ducked out of sight behind the row of parked cars.

"What was that?" I asked, instantly on alert.

"I don't know. Someone's kid probably thinks he's being funny."

We put out our cigarettes and stood in companionable silence, waiting for the culprit to reappear. When nothing happened, we headed into the chapel.

I hung back while Andy joined George and the management team in the second row. A large painting of Alma was angled on an easel next to the closed casket and I started toward it, up the wide central aisle. Seated on my left, Lieutenants Young and Leblanc watched the guests. When they saw me, they looked away. The temperature was on the tepid side of warm with the fragrance of bouquets in the air, the organ music tastefully faint.

The portrait turned out to be a picture rather than a painting, the same picture Bombardier had gotten from Alma's parents. It had been blown up to fit a large gilded frame. Alma's long black hair flowed around her beautiful face. Here, the delicate turquoise blouse seemed to show more color.

I turned back, looking for a place to sit, but stopped when something caught my eye in the last row. A man wearing a grimy business suit crouched into a lump. He lowered his eyes and flipped up his collar as though trying to make himself inconspicuous. I thought I smelled mothballs, probably a reaction to his faded, rumpled suit. He peeked at me, and what little I saw of his mouth seemed contorted into a woe-is-me grimace. The Sad Sack lowered his head again, and I stared at his scruffy gray hair and the scowl line across his forehead.

Lester Robichaux!

With recognition dawning, I spun around, hurrying up to the row where the detectives sat, excusing myself as I squeezed past the knees of people sitting. I reached the detectives, bending down to whisper Lester's name, pointing him out as discreetly as I could. The duo slid off the bench at their end near the wall. Lester moved like a shadow out the doorway, the detectives in pursuit.

A part of me felt bad for denying Lester the chance to say his final goodbyes to Alma, but the restraining order against him had been processed yesterday. He'd been served with his copy and knew not to come near Rockhold or our employees. I reminded myself that he'd made his choice when he threatened to kill Andy then sat in the pew where Lester had been. I figured he wouldn't be returning. I pulled my checkbook and a pen out of my purse and jotted notes on the back of a blank deposit slip.

There's a reason Lester is back. What does it mean? Who is Jena afraid of?

If I wanted to help find the killer, I needed to start working at it.

Millie had arrived and was standing before the picture of Alma. I'd never seen her in anything other than a Rockhold uniform, so she had my attention with her muted red suit, white blouse, and dark high heels. She joined Andy, Jena, Bert, JoAnne, and George in the second row. Alma's family had taken the front.

Bert wore something in a drab color like he always did. His head was lowered and the occasional jerk of his shoulders

suggested he was struggling with his emotions. JoAnne sported a heavy knit top that emphasized her bosom. She was, of
course, crying, composing herself periodically to blot black
mascara smudges from her eyes. Jena, wearing a tailored black
suit, looked as scared as she did sad, pilfering glances round
the chapel. George was dressed in a standard gray suit, his face
tense and his mouth drawn.

Scattered around the chapel, I recognized many faces—
our hourly employees—but except for a handful, I didn't know
their names.

Detective LeBlanc returned to his seat without his partner
and picked up where he left off, observing those in attendance.
The priest went through the ceremony, speaking a great deal
about life after death. When he finished, George took over and
talked about Alma's ten-year career with Rockhold. During the
entire service, Alma's parents labored at stifling their sobs.

Jena and Millie joined the family and close friends at the
graveside. The rest of us began to leave, heading for the parking lot. My head swung in a double-take when I saw someone
ahead in the crowd who looked exactly like Jolene Cromwell.
Even walked like her, too. I put some serious speed into my
gait and moved to the front, but once there, no one came close
to matching Jolene's appearance. Baffled, I walked to the car,
muttering under my breath, "I need to find Alma Guerra's killer. It seems Jolene won't rest until I do."

CHAPTER 13

Dan listened to every detail of my encounter with the nutria rat, concern etched in the lines of his face. The mention of Buffy's name brought her to my side.

"Miss Buffy," he said, giving her a stern look. "Shame on you for putting yourself and your mommy in danger." Too much time had passed for the dog to understand any discipline, so Dan's attempt went unnoticed. She gave a huge yawn then ran her head under his hand for a pat, wagging her tail profusely.

"You've been through hell and back," Dan said. "How 'bout dinner out?"

"Mary Mahoney's?"

He nodded then turned back to Buffy who nudged his hand again, groveling for more pats.

❧❧❧

We were standing at the bar, still waiting for a table, when Dan said, "Should we go somewhere else?" We'd expected a wait but not this long, and at this point I just wanted to get off my feet.

Hearing someone call my name, I glanced around. The stirring crowd shifted and I saw Chief Bombardier. He motioned from a tall bar table for four.

"Judy Kenagy," he said again.

"That's the police chief." I took hold of Dan's arm, leading him over.

After introductions, we hopped up onto the bar stools beside him. The chief asked me how I'd been, giving me the opportunity to review my early morning fiasco once again.

The story brought a grin to his face. "Hmm. You don't become a true resident until greeted by one of our rats."

"I watched it and my dog in a face-to-face show down," I said. "That's one heck of a greeting." Jimmie Lee's hidden boat came to mind, but I didn't bother mentioning it. It wouldn't make much sense to most people.

"By all means, don't leave out how you reacted," Dan said.

"I became hysterical, okay? Screaming and too scared to do anything but watch until it left."

Bombardier chortled. "Considering how most women react when they see a mouse, I'd say your response was fitting."

"You know those things swim, too, right? I'm never going in open water again."

"I know. Hey, that reminds me. I'm having a Halloween party next Friday. Costume only. Would you and Dan like to come?"

Dan and I swapped glances.

Bombardier removed a notebook from the empty seat beside him and pulled out a card and envelope. "Hell, ya don't have to decide now. You've got all week." He slipped the invitation into the envelope then wrote *Judy and Dan* across the front.

"Do you think George Nichols would come?" he asked.

I shrugged and waited for the punch line. I didn't expect a police chief to invite people he met because of a homicide investigation to a party.

He must've read the question on my face because he said, "One thing you'll learn about the Gulf Coast is it's big on parties. Every year I invite people I consider interesting. Makes for a great bash." He reached in for another card and wrote *George and Guest* on the front of the envelope. "Will you see that he gets this?"

A waiter in a black tux-type uniform stepped up and took our drink orders as I slipped the envelope into my purse.

"The Biloxi mayor brags about making chili out of nutria rat meat," Bombardier said. "Personally, I put them in the ranks of vermin."

"I'm with you. Although, Andy Holman claims rat burgers are good."

"How is Andy?"

"Fine. He told me he'd worked with you at the City of Biloxi."

He nodded, looking thoughtful for a moment. "How long have you known Andy?" he asked.

"I met him on my first day of work."

"What did you think?"

What did I think about what? I wondered. "Well, George promenaded me through the company and I saw Andy standing in the midst of the factory in crisp, colorful clothes."

"Pants perfectly creased," Bombardier added.

"Yes. That's how he always dresses." I pictured Andy under the fluorescent lighting. He'd stood out like a hologram in a white-lighted room. After seeing us coming, he'd dropped his arms and aligned his feet. When we stepped up, he looked like he was posed for a salute but instead, he extended his hand.

"George introduced us, and then Andy pivoted around and took a bow."

Bombardier smiled. "Andy hasn't changed—"

"Excuse me," Dan broke in. "I see someone I work with." He gestured to a cluster of people standing inside one of the dining areas and slid off his stool. "I'll be right back."

"Andy told me you were a commander at the City of Biloxi, and a good one," I said.

"Was he at Guerra's funeral?"

"Yes, along with Lester Robichaux," I said. "Did you find out what he was doing there? He'd been served with the restraining order yesterday, right?"

He nodded. "Robichaux told Kevin and Johnnie that Guerra had been kind to him and he felt bad about what happened to her. Just wanted to pay his last respects but wasn't expecting to run smack into the people who fired him as soon as he got out of his pickup."

"I thought someone whisked by Andy and me in the parking lot before we went into the chapel."

"That was Robichaux," Bombardier said. "He said he ducked behind a car until you both left."

"He didn't say anything about being smitten by her?" I asked.

"No. They asked him about Guerra inviting him over and he told them she'd been making artificial plants and selling them to co-workers out of her home. He'd gone on a lunch break to buy one. We found a number of handmade plants at her house. The plant thing could be true." He shrugged. "Don't know, but my gut says he's holding something back."

A memory flitted through my head, vanishing before I could fully recall it.

Bombardier held tight to his highball. "We're finding Guerra knew a lot of people, men in particular. Kevin sent Johnnie back in to watch the services while he continued to drill Robichaux. When he got nothing else, Kevin let him go."

"Is Lester a suspect?" I knew the answer, of course, but figured he expected the question.

"No. Found out he was in jail when Guerra was killed. He's off our list." Then with a clipped snicker, he said, "I'll let ya find out why when you get your copy of the background check."

I already know why, thanks to Millie's information.

"Do you have any suspects?"

He released his glass and rocked his hand in a so-so gesture. "A little premature to say. My staff's been working the street, sniffing out anything that might bring in clues. Guerra's neighbors have been notified and questioned, probation officers interviewed, alibis checked. And we're working the information we got from some of her co-workers. We do know the gun type—a .38-caliber semi-automatic pistol. Easy enough to come by in these parts."

My curiosity piqued, I tried to draw more out of him, taking care to keep my questions light. He'd probably already told me more than he'd planned.

Our drinks arrived. I took mine and pointed the waiter to where Dan still stood in the nearest dining area. "You never found the weapon?" I asked Bombardier.

"No. Probably never will."

"In California, they usually find missing murder victims and weapons in one of the deserts. I guess here the dumping ground is the gulf."

He grinned and shook his head. "Only if the murderer isn't from these parts. Anyone who's lived here long knows that anything discarded in the gulf will resurface at one time or another. You could tie cement blocks on the body, but everything will eventually wash up on shore. No, if the locals want something hid, they'll bury it in the mud."

Dan returned and jumped back on his stool. "It's nice living where you run into people you know everywhere you go. Those were a couple of managers from work." He turned to me. "I also saw Vernon Stiff."

"An attorney we met last night," I explained to Bombardier. "He told us something that surprised me."

"I know Stiff. What did he have to say?"

"He belongs to the same gun club as Valerie Kelm-Briscoe—said she's a good shot."

"Told us her father used to bring the whole family," Dan added.

Bombardier waved the waiter over and ordered another round. "Put it on my tab," he said. "I didn't know about the gun club, but I knew the old man was no stranger to guns— had a collection of them. I still think he was behind those murders decades ago."

"Huh?" I glanced at Dan.

"What murders?" Dan asked.

"Forgot. Ya'll aren't from here." Cajun blended into the Southern inflection in his voice.

"You told me about the Kelms," I said, "and a possible theft of intellectual property, but nothing about murder."

"There's no real proof, that's why. The owners of Wade

Machinery in Biloxi were found shot to death in their home, execution style, a quarter century ago. Gerald and Marlene Wade were friends of my parents."

"Whooh." I didn't know what else to say and, it seemed, Dan didn't either.

"The only things missing from the house were plans for new inventions. What they were, no one knew, but the daughter had seen design drawings and specification sheets two days before the murders. She inventoried her parents' home the day after they were killed and realized the papers were gone."

"And that's all that disappeared?" I asked.

Bombardier nodded.

"The killer was never found?" Dan asked.

"No, but fingers pointed to old-man Kelm as being involved. The Wades were his biggest competitor and he came out with new products shortly after their deaths. And he'd married someone raised in a nest of Dixie Mafia."

"I was just telling Dan about the Dixie Mafia," I said. "I took your suggestion and got the book *Mississippi Mud*."

"Good resource," Bombardier said. "Paul Kelm could've easily connected with a hit man through Eleanor's family to take out his competitor. The police knew this but didn't do anything—let the case fizzle. You know, the Gulf Coast has had its history of political and police corruption."

The waiter arrived with our drinks.

Bombardier took a pull on his. "No one mentions the old case anymore. Old man Kelm died with his reputation intact and Eleanor's connection to the Tillery name and the Dixie Mafia is a social no-no to speak of these days."

Just then, a woman with Loretta Lynn hair and a name badge appeared. "Your table is ready."

Dan looked at Bombardier. "How did we get a table before you?"

"You didn't. I had an early dinner with the mayor and stopped by here for drinks. I'm leaving soon." He tipped his head in farewell as we followed the hostess through the restaurant. She took us to a table against a nubby white wall in one of the smaller rooms.

As we took our seats, I leaned in toward Dan and whispered, "Can you believe all this stuff about Mrs. Briscoe's father?" Then I covered my face with the menu. "Dan, I can do without the nutria rats, but other than that, life here is definitely an adventure."

He grinned. "I'll say. Speaking of adventure, we've never tried out the oversized tub in the master bath."

I smiled and scooted our drinks to the edge of the table. "Then we'll need to stop drinking."

His grin widened. "I can do that."

CHAPTER 14

The rain came the following morning. Softly at first then in slow, heavy drops that turned into loud diagonal sheets, cascading off buildings and obscuring windows. I didn't get to the Sunday newspaper in time to salvage it, its protective plastic bag no match for the weather. The rain held up for two days. When Buffy went outside, she'd squeeze her eyes shut and do her business blind. So much rain fell, our backyard looked like a rectangular pond. A crab, with one arm larger than the rest of its body, dragged itself to the backdoor where it dropped dead.

On Monday evening, the sound of rain, something that had become the norm, finally came to an end. An hour later, stars glittered into our family room.

Tuesday morning, I jumped at the chance to go jogging. I figured the street would be okay, but knew the beach would be too wet for Buffy. I bundled up my running gear and pressed through the house, passing Buffy in my nightgown. Without my usual yellow ski hat, she didn't give me so much as a second glance. I snagged my purse off the kitchen counter and ducked into the garage. After a quick change, I climbed into my car and pulled out.

Bumping down the road, I clicked on the radio and hummed along to an old 1960s tune. When I made the turn onto East Beach Drive, I slammed on my brakes. At the end of the road, Dixie was climbing out of an ancient Chevy lodged on the bare spot where I normally parked. He was hard to miss, between his size and the brass-colored shine of his dyed hair next to the russet-colored Rockhold uniform. I pulled off the road then, afraid of being seen, hooked a left into a long, poplar-lined driveway.

Dixie dropped a brown sack into the black oil drum used as a trashcan. After a furtive glance over his shoulder, he pulled a broken broom handle from the drum. I shrank back in my seat, covering the exposed side of my face and watched through spread fingers.

Using the broom handle, he pounded the sack into the barrel, paused to glance around, then shoved the handle back in. He dusted his hands, kicked mud from his shoes, and climbed back into his car, heading north on Halstead Road.

I backed out and coasted forward for the remaining half-mile stretch. One look at the mud where Dixie had parked and I stayed on course, crossing Halstead Road. A left hook took me onto the paved parking lot of the Gulf Coast Research Laboratory.

I'd no sooner gotten out of the car than a flock of high-spirited gulls appeared overhead. As they flew westward, a pod of bottlenose dolphins surfaced in the gulf, swimming in the same direction. *A sign?*

My interest in jogging forgotten, I glimpsed at my watch. It was close to seven, Dixie's clock-in time. I returned to my car and eased it over to the trash barrel, bumping it lightly upon stopping. I stepped out onto the mud, grateful to be in exercise clothes and old running shoes.

The barrel was more than half full of trash, the brown bag nowhere in sight. Using the broken end of the broom handle, I shuffled through banana peels, beer bottles, and other sundry items until I found it. I jabbed noisily at the sack, breaking it open to discover what looked like exercise clothing. I poked around long enough to be satisfied nothing else was inside. Convinced Dixie—an odd one to begin with—was simply tossing out worn clothing, I headed home.

After parking in the garage, I whipped my nightgown off the work bench before going inside. In the kitchen, Buffy stopped me with a hound-dog yelp loud enough to be heard a block away. I tried to move past her, but she defended her ground.

Dan came out of the bedroom in pajamas, toothbrush in hand. "What the hell?"

I looked down at my dirty jogging suit and gave Dan a shrug. "Sorry."

"You know what you have to do," he said.

Hooking the leash on Buffy, I took her out, down the block then around and back. A short jaunt, but one that turned a crying dog into a content one. I was no longer the villain.

 espe

At work, I pulled out my checkbook and flipped to the deposit slip I'd been scribbling on. Under my previous comments, I added, *Does Dixie's strange behavior on East Beach mean anything?*

The morning passed without incident—quiet, almost disconcertingly so after everything that had happened the previous week. I normally took advantage of days like this and either went out for lunch or ran errands, so at eleven-forty, I grabbed my purse and left.

Josette's Costume Company was set back from the road, the wood-framed building resembling an old country store. Three warped wooden steps led to a squeaky porch. The inside looked more like a warehouse than a store.

Browsing through the racks of costumes, I pulled a black flapper-style dress off the rack and looked it over. The lack of a waistline couldn't hurt even though my figure was still hanging in there. Okay, I'd admit it had begun to sag, but just a bit. I tucked the costume under my arm and headed for the accessory department.

There, I found a long cigarette holder and a pair of black mesh nylons and left for the checkout line.

On the drive back, I turned left instead of right, not realizing my mistake for another two blocks until I couldn't find the street to turn on. I kept going, thinking to turn up a different road rather than make a U-turn, and my surroundings became increasingly familiar.

My heart began to pound. "Oh gawd," I said aloud. I'd pulled onto the road that ran behind Kelm Machinery.

Across the spacious parking lot, at the back of the company, a small group of employees gathered, some smoking.

Calm down. You just have to get to the end of the street and turn around.

But at that moment, Jimmie Lee appeared at the plant's back entrance, surveying the employees on break. He craned what little neck he had and scanned the parking lot, spotting me in the process. I knew he was coming to confront me when he started walking briskly across the lot toward his truck.

I braked, hard, and spun the car around, my back tires grazing the street's dead-end curb before I tore forward, spewing mud. A moment later, Jimmie Lee's dark blue pickup was on my tail, veering left then right, backing off then pulling close.

A couple of minutes of this and I'd had it. I was running like Alice from the Red Queen's deck of cards. Why? I hadn't done anything wrong. I flipped on my right turn signal and eased onto the shoulder of the road.

Jimmie Lee guided his pickup in behind me. I got out with a hard slam of the car door and marched over. He lowered his window.

"Okay, Jimmie Lee. What's this about?"

He draped one arm over the back of the passenger seat and dangled the other out the window. "Ya tell me."

"I made a wrong turn. So, what's the big deal?"

"Ya' made a big wrong turn, Mizz Kenagy. 'Cause you don't live or work 'round here. Seems funny you'd jus' come down this road."

"It's a public street." I knew he and Mrs. Briscoe had these delusions the world was interested in their stupid little company. I had news for them. Ninety, if not one hundred percent of their employees couldn't wait to get out and away from that hellhole.

"Were ya casing Kelm Machinery, Mizz Kenagy? My job

here is to protect Mizz Briscoe's property."

"What?" My head was swimming in righteous indignation. "Get real, Jimmie Lee. Do I look like a 'caser' to you? I
stopped to get a costume for a Halloween party. All I'm guilty
of is making one wrong turn."

"Whut Halloween party are ya goin' to?"

"Huh?" I folded my arms and gritted my teeth. How was
that any of his business? Well, he wasn't getting any details
from me. I took a moment to conjure up a lie. "I don't know a
thing about the party. I just picked up the costume for my
niece who just moved here, staying with us until she can afford
an apartment." When he gave me a doubtful look, I sneered,
"What? You want proof?" I reached into my purse and pulled
out the receipt then pointed to the store's name, date and time
printed at the top.

"May I?" he asked, his fat fingers snatching the paper
from my hand, bringing it to his face for inspection.

I turned and pointed down the street. "It's that shop right
around the corner. So you see, anyone could've made a wrong
turn."

But I knew he didn't want an answer. He wanted to exac-
erbate the incident. With a condescending snort, he returned
the receipt. "Jus' seems funny ex-employees keep comin'
down this dead-end road."

Knowing Jimmie's tendency to keep popping up if he
didn't get the last word, I decided to humor him. But that
didn't mean I couldn't satisfy my own need to even the score
at the same time. "You're quite a card, Jimmie Lee," I said,
giving him an admiring smile.

"Whut da' ya' mean, card?"

"Oh, you're funny sometimes, Jimmie, that's all. A real
card. You and Mrs. Briscoe both."

He smiled. "Ya, we are kinda, ain't we? We make a good
pair." Then his smile disappeared. "She's gonna want answers
'bout this, so some kinda retribution's in order."

Retribution? For making a wrong turn? They really did
believe the world revolved around them.

Yet, I repeated what he'd said in my mind as I drove

away, wondering why I continued to let the two of them get to me. They *were* cards, fallen straight from the lunacy of *Alice's Adventures in Wonderland.*

But still, Jimmie Lee's threat of retribution stayed with me.

Back in my office, I phoned Dan to share my success in finding a costume, encouraging him to rent one that would go with mine. "Maybe a 1920s gangster outfit." I also gave him an overview of my encounter with Jimmie Lee. "We'll want to be on the lookout for him among this year's trick-or-treaters." We both snickered at the thought of Jimmie Lee passing himself off as a ten-year-old dressed as a ghost. No doubt Mrs. Briscoe would sacrifice her thousand thread count Egyptian cotton sheets for the cause.

A few minutes later, Millie came in carrying two Styrofoam cups filled with coffee.

"Hey, thanks," I said, taking one. I filled her in on my luck with the costume then recounted the incident with Jimmie Lee guarding the gates of Kelm Palace for his queen. I described the chase that ended when I decided that running scared was insane. I rehashed most of the discourse between Jimmie Lee and me and ended by disclosing my get-even scheme of calling Mrs. Briscoe and Jimmie Lee *cards.* "I don't believe he knew I was making fun of them."

Millie laughed, her bulky hair shaking. "You're such a hoot when you describe these people. They sound like cartoon characters."

"They are. They just don't know it." I leaned in. "There's something else. Dan and I ran into Bombardier at Mary Mahoney's Saturday night. He told us about a double homicide twenty-five years ago. Seems he suspects the Kelms were involved."

"Phuoof." Her hand fanned her face before dropping limp at the wrist. "That's nothing new. Lidia tells me he's talked about that ever since she's worked for him. I remember the murders."

"Oh?"

She took a sip of coffee. "Everyone assumed Mr. Kelm

was involved because of the victims' company, Wade Machinery, being Kelm's major competitor. They thought Mr. Kelm hired a hit man."

"At Mary Mahoney's, Bombardier mentioned that, too. Said it would've been easy for Kelm to hire one thanks to his wife's connection with the Dixie Mafia."

"I don't remember hearing a thing about his wife," Millie said, her expression thoughtful. "Now, I'm not positive, but I think the police had a bunch of reasons for seeing this as a professional hit. They were pretty sure the killer used a silencer, and there were some other things. I'm trying to think." Millie bit down on her lower lip. "Oh, I know. It happened at TV's prime time. The neighbors were all home, but no one heard any shots. The woman across the street was fixing something in the kitchen. She heard a car pull up in front of the couple's home and looked out the window in time to see a man in baseball gear and a ball cap get out of a car. He walked up to the couple's door. When Mrs. Wade opened it with a smile and let the man in, the neighbor didn't think much about it. But when he hurried out a little more than five minutes later, hugging a bundle of file folders, she tried to get a plate number. But the car was parked where she couldn't make it out, plus it was dark. When he pulled away, she said it looked like the license plate was missing."

"That would draw immediate police attention."

"Yes, but only if a patrol car was right there. The fellow could've pulled into an isolated area and quickly put the plate back on."

"You're right. Would've been a gamble."

Millie shook her head. "Murder is the biggest of gambles."

"Did they ever think the man might be Paul Kelm himself?" I asked.

"Not that I'm aware of. Mr. Kelm was over six feet tall. The neighbor distinctly remembers this man was on the shorter side. Not short-short, but no way near Paul Kelm's height. I remember lots of chit-chat about Mr. Kelm being behind the shootings. Who else would profit from the death of the

Wades? But then time passed, and the Kelms became rich and highfaluting and the rumors cooled. It was like that back then. The Kelms' wealth and success tempered any suspicions. The chief's about the only one still interested. Lidia said he was real disappointed when Paul Kelm died. Swore he'd pin it on him some day, but that it would be more fun if the man were alive when he did."

"Sounds like a case gone cold."

"Real cold. I doubt the chief or anyone else is gonna resurrect that ol' thing. Even if they did, it's been so long, what would really come of it if they did?"

My phone rang. Millie nodded goodbye and left as I hit the speaker button.

"Busy?" Dan asked.

"Not really."

"Just found out the national resort conference is in Chicago this year, in December. Any chance you can go?"

"December?"

"A slight drawback. Ratzel said they chose December because last year so many members of the industry complained that their managers were taken away during peak season."

"Still, Chicago in December? I'd like to think Ratzel tried to change that."

"Hey, he's a good boss, but he's smart enough to avoid the politics."

I sighed. "Well, I have that conference in Phoenix and then the Christmas party. There's no way."

"When's the party?" he asked.

"December 16th."

"Same day as my conference. One Christmas party of yours I'll be excused from." Over the years, work-related events had become more of an obligation to us than fun. I was hoping this year would be different.

An hour later, Wilma called. "The police are here to see you."

Lieutenant Leblanc sat in the little lobby with another officer I hadn't met before, a young, blond fellow. They rose when I entered.

"We've got to bring in one of your employees," Leblanc said, sounding as military as he looked with his cropped hair and stiff stance.

Before I could answer, a phone line rang, and kept ringing. "Wilma," I said, glancing over at her. "The phone?"

She stared blankly then said, "Oh, ummph." Still focused on us, she fumbled for the button.

Not about to discuss this where her over-eager ears could hear, the men followed me to my office. The lieutenant introduced the baby-faced blond as Sergeant Chip Gentry.

"I know you," I said. "You were there the day I found Alma. You secured the crime scene."

"Yes," he said. "You look better than you did then."

"For obvious reasons."

Leblanc shoved his freckled hands into his pockets. "We have an issue. The wife of one of your employees had an accident. At least, that's what we're calling it."

"Who?"

"Michael Ledet," he said. "A neighbor found his wife on the front porch steps of the Ledet home. Could've been a fall, we don't know. But she's dead."

"No," I gasped. "I'll get him."

"Don't tell him anything. We have to take him to the station."

I headed toward the cutting department at a quick pace. Over the years, I'd pulled employees from their work to be arrested. But I'd never brought one up front to hear about a death in the family.

Dixie was working at a steady rate. I stepped up to his cutting machine and asked him to come with me. He looked up, his blue eyes questioning, then reached high and pulled a lever.

The machine began to slow and his eyes looked down under lowered lashes. I turned and began walking back toward my office. He followed close behind. With a glance back, I saw his brassy-blond head down, his right hand opening and shutting against his pant leg.

Dixie ducked into my office after me. He filled up so

much space the officers flinched. Sergeant Gentry took a step back.

Fast, factual, and to the point, LeBlanc informed Dixie about his wife. Dixie covered his face with his hands while the pair steered him out of the building.

I told George then headed to Andy's office.

"There's not much we can do but wait and see if it really was just an accident," I said him. I felt guilty for being the one to bring him more bad news. He looked so worn out.

Then I remembered something. "Ohmygawd, Andy. I saw Dixie this morning, putting a bag in a trash barrel on East Beach."

"Say what?"

"I thought it odd at the time, but now—"

"Real odd," he finished.

"I've got to call the police."

Lidia answered on the second ring.

"Bombardier, please. I'm Judy Kenagy from Rockhold Packaging."

"Hello, Judy," she said. "Millie speaks of you often. I'm looking forward to meeting you. Do you have your party costume yet?"

"Well, yes, but…"

"I have mine and—"

"I'm sorry but is the chief available?"

"Oh yes, sorry. I'll get him now."

A moment later, the chief was on the line. "Bombardier here."

"Your officers just left a few minutes ago with Dixie— uh, Michael Ledet, and I should've reported something I didn't think of until after they'd gone."

"Go on."

I gave him the details of what I'd witnessed that morning—Dixie's strange behavior on East Beach, the bag of clothing I found in the trash.

I could hear the sound of scribbling through the phone then he mumbled something. "Let's see. It's three forty-eight." Another squiggle noise, as he logged in the time and date of my call. "Thank you," he said then the line went dead.

I tore the scrawled-on deposit slip out of my checkbook. I didn't have much room left on the one side, so I turned it over and wrote *Jena afraid of someone. Lester shows up at murdered victim's funeral. Dixie's wife killed same day as strange behavior on East Beach. A connection?*

ფიფი

I arrived home, itching to tell Dan the story about Dixie.

He stood in front of the refrigerator, the door hanging open. "What's for dinner?" he asked, glancing over at me as I came into the room.

"I didn't plan anything," I said. "But you've got to hear this."

"Taco salad sounds good."

"We don't have everything to make it. How 'bout leftover lasagna? But before that, let me tell you what happened."

"Go ahead," he said, his attention still on the contents of the fridge.

I started by telling him about Dixie at the trash drum and took it from there.

"You did have a busy day," he replied vaguely. "I don't see the lasagna."

I sighed. "The lasagna's in the red-topped Tupperware bowl, middle shelf. Anyway, when I learned of her death, I'd forgotten about seeing Dixie on East Beach. After the officers left, it hit me so I called—"

"Do we have stuff for salad?"

"Damn it, Dan. You're the one standing at the refrigerator. Why don't you tell me?"

"Boy, you're cranky."

"Just go sit down and I'll make dinner."

Obviously that was the answer he was looking for.

He sat. "You were saying, you called—who?"

While I set out ingredients for a tossed green salad, I told him about the police showing up at Rockhold.

I laid out several types of salad dressing, so Dan wouldn't

interrupt with a request for a different kind.

"I guess we'll read about this in the paper," he said. "Do you know where the bacon bits are?"

I sighed again. "They're where they always are."

But I knew what he meant was, will you get them? So I did. Appeased, he listened to the rest of my story. I learned a long time ago that marriage was a compromise. He got dinner and I got a captive audience.

CHAPTER 15

An Ocean Springs resident was found dead on the steps of her front porch yesterday afternoon. The cause of death is still under investigation." ~ Police Chief Carl Bombardier, the *Sun Herald.* Wednesday, October 27, 2004

၄၁၄၁

The news of Mrs. Ledet's death tore through the plant Wednesday morning like a cattle stampede in an old Western flick. Wilma filled me in on all the gossip at the reception desk. JoAnne stopped me in the hall, chattering, breaking off only when I walked away.

I was closing in on my office when Millie stepped between me and the door. "If you're smart you won't go into the plant. You'll have employees all over you."

"Thanks. I plan to hide out here," I said, sliding my key into the lock. "I'm sure they feel bad for Dixie."

Millie shrugged. "Not really." She had her finger on the pulse of employee relations and never hesitated to let me know what was up. "They're surprised and curious, but Dixie's been distant for such a long time, I doubt they empathize. I'll come by later." She turned and started toward the plant.

As I dropped my purse onto my desk, I noticed my message light winking cheerfully. I rounded my desk and sat down then tapped my phone into speaker mode and dialed into my voicemail. An applicant asked about the status of her resume. An employee had a question on medical insurance. Same old, same old until I got to the message from Jack Thornton. Instantly, my guard went up.

I hadn't spoken to Jack since my last day at Kelm. People from Kelm, a company cosseted in paranoia, weren't likely to contact prior employees. A personal phone call in or out of the place could get them fired. So if he was calling me, something had to be up.

I keyed in Jack's number, hanging up on a recorded voice, and moved onto my other calls.

With the next redial, he picked up. After an exchange of greetings, he asked, "Can you meet me for lunch?"

I hesitated, letting my schedule skate before me. "Sure," I said. "Still at Kelm?"

"Lord, no." He chuckled. "If I were, I'd never ask you to lunch. Jimmie Lee would follow me and turn me in, and then—" He made a swishing sound. "—off with my head. I'm at Hilliard Products in Biloxi, but I have this…issue with Kelm."

"Does it have anything to do with a missing burgundy three-hole punch?"

"A what?"

"Apparently, not," I quipped. "How about McElroy's—noonish?"

"You're on." Jack clicked off and I lifted my head to a knock on the inside of my open door.

Millie breezed in and took a seat. "I'm still in shock over Dixie's wife."

"Yeah, but I wonder about him."

Millie waved me off. "Oh, he's okay. Been here forever and I never heard of any marital problems." She stopped and looked skyward, as if searching for her next words in an invisible balloon, the kind that float above characters in comic strips. "Yet, getting killed on porch steps?"

I pictured Dixie on East Beach, skulking around the trash barrel. "Not an everyday event."

Millie had no sooner left than George stepped in. "I just

emailed you and the other managers about my trip to Corporate." Except for the occasional use of the word *ya'll*, George didn't sound like a Southerner. "They've summoned all of the GMs to an emergency meeting."

"Any idea what they're calling an emergency?"

"None," he said over his shoulder on his way out.

My instincts told me nothing good would come out of it. Not wanting to think about it, I pulled out the Christmas party project file.

Thanks to my husband's position at the Gulf View Hotel, I'd already secured their ballroom, a popular venue, on a date close to Christmas. But then Corporate issued a directive to HR Managers nationwide to attend a meeting in Arizona the day before our party, and I panicked. Even with Dan's connections, a new reservation at this late date would be impossible. But my HR manager peers, in the same boat, waged an email attack on Corporate and they moved the meeting up a week.

My predecessor had printed off emails she'd received criticizing last year's event. Some employees complained the band produced more noise than music. I scribbled on an index card. *Find freelance DJ who'll bring CDs. Ask Christmas party committee to select music.*

There were varying complaints about the sit-down dinner as well. A few employees asked why they didn't have a choice of entrées. A number of them didn't like sitting in one place all evening. George had told me about this earlier and I'd passed it onto the events director at the Gulf View Hotel. She suggested a buffet with filling hors d'oeuvres—high-end finger foods like Swedish meatballs, jumbo shrimp, egg rolls, and mini-sandwiches. We'd sprinkle the ballroom with tall cocktail tables and high barstools. The stools, designed for short-term sitting, would soon become uncomfortable. She told me she'd used this arrangement in the past and found it encouraged guests to mingle.

A section of my predecessor's notes summarized the traditional agenda. Each year the Christmas party committee selected the employee of the year from the four quarterly winners. The theme song from the musical *Moulin Rouge* would blare in the background as George announced the winner. Last year's prize was a Caribbean cruise for two or the cash equivalent. This year's would be the same or similar. The winning employee always initiated a champagne toast and led a dance.

Also on the agenda was a PowerPoint presentation of pictures from other company functions, normally handled by the HR manager. A large pocket inside the file folder held this year's CDs, with pictures labeled by date and company event.

I slipped the CD from last year's Christmas party into my computer's disk drive then flipped through the files. Group takes of employees dining and dancing appeared. I began uploading the good shots, deleting the bad, and saving the maybes in a separate file.

Pictures of the employee for the first quarter were stored on the next CD. I recognized the thick-set black man with the sunbeam smile. I'd seen him in the plant and also at the funeral, but didn't know his name. I removed the CD and moved on to our summer picnic—employees tossing horseshoes, playing volleyball and eating hot dogs. But these pictures also singled out individuals.

The company picnic was the only event I'd attended at Rockhold so far. It took place on the Saturday my first week with the company when I hardly knew a soul. I still didn't know the names of most of the hourly employees. I found a couple shots of Bert and Andy, uploaded them, then put the file away.

I pulled out the deposit slip with my notes and read both sides. Not real organized, but it was to remind me of the details more than anything else. Jena's fear and Lester showing up at the funeral were both connected to Alma's death in varying ways.

But what about Dixie and his wife? I wrote *Dixie killed his wife. Could he also be the person Jena is frightened of? Is he Alma's killer?* Then I tucked the little form back inside my purse.

❧❦❧

Crossing the drawbridge section of the Ocean Springs Bridge, my car vibrated over the steel grating. Then I bounced back onto smooth pavement and drove the remaining distance to Point Cadet, the eastern peninsula of Biloxi. Once filled with shrimp factories and row houses, Point Cadet had been leveled to allow for the addition of dockside casinos. I passed the Maritime and Seafood Industry Museum, the Isle of Capri, Casino Magic, and the Grand Casino Biloxi. Each casino sported a unique structure, floating on the gulf like luxury cruise liners.

Together, they carried the name Casino Row. A mile long stretch of beach followed the trio up to where McElroy's Harbor House restaurant stood.

I mounted the sand-smeared steps of McElroy's and went inside. The waiting bench was packed and people milled about the hostess stand. I looked around and spotted Jack at a table for four, his head bent over a menu.

I walked over and he flashed me a smile. "Hey."

"It's been awhile," I said, taking a seat across from him. "First time I haven't seen you in a suit."

He glanced down at his burgundy long-sleeved sports shirt. "Yeah, we have dress-down Fridays." He looked at the Rockhold emblem on my polo shirt. "Looks like you do, too."

I nodded and glanced out one of many windows. Fishing, tour, and shrimp boats all bobbed in their designated spaces. "You must've gotten here early."

"I did," Jack said. "Anxious to discuss this Kelm issue, but also interested in what's happening at your workplace."

"Yeah," I sighed. "I found a good place to work and then one of our employees is killed."

"I heard. And this morning, I read the wife of another one was found dead. An accident?"

I raised a brow. "Maybe—though it's a little early to speculate."

"I understand. I'll wait for the news update."

"Lots of strange goings on," I said. "One of our employees is frightened silly of someone she's afraid to name. The plant manager feels certain the person is an employee, and considering how often she calls in sick, I'm inclined to agree."

The waitress stepped up and I grabbed my menu, looking down the list of lunch items.

"Seafood Po-Boy and iced tea," Jack said.

"Make that two." I handed her my menu and she hurried away. "So, what did the wicked witch do?" I asked.

"A month or so after you left, I found another job. Things were good until my boss ran into Mrs. Briscoe at a manufacturing conference. Judy, she said she pitied him for having hired me."

I rolled my eyes. "Why does that not surprise me?"

"He told me he asked her why and she said, 'you'll find out soon enough.'" Jack looked outside and my gaze followed. A pelican plummeted into the gulf, clumsily splashing about in chase of a fish. Near the water's edge, egrets and cranes moved slowly about on long, twiggy legs. "This happened my first week on the job. Upset me so much I didn't respond well—stuttered and stammered."

I shook my head in disgust. "Phooph."

"I thought about dropping the matter, but it's been icy. I considered asking him to call you to verify how wacky she is, but how weird would that sound?"

I thought for a moment. "My boss has ties all over the community. I wonder if he'd have any suggestions." The waitress brought the tea and I glanced at a pair of white and blue herons nuzzled on floating driftwood. "Remember the day I called her Val-*er*-ie?"

"Yeah, and Nora dropped the lemonade."

"I love rolling those vowels around, knowing she'd go balmy if she thought anyone called her anything other than *Mizus* Briscoe."

Jack chuckled.

I sat back in my chair. "You're in a real bind. Looking for another job would be impossible. Even though you don't work for her now, other interested employers would call her for a reference. A real kiss of death."

The food arrived and our attention shifted to the Po-Boys. After a few hearty bites, I said, "I assume Jimmie Lee is still peeking around corners and listening in on conversations."

"For certain. He took on some secret assignment for Mrs. Briscoe right before I left, started slipping me snatches of information about searching for her brother. Not the one who came to the Christmas party, but one missing for what's been a very long time."

"Dan and I heard something about the brother, too. The eldest Kelm son—sort of skipped town, I heard."

"Yeah, last seen at the University of Southern Mississippi in Hattiesburg twenty-five years ago. As soon as he had enough credits to graduate, he vanished, a no-show at the graduation ceremonies. Mrs. Briscoe's parents told her he didn't want to be part of the family anymore."

"What kind of explanation is that?" I said, rising. "Well, I've got to get back, but I'll ask my boss if he has any suggestions."

"Thanks," he said, his smile grateful.

Chapter 16

"Michael Ledet of Ocean Springs has been arrested and charged in the death of his wife." ~ Police Chief Carl Bombardier, the *Sun Herald.* Thursday, October 28, 2004

Dixie's confession of killing his wife made headline news. Not a surprise to the police, who'd responded to numerous domestic dispute calls.

He'd put her in the hospital twice, yet she'd never filed a complaint.

Dixie asked for leniency because he killed her accidentally during what he called a routine quarrel.

I'd no sooner settled at my desk than Millie excitedly marched in and plopped down across from me. "Guess who's been causing Jena to shake in her hard hat."

"We don't wear hard hats here."

"Judy. This is serious."

I sighed. "Dixie'd be my guess."

"Yep," she said. "Now that he's locked away, she's talking. Apparently, he'd been stalking Alma and Jena's certain he's her murderer."

A touch of disappointment surprised me. If he killed

Alma then my fantasy of catching the murderer was over. I knew it was a pipe dream, but one that gave me hope of atoning for what I'd done to Jolene Cromwell.

"Jena had told us Alma swore her to secrecy. Now, she's beating herself up for not reporting it sooner and saving Alma's life."

"Or more likely, getting killed along with her friend."

She nodded her head in affirmation. "Jena said Alma borrowed a gun—protection from Dixie. The gun part is what she shared with Rusty Shaw."

"So, that's what sent the police to her home?"

Millie took a gulp of air. "Yup, and that's when she told them about Dixie. The police advised her to remain clammed up for her own safety."

"Who loaned Alma a gun?" I asked. Suddenly overcome by a fuzzy twinge of déjà vu, I shivered.

"Judy, what is it?"

"I don't know. The association of Alma and the gun reminded me of something. We've never talked about this before, correct?"

"We didn't know anything about it until now."

I shook my head. "I think there was more said in that conversation between Lester and Alma in the break room, but for the life of me I can't remember. Sorry. Go on."

"Well, the only thing Jena knows about the gun's lender is that Alma referred to him as her secret friend. Since Alma wouldn't give her a crumb regarding who he was, Jena says he must've been a lover—a married one."

Another fleeting sense of something tingled in the back of my head. "Secret friend? Didn't someone use that term recently?"

Millie chuckled. "Yes, dummy. You did."

"That's right. The words coined by the anonymous caller."

Millie put her hands on my desktop. "You only told me and Andy about that call, right?"

"And Chief Bombardier."

"So then Jena has no knowledge of it. Hmm. And Jena

swears no one else knew about the secret friend. But the caller specifically mentioned him."

"Rusty Shaw? Maybe she told him?"

"I don't think so," she said, "but I'll ask and let ya know."

"Or maybe Jena was the anonymous caller." But hadn't Dan said it was a man's voice?

"No way," Millie said. "Jena didn't know you from Adam then and besides, that's not Jena's style." Once more Millie let me know she had the scoop on each and every employee. Dixie, of course, the odd man out, having slipped through her feelers big time. "Also," she said, "the caller said it was not an employee. Jena told me she's thought Dixie killed Alma all along, so the caller couldn't be her. Alma told her Dixie'd shown up at her house more than once, asking for a date. He didn't take it well when she turned him down. There were threats." Millie spilled details about Alma's encounters with Dixie for another few minutes. I listened and nodded until my neck ached and my attention span dwindled. When her break time ended, she wrapped it up, saying, "Jena may finally get some sleep."

I still needed to talk to George about Jack Thornton. How I'd present this, another matter.

Before I could get up from my desk, a familiar voice boomed the theme song from *Annie*.

Andy sailed in, arms spread and his head turned up to the ceiling. "Tomorrow, tomorrow…"

I chuckled. "An–dy."

"I'm celebrating."

"We don't know if Dixie is Alma's killer."

"I do and they'll prove it. Jena told Millie—"

I held up my hand. "I've already heard all about it." Millie had worn me out with her soap opera account of Dixie's and Alma's lives.

Andy's smile shriveled. "Everything?"

"I'd say. Millie was pretty long-winded."

My phone rang. Robbed of his late-breaking news moment, Andy bounded down the hall toward George's office as I picked up the phone.

"Lieutenant Young here."

"Hi, Lieutenant."

"I need to review Ledet's time records again. When's a good time?"

"I thought you—" The buzz of my fax machine distracted me. I glanced at the paper slowly emerging. "Don't you have his confession?"

"We do, but if there's evidence to back it up, we want it."

"I'll be here until five."

As soon as I hung up, it rang again. The extension light indicated it was Millie. I hesitated a moment then picked up.

"Judy, I grabbed Jena and asked about Rusty. She only told him about knowing Alma had borrowed a gun from someone. Out of respect for Alma, she didn't want to give her opinion about an illicit affair. She also can't imagine Alma mentioning this man to anyone else but her. So I have no idea about that anonymous caller."

"Okay. I guess we'll stay confused on that one. Thanks for the info."

Wheeling my chair over to the fax machine, I lifted the long overdue Hancock County background check on Lester Robichaux. Charges listed over a ten-year period riddled the report. One shoplifting arrest but no conviction. Loitering. The remainder were listed under the general category of lewd and lascivious behavior. The arrest on Monday, October eighteenth, the day before I found Alma, contained commentary that Robichaux had exposed himself to people at a bus stop in Bay St. Louis. This resulted in his rock-solid alibi, an overnight jail stay. His outburst at Rockhold the following day didn't make the sheet, but the subsequent car accident did, recorded as a reckless driving conviction.

George's voice bellowed over the paging system. "All members of the management team to the conference room."

Andy stepped inside my door. "Guess we're gonna be enlightened on George's latest trip to Corporate."

I picked up my planner and walked over to the conference room with Andy.

"We're being sold," George said without preamble. "The

buyers are investors out of Canada. My guess is this will bring changes to operations nationwide, but I'm hopeful there won't be any local personnel cuts. Get the employees together tomorrow at two p.m. I'll make the announcement." Then George left, giving us no opportunity for questions.

I caught up with him in the hallway. "George, do you have a minute?"

"After four," he said, without slowing.

Andy was waiting outside my office and followed me inside. "What's your read on the sale?"

"It sucks," I said. I fell into my chair while Andy remained standing. "I've been through this before," I said. "Things can get ugly."

Wilma stuck her head in, her heavily-sprayed hair frozen into an orb. "The police chief is waiting in the reception area. I'm on my way to break."

"The chief? I was expecting Lieutenant Young."

"He said he sent him on another case. That's all I know," she said and left for the break room.

"Why are the police here?" Andy asked.

"They want anything they can get to support Dixie's confession."

"Ah, yes, police procedure. False confessions do occur, believe it or not."

"You'd think the county sheriff would get involved," I said. "This *is* a little town."

"I learned a few things during my stint with the Biloxi PD. If a crime occurs inside the city limits, the police have jurisdiction. When it happens within the county, but outside city limits, the sheriff has jurisdiction. In this case, that would be Sheriff Ralph."

"Sheriff Ralph?"

"Ralph Broussard. You'll see him on TV eventually, if you haven't already. A real abrasive dude. The chief holds the control here but—" Andy sniggered. "—even if Alma had been killed in a field outside city limits, there's no way he'd let Sheriff Ralph in on this case. Hates the sheriff and he'd find some way to take over."

He hovered by my desk as I tapped in JoAnne's extension. When her hearty greeting burst through the speaker, I said, "I need the time records for October again. I'll be over in a couple of minutes."

"Oh, Miss Judy, this is so——"

I clicked off, pretending I hadn't heard, and blew out an annoyed snort.

Andy chuckled. We got to our feet and left my office, heading in opposite directions.

"Find out if they think Dixie killed Alma," Andy called after me.

Grrrr. Enough of Alma and Dixie.

ↀↀↀ

Bombardier sat across the desk from me, browsing over time records. Dixie had clocked in on time the day his wife was found, but didn't clock out because he left with the police.

I stared at Bombardier's full face and crooked tie, not knowing how to broach Andy's question.

By the time I decided to gut up and just ask, Bombardier came to my rescue. "Ledet's now a suspect in the Guerra case, thanks to your call this morning."

"You found something in the trash barrel?" I said.

"An old T-shirt and loose cotton shorts. Probably what Ledet slept in. But they were splattered with his wife's blood."

The thought of blood had never entered my mind. I'd assumed the speckles were mud or trash.

"We were holding off on questioning him to protect Doggett," he said.

"We knew Jena was scared of someone," I said, "but she didn't say who until this morning when she learned Dixie had been arrested. Apparently, Dixie had been stalking Alma. We also found out Alma had borrowed a gun from her secret friend. The anonymous caller used the same term for the killer."

He nodded. "We took note of that, too."

"Chief, I was wondering. Will the Jackson County sheriff help in this investigation?"

He placed a hand on each thigh and his elbows jerked perpendicular to his waist. "The sheriff's an idiot." He shifted in his chair and gestured with one hand in the air. "Broussard got his job through politics, not expertise. He's not someone I'd want working on an investigation in my town."

I held back the smile.

Bombardier returned to the time reports. "Can I get a copy of this page?"

I got out of my seat and stepped around the desk, taking the binder out of his hands.

"Oh, wait," he said. "Let me check Ledet's hours for the eighteenth and nineteenth, the day of Guerra's death and the day you found her."

"Your detectives already checked the employees' hours for those dates."

"They did, but made copies for only those with time exceptions. Since he's a suspect in Guerra's case, we need documentation of his whereabouts."

I gave the binder back to him. "Did Alma work a complete shift that day?"

"Yes. Seven to four."

"Do you know the time of death?"

"The ME said before ten p.m. on Monday the eighteenth, more likely in the late afternoon not long after she got home from work."

"Did the late-afternoon theory come from something in the autopsy, or simply from the fact she died while still in uniform?" I asked.

"The work uniform, mostly. They also found crime scene evidence indicating she probably hadn't been home long when the killer showed up." Bombardier pored over the pages.

"Ah, here we are. October nineteenth," he said more to himself than to me. "He clocked in at 7:03 a.m. and out at 3:59 p.m. She was killed sometime the evening before, so…okay. Now, October eighteenth Hmmm. Yes, he clocked in at 6:59 a.m. and out at four p.m. Would you make copies of these?"

He put a yellow sticky on the pages and closed the binder.

I took it from him and left. But when copying the page for October eighteenth, I saw the asterisk next to Dixie's time-out punch.

I set his copies in front of him. "Dixie didn't clock out on October eighteenth."

Bombardier angled his head and stared up at me.

I pointed to the little mark next to Dixie's clock-out time. "That's what this asterisk means. When the employee doesn't clock out, payroll handles it manually."

He glared at the mark. "Ledet didn't clock out?"

"Right. When an employee forgets, the supervisor sends payroll an override form and they make the entry."

I used the intercom to page Bert. In a matter of minutes, he appeared, gasping. I chuckled, "Bert, I didn't mean for you to run. It's not like the police are after you."

"Sorry," he said with a wheeze. "It–it's just, this day's b–b–been one nightmare after another."

"I need to verify a manual clock-out for Dixie. Did you approve this?" I pointed to the time-out on the form. "October eighteenth. The day before I found Alma."

"No. This-this is the first I've heard of it."

"Do you know if he was in the building until the end of his shift?" Bombardier asked.

"No idea. I was w–working on a report. Didn't go into the p–p–plant until late that afternoon."

"That was two weeks ago," I said. "How can you be so sure?"

"Judy," he sputtered out my name like he always did. He never said it in less than three syllables. "I remember because I p–p–planned to turn that report in the next day. And the next day, Alma turned up d–d–dead." He shook his head. "Same day we had that incident with Lester and my g–g–glasses got crushed. Needless to say, I didn't f–f–finish the report on time. And Dixie hasn't missed a clock in or out for years. There's no way I'd have f–f–forgotten if I'd been told."

Bombardier looked from Bert to me then scratched one side of his head through his black hair. "Can ya'll talk to some of the employees—pin down a time?" he asked.

"Sure," I said.

The chief set the binder on my desk. "I'll need to check for these symbols on all the employees' punches."

"They're rare. Won't take long," I said.

"I'll talk to D–D–Dixie's co-workers about his time," Bert said as he walked out the door.

Bombardier went to work on the list again and, in less than five minutes he rose, removed his suit jacket from the back of the chair, and shrugged into it. "Ledet's your only asterisk for those two days." He handed me his business card. "Let me know what ya'll find out. If you can't reach me, call Kevin Young. I'll brief him."

After he left, I added a note about the missed punch to the deposit slip. The paper looked more like the other junk floating around in my purse than any sort of record. But for now, it worked.

CHAPTER 17

George had said he'd be available after four. So, at 4:10 p.m., I peeked through his open office door. He had his back to me, staring at his computer screen. When I stepped in, he spun around and flinched.

"Sorry," he said. "Thought you were my daughter. She's on her way over to drain me of cash. Just got her driver's license."

I smiled. "Good for her—about the driver's license, not about taking your money. Is this a good time?"

"As good as any."

I took a seat and told him about finding the unsubstantiated manual clock-out for Dixie for Monday, October eighteenth.

"Keep me posted," he replied.

"Sure."

When I hesitated, considering how I might sound running down an old boss to a new boss, he gestured for me to continue.

"This is awkward."

"Take your time, Judy."

I lowered my head. "Okay. See, I had lunch with someone I used to work with at Kelm Machinery. He's got a problem and I'm trying to help. I thought you might have a suggestion since you have connections..."

"Yes?"

I took a breath. "My friend—Jack Thornton's his name. He quit Kelm Machinery about a month or so ago. He's working at a place in Biloxi called Hilliard Products."

"I know the CEO there."

I looked up. "You do?"

His eyes turned questioning but he held his tongue.

"Well, the owner of Kelm Machinery, Mrs. Briscoe, is…well, to put it bluntly a nut case."

George glanced at my quivering hands.

I moved them out of sight and squeezed my knees. "She ran into Jack's boss, at a manufacturing conference and told him Jack had been a poor employee, which is an outright lie. Jack knows his nuts and bolts." I took a breath, hoping George would say something, but he didn't. Sweat dripped between my breasts. "Jack's concern is his boss doesn't know him well, and…" I stopped when George smiled.

"I'll speak to Thomas," he said, "That's who Jack's boss has to be."

"You will?"

George nodded. "And don't worry. I won't say anything that will hurt your friend's career." His smile widened. "If you promise not to tell, I'll let you know what she said about you."

"Me?" Dumbfounded, I stared at him. "When?" *Was this about that stupid three-hole punch?*

"Valerie's reputation precedes her," he said. "I ran into her at the drug store and she started a conversation. She made a point of telling me she never understood what you did all day, implying you were lazy."

"That's exactly what she said about her previous HR Manager." My voice sounded so shrill it surprised me.

"Judy, her turnover rate alone sings out there's a problem. A big problem. And bosses who say they don't know what their employees do all day are just admitting their own incompetence. If it's okay with you, I'm calling Thomas now to bring him up to speed on Valerie."

"Thanks so much, George."

"I'll give you a little insight into the woman—just between you and me. Okay?"

"Sure."

He leaned over, elbows resting on the desk, his hands clasped together as if in prayer. "I went to a manufacturing conference a few years back. About a hundred and fifty people attended. Valerie came with her mother, Eleanor Kelm. Eleanor got up in front of the group and publicly criticized her daughter. Pretty damn brutal if you ask me, especially coming from the woman's own mother."

"Well, it kind of makes sense. Something or somebody hurt that woman," I said. "She's totally untrusting and hateful as hell. Thanks, George. I really appreciate the information and your help with Jack. He won't do anything that will embarrass you or your friend's company. I know you're busy, so I'll get out of here." I stood to leave, but turned back. "Are you nervous about the sale?"

"Oh yes, but I think ya'll will be okay." He rolled his eyes. "It's the people in positions like mine who are the most vulnerable."

"Nah, that can't be. We have to have a general manager, and you're good at it."

"Thanks. And Judy, if you ever need to talk just come on in. I'm not Valerie Kelm-Briscoe."

"That's for damn sure." I gave him a big, affectionate grin then hurried to my office where I phoned Jack.

∽∾∽

After pulling into the garage, I opened the door to the washroom and instantly smelled something cooking. Walking into the kitchen I found Dan standing over the stove, stirring something in a large pot. "I have dinner half-made."

"Really?" I felt a shred of guilt, remembering my annoyance about waiting on Dan. I'd forgotten how often he surprised me with a full service dinner and drinks.

"Yep, I left work early and went to the costume shop, and then stirred up my homemade meatballs and spaghetti sauce."

"Smells good," I said. "Any luck with a costume?"

"Nothing fit in the rentals, so I bought one. I'll show

you." I followed him to the coat closet where he pulled out a priest's robe.

"Dan, that's not a Halloween costume."

"Actually it is. See the cross around the neck?"

It was big and made of shiny white plastic. "But most of the coast is Catholic. Why would someone wear a priest outfit for Halloween? Besides, I'm going as Betty Boop."

"I'll say I'm an exorcist priest. Don't worry, the people at the costume shop thought the outfit looked great."

I gazed at the authentic-looking priestly robe. "Well, I guess. I hope we don't offend anyone."

❧❧

Friday afternoon, we stopped production so George could speak to the employees. The operators joined the administrative staff in an open space just inside the plant.

George came through the door from the administrative offices and raised his voice to address the standing group. "I have an announcement to make." He waited for the chitchat to die down. When he had their attention, the plant acoustics did the rest, his voice bellowing. "Our company has been sold to Brimloew International, an investment firm out of Canada. Rockhold management sees this as a positive move." He paused, allowing his words to sink in. "Brimloew will bring financial support to our operations nationwide. The news of the sale will become public over the next few weeks. Until then, I'll continue to give you updates. Any questions?"

Eddie Sutter's hand went up and George pointed to him. "Yes."

"Do you think any of us will lose our jobs?"

"I can't say for sure, although I doubt they'd cut any production positions. The plant can't operate without its front line."

Jena tugged on my sleeve. "Miss Judy, look!" she said a little too loudly. She turned around and I followed her gaze to see Lester Robichaux leaving the plant. "I saw him standing behind us, listening in."

Employees turned and looked, murmuring.

I started to go after Lester only to be stopped by Jena hugging my upper arm. I gently peeled her off and took long strides toward the back. At the exit, he began running. By the time I got there, his pickup was peeling out of the parking lot.

Returning to the group, I heard George remind everyone of our policy on terminated employees not being allowed on company property. Then he got everyone's word they'd report Lester if he ever returned before dismissing the group to return to their stations.

Policy or not, we have a restraining order against him.

I hurried to my office to call Detective Young.

"This is another nick on Robichaux's record," Young said. "After his appearance at the funeral last Saturday, he's looking at jail time."

"Geez. Why would he want to hang out at a place where he was discharged?"

"We don't get it either," the lieutenant said, "but Robichaux's a minor fish. Our attention's locked in on Ledet in the Guerra case. Or should be."

"He was so quick to admit killing his wife," I said. "Being so adamant about not killing Alma makes you wonder. At least, that's what his attorney is preaching."

"An admission to killing Guerra could make the difference between life in prison and freedom. If he gets off on killing her, his attorney's next move will be getting the charge for his wife's death reduced to manslaughter. He made a smart move confessing to killing his wife. We have hard evidence on her death, but none with Guerra."

"Is he officially a suspect?"

"Oh, he's a suspect, all right," he said in a surly tone. "I'd like to see him charged, but for some reason…Let's just say we can't get Bombardier to budge."

"Lack of evidence?"

"Ma'am, we've had convictions with less. Ledet was Guerra's stalker for gawd's sake and he didn't even clock out that day. Bombardier's got something up his—" He broke off and I pictured his thin upper lip drawing up into a contemptuous curl. "What I mean is the chief still wants to delve."

After hanging up, my mind did a quick review of the situation. Andy, Millie, and Jena felt certain Dixie was the killer. Bombardier's staff seemed to have homed in on him as well. Like the lieutenant said, Dixie had been Alma's stalker, so there was motive. He hadn't clocked-out on the day Alma was killed, something Bert told us never happened with Dixie. Yet Bombardier, a man who didn't drag his feet, seemed to be stalling. Why?

CHAPTER 18

Dan and I pushed through the door of the Bayview Gourmet, the only Ocean Springs restaurant that offered brunch on Saturdays. The sweet smell of baking pastries mingled in the air with the bold aroma of multi-flavored coffees.

The hostess took us past the glass case of carryout goodies to a wooden table for two. Decorative arrangements of fine china on white doilies covered cabinet tops. Champagne glasses circled a Mikasa vase filled with fresh daises. A hardback book leaned against an antique jewelry box, the book's cover showing a weeping willow in the midst of shadowy fog, a title written in a black, dripping font.

I ordered the Crème Caramel, the specialty coffee de jour while Dan stuck with a rich Colombian blend.

When our orders were placed and our coffee in hand, Dan leaned toward me. "Don't turn around," he said under his breath. "The Briscoes are coming in."

"Damn," I muttered, keeping my eyes on Dan.

"Do you want to pretend we don't see them?"

"Of course, though I'm not sure what good it'll do," I said.

With as small as the Bayview Gourmet was, going unnoticed was unlikely. And walking out would only draw attention.

Dan monitored the Briscoes' movements then nodded his

head to his right. "They're sitting at that table by the window. Let's enjoy our food and forget about 'em."

I worked at not turning around as Dan's voice returned to a conversational pitch. "Excited about the Halloween party tonight?"

I shrugged. "I don't know. I'm so tired from this past week. The fall-out from the company's sale has been brutal." I lowered my voice to a murmur. "Not to mention Dixie killing his wife and becoming the prime suspect in Alma's death."

"Yeah, that's a big one. I think we'll have fun. Spiked cider, bobbing for apples, trying to guess who's in the clown costume."

I chuckled. "No way am I going if we're drinking spiked cider and bobbing for apples."

"But you've got to find out which guy comes in drag with balloon breasts."

We both laughed.

"George told me he didn't want to go," I said, "but will for PR reasons. Apparently, Bombardier's well connected to influential folks on the Gulf Coast and George sees a chance to bring in a new customer or two."

Dan stirred his coffee with a little plastic stick. "I wondered if I'd ever meet him since I'll be in Chicago when you have your Christmas party."

"You could stop by my office," I said. "See where I work for a change and meet some of my friends."

"Yeah, well, I spend enough time at my job. If I can get away, going to where you work doesn't sound appealing. Sorry." He pitched me a crooked grin. "Is George bringing his wife?"

"No. He said she wasn't interested."

He smiled. "See? You're lucky to have me. I go whether I want to or not."

The waitress delivered our plates and I savored the first bite of the Eggs Benedict, letting the mix of sweet hollandaise, muffin, and warm egg melt into a tangy cream on my tongue. "This is like having brunch at Brennan's in New Orleans."

"I'd say better," he said, "if that's possible."

We spent the rest of the meal in silence. Dan was dropping dollar bills on the check when I stole a look at the Briscoes. Mrs. Briscoe, deep into an animated conversation, gestured wildly with her hands, her fingers wiggling as if playing an invisible piano.

"She's having one of her snit fits," I said in a low voice. "Take a trip to the men's room and when you come out, watch her."

"Why?"

I shooed him away with a hand gesture. "Just do it. You'll enjoy the performance. They won't see you from that angle." I nodded to the hall behind him. He rose and moved that way.

I waited. The waitress picked up the check and returned a few minutes later with the change. I took the coins and left the bills on the table as a tip.

Dan appeared in the hall, stopping a moment to look at the Briscoes before moving back into the restaurant. We paired up and headed toward the exit. As we passed, Mrs. Briscoe leaned into her husband's ear, screening one side of her mouth to whisper. A second later, they turned and watched us leave.

Dan snapped on his sun glasses. "I think it's time for you to let go of your issues with that woman."

I moved to my side of the car. "You saw her in action. That's what I've been telling you about."

"Yes, Judy." His harsh tone surprised me. "But you don't work for her anymore. Just scrape her off." He slid into the driver's seat.

Dan didn't understand what I'd put up with. "What about the time Rhonda Curtain complained others treated her differently because of her race and Mrs. Briscoe laughed?"

He chuckled. "I forgot about that. She is a psycho."

"See? She told Rhonda it couldn't happen at her company because while growing up, she'd dined with black and slept with black. Of course, the people she spoke of were nannies and family servants."

He fired up the car. "Judy, you've told me this already."

"Sorry," I said, a familiar feeling of isolation surfacing.

Dan glanced over. "You're right about her hair and jewelry," he said with a smile. "When she talks, she uses them like weapons."

"You noticed. Thanks, Dan."

CHAPTER 19

Gluing the eyelashes on proved to be the hardest part of dressing for the party. I had sprayed my hair Elvis-black and created spit curls. After swiping my cheeks with ruby red blush and my eyelids with iridescent plum shadow, I spun around to face Dan. "Ta-dah. I'm Mrs. Briscoe's assistant, Nora Flint."

I reached for the mascara, but Dan whisked it away.

"Let's not go overboard. She must use a paint brush."

I giggled.

Dan's gray head of hair looked snowy white, even glowed, when contrasted against the black priest robe. He glanced in the bathroom mirror and straightened his robe. He definitely looked the part. I could almost hear church bells ringing for seven o'clock Mass. He would never pass for a Halloween partygoer.

My flapper dress proved to be a good decision. The waist-free cut shielded my little tummy roll. The dress fell slightly above my knees, revealing legs adorned in fishnet hose, taut from standing on stiletto heels.

On our way, we pulled in at the liquor store next to Broome's Market.

"Let's take a bottle for Carl," Dan said. "Do you know what he drinks?"

"He ordered Crown Royal at Mary Mahoney's."

"I'll get a fifth," he said, opening the car door.

Five minutes later, the door to the liquor store flew open and two young men tumbled out, doubled over from uncontrollable laughter. I cracked the car window and heard one of them say the word *priest*.

Dan walked out a moment later.

"What did you do to those guys?" I asked as he handed me the bottle and got into the car.

He slid the key into the ignition and grinned. "I left the gag part of the costume, the plastic cross, in the car. Those two were putting Mad Dog 20/20 and Ripple into brown paper bags and in walks Father Dan. They looked startled."

"I don't know why," I said. "Catholics believe in drinking."

"Maybe they were Baptists. They asked for absolution in a half-kidding way, but then made excuses for their purchase. I picked up the Crown Royal and touched my fifth to their bagged bottles, and said, 'Brothers, we are all sinners.' That's when I admitted I was on my way to a costume party."

❦

The front door to Bombardier's home opened to a spacious room with high ceilings, no foyer or entrance hall. Life-sized mannequins stood in two feet deep alcoves in the upper portion of the walls—Count Dracula, a witch on a broomstick, skeletons holding hands, and a grotesque man with a sword running through him. Scattered about on side tables and counters were pumpkins, their faces carved with expressions ranging from horror to laughter. A Casper the Friendly Ghost balloon bounced against the vaulted ceiling.

Bombardier came to greet us in a dust-colored uniform, bedecked with fake medals and stripes. A nametag clipped to the lapel read *General George Patton*. He took the bottle of Crown Royal and held it at eye level. "My favorite. Thank you."

After exchanging compliments on costumes, he directed us through a pair of open French doors to what he referred to as the Florida room. The slim, rectangular room looked out on the backyard through a wall-sized window. In the right corner, near a makeshift bar, a one-man band played soft music on an acoustic guitar. A table lined with steaming hot hors d'oeuvres filled the opposite end of the Florida room.

"Help yourselves," Bombardier said before wandering away to greet other guests.

With drinks in hand, we returned to the great room and moved from one cluster of people to another. Not really knowing anyone, we stopped at the fireplace and watched the flames, taking in the warmth.

On the other side of the room, a young woman, standing with a large group of people, glanced our way then, in a delayed reaction, looked back, her face beaming. She scurried over, the pleated skirt of her cheerleader's costume bouncing merrily, and started talking before she reached us. "You must be Judy Kenagy. Why, Millie's told me you came from California and that you—"

Who on earth...

Her words ran together, broken up by only the occasional crack of chewing gum. She radiated so much gusto that if she'd jumped into the air with a split and chanted, "Go, team, go," I wouldn't have been the least surprised.

"Millie told me you'd be all gussied up as Betty Boop." She stretched out a hand for a shake. "I'm Lidia Trash."

Ah, yes, I thought. "Glad to meet you. This is my husband, Dan."

He smiled and shook her hand.

"You look just like a priest."

His grin turned devilish. "My costume might be too realistic."

"Might be?" I smirked. "People mistook you for a priest before we got here."

Lidia waved her hand in front of her, as if swatting a fly. "Hey, that's okay. I'm Catholic and I'm not bothered that you look like the real thing."

"Well, I'm an exorcist priest," Dan said. "I get rid of demons. And cheerleaders."

"Very funny, Dan," I said.

Lidia bent near my ear and I breathed in the familiar smell of bubble-gum. Not spearmint or juicy fruit, but original Double Bubble. "Tell Millie I said hi, will ya? And tell her I'll be calling her soon." Lidia teetered when she spoke as if she were about to start dancing or somersaulting out of the room.

"Sure."

"I wish I could see her more often," she said devilishly, her curly, gold hair bouncing around her sparkling eyes.

"I'm glad I could put a face to a name," I said. "Millie speaks of you often."

She smiled. "Glad to meet you both. And Judy—boop-oop-a-doop." She scampered back across the room.

"Lidia is Bombardier's admin assistant," I said to Dan.

"She's cute," he said then nodded toward the hors d'oeuvres table. "The mayor of Biloxi is here. He's talking to Carl."

I looked over, recognizing several other prominent town figures all gathered around the mayor. "Bombardier's well connected."

We were at the bar, getting refills, when George arrived. I nudged Dan and we turned toward the door.

My boss wore a scholarly sorcerer's hat and a black choir robe. He'd pasted a fake mustache to his face and a long, thin beard. Letter-sized white sheets of paper stuck to the front of his robe.

We made our way in his direction, dodging werewolves and vampires. Closer in, the print on the pieces of paper became legible. One sheet read, *Nostradamus Prophecy Number Two.* Dan and I laughed.

"George, how creative," I said.

George raved over Dan's outfit and Dan repeated his story about being an exorcist priest. When the conversation turned to golf, I looked around for my exit.

Bombardier stood at the makeshift bar, accepting a highball from the bartender. He turned and, seeing me, started in my direction. I met him halfway.

"Thanks again for the Crown Royal," he said. "Not necessary but definitely appreciated."

"That's the least we can do." I gestured around the room. "You've gone all out."

A rascally smirk appeared on his face and he whispered, "Don't suppose you've gotten the background check on Lester Robichaux?"

"I have."

We stared at each other a moment then the darnedest thing happened. We both broke out laughing, so hard we had to hold our sides. We knocked into one another and wine sloshed over the top of my glass.

"I'm glad I didn't receive the report before we fired him," I said, wiping the tears from around my eyes. "He had no felony convictions, so I couldn't discharge him just based on the report, but who would've wanted an employee around with a record like that?"

"What about those poor people at the bus stop in Bay St. Louis?"

"Yeah," I said. "I certainly wouldn't want to see something like that. I could see why you eliminated him as a suspect, his being in jail when Alma was killed."

"You'll always remember him, Judy, if for no other reason than he made that scene the day you found Guerra."

"Believe me, I'll never forget him no matter what." I moved closer and in a low voice, asked, "How's the investigation going?"

"Ledet's the suspect, but..." He trailed off and rubbed his chin. "My people are pressing me for an arrest, particularly Kevin—always in a hurry, that one. This is a dangerous stage in any investigation. My staff can push all they want, but I've seen police waste valuable time tunneling in on one person while the true criminal gets farther out of reach. I won't let that happen. Not again," he muttered.

"Do you believe Dixie's insistence that he didn't kill Alma?"

He shook his head. "Too premature to tell."

I smiled. "But, Chief, in the movies, the police all have gut feelings."

Bombardier rolled his eyes. "Okay. Then I'd say he didn't

do it, but my staff says differently. Either way, I won't rush into judgment." He looked around before directing me to a nearby wall, away from others. "As soon as Doggett reported Ledet was stalking Guerra, we started digging into his background. Appears he never owned a gun or used one. No history of hunting, not even to get rid of gophers in his backyard. After he admitted killing his wife, we grilled him about Guerra. He claimed he fell in love with her, but she rejected him from the start and there was never an affair. As for guns, he said that all he knows about them was what he saw on TV—credits this to being raised by a single mother who taught her children to stay away from them. This whole business of Ledet being the killer feels off, anyway. The man's body is a human weapon, so why bother shooting the girl? And the theory of a silencer puts it farther out."

"Silencer?"

He cleared his throat. "Umm, yeah. We have reason to believe a silencer was used. Normally the use of them is tied to a professional hit, but there's nothing to link either Guerra or Ledet with any organized crime or professional killers."

The mayor sauntered past and Bombardier stopped talking long enough to wave in his direction. The mayor returned the greeting with a nod and passed by, giving Bombardier a curious stare.

"Did you find out when Dixie left work October eighteenth?"

"Not yet," I said. "I asked payroll to look for a payroll override form for Dixie on that date. They were tied up with month-end, but I'll know on Monday. They're not allowed to punch someone out without supervisory approval. Bert said he didn't authorize it, but someone in management must have." I took a sip of wine. "Remember the double homicide you told us about at Mary Mahoney's? I mentioned it to someone at work and she remembered the case—heard the rumors about the Kelms' involvement, too. You told Dan and me you thought Mrs. Briscoe's parents, the Kelms, had hired a hit man. Millie Landry—you've met her—she said she heard the hit-man theory, too, that a silencer was also used in that case."

"She's correct," he said. "That's the only other local case where we think a silencer was used. I always take note of co-incidences."

"Coincidence? But that case is so old. The silencer couldn't be a meaningful coincidence. As you said, neither Alma nor Dixie were involved with organized crime and, as far as I know, neither have any connection with the Kelms."

"Ocean Springs is still a small town, Judy."

"But twenty-five years ago is a long time."

"Maybe," he said.

His *maybe* gave me pause and I stared at him blankly for a moment. "Are you looking into that old case?"

"I'm always looking into it."

"Are there more details to why you think Paul Kelm had something to do with it?"

He thought for a moment. "Paul Kelm already owned Kelm Machinery at the time he married Eleanor Tillery. He made a good living and came from a prominent Ocean Springs family, but he wasn't a rich man. His wife's family, the Tiller-ys, were scum and, like I told ya, tied in with the Dixie Mafia." He fell silent as someone in a clown costume walked by then said in a lower voice, "My dad always thought Eleanor went after Paul Kelm because of his name. She got what she wanted in that marriage, to climb the ladder to Gulf Coast high socie-ty. Dad talked about the murders for years. He gathered every bit of information, literally boxes of it. Left them to me when he passed. I took it as his deathbed wish for me to solve the case."

I thought about the people I'd met in the South and their adoration of fathers. In the West, loyalty seemed reserved for brothers, at least that was how it played out on old TV west-erns.

I glanced up to find Bombardier studying me. "Sorry," I said. "Just thinking about what you were saying."

"Unfortunately, that's all I have."

I took a sip of wine. "I heard the oldest son disappeared around the time of those killings."

His head swung around. "You're kidding? Where did you

hear that?" he asked so forcefully I shrank back.

"Uh, from someone I met. Vernon Stiff, I think. That's right, you know him, too."

Some of the tension eased from his face. "Stiff's a casual acquaintance. I run into him periodically."

"Dan and I met him at the Biloxi Yacht Club. He told us Valerie Briscoe belonged to a gun club where he was a member, and that her father used to bring the entire family. Then he told us the eldest Kelm son—there were two—stopped going when he dropped out of sight some twenty-plus years earlier. Someone I used to work with at Kelm told me Mrs. Briscoe asked one of her employees to search for her missing brother. My friend was more specific on when he disappeared, said it was twenty-five years ago."

Bombardier's eyes widened. "What was his name?"

"Paul Kelm, Junior, I believe. He was around twenty-one or twenty-two at the time. Fresh out of college."

He stared into the air above my right shoulder. "Thank you for that information."

"Sure," I replied hesitantly.

Downing the last of his drink, he said, "I'm going to freshen this." Then he pulled out his cell phone, but instead of going to the bar, he went into a bedroom and shut the door.

I stared after him, wondering what had triggered his reaction. I shrugged it off and circulated, looking for a niche.

Dan was talking to two men I didn't recognize. Based on his wild hand gestures, I assumed their conversation was about football or golf, so I kept walking. George Nichols sat on the sofa against the far wall, his drink on top of his knees, cradled loosely in his hands. I moved over and sat beside him. "Good party, huh?" I offered.

"Yes. I'm glad I came."

I took the last sip of my drink and set the wineglass on a side stand. "I don't know many of the guests, though."

"Your husband's talking to our sheriff, Ralph Broussard," George said. "I don't know who the other person is."

"Andy told me Chief Bombardier hates the sheriff."

"He probably does." George smiled. "Most people do."

"Then why would he invite him?"

George laughed lightly. "The fact you're not from these parts shows. In the South, we're trained as children to abide by a certain set of social customs that don't make any damn sense. Two people might hate each other and know how the other feels, but in social circles they'll carry on like best buddies. They're true Southern gentlemen."

"I thought you were from up north, George."

He leaned back, his eyes boring into mine. "Born and raised in Biloxi. Went to college in the northeast, though, did a stint in the military, and then returned."

A childhood memory surfaced. News reports of the segregation in the South flashed onto a teeny TV screen inside my head. "Mind if I ask how you dealt with the racism?"

He shrugged. "I grew up with it. I sometimes think accepting your circumstances makes it easier to change them."

"I have to give you credit," I said. "Mississippi was once a brutal place to live."

George grinned and, when he did, he looked as intuitive as the scholar he was dressed to be. "Kinda like working for Valerie Kelm-Briscoe, huh?"

I shifted my angle on the sofa, so I had a better view of George's face. He watched my reaction with perceptive amusement. Was he suggesting I accept Valerie Kelm-Briscoe in order to get over her? I started to ask then thought the better of it.

Changing the subject, we talked another ten minutes before I found Dan standing by the fireplace and pulled him back into the party. We joined in on a few more conversations then said goodnight to Bombardier.

Once settled in our car, I said "Bombardier doesn't think Dixie killed Alma."

"He told you that?"

"Basically. I won't share this with Andy or Millie, though. They're content believing her murderer is locked away, but I think he's still out there."

CHAPTER 20

Sunday morning, I woke to Buffy's face in mine. She stood on her hind legs, whimpering, one paw on my arm and the other on the mattress. Begrudgingly, I heeded her command for a bathroom break and food.

After making coffee, I settled at the kitchen table with my steaming cup, the *Sun Herald* spread out before me. Buffy curled herself around my feet.

Half an hour later, Dan appeared in his PJs and bare feet, stretching his arms and yawning. "You're up early."

"Yeah, thanks to the dog again," I said and went back to the newspaper. He poured himself a cup of coffee and sat beside me. I pushed the newspaper over to him then got up for a refill. "Check out the Halloween story on the first page," I said. "They're predicting a record number of trick-or–treaters this year."

With the holiday falling on a Sunday and perfect weather predicted, it was bound to be busy. But the news report credited the expected increase to the Gulf Coast population surge over the past year.

"Buffy and I are going to the beach for a run. I'll fix breakfast when we get back." I bent over and pinched Buffy's face. "We get to go jogging!"

She sprang up and spun in jubilant circles. Dan peered over the newspaper and smiled.

As usual, the beach was empty when I arrived, something

unheard of in California. In the midst of my warm-up exercises, a vehicle roared behind me and I turned around. Buffy did, too. A late model black sedan slowed, eased through the GC Research Lab gates, and made a U-turn. *Probably lost*, I presumed. It disappeared behind the little copse of maples surrounded by the underbrush, home of Jimmie Lee's boat.

I turned back and began touching my toes while Buffy kept staring at the underbrush. Then her ears rose and fell.

"Uh-oh."

I made for the little fence where I'd hung her leash, Buffy whizzed past. Seizing the leash, I ran after her, stopping before the maples when I heard a car door slam. I started again, this time walking. On the other side of the tree cluster, a Volvo came into view. It was parked in the shade of an elm that hovered over the edge of the research lab's parking lot.

Buffy was nowhere in sight, but thinking whoever was inside the car would've seen which way she went, I picked up my stride. As I neared, I saw the shadow of the driver behind heavy-tinted windows. Putting on a sociable smile, I stepped up to the door, but the engine revved and the car began to move. Stunned, my smile shriveled as the sedan eased away, turning north onto Halstead Road. It dropped out of sight over the hump in the road.

The only car Buffy would get into without a fight was my Camry, so I ruled out any chance of her having been dognapped. But then where was she?

I moved toward the Gulf Coast Research Laboratory's empty parking lot, scrambling across it to the buildings. I went up and down the sidewalks, ran to the wooded area behind the facility and screamed her name until my throat hurt. I ran down the mostly barren stretch of ground between the parking and the gulf, looking behind patches of brush.

I jogged over to the beach, leaning against the fence and stretching my neck. I looked west, down the length of East Beach Drive then north up Halstead Road. But Buffy had vanished.

Dan rose from his chair. "How do you lose a dog?"

"I told you. She simply disappeared."

"Get in the car," he said, heading for the garage. "We're gonna find her."

We tottered up and down East Beach Drive in Dan's Buick to the research lab then north on Halstead and back. He parked behind the buildings and we went deep into the wooded area on foot, both of us hollering Buffy's name. We returned empty-handed.

"Buffy's run away before," Dan said.

"She was a puppy then. I assumed she'd have more sense now."

He slapped his palm on the dashboard then wrapped his hands around the steering wheel. "She ended up in the next county. If someone hadn't picked her up and called our number on the tag, we'd never have found her."

I started to cry. "I didn't let her out of my sight. Not for a minute." My words came out in a nasally whine. "I can't help it if she decided to chase some car." I pulled a tissue from my purse and blew.

"Car?" he said. "Could someone have taken her?" His gaze floated over my face then out the windshield as if something out there might provide a clue.

"Huh? No one's gonna steal a dog. The pound is full of them."

He sighed, one corner of his mouth squishing down.

"Although…" I trailed off and he stared at me expectantly. "I walked over to ask if the person in the car had seen her, but they took off as soon as I got to it. It's a stretch, but—"

"Stretch nothing," Dan said. "It makes more sense than her evaporating."

"But we can't even get her into your car without a hassle."

"Someone could've bribed her with a treat or put a net over her. Call the police. While you're doing that, I'm going to Broome's for more Halloween candy and then to the Master Grill for breakfast. Try to get my mind off this."

He dropped me off at home and I dashed into the office,

flipping open a phone directory for the non-emergency police number. Knowing some people consider pets of minor importance, I drew on my political savvy. "I'm not asking you to find a lost dog," I told the officer who took the call. "I'm reporting the theft of my personal property." I didn't like calling Buffy personal property, but finding angles that worked transcended semantics.

"Ma'am, the only clue you have is the late model black Volvo. This sounds more like a runaway than a theft."

"But my dog wouldn't run away." At least I was pretty sure she wouldn't, but he didn't need to know that.

"I'm sorry, ma'am. There's not much I can do," he said, his voice sounding young. "If your dog's been stolen, the thief is probably a neighbor, relative, or friend, which makes this a civil matter. I can't help you."

My loss overrode any self-respect and for the second time that day, I started to cry. "You've got to help me."

When the officer didn't answer, an idea popped into my head. "Call Chief Bombardier. He'll help."

"Ma'am, I…it's the chief's day off—"

"Call him. Tell him Judy Kenagy demanded to speak to him."

Within minutes, I had Bombardier on the line, making every effort to convince him police assistance was in order. This time I didn't offer up the theft as a possibility, like I had with Dan, but rather as a fact. "Like I said, Chief, my dog's been stolen." My automatic response was nothing short of an Emmy-Award winning performance. "A late model black Volvo pulled up, someone inside snagged her and then drove away. Do you think there's a tie between this and the Alma Guerra murder?"

"I don't see how," he said.

"But someone's already tried to engage me in the murder investigation," I said carefully. "Remember, the anonymous call? I don't know why, but the point is they called me directly."

"Yes, but…Where are you going with this?"

"It's unusual to have one's dog stolen," I persisted. "It's

not like golden retrievers are hard to come by, so you have to admit it's odd. It's got to be connected to this murder case. First, I find the body then get an anonymous call, and now my dog's been stolen."

Bombardier laughed in a slow ho-ho way. "Hold up, Judy. You're jumping from one possibly false conclusion to another. You can't be certain someone stole your dog just because the car pulled away the moment you walked over to it. And tying this to Guerra's death, which we're still unsure was murder—"

Holy shit. She was shot in the face and the weapon's missing and he's still saying this may not be murder? What else could it be? "All right. Maybe my missing dog has nothing to do with Alma Guerra, but I witnessed her theft in broad daylight. Chief, what are you going to do about that?"

His tone became all business again. "Perhaps the thief, if there is one, is a disgruntled employee. Human resources managers are often targets of employee retaliation, sometimes even workplace violence."

I thought for a moment. The chief had a point, but I couldn't think of anyone—*Wait! Lester Robichaux.* But Andy seemed to be the focus of his contention.

I sighed. What was I doing? No one had stolen Buffy. Even if someone had tried, I would've gotten around that tree cluster fast enough to see the struggle and there would have been a struggle. My despair was making me desperate and irrational.

"Judy? Judy." Bombardier repeated. "I've got to go. Drop off some pictures of the dog at the station. I'll look into this and get back to ya."

I gathered enough pictures of Buffy for every police cruiser in Ocean Springs and the rest of the Gulf Coast. Buffy was lost and, with a little help, I was going to find her.

CHAPTER 21

Dan and I doled out candy to a record number of trick-or-treaters, without the usual chorus of barks from Buffy every time the doorbell rang. Our house felt quiet and empty.

Around nine o'clock, we emptied the remains of the last bag of Snickers into the hands of a headless horseman and a pumpkin who'd trailed up to our door a half-hour after the last batch had come and gone. Then we turned off the porch light, locked up, and hit the sack, taking with us more than our usual dose of Sunday-night-before-work blues.

The next morning, JoAnne dumped the unfiled exception reports on the middle of my desk. "Bert was right," she said. "There's no authorization for the manual clock-out for Dixie."

I stared at the pile. "This means LaShunda falsified payroll records."

JoAnne's eyes widened. "I'm sure there's an explanation. LaShunda knows when to get written approval."

I shook my head. "She has to be written up. If this is a regular occurrence then it's a terminable offense."

"Oh, dear Jesus," JoAnne said, one hand flat atop her formidable breasts. "LaShunda's as honest as the day is long. Miss Judy, that girl supports her pathetically ill ol' grandmother. It will break her poor, dear heart if we accuse her. If we pray on this—oh, yes—that's right, I'll have to do that at home, but Judy, please—"

I was in no mood to listen to JoAnne. "I'll do the talking," I said. "It won't be that bad. Right now, I have to meet with Dixie's co-workers—find out when he left work on the eighteenth. We'll deal with LaShunda afterward."

Before she could protest further, I hurried to Bert's office and crumpled into a chair. "Geez. I have JoAnne up front, practically on hands and knees, begging me to free LaShunda from any discipline. She'll burst into full public prayer session if I don't get back there soon."

Bert took his thick-rimmed glasses off, looked at them, then set them back on his nose. The only color on him came from his Rockhold identification badge. His pale skin and light hair blended with his monochromatic clothing, making him look like a blob of beige.

"It p–p–pisses me off. Someone in administration screws up and we have to f–f–fix it."

I nodded. "If Dixie hadn't been implicated in the murder, we'd never have known."

Bert glanced at his watch. "Hate to say, b–b–but I won't have time until later today."

"We'll start interviews at three then."

The first employee we brought in was Rusty Shaw, the one who'd told the police that Alma had borrowed a gun. Once he'd sat down, I recognized him as the nameless employee-of-the-quarter on the disc I'd wanted to upload for the Christmas party's PowerPoint presentation.

"We're trying to f–f–find out what time D–D–Dixie left work Monday October eighteenth," Bert asked him. "C–can you help us?"

His gaze moved over our heads. "Hmm, it's been a couple of weeks. The eighteenth was a Monday, right?"

"Uh huh." Bert nodded. "The d–d–day before Lester Robichaux made that ruckus and we f–f–found out about Alma."

I fell back against my chair and tossed Bert an aggravated stare.

With wide eyes, Rusty glanced from Bert to me and back. "Do you think Dixie had anything to do with Alma's death?"

I waited for Bert to backpedal. He'd carelessly connected Dixie's departure to the timeframe in which Alma was killed. When Bert remained slumped and silent, I took a stab at damage control. "It's just a payroll matter," I said.

Rusty gave me a dubious look then, after a pause, he said, "That whole week was jam-packed with happenings. Let me think…If it was the day I'm thinking, I remember it was odd 'cause Dixie went to break for only a few minutes. Usually takes the full quarter-hour like clockwork. Then he returned, turned off his machine, and left. It had to be 'bout two-thirty because my break came afterward."

Bert jotted notes on a piece of paper then asked Rusty to review and initial.

As we called more employees in, I made an effort to remember their names. Each of their statements were comparable to Rusty's. Satisfied, I straightened the stack of paperwork and headed back through the plant toward my office, but try as I might Buffy was still heavy on my mind.

I didn't pull my gaze off the floor until I fell into my desk chair. The first tear dropped and I wiped my cheek with the back of one hand, dabbing a tissue under my eye to stop the next one. If I were a kid again, I'd go all maudlin, bringing me all kinds of comforting attention, but at my age I opted for a show of control.

Crying won't get Buffy back.

I went through the investigation statements and prepared a summary. When I finished, I faxed the information to Bombardier then phoned JoAnne who picked up right where she'd left off.

"Pleeeze Judy, let me have one night to go home and pray about this."

I tapped my nails on the desk. "JoAnne, God's got bigger things to deal with. Let's get this over with. Bring LaShunda in."

Reluctantly, she did, appearing at my door with LaShunda Parker hunched beside her like a guarded prisoner. They entered and sat before me.

LaShunda wore her black hair in dozens of tiny braids

pulled atop her head, revealing a soft, brown face.

I read her the statement from the disciplinary form and she began to cry. When I asked her to comment, JoAnne puckered up like a dry raisin. I held my breath, hoping she didn't cry, too.

"LaShunda, don't be afraid to answer the question." I picked up a box of tissues then leaned across my desk, holding the box in front of her.

She reached out, grabbed the end of one, pulled it out, and went back for another. "I didn't think it'd hurt anythin'," she said, dabbing at tears. "Dixie never forgets to clock out, so I assumed he left at four."

I moved the tissues in front of JoAnne. She fumbled in the box and pulled one out, gripping the tissue in her lap. I set the box down and asked LaShunda if she'd done this before.

"One other time," she admitted. "But that person I felt certain wasn't tryin' to cheat and I figured I was savin' the supervisor and me from havin' to deal with the exception report. I won't do anythin' here I think's cheating."

"Write out what you've said and sign the form," I said, sliding the form in front of her. "Then step out into the hallway. We'll call you in a few minutes."

She scrawled a response and a signature then left, carefully closing the door behind her.

Stuck alone with JoAnne, I asked, "What type of disciplinary action do you recommend?"

"Oh Miss Judy, do we have to give her any?"

"We need to follow policy. I know she did this as a shortcut and not fraud, so I recommend a first step disciplinary action. No big deal."

JoAnne's glossed mouth wilted. "We—ell, okay. But would you do the talking?"

Like I hadn't been? I sighed audibly and clenched my teeth. "Yes, JoAnne."

LaShunda returned to her seat and I said, "We'll keep this as a written warning for now. If this doesn't happen again, then the write-up doesn't mean much. You're a valuable employee and we hope you'll learn from this experience."

Her face relaxed. "It'll never happen again," she promised.

After she left the room, I looked at JoAnne. "See? That wasn't so bad. If you're honest with employees and hold them accountable, you're really doing them a favor."

JoAnne glared at me without comprehension. If she'd said one single word, I'd expected it to be a jaw-dropping "Huh?"

CHAPTER 22

Once JoAnne was gone, I sat in my chair and stared at LaShunda's disciplinary form, considering its probable value to the police. Without knowing it, LaShunda had reinforced Bert's proclamation that Dixie never failed to clock-out. Yet, Dixie didn't clock out at a key time in a case where he was the suspect.

I phoned the Ocean Springs police department, reaching Lieutenant Young. "I'm faxing something Bombardier will want, information from the payroll rep who covered up Dixie's missed time-punch."

"Okay, good," he said.

Someone hollered at him in the background and his words became muffled as if he'd covered the phone. The voice grew louder, mingling with Young's, then Bombardier's voice rang through, unfiltered. "Yes, Judy, fax it over, but I'm faxing something to you as well."

"Oh?" I said with trepidation.

"We haven't found your dog, but I put together a list of owners of newer black Volvos on the Gulf Coast."

I sank deeper in my chair. "Okay, thanks. *What good is a damn list of Volvos? She would've never gotten into that car.*

"If you recognize a name, let me know," he said, hanging up.

The list turned out shorter than I'd expected and in no particular order. Some of the owners were known in the community. Jackson County Sheriff Ralph Broussard made the list, as well as former mayor Pete Halat, implicated in the Sherry murders in the book, *Mississippi Mud*. A Gulfport resident, named Longnecker, stood out but only because of his name. Mississippi had more than its share of residents with odd last names, like Trash and Stiff.

Speak of the devil, I thought, seeing Vernon Stiff's name jump out at the bottom of the first page, another owner of a Volvo, a 2004 model.

On page two, my eyes stopped on the name *Keith A. Briscoe*.

Such a small community, I thought.

Like the others, I dismissed his and moved through the remainder of the list. But I found myself returning to Briscoe's name, lingering there as if the printed words held a hidden meaning. Of course, Briscoe owning a newer-model black Volvo was apropos. But it was his connection to *her* that disturbed me.

Dan may've been right. I imagined a shadowy figure luring Buffy in with a treat then using a dog catcher's net.

Shaking the thoughts away, I dialed Bombardier's direct line, wondering how to word what I was about to say. The communication turned out easier than I'd expected.

"If you have a feeling, Judy, that's a hunch. Hunches are good."

I waited for him to continue, hoping he had something to offer.

"Let's check it out," he said. "Try to get away from work. Briscoe lives off of St. Andrew's Golf Course. His address is on the list. I'll meet you there."

I Mapquested the address and started to e-mail George I was leaving. Noticing it was close to five, I cancelled the e-mail and took off.

The Briscoe's two story brick home sat on a corner lot with a generous front yard, complete with a lush lawn and a fair amount of trees. I drove past and circled the block. Bombardier hadn't yet arrived. I parked a good block away on the opposite side of the street, giving me a view of the front yard, the east side of the house and the back fence.

I'd just turned off my engine when Briscoe's Volvo appeared, backing out of the garage. The front door swung open and Mrs. Briscoe ran out in tan slippers and a floral-patterned cotton dress. She stopped halfway to the Volvo and called, "Where will you be if I need to reach you?"

He lowered his window. "You can't. I'm going to the library and then to some bookstores—research for my master's thesis. I'll be back by eight."

"Why so late?"

Instead of answering, he yelled back, "Try to find out who owns that stupid dog."

Dog? My hand flew to my mouth.

His window went up and he backed out onto the street, driving toward me. I turned my head as he passed and when I looked back, Mrs. Briscoe was still staring after him. Soon, she disappeared inside the house.

The east side of the house, with its six-foot wooden fence, ran along an intersecting street. I got out and started walking, taking a diagonal route across the road, then straight to the intersection. I cut across the street and headed toward the back fence. After an exploratory look around, I moved up along the fence and peered through the spaces between the wooden slats.

In the center of the yard, a pool sweeper bobbed in a kidney-shaped swimming pool, gurgling over blue-green water. Wisteria, bridal wreath, and cannas lilies lined the inside of the fence.

A large weeping willow, circled by a brick-lined garden of tulips, flourished near the back of the yard.

I eyeballed my way around the yard, my gaze coming to rest at the rear of the house, and did a double-take at the sight of Mrs. Briscoe and my dog on a patio. She was leaning against the metal jamb of a double glass doorway, staring at Buffy like a cat ready to pounce. Perched on hind legs, Buffy watched her expectantly.

"Bad dog," she said. "Bad dog. I've gone out of my way to give you a home. You drove your owners off and now my husband left because he can't stand the sight of you."

She's crazy, I thought. *She's lying to a dog in her usual attempt to be cruel. She knows how Buffy got there.*

Buffy flopped down on the wooden patio and covered her eyes, but sat back up when Mrs. Briscoe stepped closer in. "I may have to turn you over to the pound if my husband keeps running off."

Buffy barked and I saw the rope securing her to a post. *Wuff. Wuff.* She barked and lunged forward, straining at the rope.

"Don't you ever talk to me like that, you ugly beast," Mrs. Briscoe said. "Consider yourself lucky you're not on the street."

I turned to the soft roar of a motor behind me and the crunch of fine gravel under tires as Chief Bombardier pulled his Crown Victoria against the curb.

I caught his eye and stepped up, raising my finger to my lips in a hushing gesture.

He ducked and strained his neck to peer out the passenger-side window. "What's going on?"

I placed my hands on the open car window and whispered, "Buffy's on Mrs. Briscoe's patio, tied to a post."

"You sure it's your dog?" he asked. At my emphatic nod, he said, "Stay here."

His Crown Victoria began to move, creeping to the corner where it took an easy right. Brakes screeched, a car door slammed then heavy shoes galumphed across concrete.

I waited. Minutes ticked by. The pale pink of dusk turned into a peach colored sky. Peering through the slats in the fence, I saw the glass door slide open. Bombardier stepped onto the patio and moved toward Buffy, Mrs. Briscoe following.

"Well, what do we have here?" he said.

Buffy lifted her pale-blonde head. Her ears rose and she cocked her head to one side.

"I found it walking in circles around my front yard in some kind of stupor. Poor little thing," Mrs. Briscoe said, her bobble earrings swinging.

I could feel my face grow hot with indignation.

"I assumed its owner abandoned it," she added.

Bombardier stooped down and untied the rope from the post. "Like I told you, it's just the opposite. The owner's committed to finding her dog—posted signs and pictures everywhere. We're lucky one of your neighbors witnessed the dog entering your house."

Why doesn't he simply arrest the bitch? I thought.

"Who witnessed—which neighbor?" she asked in her best Scarlet O'Hara imitation.

"Ma'am, we can't give out that information." He rose, holding the rope like a leash and Buffy stood up on all fours. Bombardier bent down to read her tags, raising a disapproving brow. "Why didn't you call the vet's number? It's right here on these tags."

She planted a hand above her bosom. "Oh, how silly of me. I was so worried about the poor creature, it never dawned on me."

"I'll take the dog off your hands. May I keep your rope?"

"Yes, of course, Chief. And perhaps you should have a talk with the owner. They must be an irresponsible sort." She shook her head. "What kind of person loses a pet?"

Angry voices screamed in my head, my knuckles going white as my hands clenched into fists. I turned my back to the fence and hugged my arms to keep from barreling at her.

Bombardier's car eased around the corner and parked across the street, engine idling. I looked both ways, rushed over, and climbed into the backseat with Buffy.

"That woman's a piece of work," he said, adjusting his rearview mirror to talk to me in its reflection. "You'll have a better chance of getting to your car unseen when it's dark. Let's get out of here for a while."

I held Buffy, telling her how sorry I was over and over. Bombardier pulled into a strip mall and parked at the end of the lot.

"Why didn't you arrest her?" I asked. "She stole my dog."

"Because it would've turned into a he-said-she-said thing, with her coming up with one cockamamie tale after another. I'd never be able to prove it. Trust me. We got your dog back the easiest and quickest way."

"You're right. Thank you so much. I've got to get that woman out of my life!"

Bombardier twisted around to look at me. "I'm having trouble picturing Valerie Briscoe snapping up someone's dog. Her husband?"

"No. I watched him leave the house. His last words were about finding out who owned the—" I fought away a tear. "The S, T, U, P, I, D dog," I said, spelling the word so Buffy wouldn't hear. "Chief, I'm almost positive she wouldn't have taken Buffy either. She has this little creep who carries out her schemes. Jimmie Lee's his name."

"Jimmie Lee?"

"Yes. Jimmie Lee Albright. I don't know why I didn't think of him to begin with. He's her patsy. She inflates his ego then uses him as her loyal snitch and gamesman. He works at Kelm Machinery. I guarantee you he pulled off the dog-napping on her behalf."

He turned back, looking again at me in the rearview mirror. "You know, I see murders, rapes, robberies. They're horrible, but unfortunately, real. What you're telling me doesn't sound real."

"That's why I seldom talk about them. People would think me crazy. I'll give you a perfect example. When I went to the costume store to rent the outfit I wore to your Halloween party, I made a wrong turn on the way out. I ended up on the road behind Kelm Machinery. Innocent mistake by anyone's standards. But Jimmie Lee was outside the plant and recognized my car. He chased me down and accused me of casing the company. Said there'd be retribution. I'm sure the dog-napping was that retribution. Jimmie Lee knows where I go jogging with my dog."

"You've got to be kidding," he said. "What kind of idiots are these people?"

"Paranoid—and mean. At least she is. Jimmie Lee is sucked in by her praise and attention. In his own way, he's just another one of her victims."

I told him what I'd seen through the fence, how she'd treated Buffy.

"She's not physically abusive," I said. "Her thing is emotional and mental cruelty."

He wrinkled his face. "She sounds sick."

"She's beyond that," I said, relieved that he didn't accuse me of exaggerating as so many others did. Even Dan told me I was being ridiculous the first time I told him. "Chief, I'm curious…"

"Yes?"

"The night of the Halloween party, I told you about hearing of Mrs. Briscoe's missing brother. Then you took out your cell phone and disappeared into a bedroom."

He gave me a crooked smile, but remained silent as though mulling something over in his mind. I waited.

"You must promise not to speak of this," he said finally, his eyes bright.

"Of course," I said.

He tipped his head toward the windshield. "Let's take a walk."

We walked in companionable silence to the sidewalk that ran along the front of the strip mall, Buffy ahead of us, straining at my hold on the rope.

He put his hands in his pockets. "I found Valerie's missing brother."

"Where? How?" I stopped, but he continued walking, so I bounded forward falling back into step beside him.

"Turned out it was rather easy. After I left you, I called the senator, the one who lives in Pascagoula. We went to high school together. He has contacts all over and can usually find anyone. Paul Kelm, Jr. turned up in Gaithersburg, Maryland. Seems he's a photographer there. The senator was able to pin down the time he left the state. Get this. He got married a year after he split and took his wife's name."

"I've never heard of that."

"Apparently, it's as legal as taking a husband's name. He's now Paul Mayfield. Divorced now, but he kept her name." He stopped and pulled one hand out of a pocket, waving his index finger. "And it just happens he went missing at the end of the college semester following the Wade murders. I'm pretty sure he knows something."

We began to walk again.

"I'm flying to Gaithersburg Wednesday," he said.

"Have you talked to him?"

"No. I don't want him to know I'm coming. I called his business and found out he's expected at work all week. I'll let you know what happens, that is, if you won't tell anyone."

"I won't say a word, but doesn't someone on your staff know?"

"Not a chance." He came to a standstill. "It's dark. Let me take you to your car."

"Thanks again, Chief, for everything. After saving my dog, you can count on me for anything, anytime."

"Judy, you saved your own dog. Oh, and by the way, I never once believed you thought the dog was stolen. That is until you found out she really was."

The surprise must've shown in my face for a flash of ornery satisfaction showed in his.

CHAPTER 23

I ripped a page from the desk calendar, tossing Monday, November first into the trash and moving onto what I hoped would be a calmer day. Yesterday, I'd scored a point against Valerie Kelm-Briscoe. Her or Jimmie Lee's dog-napping scheme had worked, but thanks to Bombardier's help, within a day, we'd foiled any other plans she might've had for Buffy.

Staring at the words *Tuesday, November 2nd,* printed in large black font, I suddenly felt a letdown. Had I really scored anything?

Val-*er*-ie had succeeded in nabbing Buffy and putting me through hell, and I knew without a doubt she'd be back again in one way or another. I had to get her out of my life, out of my mind. For good.

An email reminder flashed across my screen. *Plane tickets.* I picked up the phone and hit the speed-dial button to Dan's office. "I'm getting my plane reservations to Phoenix," I said when he answered. "Want me to get yours?"

"No, Fred's secretary will. He's going with me, so we'll need to coordinate schedules. Did they ever tell you the purpose of the mandatory meeting?"

"I'm sure it's propaganda about the sale. They would've known we were being sold when they set it up in September."

Ten minutes later, I was printing a copy of the online flight confirmation when the phone rang. "Got your employee into rehab," Dottie said. Dottie was the most efficient EAP rep I'd ever worked with.

"Thanks. I've only dealt with a couple of cocaine addicts in the past, but we didn't get very far with them."

"Our success rate isn't good either," she said. "I told her she must complete rehab if she wants to keep her job. Outpatient therapy follows and is twelve long months."

I scribbled *Put B. Dailey on FMLA* on a yellow sticky then got to my feet and left with no destination in mind. I stopped at the water cooler for a drink, lingered there a moment watching people at work in tiny cubicles. A janitor was yanking garbage sacks out of cans. Rusty passed by, heading to the mailroom, and I followed.

"How are you?" I asked, watching him remove a stack of memos from a mail slot, a month's worth of internal communications.

"Oh, I'm fine, considering I'm working." He smiled. "You?"

"Fine, thanks." I keyed in a number and opened my box. Unlike Mrs. Briscoe, George didn't leaf through the mail or dole it out to us with instructions.

Along with the usual stack of mail was a thick, square envelope with gold embossed print. I put the other envelopes down and opened it, removing an invitation to a Mardi Gras ball, then headed for Andy's office.

"Busy?" I asked, poking my head in.

He leaned back in his chair, his fingers still working the computer keyboard. Game cards flew from one stack to another. "Girl, do I look busy? Actually, I am but I'm sick of Corporate, so I'm taking a break."

"Look." I held up the invitation. "Did you get one?"

"Oh, sure. Ever been to a Mardi Gras ball?"

"Remember, I'm from California."

"I figured you hadn't. Rockhold managers are invited every year and it's an insult if we don't show." He made a face, as cards with red hearts and diamonds, black spades and clubs moved about the screen.

"Mine says the Krewe of Neptune in late January."

"That's the one we go to, with about fifteen hundred other guests. George expects us there. The King and Queen work all year to prepare. We're not supposed to know who they are until the night of the ball."

Back in my office, I stared at the heap of paperwork on my desk. Like Andy, I felt unmotivated. All Corporate talked about was what might happen after the sale, but tagged their every directive with the words, *Remember, business as usual.* All of us had been assigned projects, some long-term, that had a ninety-eight percent chance of being dumped by the new owners.

Personally, I had other interests.

Turning to my computer, I created a new Excel folder and named it *Who Killed Alma?* I typed Lester's name over two columns, one with a header that read *Reasons Did Kill*, the other with *Reasons Did NOT kill.* I typed in Dixie's name adjacent to Lester's and created the same two columns underneath his name. I needed to find this murderer, not knowing exactly why. He'd called me personally, but I knew there was more to it than that.

In the Did-Kill column for both Lester and Dixie, I entered *love rejection.* In Dixie's, I recorded the missed time-punch on the day Alma was killed, stalking her, and the fact that he'd killed his wife. In Lester's, I added, *has criminal record. Possible serial killer we're yet unaware of.*

Under *Reasons Did NOT kill* for Dixie, I logged, *no history of guns. His body his obvious weapon. Insists he's innocent.* I hesitated a moment then added, *Bombardier thinks he's innocent.* For Lester's column, I listed only his alibi, which pretty much made anything in the Did Kill column a moot point.

I dug the scrawled-over deposit slip out of my purse and glanced over the information before tossing it. Everything there was already in my head and now catalogued in the computer spreadsheet, up-to-date, and organized.

I looked again at the pile of papers on my desk, my mind wandering. I saw myself going back into Excel and adding some big new clue, coming to a conclusion, getting excited about it, and calling Bombardier. "Guess what," I said. "I know who killed Alma." When I realized I'd said it out loud, I glanced outside my open office door and sighed in relief for the empty hallway. *What's happening to me?* I thought. *Do I believe solving Alma's murder will put Jolene to rest? Or is it something more?*

Most of my filing was in the pile before me, but Lester's background check sat alone in the top tray of a three-tiered metal file holder. I picked it up and ran down the page of charges again. The arrest date was October eighteenth, the same day the incident at the Bay St. Louis bus stop occurred and the same day Alma was killed. There was no reference to time of arrest, but Bombardier would've had that information and never cleared Lester unless he knew with certainty that Lester did not have enough time between leaving work and the arrest to get to Alma's and kill her.

Terminated employee files were kept in a file room across the plant, giving me another excuse to skip out on my work. On the way, I passed Dixie's empty cutting machine. In the file room, I looked at the background check once more and a sudden feeling washed over me that I couldn't explain. I seemed to be responding to something on the report, as if I'd seen it for the first time. I studied it again. The charge of lewd and lascivious behavior and the arrest date were both marked October eighteenth. That was the Monday before I found Alma's body. Nothing new that I could see. I shrugged my shoulders, placed it in his file, and closed the drawer.

Chapter 24

"Ms. Kenagy, I'm afraid to put this in writing, but it happened again today. Why do the owners always accuse me? They said I wrote the wrong number on an order, costing the company over two thousand dollars. I'd been helping in a different department at the time this happened. I can't win for losing. Please don't tell them I've spoken to you." ~ Jolene Cromwell, one week before she was fired.

❦❦❦

On Wednesday morning, Millie brought her disposable cup of coffee into my office and fell into her usual chair. "Lidia says the police chief flew into the Washington/Dulles Airport early this morning—some business in Gaithersburg. He refused to tell his staff the purpose of the trip, though. Really ticked her off."

"Maybe it was personal business, something he didn't want to share with them."

"Still, he could've at least told her where he was staying."

"Surely, he told someone in his department," I said, knowing he hadn't, but hoping to get Lidia's read on the matter. "What if something happened to him?"

She waved me off. "He thinks he's invincible. It really fries Lidia's grits. When the stakes are high, he keeps the trump card to himself and trusts no one." Millie wasn't as much in-the-know as she thought.

He may not have confided in his staff but, for whatever reason, Bombardier had trusted me.

She scooted forward. "I need a favor. Alma's parents want me to mail them some of her things."

"They already left?"

"Yes, back to Texas. Now that the funeral's over, they're in no hurry to come back here." She laced her fingers under her chin. "Jena's got the key, but she won't go inside. Will you come?"

"Well—uhh—"

"Come on. Please? The thought of going alone gives me the creeps. We'll go today, at the end of my shift, okay?"

Before I could answer, Millie flew out as fast as she'd come in, apparently confident she'd gotten her way. I exhaled then plodded down the hall to get George's approval to leave early.

❧❧❧

Millie and I had just fastened our seatbelts inside her car when Bert walked into the parking lot. He usually blew off work a couple of minutes before four and never a second after. He walked past, his head down.

"Have a nice evening, Bert," Millie said.

He stopped next to an old station wagon, the sad rusted fenders a match for his expression. "Where are you guys going?"

"To look for something at Alma's house," Millie said. She put her key in the ignition and began to back out. "This is not Bert's business," she muttered under her breath. "All they want are photo albums and a necklace with a locket."

"What are you looking for?" Bert asked, walking over.

She dropped the car into drive and whispered, "See? He's always pushing to be in-the-know."

I rolled down my window and called, "Nothing important. We're just running an errand for her parents."

In my side mirror, I watched Bert, fixed in place like a stone statue. Something murky moved over his face. He grew smaller as we drove away then folded himself into the station wagon and shut the door.

Millie pulled into Alma's driveway, her tires crunching over gravel. The home looked about the same as it did the day I found Alma's body, a little over two weeks prior. A Century 21 *for sale* sign was posted where the *John Kerry For President* sign had stood. The Honda Civic that had been in the driveway—gone.

On the Gulf Coast, new buildings battled rust and mildew while old buildings got tired and gave up. There were still a few vestiges of wood on the sides of the porch, untouched by green mold. Rusty nails freckled its surface. Thin posts, with peeling white paint, supported the porch's sagging overhang.

Millie slid the key into the lock and twisted the knob, but the door didn't open. She wrestled with it for a good minute, spitting and sputtering *dangs* and *darns*. Finally, the door burst open, jerking her inside with the same harsh squeal I'd heard on my first trip here.

"Lordy be," she said, righting herself. "I doubt Alma had a steady man in her life."

I followed her inside. "Why do you say that?"

She waggled her thin hand toward the door. "Because any man hanging around would've treated that door with WD-40."

Despite the state of her front door, Alma had kept an impeccable house. The thick, white curtains looked new and hung without a wrinkle. Magazines on an accent table by the door were stacked neatly. I moved to where I'd seen the body, inhaling the strong smell of cleaning fluid. Someone had worked hard to remove the blood stain from the remnants of a maroon shag carpet that covered the floor. The stain was visible, but only as a large patch of faded brown.

Millie stepped up beside me. "Where you found her?"

"Yes." I remembered how everything looked that day then suddenly pictured Jolene Cromwell alive and well. Again, I had no idea why I'd think of Jolene when I should be feeling something for the murder victim. I hadn't known Alma Guerra, but still, what happened to her was terrible.

We stared at the spot for a full minute in silence before Millie stepped toward the kitchen. A half-dozen handmade artificial plants sat on the table. I walked over and lifted one. "Supposedly employees came to her house to buy these. That was the reason Lester gave for coming here."

"That's harebrained," Millie said. "Why would she have people come here when she could just take them to work with her?"

I put down the fake orchid, studying the others laid out on the table. In my mind's eye, I pictured Alma and Lester in the break room again. "I wish I could remember why Alma invited him here," I said. "I keep thinking it had something to do with helping her. You know, a woman needing a man's help with something."

"Well, if it was to fix her front door, that didn't happen," she said.

She pointed me to a built-in book shelf, jam-packed with books, and I dislodged three photo albums. I thumbed through one and saw pictures of Alma with friends and family. "These were an easy find."

"Looks like Alma took a trip to Pier 1 Imports," Millie said, looking at the white wicker furniture scattered about the room. Three framed pictures hung on the walls in the main living area, a conspicuous hole in the wall beside one of them. "Millie, look."

"Oh, goodness," she said, her fingertips at her lips. Walking over, she touched the edges of the drywall then made a fist and slipped it through the hole. "Someone's fist did that."

In the bedroom, a Carolyn Haines book lay open on a neatly-made queen size bed. A nightshirt hung over the back of the chair and a sewing kit sat atop a night stand.

Millie began searching the dresser while I headed for the closet. On the floor of the closet, in a partially unpacked suitcase, I fingered through a bathing suit, flip flops, and a pile of clothes. In a side compartment I found a tiny sack, holding blank Destin, Florida, postcards, and looked for a receipt— none there. A colorful piece of clothing caught my attention and I lifted the fabric. "Millie, look. Ever see Alma wear this?"

She gave the top a fleeting glance before returning to her digging. "Oh, probably something she wore one dress-down Friday."

"But this looks like a man's shirt."

"Doesn't mean diddly-squat nowadays," Millie said. "Young women wear gear like that all the time."

I put the shirt back, staring. "I swear I've seen this somewhere before," I muttered. A fuzzy memory stirred of someone in the shirt, but it vanished in less than a second. I closed the suitcase and pushed it back into the closet.

From the bottom dresser drawer, Millie lifted a necklace, a locket dangling from the chain.

I skip-stepped to her side. "I bet that's what they're looking for." I took the locket from her and opened it to see a picture of Alma's parents, younger, with Alma as a little girl. "Yep. We can go now."

Millie plucked the locket from my hand and peered inside before snapping it shut and letting the necklace fall into her purse. I scooped up the photo albums and we headed back to her car.

∽∾∽

When I walked into the house, I found Dan standing in front of the refrigerator. *Oh God, I really didn't want to think about fixing dinner right now.* "Let's eat late tonight," I said.

"Okay." He waved me into the family room then sat down and slung one arm over the back of the sofa as I sat beside him. "I went to Georgina's Hobby Shop again. This time for an airbrush."

"Hmmm, a Georgina story."

He grinned. "She was working the counter and looking very perturbed."

"Isn't that how she always looks?"

"Yes, but it wasn't my doing this time. I don't think she recognized me. Anyway, I found what I wanted, but a piece was missing and there wasn't another airbrush in stock. When

I showed Georgina the broken package and asked her if she'd give me a discount since I'd have to replace the missing part, she refused just like before."

"How dumb. Who else would want it?"

"She wasn't nice about it either. Accused me of being deaf and repeatedly told me she wouldn't reduce the price. So I left the package on the counter and started to leave. Then she whipped around and screamed at a young man working in the back, holding up the broken package and calling him incompetent for not monitoring the inventory. The worker marched to the front, slapped his name badge on the counter, told her he quit, then marched out the front door. When she turned back and saw I hadn't left yet, she said, 'What are *you* looking at?'" Dan's smile widened. "I glared at Georgina and said, 'I'm looking at someone who has no business running a store or managing people.'"

"You didn't."

He nodded. "I did, and I thought of you, of how good you would've felt if you'd ever had a chance to say such a thing to Valerie Kelm-Briscoe."

I smiled. "You bet. Thank you, Dan." I leaned over and hugged him. His muscle tone, once trampoline tight, now jiggled like Jell-O. I gave him what I'd meant to be a thanks-I-love-you kiss, but Dan held me tight and the kiss turned long and warm. Buffy barked.

"Mmmm," he said, coming up for air.

I shuddered, shaking the passion away. "I haven't even had a chance to change clothes," I said and gave him the smack of a kiss I'd intended.

But he pulled me into another groping hold and kissed me on the neck. "So, go change."

He patted me on my behind as I got off the sofa and followed me into the bedroom. We shut the door in Buffy's face.

CHAPTER 25

Bombardier called me the next day, around three o'clock. "Well, Mrs. Kenagy, I promised ya an update on my Maryland trip and I'm good to my word."

"You talked to Paul Kelm, Jr.—uh, Mayfield."

"That I did. By the way, how's your pooch?"

"She's happy and I'm happy. Thank you. So, what did Mrs. Briscoe's brother have to say?"

"Nothing really. When I suggested he had information on the Wade killings, he denied knowing more than what he'd heard on the news. I questioned him about his abrupt departure and alienation from his family, timed so close to the killings. He told me his reasons were personal and would stay that way."

"*Personal* isn't much of a reason for holding back information in a murder case," I said.

"He knows something, maybe everything. I'm keeping his silence in my back pocket."

"Darn. I'd hoped you'd get more."

"Don't worry, Judy. The day will come when I'll find a way to make use of him and his secrets. We found out more on Ledet, too." A second passed in silence before his voice chimed back on the line. "Am I keeping you from anything?"

I tapped the phone into speaker mode and returned the receiver to its cradle. "No. Let's hear it."

"When Ledet left work early on the day of the homicide, he went to Guerra's home."

"Why? You told me Alma worked that entire shift."

"She did," he said. "Ledet said he became so obsessed with confronting her, he couldn't wait another minute. Apparently, she'd locked him out in the past and he wanted to head her off, so he waited on her porch steps, rehearsing his speech. But when she arrived, he blew it. Made angry demands and then broke down and cried. The woman next door corroborated his story. "When did you talk to her?"

"Last Tuesday, when she returned home. She said she was heading out for a trip to New Orleans when she heard the ruckus next door. She put her suitcase down, went to the window, and watched. Ledet's anger struck her as especially worrisome because of his size. After he peeled out of the driveway, she felt the need to check on Guerra before leaving town."

"That was the day Alma was killed. He could have returned."

"True, but Ledet swears he knew nothing about the gun she'd borrowed. Judy, the man wouldn't need a gun. Guerra was a toy doll to him, easy enough to break with his hands."

A heavy knocking sounded on my office door. "Can I put you on hold? Someone wants in."

I cracked the door open to JoAnne Necaise. She stretched her neck, looking over my head and around both sides. "Is someone being written up?"

"I'm on a conference call."

"Oh, call me when you're done. The janitors didn't clean my desk again."

I nodded, wanting to roll my eyes instead. This time, I locked the door before returning to my seat. I clicked the phone off hold. "Sorry. Go on."

"Nothing much more. I still don't think Ledet's our man."

"Other suspects?"

"Guerra's so-called secret friend sounds promising. Sure would like to find out more about him. Also, the crime scene techs found prints all over her home that we haven't been able to match. If we ever do, we'll have another suspect. Unfortunately, not everyone's fingerprints are in the data base. The

FBI collected prints from Ledet, Doggett, and Robichaux. Ledet and Doggett's prints were in the home, but only in the front living area. Robichaux's were nowhere in the house and then we learned of his airtight alibi, eliminating him anyway. That pretty well sums up where we're at."

I thanked Bombardier for the call then disconnected, noticing my message light blinking nervously. I dialed in and retrieved a phone message from one Mary Belle McNeese, LCSW. I had no idea what the initials meant, but upon returning the call learned they stood for License Certified Social Worker. She specialized in providing supportive services to institutionalized folks and was helping Dixie get his affairs in order. Hard time for killing his wife was imminent.

"Any chance you could meet with Mr. Ledet and me tomorrow?" the social worker asked. "I'm hoping to close out his employment relationship with the least loss of benefits. Right now, he's in the Jackson County jail, just outside of Pascagoula."

"I can do that. I'll let my boss know."

"Thank you. Also, does Rockhold Packaging offer an employee assistance program?"

"Yes, one of the few benefits that continues after termination."

"Great. Can we meet with the EAP rep, too?"

"It will have to be by phone, but I'll see what I can do."

❧❧

The next day, I pulled up in front of the Pascagoula jail at a quarter to two. Mary Belle McNeese met me at the entrance hall. White-rimmed glasses tempered her big eyes and her short blond hair sported a 1960s flip. She directed me to a small, dingy room with a single table. A large window beside the door provided a view of the lobby.

"I brought some of the correspondence Mr. Ledet received from your company," Ms. McNeese said. "He won't need the Cobra letter. The government will handle his medical needs. Are we on with the EAP rep?"

"Yes. Her name is Dottie Salazar and she's expecting us."

The social worker centered the phone on the table and pressed the speakerphone on. I always used speed-dial to call Dottie from work, so I'd written down the complete phone number on a sticky that I handed to the social worker. She dialed in. After introductions, Dottie began ticking off all of the assistance programs available to Dixie. I found myself mesmerized by the vast network of services she had at her fingertips, ready to trigger at a moment's notice. She gave Ms. McNeese a thorough summation.

Two guards brought Dixie in, one on either side of him. He was handcuffed and his legs shackled, his head hanging like a beaten dog. When they let go, he fell into a chair, his cuffed hands landing on the table with a thump. His tan had faded away and he looked rather pale. Two brassy-colored locks of hair dropped into his face, having grown below his ears.

I fiddled with the trio of business cards in my hand. "Here's contact information you might find useful."

He lifted his secured hands and opened one massive palm. I began layering it with the cards while he watched with an unblinking gaze.

"This is my business card. This one will get you pension fund information, and this card is the contact for the employee assistant program. EAP benefits expire ninety days from your termination date."

He stared at the cards while the social worker began summarizing the EAP services. "I can arrange phone time for you," she said.

The bear of a man put his hands back on the table, slowly coming to life. "You think they can get me a lie detector test?"

Ms. McNeese glanced at me then said, "They do have some legal services. We can try."

Dixie turned, hurling a pleading look at me. "Miss Judy, I didn't kill Alma. I want you to know that."

"I'm not here to judge."

"But I don't want no one who knew Alma to think I done that." He lifted his cuffed hands again and smeared away tears.

"A lie detector test would prove it. I was only sad Alma wouldn't love me back, not mad."

Ms. McNeese patted Dixie's huge arm. "We'll call the EAP now," she said. "They may be able to help."

Dixie looked at her, his eyes widening. "You think?"

The social worker nodded for me to leave and I gratefully took the cue.

CHAPTER 26

On Monday, Millie brought me more news. "Lidia told me the chief returned from his Maryland trip and started drawing scenarios on the whiteboard. Every possible way the killing could've occurred."

"Interesting."

Millie crooked her head and, to my surprise, not one strand of hair moved. "He used *DX* for Dixie, *SF* for the secret friend, but in some sketches, he used *SE*, an abbreviation for someone else. Then he'd erase everything and start over. His drawings showed Alma shot from several different angles. One situational sketch suggested an accidental shooting. Lidia said he paced from one end of the department to the other, with his chin pressed against his chest and his eyes scouring the floor." Millie paused only long enough to take a breath. "His staff thinks he's possessed by the case. Lidia says he rubs his chin and chants the same thing at least twice a day."

"What's that?" I asked.

"'How do I find the person who loaned Guerra the gun?'"

෴

Weeks passed and the foliage that had begun to turn in October settled into full fall colors. Wood chips burned, dry leaves crackled underfoot, and in the air was the chill and smell of autumn.

Dixie remained the single suspect in the Alma Guerra case, but without hard evidence to charge him. Word spread about the alleged secret friend and when Dixie requested a lie detector test, interest in him as a suspect waned and public opinion shifted to the newer, more interesting, mystery man. I made a note to add "secret friend" to the list of suspects in my *Who Killed Alma* Excel file.

Before I knew it, the crisp nippiness of Thanksgiving arrived, the yellow-orange in the shrubs showing. Dan and I had a turkey dinner at a casino restaurant and played the slot machines for an hour afterward.

The following Monday, Dottie called to tell me Dixie had used several of the EAP services and I'd find them listed on her monthly bill. A second employee had come forward about a drug problem, so Dottie and I spent the rest of the call talking about him.

Bombardier and his men returned to Rockhold and interviewed more employees—their goal, to find Alma's secret friend who had loaned her the gun. Bombardier hardly spoke to me while they were there. The last inside scoop I'd received from him was about his meeting with Paul Mayfield. He'd promised to share the information and, once he had, my short-lived role as confidant had ended.

An Indian summer followed Thanksgiving weekend, the temperatures holding through the first week of December before they dropped back into the forties and fifties. Dixie's court-appointed attorney denied his request for a lie detector test, citing the lack of evidence as more than enough to clear him.

"Why give a suspect with no hard evidence a chance to fail a lie detector test?" Dan said when I gave him the update. "Attorneys are paid to win, not to be convinced."

❧❀❧

On Wednesday morning, December eighth, I watched the Weather Channel on our bedroom TV while I packed for the meeting at Corporate. I planned to leave work close to noon and check-in at the airport with enough time to have lunch before my flight.

A warm front was moving into the Louisiana Gulf Coast from Texas, forecasted to reach Mississippi sometime that afternoon. Locally, heavy rains were predicted.

I had high hopes of digging into the Christmas party PowerPoint project while at the hotel. I now had a good grasp of employee names, simplifying the work, but made sure I gathered everything I would need.

I'd just settled at my desk when Dottie phoned. We discussed some open employee issues before I said, "I'm flying to Phoenix this afternoon."

"No—you'll be right here?"

"Yes, a meeting at our corporate headquarters. A quick trip." As I said the words, I couldn't help but think that in another world, another culture not so harried, it would have been nice to stay an extra night and put a face to a voice, maybe have lunch. "Maybe next time I can stay longer," I said with no conviction in my voice.

"Yes. I'm swamped, too," she said. "Maybe next time."

At a quarter to twelve, I dropped the container of discs for the PowerPoint presentation into my purse, zipped up the computer case, and started for the parking lot. A blast of warm, sticky air hit me upon exiting, giving me a taste of Deep South humidity. I tossed my laptop next to my suitcase in the trunk and climbed into the car.

As I drove over the Ocean Springs Bridge, I noticed the white-capped waves, all fishing boats and small craft scrambling into one dock or another. A glance at the sky and I pressed the accelerator. My Camry bounced off the bridge and into Biloxi, passing Casino Row, the Yacht Club, McElroy's Harbor House restaurant, and the Beau Rivage. Staring too long at the magnolias, I missed my turn, realizing it when the Biloxi Lighthouse appeared before me, its white tower against the turbulent blue-black sky.

I headed back to the I-110 viaduct that crossed the Back Bay. Northbound, past the higher part of the bridge, traffic came to a sudden standstill while the southbound lanes went unhindered. Ahead, close to the exit to Interstate 10, a couple of police cars were parked at an angle, blocking both lanes. I got out of the Camry, and like many other drivers, strained my neck to gaze down the long line of stopped vehicles.

The sky had gone from vaguely ominous to black turmoil in a matter of minutes. A motorcyclist climbed off his bike, removed his helmet, and gazed skyward. He turned around and looked at me, taking a step toward my car as if he wanted in. But then he returned to stand beside his bike. A minute later, he repeated the pattern.

I whipped out my cell phone and began punching numbers. The moment Dan answered, I unloaded all of my frustration.

He laughed. "It's December. There are no tornadoes in the winter."

"You should see these clouds. I'm just sure Chicken Little's going to show up screaming, 'The sky is falling,' any minute now. And some motorcyclist is acting like he wants safe haven in my car. Have you heard any weather reports? Sirens? Anything?"

"I'll call you back," he said and was gone.

The sky opened with blinding sheets of rain. The wall of water turned the motorcyclist into a gray blur as he rushed to the passenger side of my car. I clicked the lock open and he slid in and slammed the door.

"I should have invited you in earlier, although a car's not much safer than standing on the bridge. You're soaked."

"I know. I'm getting your seat wet. Sorry."

"They're waterproof. Don't worry about it."

"Do you know what's going on?" he asked.

Before I could answer, my cell phone chirped. I glanced at my passenger and put one finger to my lips. "We may find out."

Dan's voice charged through the phone static. "No tornados. A jail escape. Two guys. You're in a roadblock."

I gulped, swallowing the acid taste of adrenaline. "Um…the man on the motorcycle joined me."

When Dan finally responded, his words were slow and

muted. "Do you think he's one of the escapees? I could call the police—"

"Hold on," I said into the little phone. Casting a glance sideways under lowered lids, I gave the stranger a nervous smile. "My husband says this is a roadblock. Some men broke out of jail."

He flinched, surprised. "Not a weather thing?" His reaction and the sincerity in his words gave me some hope of being safe.

"Apparently not."

He smiled. "Don't worry about me. I escaped all right, but from a bad job, not jail." He glanced at his door handle. "Since the guilty parties are still out there, you might want to lock the doors."

I clicked them locked, but discreetly reopened mine—just in case—then went back to Dan on the cell.

"Judy, why did you let a stranger into your car?"

"The rain started coming down in buckets." I looked at the man. "He would've drowned out there."

"The rain is lifting," the man said. "I'll be out of your hair soon."

"I'll call you back in a while. Maybe the static will be gone," I said to Dan then folded the phone closed.

"Looks like they've started to talk to the passengers," the motorcyclist said, peering through the windshield.

"This will take forever."

He nodded and relaxed the hold on the helmet in his lap. "I'd sure like to get off this bridge."

Just then something pounded against my side of the car and I sat up ram-rod straight. It took a moment to realize that someone's body had bounced off my car. To my dismay, that someone was Jimmie Lee. He raced forward between the two lanes of parked vehicles, pushing hard off one, then another.

"What the hell?" the motorcyclist said.

"I know him. Used to work where he does."

Jimmie Lee made unusual headway for his weight and build.

"Maybe he saw the jail breakers," he said. "But if so, why wouldn't he just call the police?"

"I've never known him to carry a cell phone. I don't think he can afford one." I continued to watch Jimmie Lee barrel forward, no idea what he was up to. I thought of Dixie and wondered if he might be one of the escapees. "You said something about a bad job," I said.

"Yeah. I just walked off mine." He gestured out the window. "It's turned into one hell of a day."

"Wow." I glanced toward him then back at Jimmie Lee, scampering toward the police like a little monkey.

"Yeah, never done that before," he said. "Moved here from Denver for what I thought would be a better opportunity. My boss turned out to be arrogant, argumentative, and demented, among other things. When he fired another good employee today, that was it for me."

I would've bet money he'd worked for Kelm, except he'd referred to his ex-boss as *he*.

Yet another dreadful workplace out there, I thought.

Jimmie Lee was now standing before the police, arms flapping like a penguin in hysterics.

My passenger sat forward. "Hey, looks like that guy just got into one of the patrol cars and the police are leaving. Thanks for the company and letting me out of the elements."

"You may want to sit tight," I said, looking over the long line of automobiles. "We won't be going anywhere right away."

We sat in silence, watching the distant cars begin to move, the progress moving backward like a slow ripple over the mass of vehicles. When the closer traffic began to stir, the motorcyclist thanked me again and hopped out of the car and onto his bike.

I'd started my engine when Dan called. "He hasn't killed you yet?"

I chuckled. "He's gone, but wait till you hear this. Out of nowhere, Jimmie Lee appeared on the bridge, on foot. He hurtled through the rows of cars and up to the road block. Then he got into one of the patrol cars and they left."

"Hmm," Dan said. "I'll keep my eye on the news."

"Oh, and the motorcyclist told me he walked off his job today for the same reason that got you fired in LA."

"See? I'm not the only one who'll take a stand."

His words struck me like a punch in the gut, leaving me with a sick, sinking feeling. "I guess not. Gotta go."

I picked up speed on Interstate 10 and got to the airport and my gate just as the flight began to board. No time for lunch.

A rain squall hit us as we taxied to the runway, immobilizing the plane on the tarmac and leaving us without circulating air for forty minutes. Once airborne, things looked up. The AC released cool, concentrated air and the flight attendants offered free champagne, which I gladly accepted.

On the way to the hotel in Phoenix, the taxi driver found himself on the wrong side of a three-car pileup. By the time I arrived, the sun was slipping over the horizon and I had a booming headache.

While hauling my luggage into the room, my cell phone rang. "Hold on, Dan," I said, and angled my suitcase against the wall before plopping down on the edge of the bed. "Okay."

"How was the trip?"

"Dreadful," I sighed. "I'll explain later. I've got to get something to eat."

"Found out what Jimmie Lee was doing on the bridge."

"Really?"

"Yeah, it made the news. Some guy named Mortimer Tobert, and that Dixie you worked with, escaped from the Pascagoula jail."

"*What*? I thought it might be Dixie when you mentioned an escape, but—"

"Yeah. They referred to him as Michael Ledet, and I remembered you mentioning that was his real name. Evidently, he overpowered the guard who was bringing this Tobert fellow in to share his jail cell."

"An easy thing for Dixie."

"They took the guard's car. The police figured they'd bolt for the main highway rather than poke along Highway 90, so they set up roadblocks at Interstate 10 entry points in Pascagoula, Ocean Springs, and where you were in Biloxi."

"Where does Jimmie Lee come in?"

"Seems he heard their names aired on the radio and knew one of them. Rushed to the guy's house. Beat them there and got a plate number off a Ford Expedition outside the house then hid and waited. They ditched the guard's car and took off in the Expedition. Jimmie Lee followed. They tried the I-110 viaduct but did a U-turn into oncoming traffic when they saw the backed up cars, and headed east on Highway 90."

"That explains Jimmie Lee flailing around on the bridge. He must've abandoned his pickup to get to the police. Did they catch them?"

"Just that Tobert fellow. Dixie's still at large."

"Wow. Keep the newspaper articles for me, will you? Right now, I need food before I pass out."

I unpacked, took a shower and changed into fresh clothes then tossed on makeup. After putting the discs for the Power-Point presentation on a shelf in the closet, I headed for the hotel's restaurant. Sipping on a martini while I waited for my food, I thought about Jimmie Lee chasing the escapees. Since Jimmie Lee's thing had always been following current and ex-employees of Kelm Machinery, that Tobert guy must've been employed at Kelm at one time or another. I doubted Jimmie Lee and Dixie knew each other. Dixie had been with Rockhold nearly two and a half decades.

When my food finally came, I ordered a margarita. "Uh, could you put the drinks on a separate tab?"

My taste buds had fallen under the influence and I ate what I could. I didn't finish the giant-sized drink, so I carted the margarita off to my room, setting the glass on the nightstand before calling for a wakeup call. After changing into a loose-fitting nightshirt, I sat in bed, sipping the tart drink, the laptop at my feet. I powered up my computer but, unable to focus, left it idling on the bed beside me.

All of a sudden, I wanted to be home with Dan and Buffy. I didn't want to go to the stupid meeting. I hadn't since the beginning but, now, I dreaded it. With everything that had been going on the last few months, I felt tired—my many years in HR finally catching up to me.

And sad. I felt very sad. Snatches of memories tumbled around in my head and I stared at the ceiling, tears streaming down my face. *I'm sorry, Jolene. I wish I'd done things differently.*

<h1 style="text-align:center">CHAPTER 27</h1>

Friday morning Millie found me at the messy coffee counter in the break room, dumping powdered creamer into a cup of coffee. She reached around me for her own Styrofoam cup and said, "Got a minute?"

I nodded and she followed me into my office, settling in her usual place across from me. "How was the meeting?"

"Predictable," I said. "I've been through this before in Los Angeles. My employer there was sold and then cut to the bone and knocked out of business."

"I hope we do better than that," she said. "I can't lose this job, not at my age and with the scant opportunities there are around here."

"I found another job, but at a horrible company." Just mentioning that place made my stomach turn. That was where Jolene Cromwell had worked, where my nightmares began. "Can't say I have high hopes for our outcome."

She glanced at her watch. "What I really came to ask is if you'd heard about Dixie's escape?"

"Yes. My husband called me in Phoenix on Wednesday. Get this. The person chasing him and that other escapee turned out to be my old boss's annoying assistant."

"You're kidding. He's the one who reported seeing them?"

I dipped into my purse, fishing for the discs. "Yep. Dan said he heard on TV that Jimmie Lee knew one of them."

"I can't imagine Dixie knowing anyone outside of family and Rockhold employees. But after this, nothing about him would surprise me. Look where my radar got me on him." She paused, staring at my hand jammed inside my purse. "What are you looking for?"

"Those picture discs."

"The ones for the Christmas party presentation?"

"Yes." I pulled out tissues, crumpled receipts, and expired store coupons. "Is Jena scared again?" I shoved aside my cell phone, lipsticks, a comb, and tiny mirror.

Millie waved me off as she watched me empty the contents of my handbag onto the desk. "None of us think Dixie killed Alma anymore. He battered his wife to death—sad—but that's where it ended." She stood up. "Well, I hope you find those things. Maybe you left them at home."

Dropping the junk from my purse into the trash, I put back my wallet and keys. I knew hadn't unpacked those discs. I took them to Phoenix inside my purse and that was how I would've brought them home. I sprang to my feet and walked the perimeter of the office, trying to recall what might have happened to them.

The telephone rang. I slammed my palm onto the desk, lunging for the phone, and jabbed the button that directs calls to voice mail. I returned to my chair and punched in the number for information. "The Desert Resort in Phoenix," I said.

After two transfers, I spoke to Sal, a man with a gruff Latino accent, and explained my problem. I hung up, giving my temples a finger massage before taking a stab at working.

A half hour later, Sal called to say the discs were found, packed, and leaving by priority mail the next morning. I stammered out *thank-yous* and *so-sorrys* then got off the phone—too soon. I hadn't verified the address he shipped them to or gotten a confirmation number. That and I should've requested express mail. I needed those discs as soon as possible. I was running out of time.

When I found only junk in our mailbox Tuesday evening, my anxiety turned to panic. The Christmas party was Thursday. I called Sal.

"I mailed them myself," he said. "Saturday morning. Your mailman has them. Call him."

Buffy sat on her hind legs, watching me traipse from the kitchen to the washroom and back. When Dan arrived, I unloaded.

"Judy, you've gotten yourself all knotted up. They'll get here and, if they don't, find something else to fill up the time." He gave me a forced smile before he pulled a magazine from the stack of mail and went to the sofa. I buried my head in my hands. I had to get through this.

The next day, I drove home at three to check the mailbox. The mailman had come, but without the discs. I raced back to Rockhold and barged into Andy's office. "I've got a real problem."

"Another nutria rat?"

I folded myself into a chair. "I took the discs for the PowerPoint presentation to Corporate last week and, well, long story, but I was in no shape to work on them."

Andy laughed. "That sounds like something my friends or I would do."

"This is serious, Andy. I left Phoenix without them. I've been calling the hotel since Friday. The mail's run, but they're still not here."

"You're such a worry wart," he said. "I'll help you fill up the time. Give the mail one last chance. If you don't get them, we'll work on something else."

"Like what? That PowerPoint presentation's a tradition here, isn't it?"

He wriggled his fingers in front of his face like a performing magician. "Girl, you're looking at the genius of spontaneous reaction. In the flesh. I'll come up with something."

"Tell me. What?"

"We could do a scene from *Gone with the Wind* or…" His voice trailed off, his grin remaining, and I thought better of asking again.

I seemed to be surrounded by people who didn't worry like I did.

On the drive home, I tried to think about something else.

Maybe Dan and Andy had a point. Worst case scenario, the presentation could be postponed.

Pulling into the garage, the sight of Dan's car gave me a start then I remembered he'd hooked a ride to the airport with his boss. With Dan in Chicago, I didn't need to fuss with dinner. I'd have a stiff drink, snack on leftovers, and stare at some reality TV show.

The sound of the train that ran parallel to Government Street was distant enough to be audible without being annoying and had always reminded me I was safe and at home. Tonight was different. The train was the last thing I heard before falling into badly needed sleep, the whistle screaming in my head like a warning bell.

೧೮೧

At close to three p.m. on Thursday, I headed home for a final mail check, this time without much hope for the discs. If I still didn't receive them, I'd have to admit the problem to George.

The mail delivery truck turned onto my road at the same time I pulled into my driveway. I waited in my car, rolling down my window to cool air and gazing around our property as if seeing it for the first time. A long, cobblestone walkway snaked to the front door of our ranch-style brick home. Near the walkway, a conspicuous maple hovered over much of the front yard, still green even though it was December. I could see the half-circle window above the front door needed a good cleaning and groaned inwardly. Below the window, a small awning protected the entryway in case of rain. Then, leaning against the side of the front porch, I saw a package.

"Shit." I leapt out of the car and padded up the walkway to gather the discs. I wanted to kick myself. The mailman had chosen to drop off a package small enough to fit inside the mailbox at our front door, but Dan and I always entered through the garage. Here I was panicking when the discs had been there all along.

I parked in Rockhold's back lot and flew into Andy's

office, package in hand. "I got them! We never use our front door. I never thought—" He stared at me blankly. "I might be a little late for the party."

I rushed to my office and began downloading the discs, intending to be selective. When finished, I'd go back and cut. I needed pictures for four company events. So far, each one was taking too much time.

A glance at the clock and I reached for my cell phone, setting it beside the computer. At this hour, if Dan needed to contact me, he'd try our home number first and my cell second. The party started at seven and I still had two company events to download. I barely looked at the pictures anymore. If they weren't blurred or spotted, they went in. *Screw it.* This was crisis mode. I bumped my cell phone with the mouse and moved it snug against the side of my laptop, out of the way but close enough so I wouldn't forget it.

After downloading the pictures, I flipped through them like shuffling cards, estimating the presentation time. I chopped indiscriminately from each section.

At close to six-thirty, I packed up my equipment and headed home. The only light in the moonless sky came from the thick blanket of spangling stars.

CHAPTER 28

I pulled up to the dark house and pressed my garage remote. The door opened with a slow mechanical grind and I welcomed the light it provided.

Buffy met me in the washroom, touching her nose to the backdoor. "Sorry, Miss Buffy. I'm running late," I said, and let her outside. I changed clothes, touched up my make-up, and hurried back. Buffy came in, making her way to her dry water bowl. She stuck her nose in and looked at me with a pout. I filled the bowl and slung the contents of a can of Mighty Dog into her food dish.

I turned the TV to Buffy's favorite channel, switched on the little light over the stove, and before setting the burglar alarm, gave the house one last look-over.

The party was in full swing by the time I carted my equipment into the ballroom, pleased to see people milling about and mixing. Partygoers swarmed the buffet tables crisscrossing the room, and huddled in conversations.

Andy stood near the stage on the far side of the room, a man about his age beside him. I made my way over, unloading my gear onto a nearby stand.

"Looks like you're ready to launch your presentation," Andy said.

"Yes." I glanced at his movie-star-looking friend. "Maybe not the greatest job, but it's done."

"Good going, girl," Andy said. "Don't worry about the

quality. The way this bunch is drinking, you'll be lucky to get their attention." He turned to his friend with a gesture of his hand. "This is Dwayne Barlow."

Barlow ran his fingers through curly, flaxen hair that appeared to have been cut one lock at a time. "It's nice to meet you. Andy speaks of you often."

I opened my mouth to respond, but nothing came out. *Why would Andy talk about me to this stranger without ever mentioning him to me?* "Andy and I do share some interesting experiences," I said finally.

Barlow smiled in a boyish way and I caught the blue-green glimmer in his eyes.

Introductions completed, I wondered how to get rid of this Dwayne fellow. Andy was my friend and confidant and I wanted to talk to him without this third wheel eavesdropping. But Barlow's brown Prada shoes seemed planted on the ballroom floor.

After suffering through a few sociable minutes with Andy and Dwayne, I picked up my equipment and mounted the four steps to the platform. I took my laptop out of its case and started plugging cords into the side. I pulled down the projector screen and stepped back to inspect the layout.

Task accomplished, I left for the buffet table, wandering through a sea of familiar faces, now with names. I glanced back at Andy and his friend, still deep in conversation, and sighed.

Hearing someone call my name, I turned to see Millie wave from a raised cocktail table where she sat beside a leathery man.

I gestured that I needed a minute then speared a couple of meatballs and dropped them onto a plate. A quarter-sized sandwich soon joined them. Jamming a cracker with jalapeño cheese spread into my mouth, I crossed the room and climbed up on a stool beside Millie.

"Judy, this is my husband, Red."

His fair skin looked even more leathery close up. With a freckled face and red-grayish hair, I decided this wasn't his given name. I nodded to him. "Nice to meet you, Red."

"You, too."

Millie leaned over. "What about that PowerPoint thing you've been fussing over?"

I told her every stupid thing I'd done, leaving out the part about getting drunk. "Don't expect much. I rushed back to the office late this afternoon and hammered it out."

After a while we left the table to do our share of mingling. Millie and Red went one direction and I the other. I realized I'd chosen the wrong way when I ran into JoAnne.

"Miss Judy, I certainly hope none of our non-drinking employees are encouraged to imbibe."

"JoAnne, relax."

Her left eyebrow shot up and she put her hands on her hips. "But there's too much drinking going on."

I downed my own glass. "Maybe you should join them. I'm getting a refill. Can I bring you a high ball? Some wine?"

"Judy! You know liquor has never touched my lips."

"See? You're a non-drinker and I couldn't persuade you to imbibe."

I walked away but glanced back. JoAnne stood, staring after me, empty-handed, and sporting a creased brow.

The sound of Vicky Coupe's giggles came from a knot of employees gathered at the bar. I hadn't seen her since Andy wrote her up for leaving her machine running. She was poured into a shimmering gold-colored dress that set off her shiny black hair and fair skin.

I walked past her to LaShunda Thompson and her guest, an elderly woman. "This must be your grandmother." LaShunda had told me she was bringing her, but she didn't fit the description JoAnne had given me of *pathetically ill and old*. LaShunda introduced us and we shared a short exchange of polite conversation.

I was talking to a married couple who had met at Rockhold when a "thud-thud-thud" echoed through the ballroom—the familiar sound of someone test-tapping a microphone. George's voice could barely be heard above the din of the crowd.

The guests began to quiet and I took a seat in one of the

folding chairs lined in rows in front of the stage. Some employees and guests followed suit while others remained sitting at a cocktail table or stood.

George welcomed us to the thirty-third annual Rockhold Packaging holiday party. He praised the employees for work well done then gave us a brief update on the pending company sale and restructuring. "When I'm done here, we'll honor each employee-of-the-quarter, and then Judy Kenagy, our HR manager, will present pictures taken at this year's company events." George pressed the clicker and looked at the pull-down screen. The company logo materialized, large and colorful. He clicked again and the portrait of Alma, the one displayed at her funeral, appeared. Hushed gasps permeated the ballroom then disappeared into sharp-pointed quiet.

"I think I speak for us all when I say Alma Guerra's death brought the saddest part of our year. Let's take a moment to remember her."

Some folks bowed heads while others stared quietly at the picture.

"It's important we find Alma's killer," George said. "If you haven't read the memo I sent Tuesday, please do. The police are still searching for the person who loaned Alma a gun. If you have any information whatsoever, report it to the authorities immediately." George gazed over the crowd. "I also want to mention losing a long-term employee, Dixie Ledet. His senseless act of violence ended his career, and worse. He's still at-large. If anyone has information regarding his whereabouts that also needs to go to the police. I certainly hope the New Year will be free of tragedies and deaths. Now, on to a happier note." He looked at me and extended his arm. "Judy."

I got to my feet and walked up onto the stage.

George passed the clicker to me. "When Judy's done, I'll announce the employee-of-the-year." He moved to the edge of the platform and down the steps.

I looked at the screen and pulled up the happy face of Rusty Shaw. Employees clapped and cheered while I read their reasons for voting him the employee-of-first-quarter, then I went on to praise the winner of the second, third, and fourth quarters. Partygoers heartily applauded each quarter's winner, and with equal enthusiasm. Next, I flicked through snapshots taken at company events and employees clapped, yelled comments, or laughed.

I was moving along at a regular pace when a blow-up of Bert brought me to a screeching halt. A stunted scream-type gasp left my mouth, the microphone amplifying it throughout the ballroom. In the picture, Bert wore a Hawaiian shirt, the same colorful print I'd found in Alma's closet. The one in the half-unpacked suitcase with the postcards of Destin, Florida. Stunned into silence, I gazed over the packed ballroom, scrambling to think of how to recant my outburst.

I sputtered a contrived chuckle. "I'm—I'm sorry, all of you. I thought I saw a spider on the screen. My imagination, or one drink too many."

The room seemed quieter, the guests continuing to stare at me.

I turned and looked at the screen, pointing to the picture, my hand trembling. "As you see," I said, my words winded, "here's Bert Axelrod at the summer picnic, trying to swat that fly buzzing round him." I flipped to the next frame. "The fly is still circling and Bert, in continuing to pursue the fly, has knocked his eyeglasses off."

People laughed.

"Bert looks especially good, considering his frustration," I continued. And he did look good, almost handsome. The simple combination of the color in his shirt and the lack of his geeky glasses made a distinct difference. I remembered trying to convey this to Andy that afternoon after the grief meetings. But I couldn't remember where or when I'd seen Bert this way and Andy had only chuckled—said Bert had never looked handsome.

I looked over the audience. Millie sat beside Red, laughing, oblivious to the significance of the shirt. Andy was wrapped up in a conversation with his friend. I didn't see Bert. Weak-kneed, I moved quickly through the remainder of the presentation. I needed to call the police.

"George?" I said and lifted my purse from under the table

as he strode back up onto the stage while I started moving away, delving into my handbag for my cell phone. Not there. I bounded down the steps and tried my purse again, then hit my head with the palm of my hand. *Damn.* This happened every time I put my phone somewhere other than my purse. I set it right in front of my computer too.

I tossed my purse over my shoulder, and stepped close to the side of the platform. George was reviewing the employee for each quarter again. He had my laptop and still needed it to present the big award.

Hurry, George. Yes. Yes. He's good. She's great. Get to the point. Please.

Finally, he did. Rusty Shaw, with his dynamic smile, won employee-of-the-year. His image exploded onto the screen. A huge round of applause echoed through the ballroom, drowning out every other sound. Employees yelled *hoorays* and *attaboys*. Rusty bounded onto the stage, thrusting his hand forward to shake George's. Then Rusty raised his hands high, waving them in a Richard Nixon fashion. I couldn't have cared less, but I put on a phony smile and waited.

The music began. "Let's start the dancing," George said, his words ringing out as in a cheer.

The only dancing I had planned was out the door. I clambered onto the stage and gathered my equipment. Carrying it swiftly through the ballroom, I sensed someone moving fast, coming up alongside me from behind. By the time I realized it was JoAnne, she'd caught up and, in two long strides, had turned and stopped in front of me.

"You aren't leaving now, are you?" she asked, her face pulsating with concern.

"No, of course not." I forced a smile. "I'm just putting this in my car." I moved on at a nonchalant pace. When I got to the door, I sailed through it.

CHAPTER 29

My headlights sliced through the dark, illuminating the road ahead of me. Cloud cover had hidden every star and any possibility of moonlight. I crawled along, my mind skipping all over the place—from Bert's shirt in Alma's home to Jena's insistence Alma's secret friend was married. Bert was married, and his shirt had been in a suitcase in Alma's closet, half-unpacked from a trip to Destin.

In my head, I could hear the muffled voice from the anonymous caller—the words typed in the report to Bombardier. '*It's not an employee. The murderer is her secret friend.*'

Bert had to be the secret friend, but he was an employee. Tired of thinking, I focused on nothing but getting home where I could call the police.

After a few more turns, my Camry hurried down my street. Ocean Springs needed more streetlights. Even at close range, I could barely see my house. I'd forgotten to turn on the outside lights. I pulled into the garage, leapt out of the car, then pressed the button to shut the garage door. Inside, I turned on the light, disarmed the alarm, and was reaching for the lock when the door began to open. Instinctively, I forced the full weight of my body against it, adrenaline running hot through my veins.

"Dan, is that you?" I asked, hoping for the unlikely chance he'd returned from his trip to Chicago early.

No answer.

My heart jumped into my throat. *A raccoon?* Raccoons had wandered into our yard before, and I imagined one on the other side of the door, up on two legs, pushing. But no raccoon I'd ever heard of could be this strong.

Dixie? He was still at large. I'd certainly be no match for him.

I summoned every ounce of my strength and shoved, but a stronger heave from the other side broke my hold and the door burst open, knocking me hard against the washing machine. I teetered, grappling for something to regain my balance, and slammed my hands onto the top of the washer, steeling myself. When I turned around, Bert was standing before me, staring through thick-lensed glasses.

Buffy's nails clicked over the kitchen tile before she came into view. She paused in the doorway between the washroom and kitchen and gave Bert the once over, then sauntered over and sat down beside me, facing Bert.

"Does y–your dog bite?"

My right hand throbbed from hitting the washer while holding my ring of keys, but I clenched them tighter, the metal digging into my palm. "Uuhh—yes. All I have to do is say the right word. She's dangerous."

Miss Buffy—aka Benedict Arnold—cocked her head and scratched a floppy ear. She strolled over and sniffed Bert's pants leg, lifting her face to him and yawning.

He stroked her forehead. "I d–d–don't think your d–dog's dangerous."

I backed slowly toward the kitchen. "Bert, how did you get in? What are you doing here?"

"I g–g–guess you didn't see my car. It's parked out front. I d–d–didn't think you'd let me in, so I stood by the bushes and ducked into the garage when you opened the door. It was e–easy."

Instinctively, I looked for something to use as a weapon but found nothing. I thought fast. "There's no reason to kill me, Bert. They'll know you did it. I told Andy and Millie all about the shirt before I left the party."

"I–I–I'm not going to hurt you. I can't believe you said that."

"Then what do you want? Why did you sneak in here?"

"I wanted to f–f–find out why you screamed when you saw my picture. B–but you've already answered my question."

"The shirt."

He nodded. "Ju–Judy, I didn't hurt Alma. I wore the shirt on a weekend trip with her to Florida. I couldn't find it after we returned. I'm sure we left nothing in the hotel room, so she had to have picked it up with her things. Before I c–c–could ask, she was dead. I didn't kill her. I l–l–loved her."

"You were having an affair?"

"Yes. That's all. It's just, I've got a family and I didn't— still don't w–w–want anyone to know about m–me and Alma." Bert collapsed against the door and held his face while his shoulders heaved.

Buffy lifted her ears, tilting her head just like the RCA Dog. She stared at Bert with compassion showing in her eyes.

I took his arm and turned him toward the kitchen. He crumpled into a chair at the table and removed the heavy glasses, dangling them in his hand as he dropped his head.

I sat beside him. "Talk to me."

"I really loved her." Tears streamed down his face. Buffy rested her chin on top of his knees. "Alma understood me. She tried to help. Sometimes I think she slept with me because she f–f–felt sorry for me. She had a kind heart. But I don't want any of this to get back to my wife. I l–l–love her, too. It's j– just hard. I can't explain."

"Bert, how did you manage to cover up a weekend in Destin with Alma?"

He reached for the stack of napkins on the table and blew his nose. "My wife thinks I went on a management retreat. She didn't even question me because she's not interested in me, my job, or anything 'cept the kids and her parents."

"You've got to tell the police about this."

"No. She'll find out and t–take the kids. They're all I have."

"If you don't, Bert," I said, "I will. You have no choice.

Besides, I can't imagine Bombardier wanting to destroy a marriage. Your wife won't find out."

"But my only alibi is my wife and children. I was home that evening."

"If that's true, he'll find a way to get the information without giving the affair away. It's a risk, but you've got to take it." I reached for the phone. "I'm calling him now."

"No, Ju–Judy."

"It's okay. You can't be any worse off than you already are."

I rang the Ocean Springs police department and asked for Bombardier. Since he wasn't available, I gave them my name and my number. Two minutes later, the phone rang.

"Carl here."

"Bert Axelrod is here at my home," I told him. "He's admitted to having an affair with Alma Guerra. He wants to come forward, tell you what he knows but he has one condition."

"What's that?"

"He doesn't want his wife and children to know about Alma, but his family is his only alibi."

"Tell him I'll work with him. I'm not in to breaking up families if I don't hafta'."

Holding the phone away from my ear, I turned and repeated the message to Bert, who continued to sob softly.

"Have him meet me at the police department in ten minutes," Bombardier said when I got back on the line.

"Okay. Hang on while I tell Bert."

"What about Millie and Andy?" Bert asked before I could say anything.

"Don't worry. They won't talk. Bert, it's for your own good. The chief wants to meet you at the department downtown. Do you know where it is?"

"Yes."

"Are you okay to drive?"

He nodded. "I can drive."

Concerned he might bolt as Dixie had, I said, "He'll go out of his way to protect your family, but if he finds out you're the murderer it may not be possible to keep the affair a secret from them."

Bert sat up in the chair. "I'm on my way. I'm not the murderer but I know who he is and I hope the sonofabitch rots in hell. Tell the chief I know who the murderer is."

"Did you hear that?" I asked Bombardier.

"Sweet Jesus. Yes, I did."

I turned on my porch light and walked Bert to his car. He'd stopped crying. "Do you want me to go with you?"

"No," he said. "This is something I need to do myself."

Still clenching my keys, I returned to the house and eased into a chair, rubbing my red and swollen palm while I stared at the key fob for my Camry in the center of the key ring. That black, oblong thing with the red panic button on the back that I kept hitting accidentally whenever I got out of the car with a bag of groceries. The red panic button that set off my car alarm in the Rockhold parking lot when I tried to get my keys out of my purse while carrying home a load of work. The red panic button I couldn't seem *not* to hit when I was getting gas and holding my credit card, keys, and the gas hose.

I shook my head. I hadn't thought to press the panic button when I thought my life was in danger. And even though I was crushing it for dear life, the one time I thought I needed it to, the thing didn't go off.

CHAPTER 30

I do not feel I should be disciplined because a truck went to Bakersfield without a full load. I'm told where each driver should go and my job is to communicate the best route. If my position description has changed to include loading procedures, please let me know so I may do my job correctly." ~ Jolene Cromwell, two days before she was fired.

❦

Bert and Millie's work schedules coincided with first shift employees, so they normally arrived an hour before I did. While Millie was often in before seven a.m., Bert rarely made it by seven. I wasn't sure whether he'd come in today, but I couldn't chance his getting to Millie before me.

At a quarter to seven, I called her office from my house.

"I've gotta tell you something before Bert gets there, if he's even coming in. I have a feeling he'll pull you aside for a chat about something he thinks you know, but you don't."

"Goodness, what? And why wouldn't he come in?"

I clutched the phone close to my ear. "Remember the shirt I found at Alma's house?"

"Not really."

"The one in the suitcase in the bedroom closet," I said.

"You mean the funny-colored pattern one?"

"Yes. Last night I realized why it had caught my attention. When I showed the slide of Bert at the company picnic, he was wearing it. That's where I'd first seen the shirt." I could hear her inhale sharply through the line.

"That's why you gasped?"

"Yes. Like you did just now."

"Bert's shirt at Alma's…"

"I left the party early and went home to call the police, but Bert paid me a visit."

"To your house?" Millie asked, her volume soaring.

"Yup. He more or less broke in. I didn't know at the time whether or not he was dangerous."

"He broke—"

"Let me finish before he arrives. I was desperate and told Bert I'd clued you and Andy in about the shirt before I left the party, so that you two would turn him in if he killed me."

"Heavens to Betsy."

"I just know he's going to corner you and ask for your silence. Please, please pretend I told you about the shirt last night rather than this morning or I'll be reliving another drama.

"Sure. But what happened?"

"Turned out Bert was real hurt I'd even think he might kill me. But I had to consider the possibility with his shirt at Alma's and his breaking in. Also, when Andy arrives, get to him before Bert. He'll make the same plea to Andy."

"Okay, but what happened at your house? Could he have killed her? Should we call the police?"

"Bert already talked to them. I'll give you the skinny later. I'll try to get there before eight." The phone went silent. "Millie?"

"Oh, yes, I'm here. It's just—Alma and Bert?" she whispered.

"Gotta go." I hung up.

Thirty minutes later, I crossed the threshold into my office and planted myself behind the desk. Millie had sent an email marked urgent and confidential that read, *Bert's in the building. As you warned, he was all over me to stay hushed up. I don't know how either of us can get to Andy before he does. If I reach Andy first, I guarantee you Bert will barge in.*

I called the extension for the plant phone that hung on the wall by the back entrance. Keisha Davis answered.

"Millie Landry, please," I said in a clipped disguised voice, hoping for anonymity.

"Sure, Miss Judy. I'll tell her right now."

Damn.

After a long few minutes, I heard the receiver being lifted. "It's me," Millie said.

"Good. Look, I have an idea. Has Andy come in yet?"

"No, it's a little after eight, so any time."

"Okay. Stay on the line until you see him then send him to my office. Tell him it's urgent and he needs to avoid Bert. Andy'll pump you for more information. Don't give him any. Direct him straight to me. Bert's not likely to come up front."

Millie and I held the connection in silence. Minutes passed then she said, "He's here," and the phone went dead.

I checked the blinking message light I'd noticed when I first arrived. Millie had covered her bases, leaving the same message on my voicemail that she'd emailed.

Just then, Andy appeared. I got to my feet and met him at the front of my desk, repeating everything I'd told Millie once he'd locked my office door.

He was as surprised as she, but with a totally different re-action.

"You're frigging kidding! Alma and Bert?"

"Andy, go back to your office and let him talk to you. Make certain he thinks I told you about recognizing his shirt last night."

"What happened at your house?"

"Long story. Come up later and I'll tell you everything. Bring Millie, too. By the way, who was that men's underwear model you brought to the party?"

He snickered. "A friend."

"You never mentioned him."

"I haven't known him long. And he actually has a regular job."

ↁↁ

I collected headcount numbers and plugged them into my portion of the week-end KPI report, betting on no changes before the end of the day. Half an hour later, I sent my standard email message to the other managers. *HR portion of the Key Performance Indicators complete.*

As soon as I clicked the send button, Andy called. "Going home early?"

I tapped the speaker phone on, returning the receiver to its cradle. "No. Why?"

"You finished your KPI and the day's not over."

"I needed something routine to work on. Can't get my mind on anything else and I've been waiting for George to get off his marathon of conference calls, so I can talk to him. Did Bert get with you?"

"Oh, Girl. Yes-siree. As soon as I left your office. Gawd, can that man whine? I'm still flabbergasted. Alma had to have taken pity on him. She was like that, you know? I mean always picking up stray cats and distressed people. Uh-huh, that's the only thing that makes sense. I'm not saying Alma was some kinda' slut, but to help some poor soul, she'd think nothing of a nice mercy—well, you know."

"I'm taking you off speaker," I said and lifted the receiver. "Bert told me last night he thought Alma slept with him because she felt sorry for him."

"See? I told you," Andy said. "I mean, if she thought she could cheer up some poor, lonely dude, well—that's how Alma was. Makes me wonder now if that wasn't why she invited Lester to her home."

"Nah, she had another reason," I said.

"Are you talking about the conversation you overheard in the break room?"

"Yes. I don't remember her purpose, but I'm certain it was more pragmatic. There was no intimacy, no romance, and nothing to do with those silly artificial plants. But I do believe the visit had something to do with an object."

"Like a broken refrigerator or stove? Lester was quite the handy man, or so I've heard."

I tried to play the break room scene out in my head. "No.

Let's just leave it with her inviting him to her house. I didn't even know her and I'm lucky to have remembered that much. Once I talk to George, I'll try to get with you and Millie and tell you about last night, how I thought Bert was going to kill me."

"Bert couldn't kill a fly," Andy said.

I laughed. "Was that a pun about his picture in the PowerPoint presentation last night?"

Andy was silent for a few seconds until recognition seemed to register. "Never connected the two. I'll do my part of the KPI, too, and try to knock off early today."

Half an hour later, I rapped lightly on the doorjamb of George's office and he swiveled around in his chair.

"We have an issue," I said.

He waved at the chairs in front of his desk. "Sit down."

I shut the door behind me then sat down and took a breath. "Well, I found out Bert had an affair with Alma."

George sat upright, muscles flexing all over his face. "*Huhhh?*"

I gave him the story from the time I recognized the shirt in the PowerPoint picture to the moment I called Bombardier. George listened intently. "Then Bert told me to tell the chief he knew who killed Alma."

George's mouth hardened. "You're kidding. Who?"

"He didn't say. Bombardier wanted him at the station. I haven't seen or talked to him since I walked him to his car last night."

"He should've come forward," George said, his tenor rising. "I've been asking people to report anything and everything for over a month and you're telling me Bert knew all along who killed her. I want him in my office now."

I rubbed my temples. "He went home for lunch. I'll bring him in as soon as he returns."

After confirming Bert was still out of the building, I called Andy and Millie up front. They were sitting before me in a matter of minutes. I gave them my account of Bert's forced entry, my initial fright, his crying, and the call to Bombardier. I sped through the story, not missing a beat, and wrapped it up with George's reaction when I told him a little while ago. They said little, Millie holding her fingers to her lips the whole time. When I finished, they got up, peeked out my office door into the hallway, then, like thieves in the night, slipped out.

Ten minutes later, I tried Bert's extension and he picked up. "George needs to see you."

"Wha—what's this about?"

"I think you know, Bert. Let's get it over with." I hung up and went to George's office. Bert shuffled in a couple of minutes later.

George leaned back in his chair, folding his arms across his chest. "I hear you withheld pertinent information in Alma's investigation."

"I had my reasons."

"Selfish ones," George said. "You're a representative of this company and, as such, you've shed a bad light on us all. You know our policy on sexual relationships between supervisors and subordinates. It's grounds for termination."

"But I–I–I wasn't Alma's supervisor."

"Let's not split hairs, Bert." George leaned forward and pounded his forefinger onto the desktop. "You are a supervisor in this company and she was an hourly employee. She may not have been a direct report, but she certainly was whenever Millie was out. And you're married." He leaned back, locking his arms across his chest again. "You put the company in a vulnerable position legally. Alma might've filed a sexual harassment charge."

Bert sat erect. "She'd n–n–never have done that."

"You don't know that, Bert," George said. "Judy will prepare a formal warning for your file. I want you to sign the form and make your comments."

Bert hung his head. "I was wrong, but I didn't want my family to find out."

"You covered up evidence in a murder to safeguard your secret."

"The po–police said so, too," Bert stammered out.

"Bert," I said, "who did murder Alma? Are you allowed to tell us?"

"I don't know his name, but I know what he looks like. I saw him leave her house once, a t–t–tall, debonair chap. Kinda like an English gentleman–rigid stance. The word *guy* d–d–doesn't go with him. He was too Ivy League."

George listened then nodded. "At least we know he's not an employee." He dismissed any possibility of Bert being the murderer, if the thought had ever entered his mind to begin with.

"That's why I called Ju–Judy that night. I wanted you g–g–guys to know the killer wasn't an employee."

"You were the anonymous caller who phoned my home?" The deafening sound of my voice surprised me.

"Yes."

"My gawd. I had no idea."

"I should've known no one would take a call like that seriously."

"I told the police," I said. "Is that serious enough? It didn't seem to do much more than confuse them, though."

"That's what I thought," Bert said.

I leaned toward him. "We have an employee assistance program. Our EAP rep, Dottie, can refer you to a network of resources for you and your family." I shrugged. "It might help ease the burden a bit." Then I handed him the card I'd brought.

He stared at me silently then looked blankly at George.

"I think you should take Judy's advice," George said. "The EAP is confidential and works."

Bert closed his fingers around the card. "I–I–I'll think about it," he said, looking up from lowered lashes.

CHAPTER 31

Dan sat happily ensconced on our comfy sofa with the *Sun Herald* before him, a drink in his hand. "Your drink's in the fridge," he said as I walked in.

I wrapped my hand around the bourbon then carried the frosty glass into the family room where I settled into a chair angled near the sofa.

He handed me the mail then returned his attention to the newspaper.

"How was your trip?" I asked.

"Okay. Glad to be home." Dan was never one to discuss his work. Normally, I talked too much about mine, but so much had happened I couldn't wait to start.

"I know the last thing you want to hear is a work story but this one is way-out." I took a swig of my drink.

"The PowerPoint presentation?"

"No, that actually went fine, but I found out something during the presentation." I'd been repeating the story since early morning and it seemed second nature now. I ended with my account of Bert's admission to George and me that he made the anonymous call.

"But the guy who called stuttered," Dan said.

"Dan, Bert stutters."

"I didn't know that."

"For God's sake, Dan. Anyone would've considered that worth mentioning. When I picked up the phone, the voice was so muffled I couldn't even tell the caller's sex. I'd never have detected a stammer."

"I told you the caller was a man. That much was clear, but he asked for you as *Ju–Judy*."

"That's how Bert talks. He's never spoken my name in anything less than three syllables." I took a gulp from my drink and set it down.

"Oops."

I got to my feet and tossed my arms out, walked in small circles in the center of the room with a mincing gait. I stopped. "You knew I planned to report the call to the police and you didn't think to mention such a major detail?" I plopped back into my chair.

"Didn't think it mattered."

"If you'd told me, we would've all known about Bert from the get-go. The police would've had the description of Alma's debonair chap early on. Who knows, the whole case could've been solved by now." I shrugged my shoulders in a hopeless gesture and exhaled noisily. "I certainly don't recommend you leave your day job for any kind of detective work."

∾∾∾

When I fell asleep that night, I dreamed of being chased down a street in the dark. The thud of my bare feet on the pavement pounded in my head and my heart knocked against my chest.

I hit a sandy beach at the end of the road and treaded into gulf waters. Knee-deep in, someone yanked my hair and pulled my left arm behind my back, holding it there. My pursuer wrapped an arm around my shoulders and held a knife to my throat, forcing me forward.

In the deeper water, some kind of being rose on two legs, advancing toward me in long, intense strides. As it got closer, I realized it was a taller version of Jolene, with a ferocious stare on the person behind me.

Her arms swung mightily, water splashing about her. She dipped down, wrenched the knife away, then shoved my captor back.

Released from my stranglehold, I rolled to shallower water, hauling myself up onto my elbows. I glanced back at my attacker to see Mrs. Briscoe sitting dazed-like, leaning back on her hands. Suddenly, Jolene swooped upon her, knife in hand, and with one single hack, severed Valerie Kelm-Briscoe's head.

Then Jolene retraced her steps into deeper water and descended back into the sea. Mrs. Briscoe's head lay on the beach, blood mixing with the waves licking at the sand. Its eyes wide, the head laughed like a hyena, over and over, loud and evil.

I was screaming when Dan woke me.

Gulping in breaths, I whispered, "Are you going to divorce me?"

"If I can't get any sleep, I'll have to. Another nightmare?"

I nodded. "This one was a doozy. Mrs. Briscoe chased me with a knife and Jolene Cromwell came to my rescue and cut off Mrs. Briscoe's head. Get this—the head was laughing when you woke me."

"Maybe you should contact Stephen King and sell him some of the story lines from your dreams."

"I'm sorry I woke you."

"Judy, why do you continue to connect Jolene Cromwell with Mrs. Briscoe? Jolene lived in LA before we even thought of moving to Mississippi. She'd never been near the woman."

"Probably because Valerie Kelm-Briscoe is the epitome of every bad boss I've ever had, you've ever had, and all our friends ever had. It's easier to focus your hatred on one person."

"Then why not blame one of those jerks who Jolene worked for?"

"Because that's what they were, jerks and bad managers. Stupid and dangerous but they didn't hide it, and, unfortunately, they're a dime a dozen. Mrs. Briscoe pretends to be something dignified when in actuality she's evil. She wants to be worshiped, expects it, and wonders why her employees disappoint her."

"And you blame her for Jolene?"

A wave of sadness tumbled through me like a bout of seasickness.

"Judy?"

Another moment passed then I shook my head. "I blame only myself for Jolene."

CHAPTER 32

s. Kenagy, I'm scared. Can you do anything? I'm an hourly employee. How can I be blamed for huge mistakes that involve decisions I don't have the authority to make? Please don't put this in my personnel file or tell them." ~ Jolene Cromwell, one day prior to her discharge

ෲ

In Saturday's *Sun Herald*, Dan found an interesting piece of news. On the second page, a journalist had written an article about the Pascagoula jail escape of Michael Ledet and Mortimer Tobert.

Mortimer Tobert had gone into a rage at work and began beating on company equipment. Kelm Machinery filed charges, putting him on the receiving end of jail time. He'd started working for Kelm sometime after I left. He obviously felt like the rest of us, only didn't handle it quite as diplomatically. Jimmie Lee's stalking tendencies probably didn't go over very well with Tobert either.

As previously reported, Jimmie Lee described the getaway vehicle to the police and pointed them to the route they took. Mortimer was apprehended, but Dixie wasn't. The article reported the charges against Dixie in connection with his wife's death, but there was no mention of Alma Guerra.

First thing Monday morning, Bombardier called. "I verified Axelrod's alibi with his family. He was home the evening Alma was killed. I feel certain we got an accurate account."

"But did they suspect—"

"I was discreet, told them police procedure required us to rule out friends, co-workers, everyone, and that our questions were routine. I doubt any of them thought of an affair."

"I'm glad you don't think Bert's the killer," I said, "but it's disappointing we keep having to start over."

"We still can't rule him out," Bombardier said. "I've seen some good liars in my time. And we don't have enough evidence on Ledet. I doubt he did it either, but I've been surprised before. We glossed over Robichaux because of his jail time the night of Guerra's homicide."

"I don't know how you do this for a living. I need to see this killer caught for whatever reason and I'm scared we've lost our chance."

"Then come up with hunches, Judy. They worked in finding your dog."

"Are you sure about Lester's alibi?" I asked.

"Absolutely. It's on his criminal background check and I verified the exact time and date of arrest with the arresting officer."

With the mention of the background check, the copy I received from Hancock County popped into my mind. "Something's been bothering me about that," I said. "Why were there a number of people sitting at a bus stop in Bay St. Louis on a Monday evening? I'm in Bay St. Louis a lot. My local Society for HR Management has a dinner meeting monthly at the Marriott. I've read that weekend buses are the rage around those casinos, but I've never seen anyone at the bus stops for weekday business."

"No. No," Bombardier said. "The incident at the bus stop occurred on Sunday, October seventeenth. Your employee wasn't picked up until the next day, Monday, at 4:03 p.m."

"Huh? My copy puts the incident on the same day as his arrest, Monday. I didn't have any time of day recorded, but if it was 4:03 p.m., he wouldn't have had time to get to Bay St. Louis. His shift ended here in Ocean Springs at four o'clock. I tell you, that county is the worst with these checks. I hired an employee last week who had to prove the county had an erroneous charge on hers before she could start work."

"Judy, fax me your report."

"Sure. You'll have it in a few minutes."

I left for the file room on the other side of the plant. Pulling up Lester's report from his file, I reread the part about the bus stop. *Reported lewd and lascivious by people at bus stop #5 on October 18, 2004, arrested, and incarcerated overnight.* My copy said nothing about the arrest time. Back in my office, I scribbled the chief's name on a facsimile cover sheet, asking him to call me, then faxed our copy of the background report.

Ten minutes later, he had me on the phone. "Like our report, yours supports his alibi with the jail time on October eighteenth, but it says he was picked up the same day as the bus stop incident. Mine says the incident occurred Sunday, October seventeenth. One or both of these reports is incorrect."

I sat up, pressing the receiver closer to my ear. "Which means other things they recorded may be in error, too."

"The arresting officer was adamant they picked up Robichaux at 4:03 p.m."

"On Monday October eighteenth, correct?"

"That, the officer had to check. Instead of digging into his notes, he went into the Hancock County computer system to verify the arrest date."

"The archaic Hancock County system," I said. "Oh, great."

"We may have a serious problem. I've got some probing to do."

"Chief?"

"I wish you'd just call me *Carl*."

"I'll try, but would you keep me in the loop on this? It's important to me."

"You bet. We have a discrepancy which could prove huge. Keep pressing for the pulse of the case, Judy. You're good at this."

I'd be getting justice if I helped find the killer, and justice for Alma somehow seemed related to justice for Jolene. But would solving the case really assuage my guilt over Jolene's suicide? I felt desperate. I had to try.

Chapter 33

The closer we got to the sale of the company, the more work Corporate generated for its business units and the weeks flew by.

Bombardier began a serious investigation of Lester Robichaux for the first time. He had the arresting officer pull out his original notes which showed the correct arrest date and time of Sunday, October seventeenth at 4:03 p.m. Lester had stayed the night in jail, released early enough Monday morning, October eighteenth, to get to work on time. The problem came when a Hancock County clerk erroneously entered the Monday release date as the arrest date which was what showed on the report sent to Bombardier. Before the clerk filed the notes, he discovered the error. He knew the incident and arrest occurred on the same day, so in an effort to correct his mistake, he made another one by moving the incident date up to match the incorrect arrest date.

This was what I'd received on the later background report. It was also the information the officer saw when he went into the county's system to verify the arrest date. Noting the incident was on the same day, he accepted the arrest date as accurate. If Bombardier had asked him to verify the incident date as well, he'd have known there was an error early on, but Bombardier was only concerned with the arrest that established Lester's alibi or lack of one.

The police interviewed Alma's friends and family, neighbors, and co-workers again, this time with an emphasis on Lester's role in her life. Her co-workers all knew about Alma's artificial plants, but none of them had been asked to go to her home to look at them. Alma had done what Millie said only made sense—she'd brought them to work in her car where employees then purchased them.

Bombardier brought this up to Lester who struggled to hold onto the lie, but after heavy questioning, he changed his story. Apparently, Alma had borrowed a gun she didn't know how to use.

Bombardier called me to ask if this might be the missing piece of what I'd heard in the break room. My mind did a free-fall, coming to rest on the entire conversation between Alma and Lester. "He's telling the truth," I said. "She told him she'd borrowed a gun but didn't know how to use it. I remember now. Lester said something about being able to tell her any-thing she'd want to know about guns. That he'd come over and show her. The gun must've been why the conversation held in my subconscious."

"Robichaux said he'd never gone into Alma's house. In-stead, they drove a distance outside the county and did some practice shooting. When Robichaux had asked Guerra why her friend didn't show her how to use the gun, she told him that her friend had never shot a gun either, had sort of borrowed this one, and needed to return it before it was found missing. And get this." Bombardier paused for effect. "The gun had a silencer attached."

He gave Lester a chance to verify his whereabouts on Oc-tober eighteenth, but Lester claimed he'd left work and gone home alone.

Having no alibi after his end-of-shift worked against him, but the fact that his fingerprints weren't at the crime scene while someone else's unidentified prints were, served to Lester's advantage.

Bombardier worked diligently with Bert, hoping to get a sketch of the mystery man to release to the public. I wondered if Bert's stuttering got in his way because the artist never drew a sketch Bert could accept. Millie said Lidia told her Bert kept shaking his head, saying, "It's not him. It's still not him."

Except for what we knew about Dixie stalking Alma, no other information had surfaced connecting him to her death. He remained a fugitive, his name occasionally appearing in connection with the jail break.

Bert had taken our advice. He'd called Dottie and arranged for family counseling. Over time, he seemed less burdened, his stuttering toning down.

ↄ∂ↄ

Suddenly, we were well into the new year and the heart of Mardi Gras season. Party music flowed along the Gulf Coast, everywhere you looked now rife with purple, gold, and green. King cakes, with the traditional plastic doll inside each, made their seasonal debut. As the tradition went, whoever got the cake slice with the doll bought the next cake. Rockhold Packaging gave coupons for free king cakes to those left holding the doll.

Mardi Gras had boogied onto the Mississippi Gulf Coast with dancing, singing, and partying from Mobile to New Orleans. Like the song said, *"Laissez les bons temps rouler"* or, "let the good times roll."

The night of the Mardi Gras ball, Dan arrived home shortly after me, carrying his tuxedo. When we were dressed, he said, "I think we look pretty good—younger. Don't you?" And the glow on his face told me he felt younger, too.

Clad in our formalwear, we stepped out onto our driveway where a gentle breeze cooled our faces. A winter moon hovered low in the direction of Mobile and a zillion stars twinkled in a velvet sky.

I hugged Dan's arm. "That's a Walt Disney sky and I'm dressed like Cinderella."

He patted my arm and grinned. "And we're going to the ball."

ↄ∂ↄ

Biloxi's Gulf Coast Coliseum was packed with men in tuxedos and women in billowing gowns. Colorfully clad masked entertainers performed on a stage. We watched the jugglers, dancers, and singers from the bleachers. Some of the performers carried Flambeaux torches.

The shows were the teasers, the hors d'oeuvres before the entrée when the new Krewe royalty would be introduced.

I pulled on Dan's arm. "I heard the king and queen work all year for this event while keeping their identities secret." I stretched my neck, straining to see above the crowd.

"Who are you looking for?"

"They're here. Jack and his wife." I waved. Jack nodded in recognition and they started toward us. The four of us moved up to the top of the bleachers and leaned against a long wrought-iron railing.

Drums rolled—one long, slow beat after another, growing louder, the prelude to announcing the Krewe Royalty. Dancers somersaulted onto the stage, pausing for introductions. The riveting drum beat again, thunderous, reaching its crescendo.

The background music escalated then a man's voice bellowed into a microphone. "Ladies and Gentlemen, may I present King Neptune and Queen Venus."

Lined together, leaning over the railing, we watched in silence. With another humongous rumble of drums, two people stepped out in garb so flamboyant, Las Vegas entertainers would've looked bland beside them. The couple's bejeweled crowns rose two feet high, another three feet of feathers extending up. Their floor-length robes glittered with mirrored colors, reflections, and shiny stones like in a kaleidoscope. They carried huge feathered fans.

Follow-spotlights tracked them. I'd never seen the queen before, but the king was all too familiar.

"Isn't that Keith Briscoe?" Dan asked.

"In the flesh."

Jack screwed his mouth to one side. "A drawback of living and working in small town, USA. That means Val-*er*-ie's here."

We followed the crowd into an open section of the

convention center, filled with more white linen-covered tables than I'd ever seen in one place. "Mardi Gras Mambo" resonated from the speakers.

Andy stood alone by our table and I stepped up beside him. "Looks like Dan and I are sitting next to you," I said, looking at the nameplates.

"Bert's sitting across from us," he said.

"How about his wife?"

"He normally comes alone," Andy said. "Enough of an expense to rent the tux and all."

"Millie told me his family counseling is working."

"That's good," Andy said, looking relieved. "He can make me crazy sometimes, but Bert's basically a good person. Alma liked him, and your dog took up with him. That's always a good sign."

"Phooey, that doesn't mean anything. Our dog takes up with everyone. We hired a contractor to do some work around the house and Buffy adored him. When he left, she tried to go with him. We found out later he was an escaped bank robber."

"Why, the little bitch." He chuckled and let his gaze wander over the mass of guests. Then he wriggled his fingers with a goodbye wave and vanished into the crowd.

Jack moved to where Andy had been. "So Val-*er*-ie is here," he said, replicating my adaptation of her first name.

"She'd have to be, but you don't see me looking."

"Hmmph. You'll have to tell me sometime about those barbaric bosses you worked for in Los Angeles."

I pictured them in my mind, laughing at Jolene, calling her incompetent. I could see her writhe with humiliation, make meek attempts to explain herself, only to be called a liar.

Jack gazed over the vast breadth of circular tables. A part of me wanted to tell him I was worse than any barbaric boss. I knew how fragile Jolene was and I didn't stand up for her. I let her get hurt. If only...

But I was sick of all the *if onlys*. I had an endless supply of them. If only this. If only that.

I was shaking my head and moving my lips when I noticed Jack staring at me.

"Wow. Where did you go?" He took a step back and smiled, hands in the pockets of his tuxedo. "You seemed to be talking to someone in your mind."

I felt my face redden. "Yes, myself actually."

Wine was served along with starter salads. We talked through the salad, main course, and dessert, never running out of things to say. I didn't remember much of the conversation, but I remembered Bert participating in all of it.

An Al Johnson recording of *Carnival Time* played in the background while aimless conversations merged into a single buzzing sound. Dan dropped his napkin on his plate and disappeared among the patrons. Millie and Red rose together and left. A man I didn't know took Red's seat and began discussing the presidential inauguration with Andy. Bert got up and told us he wanted to meet the royal couple.

"There's a waiting line, Bert. It looks like a long one."

"That's okay. I think they're supposed to bless us and I can use all the help I can get." He weaved his way around tables and in between people until he'd reached the king and queen on their thrones, waving their massive fans over each person that approached.

I took a long pull on my wine and considered whether to get up and move around, but my girdle was killing me. Then raised, angry voices came from somewhere and I turned toward the noise. Bert stood before Keith Briscoe, jaw thrust forward, brow furrowed, Keith waving him off.

I stood up for a better look then nudged Andy and brought my mouth to his ear. "Take a gander. Bert's in a dispute with King Neptune."

I began making my way through the crowd, the cumbersome gown impeding my progress. Behind me, I heard Andy say, "Fudge." I pulled up my skirt, making room for my legs and, half-tripping, worked my way to Bert, Andy on my heels.

Closer in, I saw the red in Bert's face and heard him shout Alma's name. I tapped his arm and whispered, "Bert, what are you doing?" I offered a sheepish grin to the people standing nearby.

Bert pointed to Keith Briscoe. "He—he's the guy, the chap I saw coming outta Alma's house."

Before I could respond, I sensed the ol' eyes-upon-your back sensation. I whipped around. Valerie Kelm-Briscoe was staring through me. She leaned against a wall, posed like Princess Diana. She looked like her, too, and might have pulled it off if not for the evil that showed in her eyes.

People in line to greet the king and the queen shared puzzled glances, their voices murmuring. Mrs. Briscoe's back stiffened. She glimpsed from me to her husband to Bert then back to Keith.

Andy grabbed Bert's arm and yanked him off to one side. He twirled Bert around and faced him. "What do you think you're doing?"

"That's the man who I saw c—c—coming out of Alma's house." Bert raised his arm to point.

Andy slapped his arm down and pulled him farther from the spectators. I tagged along.

"Are you saying King Neptune killed Alma?" Andy asked in a low-key mumble.

"Yes."

"Then we need to call the police," Andy said. "No matter how big this is, there's no need for a scene here. That's the Mardi Gras Neptune King and this is a *huge* accusation. Remember, you're representing Rockhold Packaging."

"Do you think I'll get in trouble?" Bert asked sadly.

Andy threw his arms up and rolled his eyes.

"Bert," I said and nudged him toward a door to the parking lot, "this isn't the time. Let's go outside."

I glanced quickly around. Dan was coming toward us from across the room. I shook my head then mouthed the word *no* and tipped my head toward our table. He stopped for a moment then seemed to get the message, and did an about-face, heading in the opposite direction.

Bert lowered his voice. "T—that—that's the man who loaned Alma the gun. That's her m—m—murderer."

An aroma of *Drakkar* men's cologne hung in the air and a shadow fell on the floor before me. Andy turned as if to speak, but stopped, his eyes looking over my shoulder.

I spun around.

The last person I expected to see was the police chief in a tuxedo, his hands clasped against his midriff.

We all stood there in silence. Then Bombardier addressed Bert. "Looks like we need to take a ride to the station. Sounds like ya may have pertinent information. Do you have a coat or anything?"

"No," Bert said.

Bombardier surveyed the room then, discreet and without a word, ushered Bert toward one of the towering doorways. The old New Orleans party song, "Iko, Iko" had started to play. Someone turned the volume up and the beat boomed through the ballroom. "My grandma and your grandma were sit-tin' by the fire…" I hummed along as I watched Bombardier and Bert disappear into the hallway.

CHAPTER 34

We stood silent on the ballroom floor, paying homage to the complexity of the moment.

Then Andy broke the silence. "Let's me and you go outside."

We found the most isolated place in the convention center parking lot, under low hung moss drooping from a row of ancient trees.

"Andy, do you realize what's happened? The husband of my ex-boss must've been Alma's lover and may have killed her." *Where did they meet? When? The affair I can buy, but Keith Briscoe a murderer?*

"Girl, I know, and he's the Neptune King, no less. But right now, we have this Bert issue."

"What do you suggest?"

"Well, George won't fire Bert if King Neptune is really a murder suspect, but he isn't going to be happy. Bert just got that write-up, what—a little more than a month ago?"

"Uh-huh."

Andy shook two cigarettes from a pack and in typical Andy style, lit both at once and gracefully handed me one. "The way I figure, George would prefer not to know what happened tonight, if you get my drift."

I took a drag. "You're proposing we don't tell him?"

Andy tapped off ash. "I watched George from across the room and I can tell you, he didn't see a thing. And none of the people who witnessed the dispute seem to be making a big deal out of it. I'm not saying we cover up the incident. All I'm saying is we don't bring it up."

"I agree. Let's not," I said. "Why even worry George?"

Andy took the last puff off his cigarette then dropped it on the asphalt and ground it out with the toe of his shiny black shoe. "Bert can make me friggin' crazy. We need to talk to him Monday morning, let him know we've stuck our necks out. God knows what he may rush in and say to George if we don't get to him first."

"You've got that right."

"So, looks like Alma and the Mardi Gras king were going at it," he said. "Now, that *is* something we can tell George. After all, Jena insisted Alma's secret friend was a married man. But looks like the married man turned out to be this dude instead of Bert."

CHAPTER 35

A credible witness has come forward, identifying Keith Briscoe of Ocean Springs as the secret friend we've been seeking in the unsolved homicide of Alma Guerra." ~ Police Chief Carl Bombardier, the Sun Herald – Monday, January 24, 2005.

༺ఎఁఅ༻

Keith Briscoe didn't make big, bold headlines in Monday morning's newspaper, but he did merit a two-column report on the second page.

The news that someone had identified him as the sought-after secret friend had brought him into the public eye as the newest person of interest.

The fact he hadn't been charged with a crime didn't appear to faze anyone. Bert's name was withheld, at least for the time being.

Mrs. Briscoe made the news, too, as the wife of the accused adulterer and suspected killer. I had high hopes that Gulf Coast high society tittle-tattle would dethrone Val-*er*-ie from the queen's court at Kelm and slap her with some humility.

First thing that morning, Andy and I cornered Bert inside the corridor to the back offices.

"Judy and I don't think you should tell George about the

scene at the Mardi Gras ball," Andy said, almost in Bert's face.

"Why not? I f—f—found Alma's murderer."

"We don't know that for sure, for one," I said. "But even so, pointing and accusing was unnecessary and inappropriate."

"And George ain't gonna like it," Andy chimed in.

Bert gave us a look of comprehension. "What do you think I should do?"

Andy slipped me a sideways glance. "We won't say anything, that is, unless you go traipsing through George's door to turn yourself in. If George finds out we didn't tell him, we're in trouble, too."

Bert creased his brow. "I'll have to tell him I'm the one who reported Keith Briscoe to the police."

Andy nodded. "Yes, but you don't have to tell him the rest."

The tightening I'd seen around Bert's eyes disappeared. "You're right. T—thanks."

Andy took a breath and leaned back against the hallway wall. "So what happened at the police department?"

"I told the chief that King Neptune was the chap I'd seen coming out of Alma's house. She'd t—told me there was someone else and when he saw me, he covered his face."

"You're barely stuttering," I said.

"It's something I'm working on in counseling. My wife g—goes with me. Good thing, too. I may have to tell her about Alma."

"That's not good," Andy said.

Bert pushed his bangs off his brow. "The chief doesn't know how much longer he c—can keep my name out of the press. Keith Briscoe already knows I'm the witness. If it becomes public, I'll have some explaining to do. I could make up a story—or I can just gut-up and tell her."

"How do you think she'll take it?" I asked.

"Not well," he said, "but the support we've gotten through the counseling will help."

"Good." Glancing at my watch, I said, "We should all get to work now."

An hour later, Millie stood over my desk and I swiveled

around to face her. "I've got news," she said. "The police went to the Briscoe home Saturday."

"You've been talking to Lidia."

"Yep." She smacked an open palm onto my desktop. "The part-timer was on vacation, so Lidia had to work." She waved her hand, as if getting the words out of the way for what she really wanted to say. "They returned with nothing. The chief's been fussing at them ever since."

"Millie, sit down."

"Okay," she said and pulled out a chair. "According to the lead detective—"

"That would be Lieutenant Young."

"I guess. Well, he and the other officer tried to coerce Mr. Briscoe into coming in for fingerprinting. It didn't work. Mr. Briscoe told them they could ask the questions then and there, but in no way would he produce his prints. He said he'd done nothing more than return the girl's driver's license and credit card—claimed he found them in the parking lot at Edgewater Mall. He used her address on the license and drove there."

"That's a pretty good story. If he made it up, he made certain he didn't say he found a wallet or a purse, something he'd have to describe."

"That's what the chief told the lieutenants. Lidia said he called them gullible. They weren't happy. Mr. Briscoe said Alma had been home and she invited him in. He said he stood inside her front door long enough for her to thank him."

I chuckled. "Did he say how she thanked him?"

"Judy, really."

"Seriously though, losing only a credit card and driver's license sounds a little suspicious."

"The detectives told Mr. Briscoe the same thing. He countered, saying Alma told him she took them out to make a purchase and went to the parking lot still holding them. She had left the mall about a half-hour before he found them. Mr. Briscoe said she must've forgotten she had them in her hand when she opened the car door. You know, them being so light and all."

"Could've happened," I said, still skeptical. "Definitely something the police could check out."

Millie's eyes widened. "How?"

"Since she used a credit card they could verify whether she made a purchase in the mall shortly before the time she told Keith she'd lost them."

"Duh. Of course. Well, maybe that's why Mr. Briscoe told them she never made the purchase."

"You're kidding," I said. "He told them that?"

"He said she noticed a button missing on the blouse she'd picked out when she got to the cash register. The blouse was the only one in her size."

I tossed my hands in the air. "Millie, this is ridiculous. Anyone would know he made up that whopper." A teensy spider started across my desk and I smashed it with a yellow sticky. "I can understand him wanting to cover up the affair, but I still can't picture him killing anyone."

"Lidia thinks he's guilty."

"Why?"

"Because he refused to give up his prints—said he didn't much trust cops on the Gulf Coast. Claims he may've left a print or two inside the front door and wasn't going to let them find something accidentally-on-purpose to misinterpret."

"Doesn't mean he killed her." I glanced at my watch out of habit. "Hey, did they tell him about Bert seeing him at her place?"

She flapped her hand down. "Oh, he had that covered, too. Told them that when he left, he saw Bert crossing the lawn toward the house. Mr. Briscoe said Bert appeared bitter."

I smiled. "That's our Bert."

"Lidia said the chief's kicking himself he didn't go personally." Millie tilted backward in her chair and waggled her hand as she spoke. "That same morning, the chief asked Lidia to pull the records for the Wade murders. Lidia told me he tore through them with passion. He should be too busy with the current case to be messing with that old, cold thing."

"The only minuscule connection I can think of," I said, "is Keith Briscoe married into the Kelm family. Bombardier

always thought the Kelms were involved in the Wade murders."

"Yes, but Mr. Briscoe didn't know the Kelms way back
then."

"Bombardier must know something. He wouldn't get
worked up if he didn't. All I can think of, and it's a stretch, is
something linked to the Wades has resurfaced, perhaps connected to Alma's case."

Millie's mouth took on the shape of an O. "I can't imagine what. The two cases occurred decades apart. It's just him,
the chief, being fanatical. Listen, I've got to get back to work.
I'll let you know if I hear of anything else."

"Please do."

She disappeared, leaving me to mull over her words. My
chances of finding the killer looked bleak again. I thought for a
while then sank back into my work.

CHAPTER 36

Days passed without mention of Keith Briscoe—in the news, from Millie via Lidia Trash, *nada*. But on Monday, January thirty-first, after a weeklong information dry-spell, I blessed the willingness of Lidia to bare all to Millie.

I learned that Bombardier went to the Briscoe home himself and pushed for his fingerprints. When that failed, he took every piece of circumstantial evidence he had and petitioned for a court order. The judge turned him down. Bombardier told Lidia he'd slammed his fist on the judge's desk and yelled, "Damn. If Briscoe's innocent, why the hold-back on his prints?" The judge told him Briscoe's story of the found driver's license and credit card sounded plausible then ordered Bombardier out.

Millie offered her own opinion as usual. "If this had been some poor slob instead of a member of the Kelm family, they would've granted the court order without a moment's hesitation. And I'm sure they took into account Mr. Briscoe's role in this year's Fat Tuesday."

I knew Millie was right. People on the Gulf Coast loved their Mardi Gras—the costumes, the decorations, the pageantry, and the pride. Arresting the King of the Krewe of Neptune less than two weeks before Mardi Gras would be a major upset.

After she left, I clicked open my Excel folder. I replaced

the name *Secret Friend* with *Keith Briscoe*. In the empty *did-kill* column I typed, *wanted to cover up the affair, lover's quarrel and gun went off, refusal to provide fingerprints, seen and admitted being at Alma's home.*

I stared at the screen for a long moment. If Keith was the main suspect, this information seemed weak. I shrugged and moved on to the *Did-NOT-kill* column and typed in, *Doesn't seem a violent person, may not have known how to operate a gun.*

I added Bert Axelrod to my file as well, creating the same two columns I made for the other suspects. Under *did-kill*, I entered what I'd put in for Lester and Dixie when I first created this spreadsheet. Love rejection. Alma sure seemed to have gotten around. Under *Did-NOT-kill*, I listed, *Bert not capable of murder, he identified Keith, his family provided his alibi, he made the anonymous call.*

Under the *did-kill* column for Lester Robichaux, I added, *lied to police on reason went to Alma's home, knows guns, handled the murder weapon, zero alibi, some criminal background.* For the *did-NOT-kill*, I typed in, *came clean on true reason for trip to Alma's, criminal history lewdness instead of violence, no finger prints at crime scene.*

A reminder appeared on my computer screen. *Meeting with George.* I shoved the papers to one side and picked up my planner.

On the way over, I tried to talk myself out of the unsettled feeling in the pit of my stomach. What if George had heard of Bert's scene at the ball and the cover-up Andy and I had plotted? No way would George let me get away with saying something like we had forgotten to mention it. He'd jump all over me the way he did Bert in response to Bert's flimsy claim that he didn't supervise Alma. At the door, I stopped to take in a quick breath.

George stared out at gray, bulbous clouds. When he turned, his face had the grim look of a homeless man. "Have a seat," he said, in tone a little heavier than usual.

I did, fastening my hands to the arms of the chair. A moment passed before I became aware of the silence.

He placed his elbows on the desktop and steepled his fingers. "We're in for some changes due to the sale."

My body relaxed with the realization I wasn't in trouble, but stiffened again when new concern sunk in. "The reorganization?"

He nodded. "We've been luckier than some of the business units. Joey Chauvin, the general manager in New Orleans—his job is being eliminated. They haven't made a profit in two years. His HR manager's position will be cut, too. They'll each receive a severance package."

"Who's going to handle their work?"

"You and me. We're going to wear multiple hats. I'll run the New Orleans unit and this one, and you'll handle human resources functions for both locations. At least New Orleans is close. But there's one more change. We have to sever Bert."

"Oh, no."

"It's either Bert or Millie, and Millie's been here too long. Unfortunately, Corporate feels we only need one supervisor for the day shift."

"But he's so broke and his wife doesn't work."

"He'll get a three-month severance and unemployment benefits. Keep this under your hat," he said. "We'll drive over sometime before Mardi Gras. Corporate is emailing the severance agreements."

"That doesn't give us much time," I said. "Mardi Gras is one week from tomorrow."

"I know," he said. "I'll nail down the date soon, and tell Joey we need to meet with him. He'll ask why, but he'll have to wait. We'll talk to Bert afterward."

I sighed audibly. "Okay."

On my way back, I walked into the empty office next to mine and sat down. I didn't realize what I'd done until I heard the phone ringing in my own office. I hastened next door and lunged for the phone.

"You sound harried," Dottie said.

Bent over the desk, the phone receiver barely at my ear, I said, "I was in the wrong office when I heard the phone."

"Huh?"

The cord was stretched to the limit and I began shuffling around my desk, my thighs pressed against it. "Oh, never mind. I just need to get to my seat." Still holding the receiver, I fell into my chair and accidentally disconnected her. I punched in her speed-dial button. "Sorry, I hung up on you."

"How did you reach me so fast?" she asked. "I hadn't had a chance to redial a single digit of your phone number."

"You're on speed-dial. All my contacts are. I simply hit a button."

"Oh, I see. Well, back to the reason I called. Your employee, Brittany, she's doing well in rehab."

"That's great news, Dottie, and I can sure use some."

"Are you okay?"

"Yes. The same ol' routine, except we're starting to let people go."

"Sometimes change seems bad at first, but more often than not it will turn into a positive."

"I wish I could share your optimism."

"Don't forget, Judy, the EAP is available as part of the company's severance package."

"Believe me, I'll make the offer to each of them."

"Keep in mind it's also available to you."

"I know," I said, noting the raised volume in my voice. "Glad I don't need it with as busy as we are."

Dottie didn't respond.

"Thanks for the news on Brittany." I paused then said, "Dottie?"

"Yes?"

"Oh, nothing. I'll talk to you later."

"While you're worrying about others, Judy, make sure you take care of yourself. Goodbye."

At a little past eleven, my office phone rang and Millie's voice burst through the line. "Someone I've never seen before has come through the back entrance and is talking to the employees in the folding department."

We had a definite lack of plant security at Rockhold. I phoned Andy. "Millie says we have an intruder in the folding department."

"Meet me there," he said.

I walked into the plant from the front offices at the same time Andy came up from the rear. When I saw Jimmie Lee Albright, I was hot. No, I was more than hot. I was pissed. He stood beside Keisha Davis. She talked while inserting cardboard into one end of her folding machine while he scribbled something on a small ringed notepad.

"Bastard!" I said under my breath.

He saw me and did a double-take before wobbling toward the back entrance like a battery-operated toy. Andy stopped him and I picked up my pace to join them.

"Jimmie Lee," I said, "we're going to step quietly into the plant manager's office."

"You know this character?" Andy asked.

"Oh yes. He's my ex-boss's little snitch."

Jimmie Lee walked obediently with Andy and me down the corridor. This worked for about fifteen seconds before he stopped and turned to face us. "I ain't goin' into nobody's office. I don't even work here."

"Then why are you here, Jimmie Lee?"

He plunked hands on his hips and crumpled his brow. "Got business. Important business."

"Did Mrs. Briscoe send you?"

"She didn' hafta. I'm on a crusade for information, if you will."

"About Dixie?"

"Who's he?"

"Maybe a friend of the guy who he escaped with. The guy who worked for Kelm."

Jimmie Lee's head swiveled. "Hey, did that big un' work here?"

"Never mind," I said, putting my hands on my hips, too, and bending into his face. "You're on private property. If you show up here again, we'll have you arrested for trespassing. Get out of here, Jimmie Lee."

He gritted his teeth and shuffled out the back entrance, moving as fast as his asymmetrical body would allow.

I turned to Andy and laughed. "I can't believe that little

hick. He's on a crusade for information, if you will?"

"He talks exactly the way you told me he did. But my question is what was he doing here?"

Andy and I talked to Keisha and a couple of other employees in the folding department. Apparently, Jimmie Lee wanted information about Alma—where she lived, who her friends were. They thought he was on official business and told him everything.

"Andy, can you cover for me? I don't want George to know I'm leaving to chase after some waif, but I am. If he realizes I'm gone, act like I went on a personal errand."

"How will you find him? He left twenty minutes ago."

"Simple," I said. "He asked our employees where Alma lived for a reason."

"Of course," Andy said.

I hopped into my car and headed toward Alma's house. After four street changes and a couple of bends in the road, I'd come to the block where Alma had lived. I passed Jimmie Lee's Chevy pickup parallel-parked in front of a house next door to Alma's. I kept going, taking a right at the stop sign, and driving around the block. When I came up the road a second time, I parked at the curb two houses down from his truck. My guess was he started knocking on doors until someone opened one. I waited for him to appear.

On the far side of Alma's, the house next door had its screen door open a crack. I craned my neck. Someone stood just inside the door, facing in, keeping the screen ajar. Then the screen door flew open and Jimmie Lee soared out, running past Alma's house to his truck. He jumped in, revved the engine, and disappeared.

I had two choices. Follow him or stay in the neighborhood and find out what he was up to. Having seen the speed in which he departed, I opted for the latter.

Dropping my car into gear, I coasted four houses up. Stepping onto the cracked, wooden steps Jimmie Lee had just bounded off of, I rapped on the screen door. A gray-haired woman in a flowery housedress approached. A bobby pin clipped bangs off her pallid face.

"I'm Judy—Judy Kenagy," I stammered. "I have some questions about that young man who just left."

"Are you a detective, too?" she asked.

I flinched at her question then took a moment to gather my words. "No. I used to work with him and—"

She unlocked the screen, opening it toward me. "Come in. I have questions myself."

I went inside and she pointed me to the kitchen table. She remained standing as I pulled out a chair.

"Would you like some coffee? Iced tea?"

"No, thanks," I said. "I'm trying to find out what that kid is up to. He barged into my workplace earlier and questioned our employees about someone who used to work for us."

"Yes. The young woman from next door. Such a tragedy. He wanted information from me, too. That's his job."

I lifted a brow. *Since when?*

"I'll get his card." She moved to the kitchenette behind her, lifting a little card from the laminated counter and bringing it to me. Black print on a gold background read *J. L. Albright, Private Investigator.* An address and phone number appeared in smaller font underneath. She'd heard Jimmie Lee speak, yet didn't question his PI status?

"Are you by chance the neighbor the police questioned?" I asked.

"Yes, but they didn't talk to me until two weeks after they found her body. I'd been in New Orleans with my daughter and grandbaby. Before I left town, I'd seen my neighbor arguing with a scary muscleman on her front porch. I now know his name, Dixie Ledet, and he's escaped jail." The woman repeated the story Bombardier had shared with me in early November when he called about his visit with Paul Kelm, Jr., now Paul Mayfield, the story of the scene Dixie had made outside Alma's home three months ago. "I wished I'd called the police then," she said. "For a while there I was wondering if that might've saved the girl."

"You think something different now?"

"Now, hardly no one thinks he did it." She leaned on her elbows, rubbing her temples. "The man left in a huff and I walked over. She saw me coming and waited. She told me she was so frightened of the big man she'd gone and borrowed a gun from a friend for protection."

"Is this what you told *Detective* Albright?"

"Yes, and more. I let him know I talked to the police and brought up what her friend, Jen…Jena something told me."

"Jena Doggett? When did you speak to her?"

"The same day the police questioned me. They arrived in the morning. Later that afternoon, I saw her walking toward the back of the young woman's home. I'd never seen her around so I stepped out onto my porch for a look. Jena—Miss Doggett lifted a pot in the back and took something from underneath. When she caught me watching, she came over to show me the house key she'd taken. She said someone needed to fetch some of the girl's things to send to her parents."

"The girl's supervisor wanted the key," I said. "I went with her to collect the items."

The neighbor took a breath and exhaled. "I believed Miss Doggett. She had an honest face, pained but sincere eyes. We began talking about her murdered friend. She knew about the borrowed gun, too." The woman looked at me and her eyes widened. "I read they've never found the gun."

"That's correct," I said. "And you told Detective Albright all this?"

"I sure did. Oh, and also told 'bout the silencer. Almost forgot that part. Miss Doggett asked if I'd heard anything about one. I had, and so we discussed it. The police had asked us both not to let word of the silencer get into the press, at least not back then. I doubt it much matters now since that big man is hardly a suspect no more. A borrowed gun with a silencer attached. Isn't that the dangedest thing?"

"Hmmm, the police chief told me early on he suspected a silencer. That must've started with Jena."

"That, and the fact that no one around heard the shot," she said. "Detective Albright lit up like a Christmas tree. He asked me if the *Sun Herald* office was on Pass Road in Biloxi. I said south of there on DeBuys and he tore outta here like his britches were on fire."

"I wonder what he wanted from the newspaper office."

"I don't know," the neighbor said, "but you might wanna make a stop there. If he went in, people are gonna remember him."

Chapter 37

I hadn't planned on Jimmie Lee still being at the *Sun Herald,* so when I caught the glint of sunlight reflecting from the hood of his truck, I knew luck was on my side. I would not only be able to question people inside the *Sun Herald,* I'd be able to follow him to his next destination.

I parked my car out of view then strode over to the wall of the building south of the entrance, and waited. The sun warmed the top of my head and I figured it was close to noon. I was about to change my stakeout location to one in the shade when Jimmie Lee came out, a dance in his step and an easy grin on his lips.

I loped off to my car and started the motor. Jimmie Lee's truck wheeled into view, stopping at the exit to DeBuys Road. I stayed put until after he turned then I followed. I hung back far enough for my Camry to appear only as a blur in his rear-view mirror. He made a left onto Highway 90, going east. After the first few miles, as I maneuvered around cars that barged in front of me blocking my view, traffic thinned and trailing him became easier. He led me over the Ocean Springs Bridge, but when he flew past the little city of Ocean Springs and its strip malls and restaurants, I began to worry we were going to Alabama. But after a few more miles, his right turn signal began to blink. He slowed and turned south on highway MS 57 toward St. Andrews Golf Course. I knew his destination. That's where I'd found Buffy dognapped. Mrs. Briscoe went home for lunch on most work days and would likely be there now.

I circled back to the *Sun Herald*.

The woman behind the counter had the sparkling eyes of a girl's set in an elderly woman's face.

"I work for Detective Albright," I said. "He wanted me to review some information he got here."

"Oh, yes," she said, picking up his business card and shooing a fly off the counter. "He left not long ago—looked through some of our news articles 'bout that young woman who was murdered."

I paused a moment, marveled by the fact that yet another person had bought into Jimmie Lee's detective scheme. "He thinks he might've missed something."

The woman's face furrowed. "I thought he was simply trying to find out what type of gun killed her, which he found."

I drew on my acting skills. "Yes, that was the most important thing, but he had one other loose end to close."

"Well, he sure didn't mention it to me." She stretched her arm out toward a computer monitor set high on a table by the window. "That will get you the same news articles he looked at. The switch is the red button on the bottom."

"Thank you."

I didn't need the gun make. Bombardier had already given me that. Jimmie Lee had retrieved information at the *Sun Herald* that was already publicized news. He was probably at Mrs. Briscoe's home this very moment, reporting his day's success, sipping iced tea while he asked if Keith had access to a .38 semi-automatic pistol, possibly with a silencer. My business here was over. I hit the red button and wasted a couple of minutes in the pretense of searching through articles.

On the way out, I dialed information and was transferred to the non-emergency number for the Ocean Springs police department. By the time I got into the car, I was talking to Bombardier, laying out the sequence of events beginning with Jimmie Lee's workplace invasion. I detailed my conversation with the neighbor, told him of Jimmie Lee's trip to Mrs. Briscoe's, and what I'd learned at the *Sun Herald*.

When I finished, he chuckled. "Perhaps you should join my force, Judy. You're turning into quite a detective. Give me a description of this character's vehicle. I have no reason to go to Valerie Briscoe's home, but may need the information later."

Back in my office, I tapped a speed-dial button to reach Dan. I hit the wrong one and, at the sound of my answering machine at home, hung up and hit speed-dial number four, getting Dan's direct line at work. Speed-dial was the major method of phoning at Rockhold. It worked. I told him about Jimmie Lee's performance in the plant and he laughed heartily. But his mood changed when I said I'd followed him.

"Why did—that's not your job."

"Don't worry. I'll tell you more tonight. I just got back and I'm buried."

The next speed-dial button I poked connected me to the HR staff at Corporate. I let them know I'd mailed them copies of the employee-signed code of conduct acknowledgement forms—again. They'd lost the first batch.

Concentrating on a computer report, time passed without interruption. It wasn't until Millie sat in front of me that I looked up and flinched. "Millie—hey—hi."

"Who was that creep in my department?"

"I'm so busy. Can we discuss this in the morning? This has become a rather long story."

Her features compressed into a portrait of disappointment. She bit down on her lower lip. "Can you at least tell me who he was? Tomorrow is a long ways off."

I sighed. "His name is Jimmie Lee Albright. You know, Mrs. Briscoe's court jester."

"He certainly fits your description, but for heaven's sake, why was he here? And where have you been?"

I leaned toward her. "I followed him."

"Land sakes! You did what?"

I clicked the *save* button on my computer and closed the report. "His purpose was to gather personal information on Alma Guerra. And your employees gave it to him freely."

Millie scooted forward, perched on the edge of her chair. "I'll have to talk to them. But Judy—"

I gave her the story rapidly, gesturing wildly as I detailed each event. Millie listened, bobbing her head. Sometimes she'd interrupt with a question, raise an eyebrow, or widen her eyes. Occasionally, she'd open her mouth and cover it with her hand.

"Millie," I said, wrapping up my account, "I can't get over the neighbor and the receptionist at the *Sun Herald* believing Jimmie Lee is a detective. Your employees did the same. Am I missing something?"

She chuckled. "You might be. You're not from these parts. Mississippi has its population of local yokels. They're not stupid. Some are professionals with bad grammar and hick Southern accents. Some know better, but enjoy carrying on the culture by using local colloquialisms. And business cards impress people around here."

"Maybe Jimmie Lee's smarter than I thought."

I left work a little early and on the way home stopped at the drycleaner's on Porter Avenue. Hanging my dry cleaning on the inside of the back door, I heard the squeal of a bad transmission and looked up to see Jimmie Lee's pickup passing. He stopped at the corner, staring straight ahead, pensive. He held a tight grip on the steering wheel, leaning heavily into it. The intersection cleared and he turned right onto General Pershing, heading south toward East Beach.

On my ride home, I pictured myself chasing Jimmie Lee's pickup, the way he'd chased me. Only he'd stop with his front bumper near a tree and I'd block him from behind with my car and call Bombardier. The police chief would arrive and open the passenger side door of Jimmie Lee's truck saying something like he did when we found Buffy. *Well, what do we have here?* Then with a gloved hand, he'd pick up the murder weapon with its silencer from the passenger seat of Jimmie Lee's pickup.

In my daydream, Jimmie Lee had accomplished his mission to find the gun. He'd do with it whatever Mrs. Briscoe wanted done—use it against her husband, bury it, or plant it on someone else so they'd be charged with the murder. Thanks to me, Jimmie Lee's success would be short-lived and he'd have to tell Bombardier where he got the gun. The case would be solved.

My triumphant image ended when I walked into the house from the garage. Dan was letting Buffy in the backdoor. I followed him into the bedroom, carrying the dry cleaning and telling him about the severance packages for the New Orleans employees and for Bert. I hung the dry cleaning in the closet and continued talking while we changed clothes.

I took a breath. "And I didn't tell you everything that happened when I followed Jimmie Lee." I continued to talk incessantly, jumping all over the place, switching between work issues and Jimmie Lee. Dan didn't say a word. "And then I saw Jimmie Lee again. Tonight at the cleaners—"

"Whoa," he said. "Enough. This is interesting but you haven't shut-up since you walked through the door."

"I'm sorry. Today's been one surprise after another."

"Sounds like it. I want to hear the rest, but take a breather."

I nodded.

"And can I ask you a favor?"

"Yeah, sure. What?"

"When you're through, will you get off the subject for the rest of the evening? I mean, no more pieces that pop into your mind. No interjecting new thoughts or theories."

"Sure," I said, "but will you agree to stay up and watch the ten o'clock news? I'd hate for you to be asleep when I'm watching Keith Briscoe being hauled away in handcuffs."

"Okay. You've got a deal."

I went over the events of the day with a reasonable amount of detail. Dan listened and asked a few questions. When I finished talking, as promised, I dropped the subject and we relaxed with a pay-per-view movie. Tucking my thoughts away was another matter. They continued pushing to the surface.

The ten o'clock news came and went with nothing tied to Keith Briscoe.

"Darn," I said. "Maybe we'll hear something tomorrow."

Then, during the weather report, the anchorman broke in. "This just in. We received a report from the Ocean Springs police department—"

"Aha. Dan, this may be it."

"The body of a possible homicide victim was found this evening near the shallow gulf waters south of the Gulf Coast Research Laboratory in Ocean Springs," the anchorman continued. "The medical examiner has not yet determined cause of death. Anyone who may have been in the area and witnessed anything out of the ordinary, please contact the Ocean Springs police department. The name of the deceased is being withheld pending notification of next of kin."

"Well," said Dan, "unless Keith Briscoe is a serial killer, that didn't sound like news about him."

"Geez," I said, "that's close to home. I wonder—"

"Maybe it's a suicide," Dan said. "Let's go to bed. I'm tired."

"How tired?" I asked.

"It depends. Might there be a suggestion in your question?"

"There might," I said.

"Then I propose we slip into bed quietly while Miss Buffy is conked out on the kitchen floor."

The dog didn't miss us until the middle of the night when she jumped into bed, found a spot to settle in at its foot, and fell asleep.

CHAPTER 38

The tapping sounds of a slow, steady rain woke me at five the next morning after I'd tossed and turned, flipping my pillow over and searching for that one soft spot to sink my head and fall back to sleep. When the clock rolled to seven, I gave up, crawled out of bed, and pulled open the curtains. The maple in the front yard, now a soggy plum-black, dripped on the grass at eight-second intervals. When a pink tinge of dawn fell like fairy dust, I thought this might pass for a Thomas Kinkade painting.

An hour later, I tramped half-heartedly into my office, procrastination on my tail. I dropped my purse under my desk and lifted a report from the top of the stack of file trays. Report in hand, I wandered in and through the plant, finding Andy by the time clock, wrapping up a conversation with Bert.

"Hi, there," he said. "What's up?"

I handed him the papers. "These figures are wrong."

Bert nodded a greeting then left.

Andy took the report and turned for his office. "Come with me."

Inside, I took a seat as he descended into his swivel chair. "Um, let's see," he said, rifling through papers in his in-box. "Aah. Here it is." He nabbed a sheet of paper and spun around to a computer table where he tapped keys on a calculator. "You're right." He twirled back, scribbled a number on a yellow sticky, and handed it to me. "I plugged in one too many numbers. Glad you caught it before Corporate did. I try to stay on their good side these days."

"Okay, Andy. What's that mean?"

His eyes shimmied to one side than another, verifying our privacy. "George said he told you about the reorganization."

I released a heavy sigh. "I'm glad to have someone to share the burden with. Poor Bert."

"He'll be devastated," Andy said, making a shuddering motion. "It's too horrible. I try not to think about it." And he meant what he said, because the next thing he did was lob one foot up onto his desk and smile. "I'm coming out of this pretty good," he said. "No changes for me. I'd feel guilty if I weren't so relieved."

"Andy, it's too soon to be relieved. I've been through this before and sometimes there's a second restructure."

"Dang."

I tossed him a teasing grin and got up to leave. "Sorry."

Millie was waiting outside my office and began talking as she followed me inside. "I just heard from Lidia."

"Something else has happened?" I sat at my desk while she remained standing.

"Definitely. But we don't know what." She opened her palms. "Lidia received a Federal Express package for the chief yesterday. Nothing unusual. She held onto it until he'd settled in his office later that afternoon. She set the parcel on his desk and heard him tearing into it on her way out, and then he laughed, loud."

I waited as Millie caught her breath.

"She had no idea why, but said he sounded like someone who'd won the lottery. He whizzed past her, package in hand and said he was going to Biloxi. That he knows a judge there who'll grant him court orders. Apparently with whatever he received, she'll have no choice."

"He must've received some sort of evidence."

"That's what we're thinking. She called after him, asking why he'd go to a Biloxi judge over an Ocean Springs matter. Lidia said he cackled in that Gene Hackman way of his and said it wasn't any more."

"I wonder—what on earth?"

"Judy, I've got to get back. But trust me, if I hear anything, you will, too."

"Okay. Thanks. See ya."

She vanished almost as quickly as she'd appeared. I stared outside my office, rehashing the news Millie had brought. I'd been hit by surprises since yesterday, but this new one included a puzzle. What could've been in the Fed Ex package to persuade a Biloxi judge to issue a court order to fingerprint Briscoe? And what happened last week to reignite Bombardier's obsession with the twenty-five-year-old Wade murders. To quote Winston Churchill, this was indeed "a riddle wrapped in a mystery, inside an enigma."

Having delayed the inevitable, I returned to my paperwork and unanswered emails.

Late that afternoon, I took another break from the work grind and went into the plant. Millie stood beside a printing machine, flipping through notebook pages. I moved off the walkway and, with a tap to her arm, nudged her to the nearest aisle. "Any more news from Lidia?"

"Yes, but not about the Fed Ex package. Her attempt to broach that subject got her nothing but a cocky smirk. The chief told her he got his court order yesterday, took it straight to Mr. Briscoe's place, and got his prints."

"This must've happened shortly after I talked to him about following Jimmie Lee. He was in the office then."

We stopped talking when Jena Doggett meandered down the aisle. She flung us an I-caught-you-gossiping stare and continued past nonchalantly, her ponytail swinging wide. I bent close to Millie's ear. "I'd love to find out about the mystery in that Fed Ex package."

"No kidding," Millie said. "Hey, did you see the morning paper—the homicide in Ocean Springs?"

"I heard about it on TV last night."

"As soon as I read about it, I said to Red—" One of the folding machines sputtered loudly to a stop. "Sorry. Got to go," she said.

eɔeↄ

I entered my kitchen, arms full of Salvetti Brothers take-out, and placed the bags on the table. "Wanta eat now or wait?" I hollered to Dan in the family room.

He put down the newspaper as Buffy rose from her place at his feet. "Sure. Why mess with reheating."

I scattered plates, silverware, and glasses in a hap-hazard fashion before opening a bottle of merlot. Dan turned the TV toward the kitchen and raised the volume. The national news ended and the local news began. He took a seat at the table. In sync, Buffy settled at his feet.

"Maybe tonight we'll hear something about Keith," I said, pouring the wine.

"Shoosh. I want to hear this."

I took a seat as WLOX zoomed in on its anchorman.

"Yesterday evening, two joggers found the body of a homicide victim lying in the shallow gulf waters south of the Gulf Coast Research Laboratory's parking lot. He's been iden-tified as James Lee Albright, a resident of Ocean Springs. Al-bright was shot twice in the chest. Time of death is uncon-firmed. The police currently have no leads. They ask that any-one who heard or saw anything in connection with this crime call them immediately." The phone number appeared large on the screen.

Dan put his fork down and stared at me with an e-gads expression.

"Jimmie Lee Albright?" I said. "Murdered?"

"I'll be damn," Dan said.

"Poor kid. Yesterday evening he was headed for East Beach."

"And the news just said he was killed on the adjacent property. Judy, this happened the same day you said he was running around questioning people and driving to Mrs. Bris-coe's."

"I'd say there are a number of coincidences here. Too many." I shook my head then shook it again. "He didn't de-serve this."

As much of a snitch as he was, I still felt he was a help-less victim to Mrs. Briscoe's cruelty. I reached for the handset on the wall, pummeling in the numbers still displayed at the bottom of the TV screen.

"You're calling the police?"

"Absolutely." When a man answered, I said, "Is your chief there?"

"Yes, he's here. Can I say who's calling?"

"It's Judy Kenagy." Placed on hold, I took a bite of lasa-gna then another one.

"I'll transfer you now," the man said.

Bombardier came on the line, chortling in a slow, *ho-ho* manner. "So, Judy, once again you're connected to a local homicide victim."

"He wanted that gun-make for a reason. I'd say he found the gun and that got him killed."

"Possibly," he said, "but a little early to speculate."

I tightened my grip on the phone. "I saw him again, short-ly after five yesterday. He was in his truck heading in the di-rection of East Beach. He was in a real lather—you know?—all worked up."

"Are you sure of the time?"

"Yes. Maybe five or ten minutes after. I was leaving the dry cleaners on Porter Avenue when he drove past in the same pickup I described to you earlier. He stopped at the intersec-tion and then hooked a turn south onto General Pershing."

"Did you get a receipt from the cleaners?"

"Yes, it's still in the closet with the clothes."

"Fax me a copy," he said. "Do you recall what he wore?"

"A dark colored jacket—lightweight, I think. That's all I remember, other than the intensity in his demeanor."

✂✂✂

The next morning, George and I gave severance packages to the general manager and the HR manager in New Orleans. They took the news fairly well, but I knew the hardest one was yet to come.

I learned from Millie, via Lidia Trash, that the police had picked up Dixie and returned him to the Jackson County jail.

"How did they find him?" I asked.

"Someone called in an anonymous tip, placing him at a second cousin's home in New Orleans' Lower Ninth Ward. That's about all that will be in the news. The police took the tip and acted on it."

Lidia had also told her Valerie Kelm-Briscoe identified Jimmie Lee's body. The police had his driver's license and a Kelm work badge. They'd called Kelm Machinery the morning after and learned he had no next of kin.

That afternoon, as we were giving Bert his severance package, Andy stepped in and told us he'd gotten Bert an interview at a Rockhold plant in St. Louis. "They're in a hurry, too," Andy said. "They want you there Thursday afternoon."

"Next Thursday?" Bert asked.

"No, tomorrow."

Bert jumped to his feet. "The plane ticket will c—cost more than—"

Andy smiled. "Don't worry. They'll pick up the tab. I already asked."

☙❧

On Friday afternoon, I rang Andy's extension. When he didn't answer, I went to look for him. I was making my way to his office when I saw him come out of the cutting department.

He stopped, folded his arms, and beamed.

"What happened?" I asked.

"Your timing is perfect. I just got off my cell with Bert."

"And?"

"He got the call from St. Louis. Apparently, his interview went well. They offered him the job. He'll stay here a few more days and then transfer."

I smiled back at him. "Andy, thank you for checking the company website. There's been no supervisor jobs listed on it for over six months. Who would've thought?"

"Not me. I was so surprised to see the posting I made up

my mind that this was a blatant twist of fate. Bert told me he convinced his wife about the transfer rather easily, too, crediting her change in attitude to the family counseling Dottie got them into. I asked him if she'd dump her parents. You know how Bert is. He gasped into the phone at the thought I'd say such a thing then laughed, telling me he didn't expect her to go that far. Says that, thanks to Dottie, her parents had already taken a backseat to him. He's calling Dottie now to tell her all about it."

"Are you leaving early?" I asked.

"You bet. I'm out of here in two minutes and won't be back until after Fat Tuesday." He crouched down and began to snap his fingers, dancing to an imaginary beat. "Come with me while I close up shop."

"Any issues I should know of while you're off?" I asked as I walked with him.

None," he said, entering his office. "Any questions for me?"

He shut down his computer, piled papers into neat stacks, and slipped file folders into a slot in his lower desk drawer.

"Not about work. Wondered if you thought there was a chance Bombardier would ask the Jackson County sheriff for a little help now that he has the Albright murder case, too."

Andy chuckled and started for the door. "Oh girl," he said, stopping at the threshold, giving his office a final once over. "There's no way he'd let Sheriff Ralph into this mess, 'cept maybe to blame it on him."

I followed him out. He locked his door and, to double-check, jiggled the handle. We strode together down the hall toward the back of the plant.

I was making the turn for the corridor to the front offices as Andy opened the back exit. "Have a great time, and be careful," I said.

"Judy?"

I stopped and turned. A half-minute passed before his words rolled out. "What would you say if I told you I was gay?"

Not having seen this coming, I was stunned into silence.

My face smarted from the spontaneous grin. "Andy, you are unrelenting in your surprises."

"I just want—"

"I know," I said, finishing his sentence for him. "You just want your friends to know who you really are. Have you told anyone else?"

For the first time, I saw Andy as the youth he really was.

His face beamed. "Yeah. In the past week, I've told a lot of people, and you know what? It felt good. I mean, I thought this would be a big deal with them and it wasn't. I mean, their responses surprised me. I wasn't as sure about you—your being a little older and all."

I laughed quietly. "Ha, Andy. Thanks for the tact but I'm not a little older. I'm a lot older." Still chuckling, I gave him a pat on the back then rested my hands below my collarbone. "Andy Holman, I love you. I absolutely do. Thanks for including me in…in what I think is called your 'coming-out.'" I dropped my hands. "Way to go, Andy. I'll see you on Wednesday. Got to finish my KPI so I can get out of here, too."

I went down the hall toward the plant but hadn't gotten far when I heard light footsteps pick up their pace behind me. Before I could turn, Andy grabbed me, twirled me in a half-circle, and hugged me hard. In just as swift a motion, he rotated around on one foot and skipped down the hall and out the door. I stood there a moment, staring after him, then weaved my way to the front offices, thinking, *I'll be damned. I should've known.*

A half hour later, I'd completed my KPI and typed my usual email message to the management team. *HR portion of Key Performance Indicators complete.* I made a quick, hard click on the send button, got to my feet and started for the restroom. Most of the office staff had already left for the weekend.

Vicky Coupe dashed out of the women's restroom, her hair hastily pulled up on top so that long strands flew up and out as she made a sharp turn toward the factory floor. She'd yanked the restroom door open so hard that, when I got there, I stepped in before it had closed. *Hmmm. Probably left her machine running unattended again.*

I came out of the stall as Millie walked in.

"I thought you'd be gone by now," she said. "Did you get George's email saying we could leave early?"

I washed my hands. "Yes, but I didn't want all this work hanging over me all weekend. I'm leaving soon. Why are you still here? It's almost four-thirty."

"My car's in the shop and the earliest Red could pick me up was a quarter to five." She lowered her voice. "Hey, I'm glad you're here, I have some—" She stooped, bending her head down to peek under the stalls, the tips of her hair grazing the floor. As quick as she'd dropped, she stood erect, tossing the thick head of hair back out of her face. "Some really incredible information."

"Has Andy talked to you?"

"No. Does he know something?"

"No. Not really," I said.

"You've got to promise to act surprised when you hear the official news."

"I promise."

"Lidia called. The police are gonna arrest Keith Briscoe."

I clapped my hands then held them together. "The fingerprint results came back?"

"Uh-huh. A little while ago. Lidia says his prints match others found all over Alma's house. Get this." Millie's voice became a whisper. "They were on her bedposts, too."

"Aha. His story of returning the driver's license and credit card is out the window."

Millie's head bobbled.

I lowered mine, garnering a thought. "He really is the secret friend who loaned her the gun."

"Has to be," she said.

"Hmmm. Incriminating, but still circumstantial. So, what's the motive? To me, the only one that makes sense is if Alma had threatened to go to his wife."

Millie waved the idea away. "No. Alma would never threaten anyone. It's simply not in her nature." Except for Dixie, Millie's read on employees had never been wrong. She swiveled her head, surveying the empty restroom. "Oh, I plumb forgot. The gun that killed Jimmie Lee is the same one that killed Alma."

"Huh? Millie, how could you forget something like that?"

"I don't know. It's all gotten so big. Lidia saw the report. Shell casings at the scene indicated the gun was another .38 semi-automatic. Since that's the same make of gun used in the last murder around here, I guess they made a comparison. The police now think Mr. Briscoe is behind both murders. They won't be arresting him until after Mardi Gras so as not to mess up the big celebration. I think that was real nice of them."

"Yeah." I forced myself not to roll my eyes. It seemed ridiculous to allow a murderer loose on the streets during the biggest party this side of the Mason-Dixon line. "But what possible reason could Keith Briscoe have to kill Jimmie Lee?"

She bit down on one side of her lip. "Who knows? But something tells me we'll find out soon. Remember, don't give Lidia away. This is huge."

"Don't worry." I fluttered my hand, dismissing the subject. "I'd love to see the look on Mrs.—on Val-*er*-ie's face when Keith is arrested. Are you taking Monday off?"

"Nah, I'm covering for Andy. I'm sure he's already whooping it up."

"See you Monday," I said.

Millie nodded. "Yes. Boy howdy, we've got ourselves some interesting times ahead."

I whisked into my office and seized my purse then locked up and made a beeline for my car. When I got there, I froze. Something had been bumping up against my mind during my conversation with Millie. I stood next to the car, stock-still, letting Millie's words wash over me.

Now that the police know that a single gun was used in both deaths, won't that change the whole scenario? I held that thought as I climbed into the car and started for home.

What could Jimmie Lee have discovered that would jeopardize Keith Briscoe? Jimmie Lee had left Alma's neighbor's home and the *Sun Herald* building with no more information than the police already had. Could he have found the gun? If so, would that have made much difference?

I hit traffic on Highway 90 and put my thoughts on hold, slowing to negotiate my situation on the road. As soon as my pace was in line with other cars, my mind went back to swinging in every direction.

Keith knew of Jena and Bert's allegation that Alma had a married lover who loaned Alma a gun. He also knew Bert had seen him leaving Alma's home. Keith had to have known all along that if the police got his fingerprints, he'd be arrested whether the weapon had been found or not. Giving up his prints would be his issue, not Jimmie Lee.

A honking horn returned me to reality. I glanced at the green arrow and veered left onto Washington Avenue, but no sooner had I made the bend than lights began flashing at the railroad crossing. I gave my mind a rest while the train roared by, my car vibrating from the metal weight of the train's wheels on the tracks.

A few more turns then another mile or so and I'd be home. I attempted to change my disposition to nonchalance, but my mind jolted back into overdrive.

With no hard evidence on Lester and his lack of prints at the crime scene, he'd been put on the back burner of suspicion, along with Dixie and Bert. The surfacing of Keith worked to good advantage for the other suspects. Keith was in the limelight as the secret friend and prime suspect in Alma's case, not a good time to kill someone.

So, did Keith kill Alma and not Jimmie Lee? Alma should never have been a risk to Briscoe. Millie said Alma would never threaten anyone and no one knew Alma better than Millie. A lover's quarrel resulting in an accidental shooting? I don't think so.

And Lester had reported that the friend who loaned her the gun didn't know how to use one.

A bulb flashed on inside my brain and every piece of information came together as if I were sitting in my office with it on my desk, spread out before me. If Keith Briscoe didn't kill Jimmie Lee, he didn't kill Alma either. Someone else was toting that gun around, someone not currently under public scrutiny.

They found Jimmie Lee's body on East Beach where he kept his getaway boat. He'd probably gone there to run, but from whom?

I knew I'd missed my turn when I whizzed past the big oak tree in front of Georgina's Hobby Shop. Going home was no longer an option. The boat swirled around in my head and I knew it would tell me something.

I took a deep breath and headed for the one place I might find new evidence. I had to hurry. It would soon be dark.

CHAPTER 39

I drove fast, my brain racing. Bombardier suspected Keith Briscoe of Alma's murder, which once made sense. Now, he suspected him of both murders and nothing made sense. Andy claimed Bombardier was a great detective when he worked with him at the City of Biloxi. I had watched him take painstaking steps not to rush to judgment with Dixie Ledet. He took the same cautionary approach with Bert when he became a suspect.

I eased in beside the trash barrel and climbed out of my car. A gull walked proudly over the boat launch, but otherwise the beach was vacant. A single vehicle in the Gulf Coast Research Laboratory parking lot was leaving. I pitched my purse into the trunk and shoved my keys into a pants pocket.

Staring at the copse of maples and underbrush, I thought of the nutria rat and looked behind me. The sun was setting and my compulsion to see the boat deflated like a tire quickly going flat. Jimmie Lee hadn't made it easy to get to his boat.

But he'd been killed close by. I looked passed the maples and over the fence. Remnants of bright yellow crime scene tape marked the spot. I hustled through the gates, and cut south over nearly barren ground peppered with bushes, weeds, and one short, sickly palm tree.

Closer in, I could see the yellow tape was broken or missing in places, but still cordoning off a circular area of dirt and mud, about twelve feet in diameter. The tape had been stapled to stakes pounded into the ground, but many of them had fallen over. This crime scene had already been worked. Two dirty latex gloves and a staple gun had been left outside the perimeter, and multiple footprints marred the mud. The absence of a patrol officer protecting the scene implied the clean-up crew was on their way.

Inside the partially taped-off area, someone had outlined where Jimmie Lee's body had been. Instead of the typical chalk line, plastic pegs were pressed into the mud about six inches apart, marking where the body had fallen.

I stepped high over the tape and into the mud, grateful I'd worn jeans and flat shoes for that dress-down Friday. Trees towered behind me, the interminable water before me. I caught a whiff of mildew.

I was no sooner inside than a rustling sound came from the tangle of maples and I twisted around. The noise disappeared and I turned back, catching a glitter in the mud. It came from the waterline where the soft waves of the Mississippi Sound licked against the cryptic outline of the corpse.

That noise again.

I spun around to the whooshing sounds in the maples, my heart palpitating, but I still didn't see anything. When I turned back, the glitter had disappeared. I stooped. I was in a race with the sun, not to mention wanting to be long gone before the clean-up crew appeared. With one hand, I frantically ran my fingers through the muck. Then a final spray of sunlight illuminated the spot and the sparkle reappeared. This time, I kept my eyes fixed on it, bending, reaching, touching. Gently, I lifted a metal object, close to an inch long and about half that in width. Heavy for its size.

Twilight had deepened into dusk. I stood up and whirled round to the same rustling noise, but this time a crackling blast followed. A gun? All I knew was the sound rang through the stillness like the gong of an immense bell.

I pocketed the object and, with a surge of strength, loped through the crime scene tape. Stakes still bound to the yellow tape flew in every direction. With arms swinging wide and legs stretched for double strides that belied my age, I scrambled back toward the road.

I was closing in on my car when the second blast sounded, followed by a commotion in the trees. I threw myself down, rolled over to the car, coming up crouched at its side, and rounding the vehicle to the back bumper. I remained kneeling, my heart throbbing in strokes that thumped into my fingertips.

A bunch of boys tumbled out of the maples and into a sprint up Halstead Road, giggling and guffawing. One boy carried what appeared to be a rifle. Probably a BB gun. One of them yelled, "We didn't kill him. Don't come after us." The words sent them into further gales of laughter.

I took a gulp of air and exhaled, relief seeping through my raw nerves. I got to my feet, dusted my hands and pants then looked north on Halstead Road where the little brats had disappeared. The clean-up truck could show at any time, or the police. I opened the trunk to retrieve a towel I kept for Buffy and put it to good use wiping mud off various parts of my body and the soles of my shoes. Then I snatched up my purse and drove north.

I'd come hoping that Jimmie Lee's rowboat would offer up a clue. The mystery of the little dinghy would have to wait another day. But I had something else, something that had been at the crime scene.

The first exit took me into a motor court and I parked in a place screened by bushes of oleander. I reached for the thing in my pocket. Not easy while sitting seat-belted and in tight jeans. I tried until I felt it. Definitely something that had belonged to someone. When I couldn't get it out while sitting, I took this as a sign to wait and share the unveiling with my husband.

I pulled out my cell and called Dan.

"Where are you?" he asked. "I've been calling."

"I'm close to East Beach," I said. "I found something left at Jimmie Lee's crime scene."

"Judy, what in the hell?"

"Don't worry. The police were through with it."

"Through with what?"

"Never mind. Will you meet me for dinner? I've got lots to tell you."

Anthony's Under the Oaks was on the bayou next to Aunt Jenny's famous catfish restaurant. In the front, a colossal ancient oak hovered over the entrance, its branches stretching eerily out as if reaching for something. Oak trees with Spanish moss, cascading from branches cloaked the two sides of the building. The back dock was open to the water.

Dan sat at the tiny bar. I hopped up onto a stool beside him and he ordered two Manhattan-rocks.

"Well?"

"I don't know where to begin," I said, giving him a one-shoulder shrug. "Right before leaving work, Millie told me that the police were planning to arrest Keith Briscoe on Wednesday, after Mardi Gras. They found out Jimmie Lee was gunned down with the same weapon used on Alma, and believe Keith killed them both." I stopped talking while the bartender brought our drinks, waiting until he'd shifted out of hearing range again. "Still digesting Millie's words on my way to the car, the fist of reality socked me." I took a breath.

"And that reality was?"

"The news of the single gun. Keith Briscoe wouldn't have killed Jimmie Lee." I listed all the reasons I'd come up with as to why it was ridiculous to think he did. "Then it all hit me as I was driving home. Whoever killed Jimmie Lee had to have murdered Alma. Someone else had that gun. I remembered Jimmie Lee's intense demeanor before he turned onto General Pershing that final evening. He was going to East Beach, and a trip to East Beach meant a visit to his boat. That's when I turned and headed there, believing the boat would offer up a clue."

I knew I was talking too fast, missing and mixing words. I took another breath and slowed down. "Dusk was minutes away and—sheesh—the idea of digging around in that scrub-brush turned my stomach. So I went on to what was left of the crime scene."

Dan layered the bar check with bills. "Let's get something to eat. We can talk easier at a table."

He was right. Anthony's bar was too small and people kept coming in. "Okay," I said. "Mind getting us a table and taking our drinks over? I'm going to the restroom."

I found Dan at a table next to a windowed wall overlooking the river to the Back Bay. I pulled up a seat and took hold of my drink. "I found something at the crime scene. Maybe nothing." I let go of the drink and went for my front pants pocket. "A gunshot scared me—turned out to be some boys, about ten to twelve in age—" I reached deep into my pocket, pulling out the chunk. "One of the boys was carrying what I think was a BB gun. I thought I heard real gun shots, but in hindsight—The boys must've been at the crime scene and hid when they heard me drive up."

I laid a silver-plated piece on the white linen tablecloth and sat back. "What do you make of this?"

Dan stared curiously. He furrowed his brow then lifted the item off the table and into his palm. "Damn. It's got a bolt molded into it."

I snatched it out of his hand and held the piece close to my face, feeling my mouth falling open. "Look," I said, "it's—it's—I can't believe—how?"

"Judy, is this one of Valerie Kelm-Briscoe's charms? The ones you described to me ad nauseam."

I folded my fingers around the chunk of metal and shut my eyes. I fell against the back of my chair then looked at it again. "Yes. Yes, that's exactly what it is. Exactly."

CHAPTER 40

M s. Kenagy, they may fire me. I didn't make the costly mistake they blamed on me today, but this time I have no proof. Please remind them of how many times they've accused me when it wasn't true. Surely, they can give me the benefit of the doubt this one time. Please put this in my personnel file." ~ Jolene Cromwell, an hour before her termination

⁓⁓⁓

The back and west walls of Anthony's Under the Oaks offered customers a broad vista, the top half of each wall nothing but windows.

On this night, visibility had been limited to a web of rolling black shadows, interrupted from time to time when clouds parted and the full moon peeked through, its luminous trail reflecting off murky water. I wanted to tell Bombardier what I'd found, but Dan reminded me that the last time I'd phoned him while having dinner, my food had gotten cold.

"This time we're paying a pretty penny for the meal," he said.

Over veal Oscar and merlot, I ticked through the chronology of events—backing out of going in to see the boat, finding the charm, and being frightened by the little brats with the BB gun.

"Will you go with me in the morning when I dig into the clearing where the rowboat is?"

"Of course."

I ran through the part about Keith Briscoe's prints in Alma's bedroom. "The affair was real, but I still don't understand why that ballistics report caused the police to think Keith Briscoe committed both murders. The gun link is the very reason to turn all suspicion away from him."

"The police are notorious for homing in on a person or persons of interest," Dan said. "They think Briscoe's their killer and will likely stick to their premise."

A history of mishandled murder cases flicked through my mind. "I can't imagine Bombardier having anywhere near that kind of tunnel vision, but Millie says he plans to arrest Keith right after Fat Tuesday."

Dan shoved his plate to the side. "Your discovery's going to prove Valerie Briscoe killed them both."

I shook my head. "I can't see her hurting Jimmie Lee. He was as loyal as Miss Buffy."

"If she's the evil witch you claim she is, someone like that kid didn't matter. She killed Alma to get rid of her husband's mistress. If Jimmie Lee found the gun—"

I shook my head again. "Something's not right." I stared at the tablecloth and my mind went blank. "But the charm puts her at the crime scene."

"More than coincidence," Dan said.

I gazed out into the black, catching the flicker of a distant ferry light.

☙❧

At nine the next morning, I called the police station, finding Bombardier there. "I have something I want to show you. I'm coming down."

"Evidence?"

"Yes. I'm bringing Dan. We have a quick stop to make first."

"I'll be here," he said before clicking off.

At East Beach, Dan stooped and pulled back shrubbery while I pushed through to the clearing. The little boat was still there. "Well?" Dan said as I stepped out, sweeping weeds from my hair and dusting my hands.

"The dinghy's there, equipped to leave. All the necessary provisions—bottled water, flashlight, lunch pail, shovel."

"Looks like he planned to bury the gun on the little island," Dan said.

"Uh-huh. Poor kid, trying to be her loyal hero and she killed him with the gun he planned to hide for her."

At the police station, a stalwart woman at the front desk greeted us.

"We're here to see Chief Bombardier," I said. "I'm Judy Kenagy and this is my husband, Dan."

She gave us the once-over with mean, beady eyes then led us through the squad room, her cinder block legs pounding on faded linoleum floors. A handful of people worked at desks. Two police officers in a heated discussion with a great-granddaddy of a man paused to watch us pass.

The woman took us into a pictureless room with high pebbled windows and directed us to a rectangular table. She offered us coffee as we took our seats.

Bombardier came in accompanied by the young blond who'd secured Alma's crime scene and had also been with Lieutenant Leblanc the day they picked up Dixie. He introduced him to us.

"I've met Sergeant Gentry before," I said.

Our coffee arrived as Sergeant Gentry was placing a tape recorder on the table. They both sat down across from us. Bombardier began, dictating names, dates, and subject into the cassette then said, "Go ahead, Judy."

"I found something inside the broken tapes where the crime scene had been. And this morning we checked out the boat Jimmie Lee kept—"

"Whoa. Crime scene? Boat?" Bombardier arched a brow and darted a sideways glance at the young officer. "And what, pray tell, were ya doing there?"

I ignored his question, took a sip of coffee, and shared

what I knew about Jimmie Lee's boat. I went over yesterday's events, wrapping up my report with the morning's find of the well-stocked rowboat. "And here's what I found inside your taped-off area," I said, placing the charm before him. "This belongs on a bracelet owned by Valerie Kelm-Briscoe."

His eyes widened as he lifted the silver nugget, rolling it around like a jeweler examining a stone. "It doesn't look like a charm."

"None of hers do. They all have different micro hardware parts embedded inside, like this bolt. Each time her father invented a new part, he saved the first ones off the production line to make jewelry pieces for his family."

Bombardier leaned forward. "Why did you go there?"

"The coincidence of Jimmie Lee being killed so close to his hidden rowboat. I couldn't get it out of my head, so I went to check it out. Was the dinghy still there? Cleaned up? Moved? But when I arrived, dark was settling and I remembered the nutria rat, so I took a detour."

"Hmmph. To our crime scene," he sniped.

"To your *old* crime scene," I said. "You'd finished with it."

He gave me a look. "Go on."

"A glitter appeared next to one of the plastic pegs used to outline Jimmie Lee's body. Where his head had been. That's where I found the charm."

Bombardier clicked off the recorder and cut a look at the sergeant. "I told Kevin and Johnnie to preserve that scene and get back there at low tide. Call the lazy bastards and tell them to report to work."

"Kevin is in Pascagoula at a family reunion," the young officer said.

"Do I care?" he said. "Pascagoula is a thirty-minute drive. Kevin should've handled this right to begin with. How's it going to look when the press starts blabbering about some woman finding a major piece of evidence at our crime scene?" Bombardier hurled me a penitent glance and his cheeks flushed. "Uh, um, not that we don't appreciate what you've done here, Judy. This evidence could prove crucial."

"I'll phone them," Sergeant Gentry said, getting to his feet.

"Tell one of them to pick up Valerie Kelm-Briscoe and bring her in for questioning," the chief called after him. "Get the address from Mavis."

Mavis must've been Lidia's weekend replacement.

"Yes, sir," the sergeant shouted back from outside the door.

Bombardier pushed on the recorder's off-button a second time and looked at me with a grin. "Now, how would you like to hang around and watch Valerie Briscoe squirm?"

I didn't answer.

"Well, either way, I need you here. She's going to tell me it's not hers. You can corroborate that it is." He put his elbows on the table and smiled like the *Cheshire Cat*.

Dan rose. "Call me when you're done and I'll pick you up."

"All right," I said reluctantly and watched him leave.

Bombardier's smile waned and he glimpsed from left to right. "I can say—" He pressed his lips together tightly and I figured he was dying to share something. "Oh, why not tell ya?" he said. "Hell. You brought me this evidence. I owe ya."

I waited.

"I'd known all along the gun used to kill the Wades and Guerra was a .38-caliber automatic pistol, fairly common in these parts." He massaged his hairless chin. "But then enters Briscoe, the most-likely secret friend, the sought-after person who loaned Guerra the gun and I'm thinking…hmmm. A .38 automatic used on Guerra. A .38 automatic used on the Wades. Both with a silencer."

"But Keith was too young then," I said. "He wouldn't have known either the Kelms or the Wades at the time."

"Yes, but he had a strong connection to the Kelms when Guerra was killed. His having access to the missing pistol used on the Wades was more than coincidence. I ordered a ballistics test comparing the weapon used in the Guerra case with the Wades'."

"I assume they matched."

Bombardier leaned back and brandished a grin. "Yes. The information my father left linking the Kelms to the Wade murders wasn't enough to get a court order to fingerprint Briscoe, but with the matching ballistics comparison, I had more than enough."

Well, that solved the riddle of the Fed Ex package, I thought.

"We took the court order to Briscoe the same day and got his prints. They matched those found all over Guerra's home."

"So," I said, "the gun that killed the Wades resurfaced in the hands of son-in-law Briscoe who used it to kill Alma? This was your assessment before I brought in the charm. Correct?"

"No, but that had been my assessment at one time. Then everything changed."

"Huh?"

"I figured if we matched Briscoe's prints with those in her home, we had him cut an' dried. Since the .38 was also used in the Wade murders, I had high hopes Briscoe would lead me to the gun and I'd pin those old murders on the Kelms. Almost as soon as we'd matched Briscoe's prints at Guerra's home, the ballistics report came back on Albright, a murder considered unrelated, yet all deaths were by the same gun. And reasons to suspect Briscoe evaporated."

I half-choked on my coffee. This was at odds with what Lidia had told Millie. I almost blurted out, "But I thought you were arresting Keith for both murders!" I managed to hold my tongue. I needed to take care not to give Millie's friend away.

Bombardier beamed and a twinkle in his eye suggested I was about to hear things even Lidia didn't know. I could tell he took pleasure in laying out his case. "I knew then Briscoe didn't kill Guerra, but my staff was pushing for an arrest. I needed to buy time. His role as King of the Krewe of Neptune in the parade on Fat Tuesday helped me convince them to wait until after Mardi Gras."

I sat there frozen, wishing Dan had stayed. Everything was coming together.

"Already a suspect, what motive did Briscoe have to kill Albright? Judy, from what Guerra's neighbor shared with you,

Albright had no more information than we did. And Briscoe knew what we had on him. When you learned his purpose at the *Sun Herald* office, we knew he'd only gotten what was already public knowledge—the gun type."

I wanted to scream out that I'd already come up with the same premise. Unfortunately, the gratification of doing so would alert him that someone on his staff had leaked the Alma and Jimmie Lee gun link. So, I said nothing.

"If Briscoe had killed Guerra, he'd never have used the same gun again. He was well aware we were watching him and frightened by the information we already had. He knew the affair would come out with the fingerprints, which would lead to his being charged with murder, gun or no gun. Briscoe had no reason to kill Albright." Bombardier took a breath. "I thought about the possibility of Briscoe killing Guerra and not Albright, but that sounded way-way off. Someone else used that gun. Phfft. Yeah, the killer had to be someone who felt invincible, immune from suspicion."

I tilted my Styrofoam cup and finished my cold coffee in one long swallow. "Mrs. Briscoe, I presume."

"She's not who I had in mind, but now with this new evidence you've brought—"

Mavis marched briskly into the room. "You have a phone call, Chief. Will you take it now?"

"Yes, but not here. Tell them to hold on." Bombardier left, leaving a vacuum with his unfinished comment.

He considered someone other than Keith Briscoe, but not Mrs. Briscoe? Who would've felt invincible? Mrs. Briscoe should have felt vulnerable being the wife, with the cliché jealous-wife motive.

Possibilities nagged at my brain. Lester Robichaux? With his airtight alibi gone, he had no way to verify where he was when Alma was killed, but Bombardier still could not prove anything. Had he found something I didn't know about? Dixie or Bert? Both were suspects, lame ones now, but not if new evidence surfaced.

Dixie was still at-large when Jimmie Lee was killed.

Hmm, I thought. Jimmie Lee said he didn't know Dixie,

but Jimmie Lee had been known to lie. Paul Kelm, Junior? He was old enough to kill the Wades when he mysteriously disappeared. Maybe there was a back story I wasn't aware of. He could've slipped back to the Gulf Coast. He was the only one I could think of who would've felt invincible. But did he even know Alma and Jimmie Lee, and what would be his motive?

I tossed my hands out, palms up, and heaved a heavy sigh.

Bombardier had returned and was standing across the table. "Who are you shrugging to?"

"Myself. You've got me stumped. You're saying that after Jimmie Lee was killed with the same gun, you no longer thought Keith Briscoe was guilty and yet you didn't considered his wife. So, who?"

"Well, doesn't much matter now, does it? Valerie Briscoe is the viable suspect and she'll be here soon."

CHAPTER 41

The sound of a train whistle down off Government Street blared through the police station's old brick walls. I turned to look out the two pebbled glass windows, but they offered no view.

I sighed. "Mrs. Briscoe was close to Jimmie Lee and I find it hard to believe she'd kill him. What if she says she lost the charm some time ago?"

"She'd be lying," he said. "What are the odds of her being at that spot at some other time? Besides, shooting a .38 automatic would produce quite a jolt for a woman her size. On which arm did she wear the bracelet?"

I tried to picture her office, Mrs. Briscoe at her desk. Her earrings knocked against her neck as the bangle of charms rattled with her arm movements, all in tune to her incessant Scarlet O'Hara babbling. The charm clomped across the desk and fell. "The bracelet was on the arm to my right, which would have been..." I glanced at the blank whiteboard behind him. "...her left arm."

"Was she left handed?"

I stopped to think again, picturing her signing paychecks. "No, right handed, but she didn't need to shoot a gun to lose one. After one fell off in her office, she told me this happened quite often." I lingered a moment over the memory and something else floated into my mind's eye. I tried to grasp onto it, but couldn't quite lock on.

"What are you thinking about?" he asked.

"When her charm fell. Jimmie Lee was making noises about the bracelet's history. I'm trying to remember."

Bombardier leaned in, his hands balled up on the table. "Take your time, Judy."

Drawn back into her office, I watched Jimmie Lee pick up the fallen charm. Mrs. Briscoe took it from him and hooked it back onto her bracelet. She was telling me why her dear, wonderful daddy had made them, Jimmie Lee, in the background adding his two cents. Someone made a comment about the charms. The comment…

"Judy?"

I waved him off. "Don't make me lose this."

I folded my hands and pushed them against my cheeks, staring at the tabletop. I was back in time, to that moment. I had a panoramic view. Jimmie Lee beamed, his porky chest puffed, and his hands gesturing as he spoke, something about Mr. Kelm having them marked in the order they came off the line. Then Mrs. Briscoe chimed in about always getting the second one for each new invention.

"Carl, I got it! Give me the charm."

Bombardier passed the jewelry piece across the table.

I seized it, turning it over and around in my hand. No, Mrs. Briscoe couldn't have killed Jimmie Lee. The number would be there, but I didn't expect it to be a two and I wasn't disappointed. Engraved into one side, in Roman numeral format, the number one was clearly carved.

"Look here." I pointed to the spot and returned the charm to Bombardier. "Mrs. Briscoe's charms were second off each new production run. Her father marked them accordingly. This one shows the number one. This isn't hers." He started to speak, but I cut him off. "If this had been made for one of her brothers, it would be a tie clip or cuff link and marked with a three or a four. Another charm, marked with anything other than Mrs. Briscoe's number two, has to belong to her mother."

Bombardier smiled and his black eyes danced. He raised one arm high, made a fist, then pulled the arm down, hard, fast, as if jerking on an invisible rope. "Yes! I am *sooo* glad I came to work today. My father had a feeling Eleanor was the driving force in the murder of the Wades. Paul Kelm—lily-livered."

At that moment Kevin Young tramped up to the door, gripping the sides and leaning in with a red face. "What's this about, Chief?"

Bombardier half-turned to look. His mouth shrunk into a small straight line and he stood up, shoving his chair back. Kevin dropped his hands and backed up as Bombardier stomped toward him, burrowing his eyes into Kevin's. "Aren't you going to ask what's happening with the case?"

Kevin stood stock-still.

"If you'd done your job, none of us would be here," Bombardier said. "This case would've been solved by now."

Kevin threw his hands out. "But the case is solved. We're arresting the perp on Wednesday."

Mavis stepped into view and stood attentively behind them. She'd lost the frown.

"No, Kevin," Bombardier responded. "We're not arresting *him* Wednesday. We're arresting *her* today."

"Her?" Lieutenant Young bit down on one finger. "What the hell are you talking about, Chief?"

"Well, I'm so glad you asked, Lieutenant. I'm sending ya over with Chip to pick her up. I told you and Johnnie to make certain that crime scene got a thorough going over."

Kevin flailed his arms. "We were thorough. The place was nothing but a mud hole."

Bombardier fumed. "Well, it's too bad you didn't get mud on your lily white hands. Thanks to you, we almost arrested the wrong person. Now, grab Chip as soon as he returns, get over to Eleanor Kelm's home, and bring her in for questioning."

Kevin opened his mouth, his face a mask of dismay. "Eleanor Kelm? No way."

"Tell her she may want to bring her makeup kit and a toothbrush." Bombardier returned to the table, but didn't sit. He ripped a couple of sheets from a legal pad then wadded them into a ball which he threw hard against the wall. "That lazy bastard. I'll never trust him again. Kevin was the lead here." He walked over and picked up the paper, tossing it into the trash.

Outside the open door, Sergeant Gentry and Lieutenant Leblanc were bringing in Mrs. Briscoe. She wore a crème-colored silk blouse and a pair of brown linen slacks.

"Why won't you tell me why I'm here?" Her voice was shrill and her face blanched.

"I'll be right back," Bombardier said and left for the squad room.

Mrs. Briscoe glanced at him then crooked her neck and peered at me. Bombardier directed her in with a hand move-ment. Gentry and Leblanc sidled in to accompany her and re-mained standing as she sat next to me. She looked down at the linoleum as if checking its cleanliness before placing her purse on the floor.

Bombardier came back in and said to the sergeant, "Get with Kevin. I've given him an order and you'll need to go with him." Gentry left and Bombardier and Leblanc sat down across from us.

Mavis popped her head in, smiling. "Is there anything I can get for any of ya'll?"

The others ignored her, more important things on their minds, I assumed.

"No," I said, "but thank you for offering."

"Anytime," she said, bubbling.

Mrs. Briscoe stared across the table at Bombardier. "Why is Mrs. Kenagy here? Why am *I* here, for heaven's sake?"

When he didn't respond, she turned and glared at me, not in her usual smug way with an air of guarded superiority.

Bombardier cleared his throat. "Judy brought this to me this morning," he said, extending his arm over the table to hold the charm close enough for her to see. "Judy." He nodded for me to speak.

"I found this where Jimmie Lee was killed. I'm sure you know who it belongs to."

"I want you to tell us all you know about this piece of jewelry," the chief said.

She wrenched the charm from Bombardier and looked at the side where the marked number appeared. "It's not mine." She plunked the silver nugget in front of Bombardier.

"It's marked with the number one," I said. "You told me once your charms were made from the newly invented hardware that ran second off the production line. Jimmie Lee—" With the mention of his name, her eyelids fluttered and she exhaled. "Jimmie Lee said they were marked accordingly. If yours were second then your mother's must've been first. This has to belong to her."

She shook her head and rolled her eyes, summoning up her haughtiness. "You can take this to mean whatever you want, but I don't know to *whom* this belongs." She sighed and dusted something invisible from her slacks before checking the time on her Cartier watch. Her charm bracelet dangled next to the watch.

A subtle smile appeared on Bombardier's face. He glanced at me as if to share a joke then turned his focus on Mrs. Briscoe.

Something murky rippled over her face, altering her appearance. Something bemused and hesitant that moved behind the façade of self-assurance. She stiffened into her normal ostentatious Southern lady charade, that better-than-everyone-else look. "Mrs. Kenagy," she said, "I have no idea what you're talking about. What possible difference does it make, anyway? For all I know, ya'll could have planted the thing."

"This is going nowhere," Bombardier said, his smile converting to a sneer. "Your mother will be here any minute and we'll get to the bottom of this."

"My mother? My mother—why's she coming? You all can't think—you can't possibly think such a gracious southern lady could have anything to do with this. Why, she's a fine woman, a genuine good person, the wife of my deceased daddy, God rest his soul."

"Cut the crap, Valerie," Bombardier said. "You know they were both crooks."

We all looked at Mrs. Briscoe's empty face. Was she confused? Stunned? Could she be ignorant of the crimes of her parents or were there uncertainties she kept hidden in her un-conscious? For all I knew, she could be rehearsing another sto-ry about Daddy or her and her fine family. Hell, she could be reflecting on whether or not to go out to dinner tonight. Damned if I knew.

Bombardier kept his gaze on her while Lieutenant Le-blanc looked at his hands pressed flat on the tabletop. Another second and the chief looked past Mrs. Briscoe into empty space. Using his index finger and a thumb, he gripped his chin. Slowly, he slid his thumb and forefinger underneath the slight-ly double chin, down each side of his Adam's apple to the base of his neck. He let go and repeated the action. Then he stopped and his eyes began to twinkle, a trace of a grin coming and going. He caught me watching and transformed his expression into a serious one then got to his feet. "Johnnie, we should be out front when Eleanor Kelm arrives."

Johnnie rose and the pair left the room. The chief reached back in to pull the door closed and there it was again, that faint grin, the glimmer in his eyes.

Mrs. Briscoe shivered to the sound of the door shutting. I wrung my hands and looked away while she repositioned her-self and gazed at a waste can.

We sat in rigid silence, the soft ticking from the clock on the wall the only sound. Then Lieutenant Young's voice came from outside the door, barely audible, but I heard enough to know he directed someone into another room then a door closed.

A few minutes more and the tick-tock from the clock grew louder. Mrs. Briscoe shifted again in her seat. I sneezed once and excused myself. Another five minutes and the tick began to sound like a knock. The thought of jumping up and beating the clock lifeless entered my mind, but disappeared when the door burst open and slammed against the wall.

Eleanor Kelm stormed in, Bombardier, Young, Leblanc, and Gentry on her heels. "You," she screamed at her daughter. "You! I told him you should never have been born."

Mrs. Briscoe sprung up, grabbing the back of her chair. "Mother, what are you talking about?"

I got up and backed myself against the far wall. Eleanor unclenched one wrinkled hand, bound forward, and slapped her daughter's face so hard Mrs. Briscoe's nose began to bleed.

She fell into her chair, holding the pained side of her face. She seized a tissue from her purse and daubed at the blood. "Mother," she shrieked. "Why are you saying these things?"

"Your father was gutless." Her Southern accent shook with age. "The boys I could influence. Teach them backbone, savvy, but I knew how he'd spoil a daughter." Eleanor gripped the back of a chair, inhaled, and released her breath with a rasp. "When I found out I was carrying a girl, I wanted an abortion. He threw a fit, threatening to expose my family's secrets. And just as I'd envisioned, he treated you like a princess. He gave it all to you, every last piece of Kelm Machinery."

Tears flooded Mrs. Briscoe's face. "Mother, please. You don't know what you're saying."

Mother and daughter seemed to be the only ones in the room, the rest of us brought in like mud on the soles of shoes.

Eleanor hammered the tabletop with age-spotted hands. "You stupid little bitch. You're just like him." Her voice rose to a point of frenzy. "I tried to help you, tried to save the good Kelm name, and what do you do? You run down here and identify my charm without calling me or our attorney."

"But Mother—Mother—"

Eleanor Kelm turned to Bombardier, eyes scared and helpless. "I didn't mean to kill that woman, that Alma—or, whatever her name was. I went there to buy her off." She wagged a hand as if shooing something dirty away. "The little tramp lived in squalor but stupidly refused my money. I didn't know Keith had loaned her one of our guns. She pulled the thing on me. She threatened me!"

"How was she killed?" Bombardier asked.

Her words spilled out in a guttural whine. "It was an accident. I tried to take the gun from her, a true struggle for a woman my age. We got all twisted up. My hand wrapped close to the trigger and the gun went off. I ran, taking the gun with me."

"Mother," Mrs. Briscoe bleated like a goat. "Don't say any more. Get an attorney. Why are you doing this?"

"Why am I doing this?" she snapped. "Valerie Lynn Kelm-Briscoe, I am doing this because my *daughter* came here to identify my charm. I tried to get the other woman out of your life, help you save face. I was doing this for you! But you've always been an idiot. You shared private family business with that ignorant, worthless troll, Jimmie Lee. Sent him snooping on your behalf. He came to my house, looking for the gun, and found it. That rubbish in my house." She lowered her voice and it turned throaty and intense. "In a short matter of time, he would've been running his mouth."

Mrs. Briscoe wailed at the ceiling then fell folded into a chair, holding herself. A once-poisonous flower now wilted into a defenseless weed. Bombardier directed Leblanc and Young to read Mrs. Kelm her rights and handcuff her. They hesitated then started to approach her.

"Wait a minute!" Eleanor screamed. "I told you it was an accident!"

Bombardier folded his arms and hovered over her. "Was the murder of Jimmie Lee Albright also an accident? Same gun used—your charm found at the murder scene. Or tell me, Mrs. Kelm, will you plead his murder doesn't count? After all, like you said he was worthless rubbish."

"Mother, how could you?" Mrs. Briscoe caterwauled like a baby, her features compressed like wax melting on a candle.

"I want my attorney," Eleanor demanded.

Bombardier got right in her face. "Make sure you tell your attorney I've spoken to your son, Paul Junior."

She gasped and a shrill animal-like sound ripped from her soul. "My son." She collapsed into a chair like a body without bones. "Junior would never—"

"Where is my brother?" Mrs. Briscoe pleaded.

Bombardier's gaze bounced from mother to daughter and back. "He's in Maryland and he wants nothing to do with either of ya."

"But why?" Mrs. Briscoe asked.

He caught my eye with a watch-what-I-do-next glance before turning back to Mrs. Briscoe. "Maybe you'll want to ask your mother how the gun that killed Guerra and Albright also killed Marlene and Gerald Wade twenty-five years ago. That might help you understand why your brother disappeared."

Mrs. Briscoe bent over and held her stomach, tears smearing her mascara as they streamed down her cheeks. Her eyes, once blue, were drowned and faded, her mouth loose like gelatin.

Eleanor put both elbows on the table while Mrs. Briscoe's head flopped about, her eyes rolling up and around like someone having a seizure.

"I want amnesty for Junior," Eleanor declared.

Bombardier nodded to Leblanc who cuffed Eleanor's hands in front of her while quoting her Miranda rights.

"Are you certain you don't want an attorney before you speak?" Bombardier asked.

"Maybe later, but not with what I have to say now."

"To consider amnesty for your son," Bombardier said, "I must know he had nothing to do with the Wade murders."

"Of course not," she snapped, "but he knew about them after the fact. I want your word he won't be touched. With that, I'll tell you everything."

Bombardier smiled. "That's a reasonable request."

"He knew nothing until that day." Eleanor clutched her cuffed hands underneath her chin and leaned over the table. "USM in Hattiesburg closed early that week and Paul, Jr. came home unexpectedly. The design drawings for the Wades' new products were scattered over the dining room table where I'd left them. He'd heard about the Wade murders on the radio on his drive home. When he entered the house, he saw the file folders and took a closer look. The Wade name was all over the paperwork, confusing him. He wandered through the house looking for answers. My husband and I were in the bedroom arguing."

Eleanor stood up and kicked her chair back. "I'd told my husband we had to take the Wades out. His business was losing money. We needed to eliminate the competition and take their intellectual property. He considered it then backed down. Like I said, he was a wimp. Pfft! I wanted a good life and so I handled it myself, without Paul's consent. He wasn't happy."

"Did you hire a hit man?"

She gave the chief a sneer. "Didn't trust anyone, even those who were family members. Didn't need to. I knew how to handle a gun. My brother had given me an unregistered one with a silencer. I knew when and where Marlene Wade had her hair done and waited outside in my car. When she came out, I climbed out and acted like I'd run into her accidentally. We talked. She'd been on me about coming by for a preview of a new Claude Monet painting she'd purchased at auction. I asked if I could stop by that evening. I warned her I'd be dressed in baseball gear since I'd be coming from the little league game where I volunteered. After that, I walked into the same beauty salon she'd just left and had my hair cut as short as a man's. When I rang her doorbell, she recognized me even with the ball cap and men's sports clothes."

"So, Paul, Jr. heard ya admit to a double homicide?" Bombardier asked.

"Yes. I didn't expect to see my son standing in the doorway." Eleanor covered her face and bawled without control. "Paul told Junior he didn't like it either, but we had to face facts. What I'd done was done," she wailed. "Junior cried and told us he'd return to school, finish the semester, and go somewhere we'd never find him. I begged him not to."

She looked up helplessly at Bombardier. "Tell me he's okay and happy."

"He appeared to be doing fine," Bombardier said.

"The gain from the murders cost me dearly. I lost my wonderful boy."

Bombardier leaned forward as if to get in her face. "You got off easy," he said, spitting out the words. "Ya took the lives of two people back then. The number's now risen to four."

Eleanor held her eyes on him, wide with fright. "I'm ready to go now," she said, in a voice suddenly old again. Her countenance turned dark and she looked back at her daughter, hurling one last vile glower. "You," she hissed then cursed at Valerie while Young and Leblanc shuffled her out.

Bombardier ordered Gentry to take Mrs. Briscoe to the hospital for observation and call her husband to update him on the events. Reluctantly, Gentry moved to where she sat lifeless. He put her purse into her hand and assisted her in standing before leading her out of the room.

I returned to my seat. Mavis stepped up to the doorway and peered in.

Bombardier strode over and slammed the door in her face. He turned back, giving me a devilish grin. "Well, well. This day went fine—just fine." He sat down.

I was emotionally drained and let Bombardier, who seemed unscathed, call Dan to come get me. While we waited, I asked, "What did you tell Mrs. Kelm that made her think her daughter exposed her, instead of me?"

"The truth," he said, his grin taking over his face.

"I have to know. What did you tell her mother?"

"Judy, I had to get innovative. The first thing a defense attorney would do is have the charm thrown out since you found it instead of us. I told her we had her charm, the one that fell off her bracelet when she shot Albright. I told her someone had pointed out the history of those charms and their markings. And that, Judy, is exactly what you did. That's when I told her we had her daughter in the next room." Still holding the grin, he lifted his round shoulders and with a buckling of lips, continued. "Hey, I can't help it if she misunderstood. That's when she lost it. I wanted evidence on her so badly and you brought it. I had to find some way to assure we could use it. Judy, without you we'd never have nailed her."

"What's going to happen to Mrs. Briscoe?"

"Who knows?" He shrugged. "Who cares? She'll hear about her father's scams, encouraged by her mother. She'll learn that once he got hooked into Eleanor's Dixie Mafia ways, there was no going back. And, if she ever thought her mother loved her—well, I guess after today that myth exploded."

Dan arrived.

Tired, stressed, and still filled with questions, I left the police station with him. On the drive home, I told Dan how the events played out and about Eleanor's confessions. "I would've suspected Eleanor, too, if I'd known about the single gun in all three cases. He'd never have been able to pin it on her though, without my finding the charm. Millie told me a neighbor saw Gloria Wade open the door to a man the night of those old killings. He wasn't a tall man, but not short-short. Eleanor is of good height and, in the right disguise, could look like a male of about five-eight, five-nine."

I stopped talking when we turned onto our road, my mind filled with the eruption at the police department. Bombardier had baited Eleanor Kelm then pitted her against her daughter. What followed was something I couldn't stop tossing around in my head.

"Why don't you look happy?" Dan asked. "Isn't this what you wanted? The case is solved and Valerie Kelm-Briscoe ruined. I'd say completely. One less monster boss in the world."

"There's no way to be happy about what I witnessed. That was a dreadful scene, one I wouldn't wish on anyone."

"After how she's treated others? Give me a break." He tossed me a glance then looked back at the road. "Judy, take a lesson from the police chief. I bet someone could take his blood pressure at a gruesome murder scene and it would be normal. You look at the same bad scene and see only the loss, the sadness, and empathize with the victims. Bombardier sees a puzzle to solve, part of his job. He really has the healthier approach."

"I know, Dan. He doesn't, I guess I'd say, internalize things."

"That's right. You hold everything inside. It's wasted energy and doesn't do you or anyone else any good."

CHAPTER 42

I don't understand. I was a good employee. I worked very hard and the reasons given to me for my discharge were all untrue. Why did this happen?" ~ Jolene Cromwell's suicide note, shown to Judy Kenagy by Jolene's parents.

❧❧❧

The weather Tuesday was ideal for Mardi Gras festivities—a cloudless sky, beaming sunshine, and a cold, dry wind blustering in from the gulf. The Mississippi Gulf Coast looked as beautiful as it did the first time I saw it. The weeping willows, their wispy leaves dangling to the ground, mimosa trees, overpowering oaks, and of course, the magnolias all still in shades of green. Sprinkled in between magnificent trees, Southern mansions flaunted their tall white columns, and a long strip of sand flanked the shimmering water. I loved every part of the Gulf Coast and now I called it my home.

But as beautiful as the area was, I wasn't interested in the Mardi Gras parades. Folks arrived at four and five a.m. to secure a parking place. Tailgaters began staking out their spots days in advance to guarantee their vantage points. One long party, where beer ran like water. Neither Dan nor I had been raised with the tradition, so watching the event on TV worked fine for us.

Jack Thornton and his family would be there. He'd mentioned this on the Christmas card he sent six weeks earlier. Jack said his kids were excited about being part of the uniqueness of their new turf. Millie told me she and Red would take their grandchildren.

And apparently George went every year with his wife and daughter, part of his heritage.

Carl Bombardier was out there somewhere, too, with a few of his men. He assisted the City of Biloxi's police department at the function every year. He'd told me he didn't mind working that gig because Biloxi personnel always cordoned off a section along Highway 90 for them. Unlike everyone else, they didn't have to get up early to get crème-de-le-crème seating.

Bert and his family would enjoy the parades one last time then he'd leave for St. Louis at the end of the week. His wife planned to stay behind long enough for the kids to finish their school term.

I knew Andy would be there, perhaps tipsy, but undoubtedly happy. Maybe he'd be with Dwayne Barlow, maybe someone else. Keith Briscoe would be on a float gliding down Highway 90, his role as the Neptune King scarcely touched by recent events. I had no idea whether Mrs. Briscoe would show and I didn't care. She no longer had an effect on me.

The first report of Eleanor Kelm's arrest aired Saturday on the evening news. She was charged with manslaughter in the shooting death of Alma Guerra and first degree murder for James Lee Albright. Additionally, she was charged with the twenty-five year old double homicide of Gerald and Marlene Wade. The same information appeared in Sunday morning's *Sun Herald*.

Bombardier had called me at work on the Monday before Fat Tuesday. "I thought you'd want to know firsthand what I got out of Eleanor."

"Thanks," I said. "I've been curious. Hold on a sec." I got up and whipped my *Currently on a Conference Call* sign from the top of one of the personnel file cabinets and hooked it to the front of my door then shut and locked it. I returned to my chair and pressed the phone's speaker button. "Let's have it."

"Eleanor found out about Briscoe's affair with Guerra by happenstance. She was driving down Washington Avenue and recognized his car turning onto an out-of-the-way road. He had a young woman with him and Eleanor followed at a distance. She watched them go into Guerra's house, said they were all over each other. The next day, she went back with five grand in an attempt to buy Guerra out of the affair. Her claim that she accidentally shot Guerra is credible. Her bank confirms the cash withdrawal on the day Guerra was killed. Her hair dresser also verified Eleanor was a no-show for her hair appointment the same day. And there's the single gunshot, normally the case in an accidental shooting. And I knew—if a woman had killed her, it likely was an accident."

"Because women aren't prone to shoot other women in the face?"

"I never underestimate you, Judy. Yes, some female vanity thing. Her mistake was not stopping there. She'd gotten away with murder all those years ago. I think she convinced herself she could do it again, this time with Jimmie Lee, up close and personal. After all, who would think of a little ol' lady of Gulf Coast high society to be involved in murder?"

Bombardier paused and I reflected back to my first impression of Eleanor Kelm. Her aging Southern grace and poise had fooled me but only for the moment. Her voice, with its tone of Southern upper-class vanity, the pursing of her lips—it hadn't taken long to sense the evil that emanated from her.

"How did you come to suspect Eleanor Kelm?"

"I always suspected her involvement in the Wade killings. I knew, thanks to you, Albright was looking for the gun that killed Guerra, not knowing of its link to the old double homicide. Eleanor was the only one who had a stake in keeping the gun hidden. When Albright was killed, I figured her for the guilty party. Keith Briscoe had nothing to gain. I was stumped as to why she'd kill Guerra, but knew there could've been some connection if Guerra was his mistress. Regardless, Eleanor had to be the killer. The thread of the single gun, reaching all the way back to the Wades was more than coincidence."

"So, she killed Jimmie Lee to silence him?" I asked.

"Yes. She hadn't even bothered to hide the pistol. The arrogance of the woman. When Albright left the *Sun Herald* office, he went to Valerie's home and asked if she knew of a .38-caliber semi-automatic pistol. Valerie must've wanted to halt Albright's investigation because she told him she hadn't seen any .38. He believed her."

"Wait. I'm a little confused. Did Mrs. Briscoe tell you this?"

"No. Eleanor got the information from Albright when she grilled him, making certain no one knew of his visit to her home. He told her that only after he drove away from Valerie's home, did he remember her telling him, some time ago, about her father's gun collection. He knew Keith Briscoe had a key to Eleanor's home—took care of the cats when she was away. Albright made the biggest mistake of his life when he drove to Eleanor's, knocked on her door and, in her words, had the impudence to ask to see Paul Kelm's gun collection. She asked why and he said he wanted to see if one was missing. He saw the guns in the glass case behind her, walked past her and opened the case. They were all there, including the .38-caliber automatic, a Walther PPK."

"That was a simple find."

"Turned out that way, but got Albright killed. Eleanor knew if word got out she had the gun, the police could tie it to Guerra's death, which she couldn't risk. Someone would likely remember those stirrings so long ago about Paul Kelm and the Wade murders and do a ballistics comparison. If she'd known I'd already done that, she'd never have bothered killing Albright."

Someone knocked on my door. I ignored it until the person began rattling the doorknob. "Hold on, Carl."

I unlocked the door and peeked out.

"Judy," JoAnne said. "I'm going to look for another pest control company. One of our employees found a live bug."

"JoAnne, there will always be live bugs."

"But, Judy—"

I shut the door and relocked it, then returned to my chair.

"Sorry," I said. "Go on."

"When she felt certain no one knew he'd gone to her home, she planned his murder."

"How did she get him to East Beach?"

"She played him. Said Valerie had lied because she *did* know her dad had a .38-caliber pistol, a Walther PPK, accessible to Keith. Albright got all bummed out, thinking Valerie didn't trust him and Eleanor began her sting. She convinced Albright that Valerie had lied to protect him. After all, as she told him, he could be charged as an accessory to murder. Once Eleanor got him puffed up, he went into his detective role, reacting as Eleanor expected. She told me he got excited and said they had to get rid of the gun. He said he'd take it to the island off East Beach in his boat and bury it. Eleanor asked for directions to his boat and said she'd meet him there with the gun, giving him a flimsy excuse that if he left her house carrying anything, her nosey neighbors would notice."

"She must've given him time to stock his boat," I said.

"She did. Albright asked for a half-hour to gather some gear. After that, she pulled in next to his truck, parked near the water just south of the research lab's empty parking lot. Eleanor said it was getting dark as she got out of her car. She pulled the gun from her purse and shot him twice in the chest. With the silencer masking the shots, Eleanor had counted on getting away with another murder. A little old lady is almost invisible as a suspicious character. End of story."

☙☙☙

Dan wanted to stay home and relax, but I felt restless so I took off for the Isle of Capri, the first casino after the Ocean Springs Bridge, and the only one totally accessible. The parade would begin at the Casino Magic next door and travel west through Biloxi, Gulfport, Long Beach, Pass Christian, Bay St. Louis, and Waveland.

When I hit downtown Ocean Springs, I drove past Georgina's Hobby Shop. An enormous sign hung at the entrance. I slowed, but I'd gone too far to read the words. I took the corner at Joseph Street and went around the block, this time pulling into the shop's parking lot. The sign read, *Closed Permanently ~ Out of Business.* I wasn't much surprised.

The casino was bustling. I found one blackjack table with an opening and hopped up on the stool. When the dealer re-shuffled, I laid down a hundred dollar bill and received a stack of chips. I stayed at the table until the hundred was gone.

On my way out, I noticed people gathering in the lobby around a big screen TV. I took a detour, turning left in their direction. When I got closer, I heard a news reporter speaking in a quick, harried voice. I stepped up to the small group and a couple moved aside to let me in.

One of WLOX's reporters stood on the north side of Highway 90, microphone in hand, Bombardier and another man in a tussle behind him. Parade goers had strung out around them, watching. Bombardier struggled, turning the other man around, handcuffs dangling, attempting to secure the man's arms behind him. The man broke free and the camera followed. The only place he could run was into the crowd which worked about as well as running into a wall. In a frantic eruption of arms and legs, Bombardier caught him again, this time cuffing him. He twirled the man around and shoved him over to Lieutenants Young and Leblanc. Obviously winded, Bombardier bent over and placed his hands on his knees, catching his breath.

The restrained man was crying and I recognized the scowl line burrowed into his brow, his hair in disarray. *Lester Robichaux.*

The camera had been focused on the upper half of Lester's body and, as the reporter continued, I understood why.

"…the police have apprehended a man exposing himself to people passing by on Mardi Gras floats," the reporter sang into the microphone.

I pictured more than I wanted to and burst out laughing. Heads turned. "Sorry," I said to the small group and covered my mouth, still snickering as I left the casino.

But by the time I reached the car, my mood had changed. I didn't know what I wanted to do or where I wanted to go. If I went to work for a while, my tomorrow would be easier to manage. Mardi Gras was an observed holiday on the Gulf Coast, not so for the rest of the United States, so most of those I dealt with via email and phone would be working today as always, all day. I drove without thought, my Camry seeming to be in control. Soon, I pulled into Rockhold Packaging's empty parking lot and sat there for a moment, suddenly missing Dan. His honesty, his emotional strength, and his body embracing mine.

In my office, I checked voicemail messages, emails, and faxes. I'd hold off on responding until tomorrow. An occasional jingle announced a new email. While I worked, I focused on what I did without emotion. But an hour later, when I took a break, a sharp sadness returned like an unwanted boomerang. I moaned and dropped my head into my hands. So much had happened.

I clasped my hands under my chin and sat still, staring at the floor, thinking for what seemed like ages. I hadn't slept well last night and I was bone weary.

Leaning back in my chair, I looked at my phone with its programmed speed-dial buttons and weighed my options. The tiny bell chimed again and I turned toward the computer screen. This email came from our corporate vice-president of human resources, the subject line in caps. *The National Restructuring.*

"Shit."

I rubbed my temples and thought of the first time I wanted out of human resources. I was coming home from Jolene Cromwell's funeral, hating my job, and feeling I'd neglected my true role in the position. I believed then, as I did now, that employees like Jolene truly wanted to do a good job. I tried to convince my employers, the efforts often in vain, and I was haunted by my failures.

The speed-dial buttons on the phone faintly glittered as I drummed my nails on the desk. Then, instinctively, I pressed the speakerphone on and tapped speed-dial button number three. The numbers clacked as each one registered then the phone began to ring.

A familiar voice answered. "Hello."

I didn't respond, the urge to hang up tugging at me.

"Hello? Who's there?" the voice called again, the choppy accent and warm composure seeping through.

"It's—it's me."

"Judy? How are you? What's the issue?"

I fought away tears that came out of nowhere.

"Are you still there?"

"Yes," I said. "I'm not totally sure what the issue is—just thought you might help."

"Well, at least tell me who the employee is."

My words came easier than expected. "Dottie, this time the employee is me."

Thank you for reading my book.
Did you enjoy it?
An author's success depends on
readers like you!

Please take a minute to post a review on
Amazon and Goodreads.
Your opinion will make all the difference.

About the Author

Linda Thorne began pursuing her true passion, writing, in 2005. Since then, she has published numerous short stories in the genres of mystery, thriller, and romance. Her debut novel, *Just Another Termination,* is the first in a planned series of mysteries that tell the story of Judy Kenagy, a career human resources manager turned sleuth. She is currently writing the second book in her series, *A Promotion to Die For.*

Like her lead character, Thorne is a career human resources manager. She has worked in the HR profession in Arizona, Colorado, Mississippi, California, and now, Tennessee. She holds a BS degree in business from Arizona State University and has completed a number of graduate-level courses in her field.